"I'm goi... S0-ARG-486 all your secrets tonight. ...every last one of them."

His hands tightened around her, forcing her closer. Then he moved against her, making her tremble in response.

"You feel so damn good," he muttered thickly. He nuzzled the sensitive place behind her ear and then found the lobe with his teeth, sampling her with exquisite care. Verity moaned and locked her arms more urgently around him. "So soft," he said, "I'm half out of my mind with wanting you." He released her slightly.

Verity looked up at him. There was enough moonlight filtering through the cabin windows to reveal the starkly aroused expression on his harsh face and the burning heat in his eyes. For an instant she knew a jolt of fear once more.

"Jonas, I..."

"Hush," he said, kissing her back into silence. "I've told you I'll take care of you. You'll be safe with me."

She wondered why Jonas was so determined to promise safety, but there was no opportunity to ask. His fingers were already working the tiny buttons of her nightgown...

"The unique touch of Ms. Krentz...sets ablaze a fierce sensuality to scorch the heart of every reader."
—*Romantic Times*

Also by Jayne Ann Krentz

A Coral Kiss
Crystal Flame
Midnight Jewels
Sweet Starfire

Published by
POPULAR LIBRARY

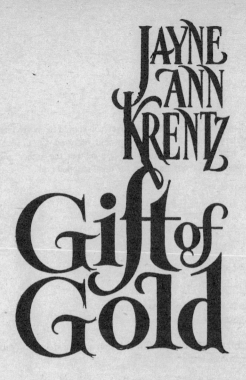

JAYNE ANN KRENTZ

Gift of Gold

POPULAR LIBRARY

An Imprint of Warner Books, Inc.

A Time Warner Company

POPULAR LIBRARY EDITION

Copyright © 1988 by Jayne Ann Krentz
All rights reserved.

Popular Library® and the fanciful P design are registered trademarks of Warner Books, Inc.

Cover design by Barbara Buck
Cover illustration by Gregg Gulbronson

Popular Library books are published by
Warner Books, Inc.
1271 Avenue of the Americas
New York, N.Y. 10020

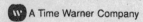 A Time Warner Company

Printed in the United States of America

First Printing: July, 1988

10 9 8 7 6 5

For my mother, Alberta Castle,
who taught me to keep an open mind.

Gift of Gold

Chapter One

The hunt was over. He'd been chasing her for two months and two thousand miles and he was finally closing in on his quarry. For the first time since the whole thing had started, Jonas Quarrel allowed himself the temporary pleasure of triumph mingled with anticipation.

The Jeep ground its way along the rutted, unpaved road until it reached the edge of the lake. Jonas halted the dusty vehicle near a cluster of tall, swaying pines, switched off the engine, and sat for a moment behind the wheel. Then he opened the door and climbed out.

He walked slowly to the water's edge and stood gazing thoughtfully out over the expanse of Sequence Lake, the visual focal point of the little Northern California town of Sequence Springs. Jonas had been in the vicinity for a few days getting the feel of the place and planning his next move. Somewhat to his surprise, he had discovered he liked Sequence Springs and its lake.

Ripples on the blue-green surface in front of him shimmered in the waning sun of a warm fall afternoon. The lake was ringed with a thick fringe of pine and fir. Most of what constituted Sequence Springs was on the opposite shore, a cheerful jumble of small shops, old gas stations, and aging houses. Here and there around the perimeter of the lake Jonas could see cabins hidden in the dark shelter of the trees.

The whole place had a subtle air of being undiscovered and picturesque, Jonas decided. It wasn't quite what he had been expecting, but then, he hadn't really known what to expect two months ago when he'd begun his hunt for Verity Ames.

At the far end of the lake an impressive, neoclassical structure painted a stark white caught the last rays of sunlight and reflected them back with almost blinding intensity. The building was unlike any other on the lake. Even from here it was obvious it had been designed to impress the viewer. The architect had clearly been given a free hand and he'd used it to create a self-consciously elegant facade that stressed arched doorways, colonnades, and courtyards. The Sequence Springs Spa Resort was as imposing and luxurious as any Renaissance villa.

Almost lost in the trees not far from the resort stood two weatherbeaten cabins and a small building that housed a restaurant. The three structures presented a blithely irreverent contrast to the neighboring spa.

From where he stood Jonas could see a couple of cars winding their way around the far side of the lake toward the gleaming white resort. The cars, Jonas knew, would be of the Porsche or BMW or Mercedes persuasion.

It was Friday afternoon and the weekend crowd of stressed-out, upwardly mobile types from the San Francisco Bay Area were arriving for their fashionable fix of mud baths, mineral soaks, workouts, and massages.

And after they had been through the spa's luxurious torture program, they would be in the mood for expensive wine and gourmet food that could be eaten with a reasonably clear conscience. The resort offered carefully controlled, reasonably stylish cuisine. But a number of resort guests who were in the know would head for the cozy little restaurant located a short distance from the main resort facilities. The No Bull

Cafe did a landslide business on the weekends serving elegant and expensive vegetarian cuisine.

The No Bull was Jonas's goal this afternoon. He had made his decision on how to close in on his quarry. She owned the cafe and had been advertising in the local paper for a combination dishwasher, waiter, and handyman.

Jonas was presently unemployed and happened to be an expert in the field of dishwashing. Hell, he thought, he could have gotten his Ph.D. in the art if such a degree were offered. It would have been far more useful than the Ph.D. he had gotten in Renaissance history a few years back.

He had never been certain if pursuing the kind of career the history degree had established for him would have killed him outright or just driven him insane. A sense of self-preservation had kept him from experimenting.

Once upon a time, he had come very close to becoming a murderer because of his talent. He had decided then that the fascination of history was better left to those who had less affinity for it than he had.

So he'd washed a lot of dishes in the last few years, mostly bar glasses. He'd also served a lot of liquor, which should have given him the skills of a waiter. And there was no doubt that he'd picked up a few skills as a handyman. He thought of the knife packed away in his duffel bag in the back of the Jeep. . . .

He was a real Renaissance man, he thought wryly. All the benefits of a classical education coupled with a lot of experience in the real world. What more could a potential employer ask? Four hundred years ago he wouldn't have had any trouble at all getting work.

His mouth was edged with a hint of laconic amusement as he reached into the pocket of his jeans and curled his long, lean fingers around a small circlet of gold. As soon as he touched it the earring seemed to warm his hand and a faint, tantalizing sensation that was both peaceful and pleasant and oddly anticipatory tingled deep within him.

Jonas had discovered that the earring was as effective as a

shot of tequila or a couple of bottles of beer when it came time to soften the rough edges of a hard day. He withdrew the tiny piece of feminine jewelry and examined it as it lay innocently in his palm.

It wasn't the first time he had looked at that earring and tried to fathom its compelling mystery. The truth was, he hadn't let it get out of his reach in the two months he'd had it. Jonas felt distinctly possessive and protective toward the earring.

The odd thing was that the possessive feeling extended to the woman who owned it, even though he had never met her. Somehow, in a way he couldn't yet explain, she was part of his future. And it was now time to meet her.

The compulsion to locate the owner of the golden earring had brought Jonas a couple of thousand miles from a Mexican waterfront bar to Sequence Springs. The distance he had traveled meant little to him. He would have come from the other side of the world to find the woman who owned it.

He had gotten only a few brief glimpses of her the night she had lost the piece of jewelry, but he remembered well the copper fire of wild curls that framed huge eyes and a finely boned face. He recalled, too, her soft, slender, feminine shape in the golden light spilling through the open door of the cantina.

She had never seen his face. Verity Ames had been too busy fleeing back to the safety of her hotel. He could still hear the echo of her high-heeled sandals disappearing into the darkness.

It had taken Jonas a week to find out the name of the earring's owner. In true Mexican tradition, money had crossed palms just to get that elemental piece of information. That had been the easy part. It had taken nearly two months to track her down to Sequence Springs, California. All the while the earring had burned in his pocket.

When Jonas had picked up the tiny local newspaper he'd been pleased to find the ad for the position at the No Bull Cafe. It had seemed like fate. Working for someone was one hell of a good way to learn her secrets. And he badly needed to explore the mysteries of Verity Ames. His future was tied up with those mysteries.

Jonas stood at the edge of the lake, his fingers moving absently on the earring, and wondered what it would be like to work for this flame-haired woman.

One thing was certain, he decided: she was bound to be an easier proposition than some of his past employers. After all, she was small, female, and not yet thirty. How much trouble could she give him?

Dishwashing at the No Bull Cafe was going to be a piece of cake.

Verity Ames groaned in frustration when she heard the demanding knock on the locked front door of the No Bull. She put down the bottle of extra virgin olive oil she had been about to uncork and stalked out of the kitchen into the small dining area.

"Too bad they don't teach tourists to read signs," she muttered, wiping her hands on her apron. "The American educational system is obviously failing somewhere."

Ever mindful of future business, however, Verity managed a polite smile as she unlocked the front door of the restaurant. She began speaking before she had the door more than halfway open.

"I'm sorry," she said in a cheery tone, "we don't open until five-thirty this evening. We stopped serving lunch at two. If you want to make reservations for tonight, you're welcome to call. I should warn you, however, that we're almost booked. The only time open is after nine o'clock."

"I'm not here for a meal," said a male voice that was astonishingly dark and soft and faintly amused. "My name is Jonas Quarrel and I'm here for a job."

Verity had the door fully opened now and was already regretting her impulsiveness. She should have peeked through the window first.

She found herself looking up at a tall, lean man with hair

the color of midnight. His surprisingly broad shoulders were covered with a well-worn blue denim work shirt. The sleeves had been rolled up, revealing sinewy forearms sprinkled with dark hair. The man was wearing a pair of jeans that were at least as old and almost as faded as the shirt. The scarred leather belt that wrapped his narrow waist looked as if it had been run over by a truck at some point in its existence. It went well with the low, scuffed boots that clearly hadn't been exposed to a jar of shoe polish in years.

But the faded, worn garments were only minor disturbances compared to the hard-edged planes and angles of a face that had obviously seen more wear and tear than the clothes. He was not a handsome man by anyone's standards, but Verity was curiously aware of the quiet power she sensed in him. She did not recall ever having met a man who had impressed her in quite this way before. For some reason she found herself thinking of legends, and her dark red brows drew together in a small frown.

As Verity met his eyes, she discovered gold. Not new, shiny, jeweler's gold, but rich, ancient gold. It was the gold of history, of pirate treasures and Florentine coins. It was the first time in her life that she had seen eyes that color and she was shocked at the impact they had on her senses. There were ghosts in that gaze, she thought with unaccustomed whimsy. This man knew what it was to live with wraiths and shades and phantoms.

The realization that she was staring open-mouthed at the stranger on her doorstep brought Verity back to herself. Common sense took over, as it always did. Verity prided herself on her abundance of level-headed, practical common sense.

And common sense told her that men such as this did not wash dishes for a living.

"I'm sorry, Mr. Quarrel," she said briskly, "the only position I have open is that of dishwasher-waiter, and I doubt you'd be interested in that sort of work." She started to shut the door.

Jonas Quarrel shoved one booted foot across the threshold and effectively halted the advance of the door. He smiled faintly. It was not a reassuring expression.

"The dishwashing job is the one I'm after." He dug a scrap of newspaper out of his pocket and glanced down at the tiny print. "Dishwasher, waiter, and handyman."

"Handyperson," Verity corrected absently as she automatically leaned forward to peer at the newsprint. "I'm an equal opportunity employer."

Quarrel's smile widened slightly as he watched her reread her own ad. "You're in luck," he murmured. "I'm an equal opportunity employee. I'm even willing to work for a woman as long as she signs my paycheck on time."

Verity pulled her gaze away from the ad and eyed her visitor with wary speculation. She knew beyond a shadow of a doubt that this man did not belong behind a sink full of dirty dishes. She couldn't begin to imagine what had brought him here in response to her ad but she was certain she wouldn't like the answers if she were to ask. No doubt about it, the safest course of action was to get rid of him.

"You really don't look the type to be content with the sort of job I'm offering," she said with polite firmness.

"Let me worry about how content I'll be. I've washed dishes before and I can do it again."

"I'm only offering minimum wage."

"I'll make up the difference in tips," he replied with a nonchalant shrug.

"I need someone who will be around for a while," Verity said, clutching at straws. "My summer staff just left to go back to college, and I require someone who will be here through the winter and spring. I don't want to be bothered training an employee who will be leaving in a month or two."

Jonas pushed the newspaper ad back into his pocket and nodded. "I can give you a fairly firm guarantee that I'll be around for a while."

Verity was getting nervous. "Look, Mr. Quarrel, you're

not quite what I had in mind. I had intended to hire a local person."

"I thought you said you were an equal opportunity employer."

"Well, I am, but I . . ."

"Seems to me a newcomer to the community has as much right to apply for this job as someone who lives nearby."

Verity narrowed her eyes as she glared up at him. "Are you a newcomer to Sequence Springs, Mr. Quarrel? Or just passing through?"

"Don't worry, I told you I'll be around for a while."

"But you just got into town?" she persisted.

"A few days ago."

"Then I'm sure you'll want to study the job ads for a couple of weeks before you make up your mind about employment. I have a feeling something lots more interesting than an opportunity as a dishwasher will come along soon. You might try one of the wineries up in the hills. You look like you might enjoy outdoor work."

Quarrel's eyes gleamed as he looked down at her. For some reason the image of a gilded rapier hilt popped into her mind. Florentine gold beautifully etched on the handle of a blade meant to kill.

"As it happens," he explained in his low, shaded voice, "I'm looking for indoor work."

Verity began to panic. Something was very wrong here and she was no longer sure she could deal with the situation. The man didn't actually frighten her, for all his quiet power, perhaps because she sensed that that power was very controlled. But Verity was also certain this was no casual laborer willing to eke out a living at minimum wage. There was too much intelligence in those gold eyes, too much hooded awareness of both himself and the world around him. But the factor that alarmed her the most was her own too-vivid awareness of him. She struggled to suppress it. This man was dangerous. She knew it intuitively in a way she could never have explained with words.

It was becoming obvious that Jonas Quarrel wasn't going to take no for an answer, however. She would have to find a more subtle way to get rid of him.

"I presume you have a resumé?" Verity asked in a quelling tone.

"A resumé?" He eyed her thoughtfully. "For a dishwashing job?"

She was onto something, Verity decided in relief. Obviously he did not have a resumé.

"Well, naturally. You can't expect me to just hire you on the spot. I'll need a complete work and education history, including dates of previous employment, names of supervisors, addresses and phone numbers. You'll have to fill out an employment application, too. I'll add it to the stack I'm collecting. When I have a lot of them I'll go through them all and make my selection."

"Sounds like a lengthy process," Quarrel observed dryly.

"Oh, it is," she agreed quickly. "Might take a couple of weeks or more."

"Is that right? What are you going to do for help this weekend?"

Verity froze. "I beg your pardon?"

"You heard me. You need help now. Tonight, in fact. You're going to be swamped in a few hours."

"I'll make do," Verity said through clenched teeth. "The managers of the Sequence Springs Spa are friends. I used to run their restaurant. They'll be glad to loan me someone from their kitchen."

"Why borrow temporary help when you've got an opportunity to hire the best on a more permanent basis?"

Verity's hand tightened on the doorknob. "I had no idea dishwashers took so much pride in their craft. You consider yourself the best, Mr. Quarrel?"

"Trust me," he said blandly. "I've got more experience and skill in the art of dishwashing and waiting on customers than anyone else who's likely to show up on your doorstep between now and five-thirty tonight."

"What about your handyperson experience?" she demanded, beginning to feel as if she were getting backed into a corner. Time was wasting. She needed to get back to the kitchen.

"I'm very handy to have around," he assured her. "I'm capable of just about anything from unstopping a toilet to bouncing a drunk. You'll see. I'm useful."

Verity straightened her shoulders. "I only have a beer and wine license. We do not have a problem with drunks here at the No Bull. Furthermore, I have a plumber I can call if something goes wrong in the restrooms. I don't know what sort of establishments you've worked in before, but it sounds as if your job skills might be better used down at the local tavern. Why don't you try there? I'll give you the owner's name." Milt Sanderson, who owned The Keg, could deal with this man, she thought. Milt was used to dealing with construction workers, truckdrivers, and similar types.

"I'd rather work here," Jonas said simply.

"Why?" Verity demanded boldly.

"Let's just say I'm anxious to improve my lot in the world. I've got ambition."

"Uh-huh. Let's just say you try another restaurant, Mr. Quarrel. Don't bother coming back here until you have a proper resumé." Verity made another attempt to close the door.

"Not so fast, Ms. Equal Opportunity Employer."

He was in the room with her before Verity quite knew what had happened. Instinctively she backed up a step. She had to get control of this situation. It was getting ludicrously out-of-hand. "Now just hold on a minute. The restaurant is closed, I've told you that. I have a million things to do before I open for the dinner crowd and I haven't got time to waste calling the police. Kindly take yourself out of here."

"A job applicant has to demonstrate perseverance. Employers respond to that. They're impressed by it." Quarrel glanced around the dining room. "Have you got an office?"

"Yes, but I don't see what that has to do with anything. Mr. Quarrel, I would appreciate it if you would . . ."

"Through here, right?" He was already making his way between the maze of country French chairs and small, intimate tables toward the kitchen.

Verity's temper overcame her incipient nervousness. "What do you think you're doing?" She leaped after him.

"You want a resumé? I'll give you a resumé." He paced through the small tiled kitchen, past the large gas stove, the immaculately clean stainless steel counters and the sink, which was still full of dishes from the lunch crowd. Quarrel gave the sink a knowing glance. "Looks like you need me, lady." Then he was at the door of her tiny office. "Ah, just as I thought. A typewriter."

Verity stared at his sleek shoulders and back as he dropped down into the chair at her desk, reached for a sheet of typing paper, and inserted it into the machine. "You're going to type out a resumé? Right here in my office?"

"Right. Now go putter around in the kitchen and stop nagging me while I work on this. It's going to take a little concentration. Been a while since I had to put a resumé together. Christ. A resumé to wash dishes. What's the world coming to?" He was already flexing his fingers over the keys.

Short of calling the police, Verity was unable to think of anything else to do. She found herself looking at his hands as he began typing with quick, deft strokes. He had fascinating hands, she thought. Long, supple fingers and strong-looking wrists. A swordsman's hands.

A lover's hands.

That last impression made her frown. She stepped back out of the office and headed for the kitchen, trying to decide what to do next. This whole situation was bizarre. She didn't feel personally threatened, but she did feel astonishingly helpless.

Maybe the poor man really was desperate for a job; any

job. Verity picked up the bottle of olive oil and went back to the tortellini salad she had been making.

There was no denying that she needed help tonight. True, Laura and Rick Griswald, the husband and wife team who managed the Sequence Springs Spa, would be glad to send someone over, but it would be easier if Verity solved her own staff problems. It was unfortunate that Marlene Webberly had given so little notice before running off to get married three days ago. Amazing what love could do to a woman's common sense. Marlene had always seemed such an intelligent young woman.

Good help was hard to get.

Verity was almost finished with the salad when the typewriter hushed in the small office. There was a long silence while her erstwhile job applicant apparently proofread his work, and then Verity heard a few more desultory keystrokes. Obviously Jonas Quarrel's typing was not letter-perfect. He walked into the kitchen a moment later, thrusting his resumé into her oily hands.

"Here you are, boss lady. Read it and then tell me I haven't got the right qualifications for this job. In the meantime, I'll finish off those dishes for you."

Verity clutched the resumé and stared at the opening typewritten lines. Frantically she searched for discrepancies, outright lies, or any other reason she might be able to find for ash-canning the piece of paper.

"Age thirty-seven? I would have guessed you were a few years older." *Because of the ghosts in your eyes*, she explained silently.

"Thanks," he growled. "I didn't think I had that much gray in my hair yet."

She shook her head, glanced at his night colored hair and spoke without stopping to think. "It's not the gray in your hair. You hardly have any. It's the look in your eyes." Her own eyes widened as she realized what she had just said. "Never mind. Forget it." But her eyes widened even further in disbelief as she read the next section. "'Education: Ph.D. in history from Vincent College.' You have a Ph.D.?"

"Yeah. Don't hold it against me, okay?"

"What area of history did you study?" Verity demanded suspiciously.

"The Renaissance, with a specialization in military history. I'm an expert on arms and strategy." He seemed totally occupied with the dishes he was rinsing.

"Sure. And if I believe that, you've got some waterfront property down in Arizona you can sell me, right?"

Water splashed in the sink. "It's the truth. You can check it out with a phone call to the records office at Vincent College. I taught there for a while after I graduated."

A scholar in the field of Renaissance history. Verity was hopelessly intrigued in spite of herself. A part of her had always been deeply fascinated by that bloody, brilliant, world-changing era. She suddenly realized that she had been right earlier when she had looked at him and found her head filled with images of gilded rapiers and Florentine gold.

She forced the mental pictures from her mind and said sternly, "I'll check it out here and now. Tell me something about Renaissance history."

"Do you speak Italian?" he asked politely.

"Not much."

"Okay, then I'll translate for you." Jonas paused, apparently gathering his thoughts, and then he quoted smoothly:

"My Lady wounds me with her doubts.
    Each sigh, each glance, a rapier's thrust.
I yearn to give her love's sweet joys,
    But she must first gift me with trust."

Verity leaned against the doorway, crossed her arms over her breasts, and tried for a fierce expression. "What is that supposed to be?"

"A quick, rough translation of a bit of little-known

Renaissance poetry. Impressed?" Jonas gave her a hopeful glance.

Verity's sense of humor was threatening to get the better of her. It was hard to dislike a man who could quote Renaissance love poetry. Of course, it paid to remember that some of the most ruthless men of the fifteenth and sixteenth centuries had not only quoted such poetry, but had written it. There was no law in nature that said killers couldn't write poetry, and in those days, Verity knew, a true gentleman was expected to be as good at composing verse as he was at wielding a rapier.

"The poem must be quite obscure. I've read some Renaissance poetry and I don't recall that little ditty."

"All the more reason for you to be impressed," he retorted smoothly.

"I'm impressed, but I'm not sure if knowing a smattering of Renaissance love poetry is much of a qualification for dishwashing," she murmured.

"I can quote a little Machiavelli if you'd prefer. Perhaps something on the art of governing through fear? He taught that it was politically more expedient for a leader to be feared rather than loved. I suppose that applies to running a restaurant."

"Never mind. I've read enough Machiavelli to know I don't run this place along his principles."

"I'm not so sure about that," Jonas drawled meaningfully. "How did you happen to read his stuff, though?"

"My father always claimed Machiavelli's theories on how to survive politically are still the foundation of modern government. He thought I ought to study them," Verity answered absently. She examined the resumé again. "You've done a lot of bartending, I see. The Green Witch Bar in the Virgin Islands?"

"A tourist trap. I've had a lot of experience with tourists," Jonas said modestly.

"The Harbor Lights Tavern in Tahiti?"

"We catered to a slightly less genteel crowd there."

"The Seafarer Bar and Grill in Manila?"

"The clientele there consisted mostly of U.S. sailors on shore leave. I picked up a lot of diplomatic techniques. I'm very good at quelling brawls and riots."

"I'll bet," Verity said mildly. She was fascinated, in spite of herself. If nothing else, Jonas Quarrel had a vivid imagination. "How about The Get Leid Tavern in Hawaii?"

"Another military hangout, although we got our share of tourists. A little classier than the Seafarer."

"You'd never know it from the name. The Crystal Bell in Singapore?"

"A place where expatriates gathered."

Verity scanned the next entry on the resumé and caught her breath. Then she looked up slowly. "The El Toro Rojo Cantina?"

"Got a lot of expatriates there, too. You know, the would-be writers and artists who go to Mexico to create their art and wind up swimming in cheap tequila instead."

"I know the type," Verity said stiffly. "I also know this cantina. I was in Puerto Vallerta a few months ago and stumbled across it."

Quarrel gave her an unfathomable look as he efficiently stacked dishes. "What were you looking for in a place like the El Toro?"

"I was looking for my father." Verity frowned and tapped the resumé with a fingertip. "You didn't make these places up in a spurt of creative writing, after all, did you? You really have worked in all these sleazy dives."

Quarrel ignored the question and asked one of his own. "Did you find your father?"

Verity shook her head. "No. But that's no big deal. He'll show up sooner or later. He always does." She came away from the wall and started toward the office. "Excuse me for a few minutes."

Jonas dropped a pan back into the sink. "Hey, wait a minute. What are you going to do?"

"Make a few phone calls," she explained sweetly. She smiled at him.

Jonas stared at her for a long moment. He seemed momentarily disconcerted by her smile. Then he pulled himself together and asked slowly, "You're going to call some of those bars?"

"I always check references. What's the matter, Mr. Quarrel? Did you think I'd hesitate to call places like Tahiti and Manila and Mexico?"

He wiped his hands on a towel, studying her intently. "Well, yeah. Most people are a little intimidated by that kind of long-distance dialing."

"I've got news for you. You're not the only one who's had the advantages of extensive world travel. I spent a year and a half in Tahiti, three months in Manila, a year in Mexico, and another year in Hawaii. My memory is a little vague because it's been a few years, but I think I've even been in a few more of these dives than just El Toro Rojo. The Harbor Lights Tavern has a familiar ring. I hate to admit it, but so does the Get Leid."

Quarrel looked genuinely startled. "You're kidding. You know some of those places?"

"My father gave me a very well-rounded education." Verity walked into her office, vaguely pleased at having finally been able to turn the tables on Jonas Quarrel.

"It'll cost a fortune to call those taverns," Jonas pointed out.

"I'll take it out of your first week's pay." Verity smiled slowly as she sat down at her desk and reached for the phone. This was going to prove interesting.

An hour later she had her answers and Jonas had the dishes done. They faced each other in the small kitchen.

"All right," Verity said calmly. "You've got the job. Everyone spoke very highly of you. They said you could be relied upon to open a bar on time, you aren't into drugs, you don't have the bad habit of helping yourself to the contents of the cash register, and you don't drink on the job. High praise, indeed, considering the sources. Oh, and Big Al at the Sea Siren said to give you his best and swears he'll send along the money he owes you now that he has a current address."

Something in Jonas's eyes seemed to relax. It was replaced with a curious expression that was part anticipation and part satisfaction. "Thanks, Verity," he said. "I appreciate it."

"Since you've finished the dishes, you can start chopping onions for the vegetable tart I'm going to make. I'll do the pastry."

"I'll get right on it, boss lady." Jonas reached for a long-bladed knife, hefting it with an easy familiarity. "There's just one more small problem."

Verity paused warily in the act of taking a ball of chilled pastry out of the refrigerator. "What's that?"

"I'll need a place to stay." Jonas smiled at her. "Any ideas? Since I'm going to be working for minimum wage, I won't be able to afford anyplace fancy. I checked out of the Lake Motel this morning. I was running low on cash."

Verity sighed in resignation. "You can have the cabin my father uses when he deigns to visit. It's in back of the restaurant."

"What about your father?"

"Don't worry. I haven't heard from him since I got the message inviting me to meet him down in Puerto Vallerta. He'd already left town by the time I got there and I haven't heard from him since. I don't think he'll be disturbing us anytime soon. If he does, you can flip a coin for the bed. Both of you have probably slept on more than one floor in your life."

"You're a generous woman, Verity Ames."

"It's not that. I think the real problem is that I'm just a little soft in the head when it comes to professional drifters who spend their lives running from their talent."

Jonas's head came up and his eyes narrowed. "What's that supposed to mean?"

Verity looked at him as she rolled out the pastry. "I called Vincent College after I checked with a few of your previous employers. You really did teach Renaissance history there. What's more, you were damn good at it. Lots of impressive publications and one book on ancient armory to your credit. And then you gave up teaching for no apparent reason. Have you been drifting around the world ever since?"

"What does all this have to do with your father?" Jonas asked coolly.

"He's a professional drifter, too. Does the name Emerson Ames mean anything to you?" Verity realized she was wielding the rolling pin with too much force. Deliberately she made herself relax.

Jonas flicked off the end of an onion with a negligent slash of the knife. "Yeah, it does, as a matter of fact. Are we talking about the same Emerson Ames who wrote *Juxtaposition* a few years back?"

"One and the same."

"Well, I'll be damned. I seem to remember that book caused a certain, small sensation when it was published. Anybody who had any academic pretensions at Vincent College had it on his coffee table. What ever happened to him? Has he written anything since *Juxtaposition*?"

"Unfortunately," Verity said tightly, "Dad decided *Juxtaposition* wasn't his kind of book. He vowed not to waste his time doing another one like it and went back to writing what he claims he likes writing best."

Jonas glanced at her. "What's that?"

Verity wrinkled her nose. "Paperback westerns. Can you believe it? The man who was once heralded by *The New York Times* as the author of the year. A writer who had 'boldly and decisively examined and illuminated contemporary uncertainties and paradoxes,' they said. And this bold genius ups and decides he would rather write westerns."

Jonas stared at her for a moment longer and then began to laugh. It was a deep, masculine roar that filled the kitchen. His golden eyes gleamed with it. "I think," Jonas finally said through his laughter, "that I would like your father." He lopped off the end of another onion. "I hope I get a chance to meet him while I'm here."

"Something tells me the two of you have a lot in common," Verity grumbled.

Jonas laughed again and flipped the knife into the air. Verity sucked in her breath as the blade spun end over end. Visions of blood and sliced fingers made her clutch at the counter top. But an instant later Jonas neatly caught the knife by its handle and went back to slicing onions. Verity repressed a shudder.

"I have a hunch that what your father and I have in common is a mutual decision to live in the real world instead of pretending we actually enjoy the academic and literary establishments."

"It looks to me as if you both got lazy and took the easy way out," Verity retorted in an upbraiding tone.

All traces of humor vanished from Jonas's face. When he spoke, his voice was dangerously edged, just like the knife in his hand. "Lady, you don't know what you're talking about. Not all talent is a blessing. Sometimes a thing like talent can kill you. Or it can drive you crazy. Maybe in your father's case, it simply bored him to death. You've got no right to sit in judgment."

Verity shivered. She didn't doubt that Jonas knew what he was talking about. Instinctively she sought refuge in a change of subject. "This is a stupid argument. You'd better get busy on those onions," she said briskly. "When you're finished with those, you can start chopping the carrots. I want them done julienne style. Do you know what that is?"

"Sure, boss lady. Whatever you say. I've got a question, though."

Verity eyed him warily. "What's that?"

"I've never worked in a gourmet vegetarian kitchen." He smiled a little too innocently. "What do you use the extra virgin olive oil for?"

"Salad dressings, among other things," she explained

tartly. "And please spare me your sophomoric jokes. Extra virgin refers to the fact that the oil is of very high quality from the first pressing of the olives."

"Oh. I thought maybe it meant oil that had been aging on the shelf for a long time. Like some poor spinster who has never had a lover."

Verity could not halt the fierce rush of blood into her cheeks. He was just making a crude joke. He could not possibly be aware of her sexual status.

"That's a typically chauvinistic remark. I hate to break this to your male ego, but there are worse things in life than never having had a lover," she declared rashly.

Jonas's mouth curved faintly at the corner. "Such as?"

"Such as discovering you just hired someone who doesn't know the first thing about something as basic to a good kitchen as olive oil!"

"Don't worry, boss. I'm a fast learner."

Chapter
Two

*L*ife in the gourmet vegetarian lane wasn't half bad, Jonas decided on Sunday night as he finished off the last of the dishes and prepared to help Verity close the restaurant. He'd worked in worse places. The clientele at the No Bull Cafe was trendy but harmless. They tended to be clean, chic, well behaved, and definitely upwardly mobile. And they tipped well. A man could do worse.

On several occasions in his life, Jonas reflected, he had done worse. Much worse.

The crowd had been light that evening, but Verity ran out of broccoli bisque around nine nonetheless, and that had caused her to fret somewhat. Jonas had experienced an almost overpowering compulsion to cuddle her a bit and kiss the tip of her lightly freckled nose and tell her not to worry about the miscalculation on the soup. He had resisted the temptation. He was no fool.

Kissing the boss would no doubt be a good way to get himself flayed alive. The lady had a cutting edge on her tongue that made the knife in his duffel bag appear dull in comparison. Verity had a temper and she had no compunction about delivering an admonishing scold when she felt it was required. There was, in fact, Jonas had decided after due consideration, a side to Verity's nature that brought the word *shrew* vividly to mind.

It was not a scolding Jonas wanted to elicit from her. What he wanted was to be allowed to overdose on her smile.

Verity had a smile that dazzled the senses. He was fascinated by it; captivated by it. When it appeared—brilliant, warm, sensual, and genuine—he found himself staring at her in bemused wonder. There was a sweet, feminine honesty in that smile that drew a man the way honey drew bees. A man could be excused for thinking he was the most important male in the universe when Verity smiled at him. That smile drew Jonas more compellingly than even the dangerous secrets of his past.

That smile declared Verity to be a woman who would give herself to a man completely. At the same time, it proclaimed her to be a woman a man could trust with his life, his passion, and his honor. Verity's smile was a temptation to believe that chastity could walk hand in hand with an earthy sensuality. It was a smile of indescribable innocence and a haunting vow of total surrender. That smile promised everything and furthermore promised to deliver it with such innocent, passionate generosity that a man could not be blamed if he committed a few small murders to possess the owner of that smile.

But that smile left Jonas wondering why there weren't men standing ten deep around the No Bull Cafe begging for the chance to commit murder. It was hard to believe that every available male in the vicinity was so afraid of the shrew that they had given up trying to possess the sensual angel. But that appeared to be the case. Jonas didn't understand it; after all, what were a few thorns when you were hunting a real treasure? But he was grateful he didn't have to worry about a lot of competition.

Jonas figured the reason he had the field to himself probably involved more than Verity's shrewish tongue. It was probably that part of her basic nature that hinted at a certain fastidiousness. A man sensed instinctively that this was a woman who would never be promiscuous. In the short time he had been working for Verity, Jonas had clearly noticed that she had a remarkably prim and proper and unadventurous lifestyle. What was more, she seemed quite content with that lifestyle.

The weekend rush was over and Jonas felt he had acquitted himself well. At least his lady boss was not complaining too loudly.

He knew enough about her by now to realize that she certainly would complain if he didn't fulfill his duties to her satisfaction. She ran the little kitchen like the redheaded tyrant she was and she did not tolerate any laxity in cleanliness.

"The last thing I need is to have some of my customers get sick because the kitchen help failed to properly reheat the soup," she had told Jonas as she instructed him in soup preparation. "Everything has to be either chilled or hot. I don't want to see any food left sitting around at room temperature, and neither do the health authorities. They have a habit of paying unannounced visits, you know."

"We didn't worry too much about the health authorities down in Mexico," Jonas had remarked as he obediently stirred the soup.

"I'll bet you didn't worry about them in most of the places you've worked."

"True. A reasonable bribe usually took care of awkward health regulations."

"Things are different here," Verity had explained loftily.

"I'm learning."

And he was, Jonas thought on Sunday evening as he watched Verity walk up the path to her small cabin in the trees. No doubt about it. He was learning a lot about Ms. Verity Ames, skilled chef, small-time tyrant, and savvy businesswoman.

One of the things Jonas had learned was that he wanted her. Badly. He had sensed it first down in Mexico, but ever since he had arrived on her doorstep Friday afternoon, the need had been growing within him. He had told himself at first that it had nothing to do with sex. The need within him was all tied up with the mystery of the earring and the strange compulsion that had made him follow Verity out of Mexico.

But by Sunday night Jonas knew better. He wanted her in some way that was both sexual and psychic. He was beginning to wonder if taking Verity to bed might solve some of the mystery she held for him.

A quote flickered in his mind—a short passage from Castiglione's *Book of the Courtier.* Something about whoever possesses a woman's body also wins the fortress of her mind and soul.

It had been a while since Jonas had studied the sixteenth century Renaissance guide to gentlemanly behavior. He seemed to recall there had been a counterargument made in response to that particular statement about dealing with women, but he couldn't remember exactly what it was. At the moment he didn't care. The old words suddenly seemed to make excellent sense to Jonas.

Jonas sat on the steps that led up to the deck of his small cottage and fingered the earring in his pocket. He listened to the soft sigh of the breeze in the dark pines. He was waiting to see if Verity would follow her usual nightly routine.

This was the third night he had watched her walk back to her cabin alone. The first night, he had offered to escort her but she had just laughed and told him to get some sleep. She was quite accustomed to seeing herself home.

She was telling the truth, Jonas knew. It was becoming more and more obvious that Verity did not have a lover. Nor did she seem to care about the lack of a love life.

He had discovered her nightly routine on Friday when he had glanced out the window of his cabin after turning off the lights. Verity didn't turn off her own lights as quickly as he had expected. He had stood at the window and watched and after a few minutes he had been rewarded with the sight of his new boss coming back out of her cabin.

She had changed into a bathing suit and terrycloth robe

and she made her way briskly along the unlit path toward the resort.

Jonas's first thought was that his boss lady had a midnight swimming rendezvous with a man. The idea had made him strangely restless. He had been unable to resist the impulse to follow her.

He had discovered, to his secret, overwhelming relief, that Verity was not meeting a man. She was using the resort's spa pools after hours. The bathing rooms were distinctly marked with a "closed for the night" sign, but Verity had let herself in through a back door and had walked right into the women's section. Jonas had been fascinated as he stood out of sight and watched Verity ease into a steaming, bubbling pool. It had amused him that she wore a swimsuit into the spa bath, even though she had the place to herself.

It was a very prim and proper little bathing suit. It was cut high across her small, rounded breasts and it even had a modest ruffled skirt around the hips. It made Jonas think of the bottle of extra virgin olive oil that occupied a shelf in Verity's kitchen.

Tonight he had decided to join the tyrant in her after-hours relaxation program. Jonas figured he deserved it after the way she had lectured him earlier that afternoon about the evils of fast food. It had been his own fault, of course. He should have been more discreet with the greasy hamburger he had brought back from the chain restaurant in town.

The problem was that there were occasions when he couldn't resist deliberately provoking the little tyrant. He was rapidly learning just what sort of provocation it took to get a rise out of Verity. A part of him had guessed that the sight of the hamburger would do it and he had blandly let her see him eating it.

Jonas was perceptive enough to realize that provoking the lady was a poor substitute for what he really ached to do with her. He wondered if she would fire him on the spot if she realized that while he scrubbed her pots and pans he was fantasizing about taking her on the kitchen floor.

Once again Jonas wondered if he really could get faster answers to the mystery of Verity Ames if he did get her into bed. He was turning that over in his mind when he saw her cabin door open. Right on schedule. He pulled himself out of his reverie and watched her as she stood silhouetted for a moment in the light that shone through the open doorway.

She was dressed in her usual discreet bathing suit and robe, her red hair caught up in a loose cluster of curls on top of her head. As Jonas watched she closed the door behind her, not bothering to lock it, and started down the path to the lodge.

Jonas gave her a few minutes and then got to his feet. He reached down to pick up the two cans of beer he had put on the step earlier and then he set out after her.

As he paced down the path behind her, Jonas studied the sweet, unconsciously seductive sway that characterized Verity's stride. No doubt about it, the lady had one hell of a sexy tail. There was a gentle glide to her movements that appealed to him on a visceral level. It made him wonder how she would feel moving beneath him in passion. He could visualize those nicely curved legs wrapped around his waist, and he had no trouble at all imagining the lush globes of her buttocks filling his hands. Now he wanted to know the reality of what it would be like to make love to Verity Ames.

Jonas had tried to be realistic during the past three days. He had told himself that, objectively speaking, Verity was not a great beauty, not by a long shot. She could have been a little taller, for one thing. Furthermore, she was a bit small on top, and overall she was much too thin, although Jonas didn't fault her tiny waist. Verity's slenderness was a direct result of the fact that she worked too hard, in his opinion.

Her features were delicate but not classic. Her aqua-green eyes tilted up at the corners like those of a playful cat, and her nose was a bit sharp. There was a stubborn, feminine strength in the line of her jaw and firm little chin. It was a face that reflected intelligence and energy and a unique kind of sensuality.

Jonas's fingers tightened around the cold cans of beer and he quickened his step as Verity disappeared through a door at the back of the resort's main building.

Verity eased herself into the hot, bubbling water of the spa pool, sank down onto the bench seat, and leaned back against the white tile. She closed her eyes and exhaled slowly, a long, satisfied sigh of relief. Her feet hurt tonight. A peril of the restaurant business. The weekends were moneymakers but they took a lot of energy. She was never really sorry to see the arrival of Monday. Monday was the one day of the week the No Bull Cafe was closed during the summer and early fall. Soon she would start closing Sunday evenings, too. Winter was a quiet time in Sequence Springs.

As Verity let the frothing hot water soothe and relax her weary muscles, she mentally chastised herself for running out of broccoli bisque earlier that evening. Jonas had seemed to think it was no big deal. But then, it wasn't his restaurant.

Nevertheless, he had handled the situation with casual aplomb. He had simply removed the item from the chalkboard that listed the evening's specials and informed anyone who asked that there hadn't been enough good broccoli to make more than a limited quantity of soup. That last bit had been a small fib. There had been plenty of excellent broccoli. Verity simply had not properly estimated the amount she would need for Sunday night.

Mistakes such as that generally annoyed her. But Jonas's calm attitude had made it easier for Verity to take the miscalculation more or less in stride tonight. It was almost as if Jonas had somehow shared the responsibility with her. That was a highly unusual sensation for Verity. She was accustomed to assuming all the responsibility for everything that happened in her life. Growing up as Emerson Ames's daughter had taught Verity how to take responsibility early on.

Odd that Jonas had given her the impression she could share with him some of the difficulties of running the No Bull Cafe. From every indication he was just another irresponsible drifter, like her father. A man with too much intelligence and too little personal motivation. The combination of ability and lack of drive never failed to irritate Verity. But Jonas was giving her her money's worth and more at the No Bull, so she supposed she shouldn't be too critical. After all, he would soon drift back out of her life the same way he had drifted into it. Men such as Jonas never hung around any one place too long.

The realization brought an unexpected rush of unhappiness. She wondered how she could have already gotten used to having Jonas around. It was a dangerous sign.

But then, she had known from the beginning that Jonas Quarrel was a dangerous man. She had seen the ghosts in his eyes and she had felt the pull on her senses the first time she had opened the door to him. Instead of slamming that door in his face, she had allowed him to push his way into her serene, carefully controlled life.

A wary part of her was beginning to wonder how big a price she would pay for her recklessness. But another part of her was already wondering just how reckless she could be with Jonas Quarrel. She had never asked that question in regard to any other man; had never needed to ask it; had never wanted to ask it. A thrill of anticipation went through her at the thought. Verity fought and failed to suppress it.

"Is this a private party or can the hired help join in?"

Verity's eyes snapped open at the sound of Jonas's dark, lazy voice. She blinked and saw him lounging with the grace of a Renaissance courtier against a white stone pillar, two cans of beer cradled in one lean hand. He was wearing his usual outfit of faded jeans and work shirt, but somehow he looked very much at ease in the elegant blue and white spa room.

It struck Verity that Jonas had a knack for looking at ease, regardless of his attire or his surroundings. That indefinable air of nonchalance had been a prime goal of every Renaissance aristocrat, she knew. Whole books had been written during those years giving instruction on how to obtain the proper aura of casual power. The man who had it was quietly telling the world that he could and would handle everything that came his way. It betokened a controlled strength that did not need to be flaunted. It was the four-hundred-year-old version of the modern desire to appear cool. She wondered if Jonas had picked up the technique through his studies of Renaissance history or if it just came naturally to him. She strongly suspected the latter.

"The spa is officially closed at this time of night," she said rather stiffly. She wasn't quite sure she wanted to invite him into her private bathing retreat. On the other hand, he was already in the room. "This is the women's section, you realize."

"I'll take the risk of getting caught trespassing. I've been thrown out of better places than this." Jonas smiled faintly and came away from the pillar with a lithe movement. He strolled to the edge of the pool and crouched down near Verity. Then he popped the top off a can of beer and held it out to her.

Automatically, Verity reached up to accept the beer. He was just being friendly, she thought. Perhaps he was a little lonesome. She eyed him warily and then thought about how hard Jonas had worked this weekend.

"I'm sure Rick and Laura wouldn't mind if you used one of the pools," Verity said with studied politeness. "And I guess it really doesn't matter that this is the women's section. At this time of night, resort guests aren't allowed down here. But Rick and Laura have always allowed me to use the place after hours."

Jonas glanced around at the half-dozen pools in the tiled room. "I'll use your pool," he announced. He unbuttoned his shirt and tossed it aside. Then he rose and tugged off his low boots. His hands dropped to the buttons of his jeans.

Verity took a much larger swallow of the beer than she

had intended. She choked as she looked up at the expanse of hair-covered male chest above her. It was obvious that Jonas was every bit as hard and lean and smoothly muscled as she had guessed.

"Uh, didn't you bring a pair of swimming trunks?" she asked weakly.

"No." He was already stepping out of the jeans, revealing a snug-fitting pair of white briefs.

For an instant Verity was half-mesmerized by the full, heavy male shape outlined by the white cotton briefs. Then she jerked her eyes back to her can of beer. She told herself the briefs covered as much as a pair of swimming trunks would. Then she reminded herself that she was twenty-eight years old; too old to be startled by the sight of a man in his shorts.

"The water's very warm," she cautioned thickly.

"Yeah." He put one muscled leg into the bubbling pool. "Feels good." He settled down close beside her on the underwater bench. "Damn good." He leaned back and rested his arms along the tiled edge of the pool.

One sinewy forearm stretched out behind Verity's head. She was vividly conscious of its proximity. She was very conscious of the rest of Jonas's body, too. She considered sidling away from him and decided that that would look silly. The man was tired after a busy night, just as she was. He only wanted some relaxation. She could hardly blame him.

"How long have you been running the restaurant?" Jonas asked conversationally.

Verity gave him a sidelong glance and realized his eyes were closed. She relaxed. "A couple of years. I worked in several restaurants including the one here at the spa before I got the money and the nerve to open my own."

"Where else did you work besides Sequence Springs?"

"Oh, here and there," she answered carelessly.

"Here and there?" Jonas opened one eye. "Such as?"

"Well, there was Claude's place on Martinique. I learned

a lot of French techniques there. Then there was a little cafe in Spain where I picked up a few pointers on vegetables. I spent a few months studying Mexican cooking at a restaurant in Mazatlán. I learned about wine while working for a woman who owned a little hole-in-the-wall place just outside of Rio de Janeiro and I learned to wash dishes all by myself." Verity smiled. "I told you, you aren't the only one who's had a well-rounded education. I just don't have any formal degrees to go along with mine."

"What did your father do? Drag you around the world behind him?"

"Ever since my mother died when I was eight," Verity confirmed. "Sequence Springs is the first real home I've ever had. When I settled here three years ago I decided it would take an act of God or an economic disaster to uproot me. What about you, Jonas? Think you'll ever settle down?"

"I don't think about it much," he said, his voice becoming surprisingly rough without any warning. His eyes opened and he looked directly at her. "I take it you didn't go to college?"

Verity gave him a wry glance. "Dad didn't think much of the formal education process. He thought he could do a better job of educating me himself. You want to know the truth? I don't even have a high school diploma, let alone a college degree."

He gave her a quizzical look. "Does that bother you?"

Verity shrugged. "No, not really. I could have gotten my GED, I suppose, and applied to college, but the truth is, by the time that occurred to me I had already decided to open a restaurant and I didn't need any formal degrees for that."

"You know something? You're one of the more interesting employers I've had in the past few years, Verity."

"I'll take that as a compliment."

Jonas's leg idly brushed against Verity's in the water and she felt a tiny thrill along her nerve endings. She took another swallow of beer and discreetly moved her leg out of the way. The last thing she wanted to do was give the hired help any ideas, she told herself. Then her sense of humor took hold. The thought of seducing her dishwasher was unexpectedly intriguing. It was also amusing.

"Why the smile?" Jonas asked. "Think of something funny?"

Verity shook her head quickly. "No. I was just relaxing."

"The restaurant business is hard on the feet." Jonas reached beneath the water and pulled Verity's foot onto his thigh before she realized his intention. He began a deep, slow massage of her calf and the sole of her foot. "In fact, I've been meaning to tell you that you work too hard. I think you need a little fattening up, too. You're eating too much vegetarian health food for your own good. You need to introduce a little grease into your diet."

She bristled. "My diet is a heck of a lot healthier than yours. Do you know how much pure animal fat was in that hamburger I saw you eating this afternoon? Have you any idea what that stuff does to your insides?"

"No, but I have a feeling that if I let you, you'll tell me exactly what it does, and I don't think I want to hear it tonight. I'm trying to unwind from a hard day's work. So are you. Relax, boss lady." His thumbs probed deeply.

Verity started to argue but suddenly she was overwhelmed by the wonderful sensations Jonas was creating with his hands. She couldn't remember anything ever feeling as wonderful as his touch on the sore muscles of her calf. "Jonas . . ."

His heavy leg settled across her lap. "You do me while I do you. Fair enough?"

A wave of pure physical pleasure that had its origin in her toes moved through Verity. There was nothing wrong with a massage. It was very therapeutic. Heaven knew they had both worked hard during the weekend. So why did his question have such sensual overtones? she wondered. Or was her mind simply running wild?

"Fair enough."

Tentatively she stroked his hairy leg, seeking the feel of

the long muscles there. When she had one shaped beneath her palms she carefully squeezed her fingers.

"Ah, yes, that's it." Jonas's hand tightened for an instant around Verity's foot in a grip that was just short of painful. "Christ, that feels good, boss lady."

She wasn't sure if he was referring to the way she was stroking his leg or the way her foot felt to him. Verity intensified her grip and deepened the massage. For a few moments they worked in silence, eventually switching feet. Verity was beginning to feel more relaxed than she had in a long while. Her eyes half-closed as she concentrated dreamily on the innocently sensual sensations of giving and getting a massage.

"I wish you wouldn't call me boss lady," she finally said after a while. She took one hand off his leg to help herself to another swallow of beer.

There was a moment of silence while Jonas did the same and then he said softly, "I don't really think of you as a boss."

"No?"

"You want to know the truth? I think of you as a full-fledged tyrant."

"I had no idea I'd made such an impact on you." Verity squeezed his calf a bit harder than she had intended.

Jonas winced. "I can just see you back in the Renaissance presiding over a Medici court salon. You'd have the courtiers falling all over themselves trying to please you. They'd call you their flame-haired lady tyrant."

Verity thought about that for a moment. "Correct me if I'm wrong, but weren't most Renaissance court salons run by professional courtesans?"

Jonas chuckled. "You did pick up a well-rounded education, didn't you?"

"My father didn't believe in the formal educational process but he insisted I do one hell of a lot of reading," Verity said reminiscently.

"You're right about some of the ladies who ran the salons.

Think you'd like the life of a courtesan?" His eyes glittered teasingly between narrowed lids.

"That career path has lost some of its luster these days, but it would certainly have been a viable option for a woman back in the sixteenth century. It was either that or the convent. Either avenue gave a smart, savvy woman a path to power, and either choice sounds better than the only other job available."

"I take it you're referring to marriage?"

"Uh-huh. Marriage doesn't have a whole lot to offer a woman now, but back then it offered even less. Just the chance to die in childbirth and the opportunity to be some man's personal, unpaid slave." Verity paused thoughtfully. "I think, on the whole, I would have chosen the career of courtesan. Sounds like more fun than running a convent. I think I might have enjoyed presiding over glitzy soirees full of intelligent, refined men and women. They used to sit around in gorgeous clothes and discuss politics and philosophy and poetry, didn't they?"

"Among other things. The definition of social refinement was a little different back in those days. It was considered the height of sophisticated elegance if a man remembered not to scratch his crotch in public. Besides philosophy and poetry, the salon groups spent a lot of time talking about how to conduct love affairs. They thrived on romantic intrigue. The Renaissance was big on intrigue, remember. Any kind of intrigue. Political, social, or sexual."

Verity sighed blissfully as the images danced through her mind. "Sounds fascinating. I'll assume the courtiers in my salons were sophisticated enough to remember not to scratch their privates in public. I can just see me now wearing a satin gown with huge, slashed sleeves. I would have worn a ring that had a secret chamber for poison, of course, just like Lucrezia Borgia."

Jonas groaned. "Figures. I've got news for you: Lucrezia wasn't the witch that legend labeled her, just a lady who had a lot of bad luck when it came to marriage. And Renaissance poisons weren't nearly as reliable or as deadly as history implies, either. People worked hard on creating and testing them, but they lacked our twentieth-century knowledge of chemistry. Poisoning was a chancy business. When it came to killing, serious men usually opted for a dagger or a rapier."

"Ah hah. I can see it now," Verity said with relish. "Duels in the street over a woman's honor. Men fighting to the death to defend their lady's good name." Jonas's hand stilled on her foot. Verity lifted her lashes halfway and found him studying her with an expression that was far too intent. His amusement had faded. In its place was something far more dangerous.

"Would you enjoy seeing two men draw blood over the issue of which one got to take you to bed?" Jonas asked in an unreadable voice.

Verity was horrified. "Don't be ridiculous. I was just joking. I'm not likely to have to worry about that sort of thing in this day and age. And I probably wouldn't have had to worry about it back then, either. I'm not the type men duel over. It's fun to think about being a glamorous courtesan, but the truth is, I'd probably have wound up in a convent. The women who ran the convents were good businesswomen, weren't they?"

Jonas nodded absently. "Sure. Running a convent was like running any large business. There was a lot of financial and accounting work. Rents had to be collected from the convent properties. Staffs had to be appointed and supervised. The nuns usually helped support themselves with some form of manual labor such as making silk thread. That required supervision and financial contracts with the outside world. And then there were the jobs of educating the young novices and cooking and cleaning. On top of everything else, the convent had a definite social and political role in the community and whoever ran the convent had to be good at public relations."

Verity wrinkled her nose. "Sounds like my kind of work.

So much for the fast-lane lifestyle of the professional courtesan. I would have been stuck in a veil."

The gold in Jonas's eyes seemed very dark and burnished with mystery. His hand slid up her calf to her thigh. He hadn't appeared to move, but Verity realized he was a lot closer than he had been a few minutes ago, and the touch of his hand had somehow become intimate rather than soothing. He shifted position beneath the bubbling water, removing his leg from her lap. She went still, uncertain about what was going to happen next and even more uncertain about how to handle it when it did.

She should definitely not allow him to kiss her, Verity told herself. Bad policy between employer and employee. Very bad.

"Don't be so quick to decide what kind of woman you would have been if you'd lived during the Renaissance. And don't be so certain you know what kind of woman you are today," Jonas muttered as he looked down into her upturned face.

"I think I know myself very well," she said bravely.

"Do you? I think you've got secrets even you don't know about, little tyrant. What do you say we explore them together?"

She parted her lips to tell him she thought that was a very bad idea but the words never formed. Jonas's mouth was somehow in the way, cutting off the protest before it had even begun.

His lips came down on hers with a captivating insistence. Lulled by the warm water, the sensual massage, and the beer, Verity decided it wasn't worth making a fuss over one kiss.

Too late she realized that this was exactly the sort of kiss a smart woman should have refused. There was something different about this kiss, she reflected as Jonas's lips moved druggingly on hers. She couldn't put her finger on it but she knew that this was special, much too special. The taste and touch of him was unique, intoxicating, something for which she had been waiting for a long, long time.

Until this moment, Verity realized, she hadn't even known she had been waiting.

Without conscious thought Verity's right arm moved to encircle Jonas's neck. She felt the hard outline of the muscle of his shoulder beneath her fingers and she kneaded his bronzed skin the way a cat kneads a silk pillow. Jonas responded with a deep groan of desire.

He urged her mouth open and when she slowly parted her lips for him he muttered something thick and sensual. Hot gold poured through her in a dizzying wave. Then he was tasting her with the tip of his tongue, inviting her to join him in a small, astonishingly sexy duel. His hand moved farther up her thigh to the edge of her bathing suit.

For a timeless moment Verity hovered at the edge of never-never land, delightfully suspended at the gate of sensual exploration and discovery. She was aware of Jonas's fingertips as they slowly eased beneath the elastic leg of her swimsuit but she didn't worry about it. Time enough to stop him later. Right now she had to sample a bit more. She was enthralled.

The hot water frothed and foamed around her as Jonas changed position again without breaking the intimate kiss. He settled back against the white tiled pool wall and lifted Verity across his thighs. He kept one hand on her hip, his fingers just barely inside the barrier of the elastic. His arm was behind her back, his palm on her side, not quite touching her breast.

Verity felt no sense of being rushed. She had all the time in the world to enjoy this kiss. Languidly she touched him, her fingertips trailing through the crisp, curling hair of his chest.

Jonas seemed content to let her explore him slowly just as he was exploring her.

All the time in the world, Verity thought. She had waited so long and now she could take her time and do it right. This was the man—the right man. She didn't understand how it could be possible, but she knew intuitively that she was poised on a precarious peak. If she took one more step . . .

The lights suddenly blazed in the pool room.

"I'm sorry, folks, no guests allowed in the spa pools after ten o'clock. I'm afraid you'll have to leave."

Verity gasped at the sound of the familiar voice. She jerked out of Jonas's grasp, flailing wildly for an instant before toppling off his thighs and falling backward into the pool. The hot, bubbling water closed over her head.

A second later she felt a pair of strong hands grasp her shoulders and pull her upright. Sputtering and gasping for breath, Verity found her footing and stood. Her hair was plastered tightly against her head and she wiped the back of her hand across her eyes to get rid of the excess water. Jonas's hands remained on her shoulders as he turned to look at the newcomer.

"Hi, Laura," Verity mumbled.

Laura Griswald stared at the pair in the pool, the expression on her pretty face registering first astonishment and then speculative amusement. "Sorry, Verity. I didn't realize it was you. I just saw two people in the pool and assumed a couple of guests had violated the rules. Who's your friend?"

Verity knew she was turning a dull red. Despite the heat of the water, she could feel the warmth in her face. She ducked out from under Jonas's hands and waded determinedly to the edge of the pool where she had left a thick white towel earlier.

"Laura, this is Jonas Quarrel. He, uh, works for me. I hired him Friday. Jonas, meet Laura Griswald. She and her husband operate this place." She made a production out of blotting her hair and face while the other two exchanged polite greetings. By the time the pleasantries were over, she had herself well under control again. A bit of embarrassment was all that remained. She smiled bravely at Laura. "Busy weekend, wasn't it, Laura? I thought things would settle down now that fall is here, but the weekends, at least, still seem to be going strong. I'll be glad to start closing Sundays as well as Mondays. Jonas and I worked hard this evening. We decided to use your spa to relax. Hope you don't mind?"

If Laura thought her friend was chattering inanely, she kindly refrained from saying so. She smiled back, her bright hazel eyes moving with open interest from Jonas's unruffled expression to Verity's pink-tinged cheeks. Beneath the lighting of the spa room, Laura's shoulder-length brown hair gleamed with health. In fact, her whole body looked quite sleek and trim and bursting with energy, as befitted the manager of a spa. She was three years older than Verity and occasionally took a somewhat protective attitude toward her.

Laura was not above trying to matchmake for Verity and had made several futile attempts to pair her friend off with a carefully chosen up-and-coming type who was vacationing at the spa. To date, all of Laura's efforts had failed, so it was not surprising that she found the sight of Verity in a man's arms quite interesting. Verity stifled a groan and finished drying herself.

"Don't rush out on my account," Laura said hastily as Jonas hauled himself lightly out of the pool. "Feel free to stay as long as you like. Verity and her friends aren't subject to the same rules as the guests."

"That's all right," Jonas said, his eyes on Verity as he reached for a towel to wrap around his waist. "Something tells me it's time to call it a night. Ready to go back to the cabin, Verity?"

Verity cleared her throat. "Yes," she said firmly, "I am. Good night, Laura."

Laura's smile was beatific. "Good night, Verity. Nice to meet you, Jonas. I'm glad Verity was able to solve her staffing problems so quickly. Good help is so hard to get."

Chapter Three

*J*onas got out of bed Monday morning with a feeling of pleasant expectation. The No Bull was closed for the day and he intended to use the free time to finish settling into his new home. It looked like he was going to be around for a while, he thought, as he padded barefoot across the cold wooden floor to the small, chilled bathroom. The notion gave him an unfamiliar sense of satisfaction.

He glanced at the floor-to-ceiling bookshelves that lined every wall of the small cabin and wondered where he would put his few personal items. Someone, presumably Emerson Ames, had already turned the place into a long-term storage facility for a private library.

Well, Jonas reminded himself as he considered the limited room available, he didn't need much space. He'd been traveling light for years. A man on the run didn't let himself get weighed down with too many belongings.

He studied himself critically in the cracked bathroom mirror while he ran water into the sink. There was no getting around the fact that he did not appear too prepossessing in the mornings. The dark stubble of his beard gave his lean face a shadowed, menacing look. Jonas wondered if Verity would mind.

Ah, well, she would get used to it. After all, he had.

He worked up a lather and applied it to the stubble while he contemplated the mental image of Verity in the mornings. Jonas decided she would look pleasantly tousled and flushed with sleep, all her normal barriers lowered.

Those barriers had begun to crumble quite nicely last night in the spa pool. Jonas felt another wave of satisfaction go through him as he picked up his razor. Given a little more time, he would have had that prim swimsuit off of her. Verity hadn't been fighting him. In fact, she had seemed as caught up in the moment as he had.

It was too bad about Laura Griswald's interruption, but Jonas was philosophical. He had plenty of time. He'd been in a rush to locate Verity, but now that he'd found her, he could afford to take things easy. He hadn't even tried to pick up where he'd left off in the pool last night after he'd walked Verity back to her cabin. He had enough sense to know when to push and when not to.

He felt he had all the time in the world. It was a pleasant feeling. The idea of getting to know Verity slowly and intimately filled him with a throbbing excitement. The only major problem Jonas could see was the very practical one of how long he could restrain himself physically. After last night, it was going to be hard to let things take a slow, leisurely course toward bed. But he was determined to try. The last thing he wanted to do was rush her.

Verity deserves a proper courtship.

Jonas frowned into the mirror, wondering where that thought had come from. Was that what he was doing? Courting Verity? No, not quite. He wanted to learn her secrets, but that wasn't the same as wanting to marry the woman, for Christ's sake.

Jonas finished shaving and took his shower. By the time he was dressed and had water on the stove for instant coffee, the cabin was finally beginning to get warm. He made a mental note to see what he could do about the lousy heating system. He was supposed to be a handyperson, after all.

And if he didn't get the system fixed, it was going to be one long, chilly winter here by the lake.

Of course, the winter would be far more comfortable if he moved in with his boss, Jonas told himself. He fingered the earring in his pocket as he stood by the stove waiting for the water to boil. From the kitchen window he could see the light in Verity's bedroom window. She was up early, as usual.

A slow smile of satisfaction and anticipation edged his mouth. The gold circlet in his pocket felt warm to the touch, and the faint pulse of the earring's vibrations was full of promise. Just like Verity.

Verity spent Monday morning taking inventory and planning menus for the week ahead. She would have to arrange for a delivery of rice and a few other staples, she noted. The supply of buckwheat was almost gone; her buckwheat crepes had proven quite popular. She sat at the desk in her tiny office and sipped coffee while she made lists, checked accounts, and paid bills.

The work was fairly routine and she found herself thinking about other things while she wrote out checks and made notes. Mostly what she thought about was Jonas Quarrel.

Verity still didn't understand quite what had happened last night in the spa pool. True, she was twenty-eight years old and still a virgin, but she was far from naïve. She had been kissed before and had derived moderate pleasure from the process.

But what she had been discovering last night could hardly be described as moderate. It couldn't even be described as purely physical. Something more had been involved, something that went beyond the physical. On one level she felt vaguely alarmed, but on another, more immediate level, Verity was dangerously intrigued. She wondered how far things would have gone if Laura Griswald hadn't walked into the spa room.

She was very much afraid she knew the answer to that question, and her insides tightened at the knowledge.

Everything had felt so right when Jonas held her in his arms. After all these years of waiting and wondering, things had finally felt *right*.

But they had felt right with the wrong man. It wasn't fair. Her father had warned her once that life was not always fair, she reflected. It was more of a crapshoot, he had explained. A game without any rules except those an individual made for himself.

Perhaps it was just as well that Laura had interrupted matters, Verity decided as she put away the large check register. She needed time to think before she became any more involved with Jonas Quarrel. The last thing she wanted in her life was another drifter, even if he did know the secret of stirring her senses.

She frowned thoughtfully, wondering if Jonas had gained any wrong impressions from what had happened last night. Then she told herself there was nothing to worry about. In all the ways that counted, she was the one in charge around here. If worst came to worst, she could always fire him.

As she comforted herself with that thought, the phone rang. Verity smiled wryly as she reached for the receiver. It didn't take much intuition to guess who would be calling.

"Hello, Laura," Verity said without any preamble. "The answers are, I don't know, no, and I doubt it."

"How did you know what I was going to ask?" Laura demanded ruefully.

"You want to know where Jonas Quarrel came from, if he's already my lover, and if he isn't, will he be."

"I'll take comfort in the 'I doubt it' answer. There's still hope," Laura shot back. "You really did hire him?"

"He showed up looking for a job on Friday afternoon. He arrived just as I was about to pick up the phone and yell for help."

"Well, he's interesting, I'll grant you that. But as much as I'd like to see you involved in a love affair, it's my duty to advise caution. These days a woman can't be too careful. Did you check his references?"

"You know me, Laura, I always check references."

"Well? What did you learn?"

"To summarize: He's an expert on Renaissance history and he's got a lot of experience washing dishes, tending bar, and bouncing drunks. He's drifted most of the way around the world earning a living with those job skills."

"You don't have a bar and you don't get many drunks at the No Bull," Laura pointed out. "Nor are you in the business of teaching Renaissance history."

"True, but I do need a dishwasher. He's a hard worker, Laura."

"He looked more like a fast worker to me. I couldn't believe it when I walked into the spa last night and saw you wrapped around him."

She heard the back door open and close and knew Jonas was in the cafe kitchen. Her fingers tightened on the phone. "Don't exaggerate. I was hardly wrapped around him. It was a simple kiss, Laura. Don't make too much out of it."

"Are you kidding? After three years of trying to match you up with a nice stockbroker or lawyer and getting nowhere for all my pains, you turn around and jump into a spa with your newest dishwasher and I'm not supposed to make too much out of it?"

Verity chuckled. "You should be grateful and infinitely relieved, Laura. For three years you've said my biggest problem was that I was too picky."

"Your biggest problem is that you're going to spend your whole life looking for a man who has all your father's strengths and none of his weaknesses."

"Laura . . ."

"Common sense, which you usually have plenty of, should have told you by now that you're not going to find that combination in any normal male. You are too picky. Much too picky. But there's no need to go crazy now that you've decided to be more reasonable in what you demand in a man. Let me find you someone interesting from my guest list for next weekend. Now, I've got a nice doctor down here, age forty, and he's coming by himself. Probably divorced."

"Or gay."

"No. If he were gay, he'd probably be checking in with another man," Laura said thoughtfully. "I think this doctor might be a viable candidate."

"Listen, Laura, I'd love to chat about my problems but right now I've got to go. I've got a million things to do and . . ."

"And your dishwasher just walked through the door, right?"

On cue, Jonas appeared in the office doorway, dark brows forming a solid, disapproving line across his blade of a nose. Verity glanced up and found her senses awash in memories of foaming water and a wet, warm kiss that had been more intimate than any kiss she had ever known.

"Goodbye, Laura. I'll talk to you later." She dropped the phone back into the cradle. "Good morning, Jonas," she said very brightly.

"What the hell are you doing inside on your day off? Let's go down to the lake. There's some leftover curried lentil loaf in the refrigerator. Not the same thing as a real meat loaf, but if I put enough mayonnaise on the bread I might be able to disguise the stuff. I walked into town and picked up some beer an hour ago. We're all set. "

Verity swung around in her chair so suddenly that she bumped one jeaned leg against the desk. "Ouch, dammit." She winced, rubbing her knee. "I thought you were going to settle in to the cabin today."

Jonas shrugged in his casual, curiously graceful way. "I've already done that. I didn't have all that much to unpack. The main problem was finding room on the bookshelves for a few of my things. Your dad apparently has what is politely called eclectic tastes. He's got everything from Nancy Drew to Shakespeare stashed in that cabin."

Verity laughed. "That's the library he used to educate me. The only thing Dad never throws away is a book. Everything else in his life is disposable. When I settled here in Sequence Springs, he boxed up all the books he'd been lugging around for years and shipped them to me to store."

Jonas grinned. "I saw a copy of Castiglione's *Courtier* on one shelf. Did you ever read it?"

"Years ago, when I had a certain interest in the Renaissance," Verity admitted cautiously. "Why do you ask?"

Jonas's grin turned wicked. "I happened to be thinking about a particular passage from it last night, and when I spotted it on the shelf this morning I thought about it a little bit more."

"What part?" Verity demanded suspiciously, aware that she was enjoying the teasing quality in his voice.

"The part where one of the courtiers—Gaspare, I think—remarks that the way to win the fortress of a woman's mind and soul is to take possession of her body."

Verity smiled loftily. "I believe the response to that stupid remark was that if that were true, there would be no unhappy married women. Every woman would be madly in love with the man who had the right to make love to her, namely her husband. But since there are plenty of unhappily married women in the world, I think we can safely assume Gaspare was full of chicken manure."

Jonas folded his arms and studied her for a few seconds. "You must have had more than a fleeting interest in the Renaissance if you remember that sort of detail from a book you read years ago. Let's go pack lunch and head for the lake, boss lady. I'm hungry."

Verity thought about telling him one more time not to call her "boss lady" but decided to tackle that at a later date. The idea of a picnic was too compelling to resist. It had been a long time since she'd been on a picnic.

They packed a lunch and Jonas put a couple of cans of cold beer into the basket. Then he led Verity through the trees to the water's edge. He made a production out of picking the perfect spot among the pines before he allowed her to settle down on the blanket he had brought along. Verity was surprised to find herself very hungry.

Jonas lounged alongside her on the old blanket, sipping beer and eating sandwiches while they engaged in easy, totally nonthreatening conversation. Verity relaxed in the warm sunlight and gave herself over to enjoying the unusual experience.

She liked listening to Jonas talk, she realized. His voice was curiously attractive. She let him finish an amusing story about tending bar in some far-off corner of the world and then she said between bites of her sandwich, "I'll bet you were a popular lecturer when you taught at Vincent."

He blinked with deceptive laziness. "What makes you say that?"

She shrugged and realized she was blushing. "You have a good voice," she mumbled. "There's something very, uh, well . . ."

"Something very what?" he prodded.

"Something compelling about it. I mean, it's easy to listen to you." She stuffed the rest of the sandwich into her mouth before she was tempted to try her foot. She didn't know why she was so embarrassed. Probably because she found his voice more than compelling. She found it distinctly sensual. It touched her in an almost physical way and she responded to it.

"Thank you, Verity," Jonas said very gently as he leaned back on his elbows and watched her through narrowed eyes. "I shall treasure the compliment."

She was even more embarrassed and covered it up by fishing around inside the basket for a pickle. "Anytime," she said with false heartiness. "I always believe in giving credit where it's due."

He smiled faintly and she knew he was aware of her discomfort. His voice dropped to a low, sexy purr as he quoted softly:

"My lady scatters precious gifts with a casual, careless
*   hand.*
She knows not how much I value the fragile gems she
*   chooses to bestow.*
Greedily, I snatch all that I can take;
*   a smile of silver, a glance of crystal.*
But still I hunger for more priceless things;
*   Treasures that can't be bought or sold.*
For I will not rest until I claim her body and her
*   heart;*
Gifts of white hot fire and rarest gold."

Verity's head came up quickly and she found herself staring into his brilliant eyes. She knew in that moment that she
was being wooed. She had never been caught in a web of
seduction before, but it was shatteringly evident that she was
rapidly becoming entangled in it now.

For a moment neither spoke. They simply looked at each
other and Verity became aware of a vibrant truth. Jonas was
the one who could give a gift of gold. It was there in his
eyes, waiting for her. And as for fire, well, she might be
inexperienced, but she was woman enough to know he offered that, too. It would be a blazing, masculine fire that
would burn her to the depths of her soul, branding her for-
ever. She shook her head a little to free herself of the dizzying images. Frantically she sought for a way out of the web
that was tightening around her.

"Would you like another pickle?" she asked brightly and
slapped it into his outstretched hand. She ignored the amusement in his eyes and began a running commentary on the
economy and social aspects of Sequence Springs.

But even as she pushed the conversation back into safer
channels Verity knew she was running from the stark truth
that awaited her. She was fascinated with Jonas Quarrel. She
wanted him. It was the first time in her life she had ever
known the full, blazing power of this kind of attraction and
it both frightened and excited her.

Why, oh why, she wondered once again, did he have to be the wrong sort of man for her?

The question was, of course, unanswerable, so she pushed it aside once more and went back to enjoying the day.

They whiled away Monday afternoon at the lake, and Monday evening Jonas suggested taking in the film that was showing at the only theater in Sequence Springs. Verity realized it had been a long time since she'd been to a film. When she mentioned that to Jonas, he tapped her chin with his lean forefinger and shook his head admonishingly.

"You work too hard," he said.

Verity bristled. "That's a joke, coming from someone who spends his life drifting from one dishwashing job to another." Too late she realized she had come close to spoiling the whole evening.

"What's the matter, little tyrant? Aren't you getting your money's worth out of me?" Jonas taunted far too softly.

Angry with herself for nearly ruining what had been the most pleasant day she had spent in ages, Verity tried an awkward apology. "I didn't say that. I just meant that you and I have a slightly different understanding of the work ethic, that's all. You're content to drift through life and never use your abilities. I don't like to see ability wasted."

"Believe me," Jonas retorted, "the world does not need another professor of Renaissance history. It'll get along just fine without me. Now stop fretting about my lack of future prospects and eat your popcorn. You need a little fattening up."

She grumbled about the greasy, salty popcorn he bought but ended up eating her share. Jonas seemed pleased. She wondered if he would attempt to kiss her again that night and spent a long time trying to decide how to react if he did. She acknowledged to herself that she was actually considering indulging in her first full-blown affair. That thought made her feel light-headed.

The question of a good-night kiss, let alone anything else in that line, did not arise, however. Jonas took her to her door, wished her good night, and loped off to his cabin.

Verity tried to tell herself it was just as well and that she was vastly relieved. The truth was that she was more than a little disgruntled. She felt off balance. She also regretted the derogatory comments she had made about Jonas's lifestyle. If she'd kept her mouth shut she might have wound up having a nightcap and a good-night kiss with her professional dishwasher. Instead, she ended up reading for an hour before she could fall asleep.

Her father had frequently told her that her tongue was her worst enemy, Verity reflected as she turned out her light. Maybe he was right. She had yet to meet a man who didn't run from it.

But Jonas hadn't really run from the sharp-edged sword of her tongue. He had simply sidestepped it, sliding out of the way in the manner of a fencer dodging an opponent's thrust. If she wasn't careful, he might easily slip through her guard with his next move.

Verity just wished she knew whether she wanted to win or lose the battle.

On Tuesday the No Bull Cafe reopened for the light but steady weekday crowd that kept it going during the off season. The local people showed up during the week, as did a few tourists who happened to be passing through town and had seen the restaurant mentioned in a guidebook. And as usual, a few spa patrons could be counted on to drift over for lunch or dinner.

Verity managed to keep herself and Jonas busy during the day to prevent any time for awkward moments during which either one of them might be tempted to bring up the subject of their relationship.

Relationship. The very word made her nervous and fretful, Verity decided that evening as she and Jonas closed the cafe. She didn't think that what she and Jonas had at that point qualified as a relationship, and, as far as she could tell,

Jonas seemed not to be worrying about the issue at all. In typical male fashion, he appeared blithely unaware of all the soul-wrenching questions that were plaguing her. That annoyed Verity.

She told herself that any man who remained oblivious to the agonizing uncertainty in which she was mired was certainly not a sensitive enough male to interest her. Unfortunately, Verity was intelligent enough to know she was lying to herself. Brains could be a great curse.

But Tuesday brought an unexpected event. Laura called late that afternoon.

"Verity? I want to make reservations for three. Rick and I have a special guest staying at the spa and we want to take her to dinner at your place. Any problem?"

"Nope. I'll put you down for seven. How's that?" Verity opened her reservation book and jotted a note.

"Sounds fine. You'll want to meet our guest, Verity."

"Who is it?"

"Caitlin Evanger." Laura waited for recognition to hit.

"*The* Caitlin Evanger? Caitlin Evanger, the artist?"

"One and the same," Laura affirmed proudly.

Verity was entranced. "I heard she was a total recluse."

"She is. She's got some physical problems. Apparently she was in a serious car accident years ago and never fully recovered. She came to Sequence Springs to take the waters, as they say in Europe."

"I'll be thrilled to meet her," Verity declared, aware of Jonas listening in on the conversation as he moved around the dining room setting up tables.

"Don't make a big deal out of it," Laura warned. "She hates attention."

"Don't worry. I'll try not to embarrass you with a lot of fawning and groveling. See you at seven, Laura." Verity hung up the phone and grinned at Jonas. "How about that? We're going to be feeding a famous artist this evening. Caitlin Evanger. Ever hear of her?"

"I think so." Jonas folded a napkin with great precision

and placed it properly on the table. "The name is vaguely familiar. I don't think I've ever seen any of her work, though."

"I have," Verity declared enthusiastically. "There was an exhibition of her stuff a few months ago in San Francisco. I went to see it. Her paintings are absolutely fascinating, Jonas. There's this incredible, hard edge to them and yet they're not cold or lifeless. You can almost feel the passion under the surface, but you get the impression that it's a very dangerous passion and therefore it's overlaid with this amazing sense of discipline, if you know what I mean."

Jonas cocked one brow and gave her an odd look. "I think I know what you mean."

Verity felt a slow warmth rising in her cheeks. She wasn't certain she wanted to analyze Jonas's glance. It seemed safer to change the subject. "Good grief, I wonder if I'd better rethink the dinner menu. Maybe I should substitute orange and jicama salad for the carrots in dill sauce. Carrots are so ordinary."

"The way you do carrots in dill is anything but ordinary," Jonas said brusquely. "Don't worry about the menu for tonight. I'm sure your celebrity guest will be able to find something on it to suit her."

Verity gnawed thoughtfully on her lower lip. "Do you really think so?"

"Tell you what. If she doesn't like what she sees on your list of specials, I'll run into town and get her a hamburger."

"Sometimes your sense of humor leaves a lot to be desired, Jonas."

At five minutes after seven that evening, Jonas found himself seating Rick and Laura Griswald and their guest, Caitlin Evanger. He had met Rick on Monday and liked him. Griswald was about Jonas's age, with thinning hair and an easygoing smile, although tonight the smile seemed a bit forced. He kept himself in good shape and had the kind of outgoing personality that resort managers need. It was obvious that both he and his wife were very proud to be escorting their important client this evening, but it was equally obvious that they were finding the honor somewhat wearing.

Jonas had to admit that Caitlin Evanger was impressive. Definitely not the kind of woman who would be overlooked in a crowd. There was a sense of drama about her that made itself felt instantly.

She was tall, almost as tall as Jonas, with short, silvery blond hair that she wore slicked straight back from her high forehead. Physically, she appeared to be about thirty, but there was something in her face, a hard, weary cynicism, that gave Jonas the impression she was a lot older in some ways.

Her features would have been riveting at any age. Her stark hairstyle focused attention on her high, aristocratic cheekbones and small, perfectly shaped mouth. Jonas wondered idly if that mouth had ever been shaped into a genuine smile. He seriously doubted it.

He didn't notice the jagged scar that marred her left cheek until she turned her head. The contrast between her beautifully classic profile and the savage line of ruined flesh was startling, but not nearly as startling as the cold gray stare that met his polite glance.

It was the kind of look that chilled a man straight to the bone. Caitlin Evanger's gaze took in everything around her and made it clear that she would never be impressed by anything the world had to offer, let alone what a mere male could provide.

This was one cold lady, Jonas decided. Not the kind of woman a man imagined curling up with on a winter's night. Verity had a few thorns on which a man could cut himself, and she also had a sharp tongue and a certain feminine arrogance, but there was no doubt about the fire inside. Caitlin Evanger was a glacier right to the core.

The artist wore a steel brace on one leg, which showed beneath the hem of her severe black silk shift. She used an ebony cane to make her way toward the table Verity had carefully chosen earlier. It was the one nearest the fireplace. Her movements were slow and deliberate because of the brace and the cane, but there was a regal quality about them. Everyone around her instinctively slowed down to match her stately pace.

"I'll tell Verity you're here," Jonas said as he finished seating the Griswalds and their guest.

Laura smiled gratefully, her eyes tense. "Thanks, Jonas."

Jonas walked into the kitchen, aware that Caitlin Evanger was watching him the whole distance. He could feel those icy gray eyes on his back. It was enough to make him shiver from the chill.

He found Verity looking disheveled and flushed from the heat of the stove. The sight of her warmed him instantly. A few curling tendrils had come loose from the knot at the back of her head. She was concentrating intently as she arranged a picture-perfect salad of endive, blue cheese, and roasted walnuts. He smiled at the image she made.

"Your star guest has arrived," he announced.

Verity's head came up quickly, her eyes sparkling with excitement. "She's here? Where did you put her?"

"At that little table near the hall that leads to the restrooms," Jonas said carelessly.

"Jonas!"

"Relax. I put her and Rick and Laura exactly where you told me to—near the fireplace."

"Thank God. This is not a joking matter, you know," she lectured severely. "I can't wait to meet her. What's she like?"

"You can't miss her. She's the one who looks like she should be wearing a brass brassiere and carrying a spear."

Verity glowered at him and shoved the salad plate into his hands. "Very funny. Here, take this out to table number three. I'm going to say hello to our new guests."

"Sure, boss lady."

She ignored that, brushing past him into the dining room. Jonas shook his head in amusement and strolled out to table number three with the salad. One cold greeting from Caitlin Evanger would no doubt wash that silly excited sparkle out of Verity's eyes. It never paid to get thrilled by a visiting celebrity. From the expressions on the Griswalds' faces, Rick and Laura had already discovered as much.

To Jonas's complete astonishment, however, it was soon apparent that Verity and her celebrity artist had hit it off quite well together. The Griswalds were obviously relieved to have someone take the burden of conversation off their shoulders, and Verity clearly had plenty to discuss with Caitlin Evanger. That didn't surprise Jonas as much as the fact that Evanger seemed quite content to talk with Verity.

Jonas found himself keeping a speculative eye on the two women as he served the other tables. Strange. He'd never thought of Verity as the hero-worshipping type. *Or should that be heroine-worshipping type?* he wondered vaguely.

Verity had to keep dashing back and forth to the kitchen throughout the rest of the evening but at every free moment she returned to Caitlin Evanger's table. It was obvious that she was fascinated with her guest.

Jonas's indulgent amusement over Verity's bright-eyed enthusiasm started turning into outright annoyance somewhere around nine o'clock. It occurred to him that Caitlin Evanger was getting a lot more attention from Verity than either he or the cafe was getting. Jonas was left to keep the dining room running. It was just fortunate for everyone concerned that Tuesday evenings were quiet, he told himself grimly. If Verity ran the place like this on a regular basis, the No Bull Cafe would have gone broke a long time ago.

By ten o'clock the restaurant was empty except for the Griswalds and Caitlin Evanger. Verity sat down at their table once again and this time she stayed there, leaving Jonas to finish cleaning up the kitchen alone.

That did it. Enough was enough. Jonas tossed aside the pan Verity had used to mix a dish of fettuccini and peapods and stalked out to the dining room. Verity's crystal laughter greeted him. She turned around in her seat as he approached.

"Jonas, you'll never believe this. Caitlin knows you."

A sudden, cold alertness washed through Jonas. He glanced speculatively at the other woman. "Is that right?" he asked calmly. He was dead certain he had never met Caitlin Evanger before. No man would ever forget this chunk of ice.

Caitlin lifted her wineglass to her lips, her eyes on him. When she spoke her voice was as cool as the rest of her. "Vincent College. About five years ago. You gave an undergraduate history lecture on Renaissance warfare techniques and equipment. You used slides of several Renaissance paintings to illustrate your points. I was taking some art-history classes there at the time and I dropped into the hall to hear what you had to say. I had heard about you."

Jonas hesitated a beat before answering. His stomach tightened as if someone had just put a sixteenth century blade in his hand and told him he might have to use it. This was the last thing he needed right now. How much did this strange woman know about him? he wondered. How much had she heard, and why was she here tonight? Something felt very wrong. Dangerously wrong.

"You have an excellent memory, Ms. Evanger."

The gilded blond head nodded once in satisfaction. "I thought you looked familiar. When Verity mentioned your background in Renaissance history I began to put it all together." Her gray eyes pinned him. "How on earth did you wind up here? You were making quite a name for yourself in academic and museum circles, as I recall."

Before Jonas could find a way to deflect the pointed question, Verity interrupted. Her gaze was on Jonas's face. "What sort of name was he making for himself, Caitlin?"

"At the time I took the classes at Vincent, Mr. Quarrel was well known on campus. In addition to his growing list of publications, he had recently exposed a fraudulent necklace that was supposed to have dated from the sixteenth century. It had actually been made in 1955. He saved a well-known museum a fortune. Apparently there had been other such instances in which he exposed similar frauds.

Your Mr. Quarrel was gaining a reputation for being able to authenticate museum-quality artifacts. Your specialty was armor and weapons, though, as I recall, not jewelry. Isn't that right, Mr. Quarrel?"

Jonas watched Verity as he answered. "Times change, Ms. Evanger. My specialty today is dishwashing. Mind if I finish clearing the table?"

"Oh, don't worry about the dishes, Jonas," Verity said quickly. "Why don't you sit down and join us? Caitlin has been telling us all sorts of juicy gossip about the art world. It's fascinating."

"It's late. I'd rather finish up, if you don't mind. I wouldn't want to give you any reason to complain about the quality of my work. I need this job." He scooped up plates and silverware and went back to the kitchen. No doubt about it, he didn't like that cold fish of an artist. He liked her excellent memory even less.

Jonas was willing to bet that he wouldn't like Caitlin Evanger's art, either.

Jonas allowed his memory to shift back to the end of his career at Vincent College. Images of himself dressed as a Renaissance nobleman, a sword in his hand, flashed through his mind. So did the image of a man lying on the floor at his feet. Blood stained the pristine white lab coat the wounded man was wearing. It also stained the tip of the sword Jonas was holding.

With grim effort Jonas shoved the pictures out of his head. He had learned to live with the old nightmare. Most of the time he could keep it buried in his mind. But Caitlin Evanger had brought it to the surface again. The sense of wrongness he felt about the woman increased.

Twenty minutes later, when the little group in the dining room finally broke up for the evening, Jonas knew he was in trouble. Verity was more than a little annoyed with him.

That didn't bother Jonas. He was spoiling for a fight, himself. Everyone smiled politely as good-nights were said, but the moment the door closed behind the Griswalds and

Caitlin Evanger, Verity turned on Jonas. Hands on her hips, she confronted him as he lounged in the kitchen doorway, wiping his fingers on a dish towel.

"I hope you're satisfied with yourself, Jonas," she began without preamble. "Are you always that rude to people like Caitlin Evanger, or did you single her out for some reason? Whatever the answer, I'd like you to know that I was thoroughly embarrassed."

"Sorry about that." Jonas tossed aside the dish towel. "Ready to go home?"

She stared at him. "You're not sorry at all. What on earth is the matter with you tonight?"

"Nothing's the matter. It's late and I'd like to get to bed."

"Don't look at me—I'm not stopping you," she snapped.

"Fine," he growled. "Let's go." He headed toward her, turning out lights as he went. When he reached the door he took her arm in a forceful grip and steered her outside. She stood stiffly while he locked up for the night.

"Would you mind telling me why you're acting this way?" Verity hissed softly as he again took her arm and prodded her in the direction of her cabin. "You're behaving like a spoiled little boy who's throwing a tantrum because things aren't being done his way."

"That's better than acting like a silly, fluff-brained art groupie."

"Art groupie!" She yanked her arm free of his grasp. "That's a stupid thing to say. Just because I like Caitlin Evanger and her art is no reason to call me names."

"You were hanging on that woman's every word tonight. Talk about fawning. I never would have thought of you as having a fan mentality, Verity. You made a fool out of yourself. 'I was stunned when I first saw *Branded*, Caitlin,'" he mocked, remembering one of the conversations he had overheard while clearing tables. "'I couldn't get it out of my head for days, Caitlin. Such a vivid commentary on the relationship between women and men in this society, Caitlin. Such artistic insight, Caitlin.'"

Verity moved before he could stop her. She yanked herself free of his grasp, whirled to face him, and came to a halt on the path in front of him. Jonas eyed her warily.

"I know what your problem is, Jonas Quarrel. Your feathers are ruffled tonight because you got an unwanted glimpse back into your own past, didn't you? Caitlin Evanger reminded you of the time you were making a success out of your own life. She reminded you of the days when you were on the verge of making it big in the academic world. You had your act together back then and you were going to be someone. People were already paying attention to you. And then you got lazy and blew it."

Jonas felt a tremor of real anger go through him. Up until now he had been merely irritated. But now he knew cold fury. Caitlin Evanger had reminded him of his past, all right, but the memories were laced with violence and blood, not the synthetic perils of academic success. He kept his voice even, but he could hear the edge in it and knew Verity must have heard it also.

"You don't know what you're talking about, Verity," he said. "I suggest you keep your mouth shut. My past is my business."

"I'll bet there's more to it than just being reminded of it," she went on recklessly. "I'll bet you're jealous."

"Jealous! Of Caitlin Evanger? Give me one good reason."

"She prevailed against all odds. She made it. She had ability and she honed and refined that ability, even though she was crippled for life. She worked hard to get where she is. She's not a success just because she had talent or because she got lucky. She *worked* for that success. Look at the difference between the two of you. You should take a lesson from her, Jonas. She's enjoying the fruits of her labors and going on to bigger and better things, while you're washing dishes."

"That's enough, Verity."

"You're just like my father. Both of you are too damn easygoing and too self-indulgent to work at achieving what you're capable of achieving. You don't even want to settle down, do you? You'd rather fritter away your whole life jumping from one place on the globe to another instead of staying put long enough to build something worthwhile of your life. You're irresponsible, that's what you are. A little boy who doesn't want to be bothered with growing up and assuming control of his life and his abilities. Here today, gone tomorrow."

"I said that's enough, Verity." He was knotted with tension as he received the lash of her tongue, but she seemed oblivious to the precarious state of his temper.

"Oh, shut up and go to bed. I don't want to hear anything more out of you tonight. The least you could have done was to show some respect toward someone who's made something of herself and her talent. Laura was right. I have been on the verge of going crazy, but I've seen the light in time. I'll start paying more attention to her stressed-out lawyers and stockbrokers and doctors." She whipped around and started up the path toward her cabin.

"Dammit, just who the hell do you think you are?" Jonas had her before she'd gone a yard, his hand closing forcefully around her shoulder. He yanked her back around to face him. He knew his words were dangerously soft but he doubted if she realized the significance of that. She had never seen him lose his temper.

"Let me go, Jonas."

He ignored the imperious command. "So you think I've got a few problems, lady? Well, let me tell you something, I'm not the only one. Take a good look at yourself. You're turning into a shrewish little spinster because you won't look twice at any male who doesn't live up to your high standards of sober, respectable, responsible manhood. No wonder you haven't got a lover, let alone a husband. What man in his right mind would want to get slashed to ribbons by that sharp tongue of yours? What man who wasn't a complete wimp would want to listen to you tell him how to run his life? Who gave you the right to sit in judgment on the male of the species? You know next to nothing about me and yet you've got the nerve to stand there and lecture me on what I've done with my life. *Who gave you that right?*"

He felt her flinch under the onslaught of his anger. Her eyes were huge and wary in the shadows. Jonas could feel her straining to escape the grip of his hand.

"Let me go, Jonas."

With a muttered oath, Jonas released her. Verity turned and fled to her cottage.

Jonas stood watching her, his hands clenched at his sides. He was almost shaking with the force of the anger and frustration sweeping through him. This woman was going to drive him over the edge.

He sensed the soft vibrations of the earring in his pocket and instinctively reached for it. The instant his fingers closed around the gold circlet he began to calm down.

When he had set out on the quest to find Verity he had not expected to find himself at the mercy of this sharp-tongued wench.

And he hadn't expected to run into an ice-blooded artist who knew something about his past, either.

Life was full of surprises.

Chapter Four

*T*he faint rasp of metal on metal brought Jonas out of a light sleep two hours later.

He came fully awake in the darkness, not moving while he focused on the sound. He had heard similar sounds before. Five years of surviving waterfront dives, back alleys, and lodgings that frequently fell short of Hilton standards had taught him exactly what that slight, scraping noise was.

Someone was trying the lock on the front door of the cabin.

Jonas flashed briefly on the remote possibility that the red-haired tyrant next door had come to apologize for abusing him earlier that evening. But the fantasy did not last long. Jonas had not survived the past few years by being anything other than extremely pragmatic.

The slight rasping sound came again. Jonas gathered himself quietly in the darkness and rolled out from under the old wool blankets. He stifled a groan of protest as his feet silently hit the cold floor. He really was going to have to do something about the heating system one of these days.

As the doorknob stopped twisting, Jonas forgot about the cabin's heating problems. He heard the scrape of a shoe on the front step and then silence. Whoever was trying to get into the cabin had obviously given up on the door and was probably searching for an open window.

Jonas reached into the worn duffel bag that had contained all his worldly possessions the day he arrived in Sequence Springs. The bag was empty now except for the sheathed knife that resided in its inside pocket. Jonas's hand closed around the handle of the blade just as the window made a squeak of protest. Jonas made another note to fix the broken lock on that window. A handyperson's job was never done.

The intruder was not going out of his way to maintain silence. Either he was very inept or he thought the cabin was empty.

Jonas padded softly to the wall beside the window. He was in position as the wooden frame began to squeak slowly upward. The large outline of a man, his face invisible in the darkness, hovered outside for a moment.

When the window was fully raised, the intruder threw one leg over the sill and grunted. He was in the awkward position of straddling the window frame when Jonas moved.

"Next time try knocking," Jonas advised as he wrapped an arm around the man's throat and yanked him through the window. Jonas could feel the hair of his beard brushing his arm. This man was large. When he hit the floor there was a solid thump.

"Shit! What the hell . . .?"

Whatever his next comment would have been, it was cut off by a muffled groan as Jonas pinned his late-night visitor to the cold wooden floor. The other man floundered briefly and furiously, showing a surprising amount of skilled strength until Jonas put the tip of the knife to his unguarded throat. Instantly his victim went still.

"That's it," Jonas said approvingly. "I think we understand each other. Don't move."

"Don't worry." The voice was a deep rumble. "I'm not going anywhere as long as you're the one with the knife."

Jonas patted him down. The man was wearing a wool

jacket, a shirt, and denim pants. There was no knife or gun strapped to his leg or hanging from his belt.

"Stay where you are." Jonas got to his feet and hit the light switch. An instant later the harsh glow of the bare overhead bulb filled the small room. Jonas found himself looking at a bear of a man.

His full beard and mustache had once been red but were now heavily streaked with gray. Ditto for the mass of short, shaggy curls that framed a small balding patch on top of his head. Aquamarine eyes glittered at Jonas from beneath heavy brows. He had big shoulders and was broad in the chest and heavy in the thigh. He was probably somewhere in his early sixties, although the short struggle he'd put up suggested the vigor of a younger man.

"Don't tell me, let me guess," the man stated as he rubbed the shoulder he had landed on. "My mercenary daughter decided to make a few bucks on the side by renting out my cabin, right? Sometimes that gal shows absolutely no respect for her poor, aging father. No respect at all."

Jonas leaned back against the wall in a casual slouch and studied those familiar aquamarine eyes. "Emerson Ames, I presume?"

"The one and only." Emerson sat up slowly. His sharp gaze moved assessingly over Jonas. "You play with knives frequently?"

"Not if I can avoid it. A man can get hurt playing with knives." Jonas decided there could be absolutely no doubt about the identity of this man. He walked over to the duffel bag and dropped the knife into its sheath. "Sorry about the unfriendly welcome."

Emerson watched him move. "My fault entirely," he growled generously. "I assumed the place was empty. It was too late to rouse Verity so I thought I'd just find my own way into the cottage for the night. I don't suppose you're Verity's lover, are you?"

Still leaning over the duffel bag, Jonas raised an eyebrow

at the undisguised tone of hope. He straightened as Ames got to his feet. "Nope. I'm her dishwasher."

Ames nodded sadly. "Figures. Give her a good, strong, solid son of a bitch like yourself who knows how to take care of himself, and what does she do with him? Hires him as a dishwasher. Lord, where did I go wrong with that girl? It's enough to make a man question the wisdom of giving female children a decent education." He glanced around the room. "I suppose by now you've probably drunk what was left of that bottle of vodka I left in the kitchen cupboard?"

Jonas grinned briefly. "Not quite."

"Good. I could use a little something to steady my nerves after that set-to on the floor. Mind if I help myself?"

"It's your bottle," Jonas said with a shrug.

Emerson Ames sighed hugely. "That's a fact. I'll pour you a shot, too. Something tells me we have a few things to talk about."

"Yeah," Jonas agreed. "Like who gets the floor for the rest of the night."

Verity saw the lights come on in Jonas's cabin. She was standing at the window in her flannel nightgown, the red, curling mass of her hair hanging down around her shoulders, when she saw the unexpected glow appear among the trees that separated her cottage from his.

Jonas was awake, too.

The knowledge gave her an odd sense of kinship, which made no sense at all. She wondered if he was regretting the harsh things he had said to her as much as she was regretting the things she had said to him.

He was right, she thought for the hundredth time. She had no business judging him. A man was free to scatter his talent and ambition to the winds if that's what he chose to do. She had better things to do than try to save him from a wasted future. He wouldn't thank her for the effort, anyway. He had made that perfectly clear.

Just as her father had made it clear that he wanted to be

footloose and fancy free to squander his literary talent on throwaway paperbacks with titles such as *Lone Star Ranger* and *Trouble at Silver Creek*.

Verity knew her father well enough to know that he had no real concept of home, at least not in the sense that she had always understood the term. She would save herself a lot of energy and grief if she accepted right from the beginning the fact that Jonas Quarrel was out of the same mold.

She watched the lights in Jonas's cabin as her thoughts drifted back over the evening spent with Caitlin Evanger. There was something fascinating about that woman. Verity had never met anyone quite like her.

Caitlin was a woman to be admired. Strong, courageous, brilliant, hardworking, and successful. It was obvious that Caitlin had no particular use for men in her life. A good role model all the way around, Verity thought wryly. Verity was willing to bet that if Caitlin ever took lovers, she didn't allow herself to get tangled up in the webs men liked to weave. Caitlin would laugh at male promises and masculine persuasion. She would always keep her priorities straight.

Verity knew that she owed it to herself to take a leaf out of Caitlin's book. For the past twenty-eight years she'd done a fairly good job of keeping her own priorities straight. If she was wise, she would not let one Jonas Quarrel, dishwasher and Ph.D., distract her.

But there was something infinitely compelling about this particular dishwasher. Too compelling by far.

A shadow moved behind the curtain in Jonas's window. He was going into the kitchen. Verity hesitated a moment longer, thinking, then she made up her mind. She went to the closet and pulled out a long wool coat that came to her knees. Belting it on over her flannel nightgown, she reached for a pair of loafers.

There were ghosts in Jonas's soul. She had known that from the moment she had first set eyes on him. She'd had no right to taunt those specters tonight, regardless of her feelings on the subject of shiftless, footloose males. Her employee deserved an apology.

A few minutes later Verity stood on Jonas's front step, the chilled breeze whipping the hem of her nightgown beneath her coat. She raised her hand, hesitated, then knocked tentatively.

The door opened a few seconds later. Jonas stood silhouetted in the light, a glass in his hand. For an instant he just stared down at her, an unreadable expression flickering over his hard face. Then his gaze turned sardonic. He gave her a skewed smile and took a long swallow of his drink.

"Correct me if I'm wrong, but I'll bet you're not here to throw me down onto the bed and make wild, passionate love to me, right?"

Verity felt most of her good intentions hardening into irritated resolve. "I came to apologize," she got out between set teeth.

He blinked, his dark lashes concealing the look in his eyes. "No kidding? Hold on while I switch on a tape-recorder. I want to make sure I get this down for the benefit of future historians. Tyrants almost never apologize."

"Look, if you're unable to be civilized about this, I'll just skip the whole thing and go back to bed."

He stepped back and held open the door. "Better come in and say hello to your father, first. We were just about to flip a coin to see who gets the bed."

Verity nearly tripped over the threshold. "My father! He's here?"

"In the flesh, Red." Emerson Ames appeared behind Jonas, a lot of teeth showing between his mustache and beard. He held open his arms. "How's business, kid?"

"Dad, for crying out loud. I thought you were in Brazil." Verity laughed and stepped into her father's bear hug of an embrace. "Where have you been? I went down to Mexico two months ago to spend some time with you and no one knew where you were. I searched for you for three days, you big idiot, before someone finally said he thought you had gone to Rio. Why did you invite me to Puerto Vallerta if you had plans to leave town before I got there?"

"Something came up, Red. A trifling misunderstanding concerning money. You know how it is. I had to make an unscheduled departure in the middle of the night. I figured you knew me well enough not to worry."

"I knew you well enough to figure out there wasn't much I could do except turn around and come back home." Verity withdrew herself from his grasp, shaking her head wryly.

"May I take your coat?" Jonas offered with mocking gallantry.

"No, you may not," Verity said, aware of her nightgown underneath the coat. She turned to her father. "I wasted three days of what was supposed to be a vacation searching for you. I thought I'd gotten the address wrong or something. I hit just about every bar in town trying to find you. I knew you wouldn't be in the tourist joints, so I tried the local spots."

Emerson winced. "Christ, Red, don't you have any more sense than to go cantina hopping in Mexico? What the hell did you think you were doing?"

"I told you," Verity retorted tartly. "I was looking for you. I know the kind of places you frequent. I should. You've taken me into enough of them."

Emerson raised his eyes toward the ceiling. "It's different when you're with me and you damn well know it. You little idiot. You could have gotten into big trouble."

Verity grinned without any remorse. "I'm a big girl now."

It was Jonas who spoke up. "That only means you can get into bigger trouble in places like a Mexican cantina."

Verity gave him a speaking glance. "You're an authority on the subject?" she asked sweetly.

"Honey, the man's right," Emerson muttered. "You had no business trying to track me down. As soon as you realized I wasn't at the address I'd given you, you should have come straight back here."

"Well, I didn't. I went out asking polite questions of several bartenders. And you're absolutely right. I got into trouble."

Emerson stared at her, brilliant eyes suddenly diamond-hard. "What kind of trouble?" he asked in a dangerous voice.

"Very big trouble," Verity admitted dryly. "I almost lost my purse, my, uh, virtue, and possibly my life. Believe me, you don't want to hear the details."

"The hell I don't," Emerson roared. "I know those places down there. I swear to God I'll go back and break heads until I find the piece of filth who put his hands on you. What happened, Verity?"

"Nothing," she said smoothly, successfully concealing the memory of shock and fear that she had brought back with her from her jaunt to Mexico.

"What do you mean 'nothing.' You just said you were attacked."

"I was saved at the last minute. It was all very exciting, I assure you." She was beginning to enjoy this. She had the full attention of both men. "I took a wrong turn down some alley. Stepped into a little cantina that catered to the local riffraff. Before I could step back out again, someone grabbed me." She shuddered in spite of herself, as the scene replayed once again her mind. Then she turned a bright smile on Jonas, who was following the tale with a riveted expression. "Got any more of that cheap vodka you and my father are drinking?"

Jonas nodded once, almost absently, as if the last thing he was interested in at the moment was getting her a glass of vodka. But he obediently headed for the kitchen and a moment later Verity heard the clink of glass on glass.

"Here you go," he said as he returned and shoved the glass into her hand. "What happened?"

"Yeah, Red, let's have the rest of the story. The suspense is killing me." Emerson took a huge swallow of his drink and flopped down onto a chair. "Fatherhood has its drawbacks. A man could go crazy from the stress."

"Stress is one thing you'll never have to worry about, Dad. I doubt if you know the meaning of the word. Your lifestyle is not conducive to stress."

"That's what you think."

Verity sat on the chair near the desk and arranged her coat discreetly over her knees. Jonas just stood where he was, watching her every move. "To make a long story short, I got away from a rather large, odoriferous man named Pedro who grabbed me as I was trying to beat a hasty retreat from the cantina."

"You know how to give your old man nightmares, don't you? Jesus, Red. How did you get away?" her father demanded.

Verity lifted one shoulder, trying for a negligent air. Heaven knew she had been anything but casual about things that night. It had been a real skin-of-the-teeth experience. She had never been so frightened in her life. "Someone else came into the alley. I didn't get a good look at him. He was tall. Taller than Pedro, at any rate. That's about all I know. It was pitch black and I wasn't in the mood to make detailed observations. I just wanted out of there. I suppose the second man was some tavern patron who apparently thought good old Pedro didn't deserve to have me all to himself. There was a fight and in the confusion I got away. The only thing I lost was an earring." She held up her glass of vodka in a small salute. "So you see? Luck follows the virtuous." She took a swallow of her drink and coughed as the raw liquor hit her throat. Her father's taste in liquor was appalling.

"Luck follows idiocy, you mean," Emerson corrected gloomily. He scowled at Jonas. "Think twice before you decide to have daughters, Quarrel. They'll drive you crazy."

"I'll remember that," Jonas said quietly. He seemed preoccupied with his vodka.

Verity caught the odd tone in his voice and wondered at it. Something wasn't quite right but she couldn't put her finger on it. For some reason, it gave her an uneasy sensation to realize just how little she really knew about this man. She turned back to her father.

"Okay, Dad, let's have it. What brings you to Sequence Springs?"

Emerson contrived to look hurt. "Can't a man get a paternal hankering to see his one and only child?"

"Sure, but you could have seen me two months ago down in Mexico if seeing me had been all that important to you," Verity pointed out carelessly. "It certainly would have been a lot more convenient for you. But the fact that you've come back to the States without any warning makes me wonder just what you're up to."

Emerson sighed and again looked at Jonas. "That tongue of hers gets sharper every time I see her. It's getting to the point where she can make a man bleed with a few well-chosen words. She used to be such a sweet, good-natured little girl. Now she's turning into an old maid before my very eyes."

Verity's mouth tightened ominously. "Odd that you should say that, Dad. Jonas was just making a similar observation not more than a few hours ago."

Jonas narrowed his eyes. "You should be grateful we're both concerned about your future."

She wasn't altogether certain he was teasing her. Deliberately she smiled at him. "Don't worry about me. If either of you had any common sense you'd spend your time worrying about your own futures."

"Hah," her father muttered. "My future will take care of itself. It always has. But if I let you continue to go your merry way, I'm not going to have any grandchildren to bless my old age and that's a fact."

Verity fought back the warmth in her cheeks. Jonas was smiling faintly. It was time to press the attack. "Answer my question, Dad. To what do I owe the honor of this midnight visit?"

Emerson swirled the vodka in his glass and looked pained. "Well, Red, to tell you the truth, I need a place to cool my heels for a while."

"Dammit!" Verity exploded. "I knew it. You're in trouble,

aren't you?" Her hands tightened painfully around her glass. "Well? What is it this time?" It was all she could do to keep from hurling the glass across the room. She sensed Jonas's brooding, watchful gaze, and the knowledge that he was witnessing her loss of control made that loss even worse. "Go on, tell me. Did you get caught with someone else's wife? Did you try your hand at smuggling refugees out of some hole-in-the-wall country again? Get behind on your gambling debts? Or is your presence here simply the end result of some barroom brawl that you lost? Who's looking for you?"

Emerson cleared his throat. "You see how it is?" he complained to Jonas. "No respect. No compassion. No concern for her old man. Just demands for explanations and answers, and when she gets them she'll probably spend half an hour chewing on me."

Jonas's faint smile broadened briefly but the intent look in his eyes did not lighten. "What is the explanation, Emerson?"

The big man shrugged. "What can I say? I owe a man a few bucks, that's all. A debt of honor."

"Debt of honor, my foot," Verity muttered. "A gambling debt is a gambling debt. No need to dress it up the way they did two hundred years ago by calling it a debt of honor."

Her father shook his head in woeful regret and turned back to Jonas. "You'd think after all the history I had her read, she'd have more respect for the subject, wouldn't you?"

"So you owe a man a few bucks?" Jonas prompted calmly.

"I do and he's getting a tad anxious, I'm afraid. I told him he'd have to wait awhile, and he told me if he was forced to wait too long, he'd send a few people out to rearrange my face. I deemed it prudent to depart from Mexico and then from Rio. My research was finished down there, anyway."

"What research?" Verity asked tightly.

Emerson's eyes brightened. "Didn't I tell you? I'm starting a new series of books, Red. Futuristic westerns."

"Futuristic westerns?" she asked blankly.

"Sure. It's a natural. Just think what I can do with the combination of traditional western story components and an exotic, extraterrestrial background."

Verity didn't know whether to laugh or cry. She told herself she should be accustomed to her father's ways by now. "You were in Mexico researching futuristic westerns?"

"Great locale and atmosphere. I was just about done, so I called you up to see if you could take a few days off and come down for a visit. You always did like Mexico. But right after I called you, I got the message that this gentleman to whom I owe a certain sizable sum was impatient. I couldn't reach you to call off the trip, but I figured you'd understand when you arrived and found me gone. In the meantime I thought I'd give Rio a whirl. Hadn't been there in a while. As it happens, all my problems were solved in Rio. Or almost solved, I should say. There are a couple of small details to work out, which is why I'm here to visit you for a while."

"What details?" Verity asked with deep suspicion.

"I have to complete a certain transaction," her father explained. "When it's finished, I'll have the cash I need to pay off this rather persistent gentleman who has been hounding me for the past three months."

Verity went cold. "What kind of transaction?" she whispered.

Emerson gave her a compassionate look and then shook his head at Jonas. "Look at her. Now she's convinced I'm running drugs."

"For a spinster, she's got an active fantasy life," Jonas observed gently.

"Shut up, both of you," Verity snapped. "Tell me about this transaction, Dad."

"I have come into possession of a very unusual item, Red. It's in my bag, which is still outside in the car. I'm told this item is extremely valuable. Normally such things are sold through auction houses, but I haven't got time to set up a

deal like that. I also lack the kind of paperwork and guarantees of authenticity an auction house likes to see. I need to
unload this item quickly for obvious reasons."

"You need a private collector," Jonas said quietly. "One
who is passionately devoted to his hobby and who won't ask
a lot of unnecessary questions."

Emerson looked at him with respect. "Exactly. A discreet
collector. Preferably one for whom cost is no object. I
thought it would be easiest to find one here in the States. But
first I need to get the item appraised. I want to know exactly
what I'm dealing. So far I've only got the former owner's
word that the item is valuable."

Jonas leaned forward, his glass cradled between his lean
hands. "What is this item you're trying to sell, Emerson?"

Emerson grinned. "I'll show you." He got to his feet and
walked to the front door. En route he patted his daughter on
the head. "Be right back. Try not to tear each other's throats
out while I'm gone."

The door closed behind him and silence reigned. Verity
studied her half-empty glass. Jonas didn't move.

"So," he said at last, "you came over here tonight to apologize?"

"I don't know what got into me," she mumbled, feeling
put upon and therefore sarcastic. "I must have been crazy."

Jonas got soundlessly to his feet and crossed the room to
stand in front of her. He took her glass from her hand and set
it down beside his on the small table near her chair. Then his
hands closed around her shoulders and he lifted her to her
feet.

"So gracious. But I'll take what I can get. Apology accepted, little tyrant," he said softly and brushed the lightest
of kisses across the tip of her nose. With his mouth very
close to hers he asked, "What have you got on under this
coat?" He ran a finger down the row of large buttons to the
sash. "It looks like a nightgown."

"Never mind about my clothes. I think you owe me an
apology, too," she announced, looking up at him warily.

"I agree," he said, golden eyes suddenly cryptic. "But my sin is greater than yours and I haven't even finished committing it yet. Give me a little time, Verity."

She thought he was about to kiss her again, this time on the mouth, but the door opened, letting in a blast of cool air. Her father came into the room, bearing an old, flat wooden case. He watched with interest as Jonas casually took his hands off Verity's shoulders. "Here, now, don't let me interrupt anything. You two got something going on between you?"

"Don't get excited, Dad; the man works for me."

"Looks to me like you're giving out some interesting employee benefits, Red."

"Forget it, Dad. What's in the case?"

Emerson chuckled. "Take a look. If your old man hasn't been had, if these are genuine, they're worth a small fortune. Enough to pay off the hound who's baying at my heels." He opened the old case and revealed two oddly shaped guns nesting in faded, aging felt.

Verity stared at the long-barreled weapons. They were both fascinating and ominous-looking. The grips were curved and the metal was blued. There was no hint of ornamentation on the guns. Unlike most handcrafted items from the past, they were stark, functional, and terrifyingly plain in design. The very lack of decorative details seemed to emphasize the purpose for which the weapons had been made.

"Dueling pistols," Jonas said calmly. He peered into the case but made no move to touch the guns. "British flints. Probably late seventeen hundreds. If they're real, you're in luck, Emerson. They're worth a bundle. How did you say you got hold of them?"

Emerson eyed his prize. "I did a favor for someone once a long time ago. I looked him up in Rio a few weeks back to see if he would be willing to loan me a few bucks to help me get out of my present predicament. He gave me these instead and said they should take care of my problem. I trust my friend, naturally, but you never know. The first thing I have to do is verify that these are originals and not reproductions. Then I'll have to figure out how to find a buyer."

"The first part of your problem should be easy to solve," Verity said briskly. "Jonas has the kind of knowledge and experience it takes to authenticate old things, don't you, Jonas?" She looked up at him, challenging him to prove that what Caitlin Evanger had said about him earlier was true. "Go ahead. Tell us whether my father has come into possession of a pair of valuable dueling pistols or if he's just been taken to the cleaners."

"I'm kind of curious myself," Emerson said easily. "The condition of my face may depend on it, not to mention my kneecaps. Do you know something about old guns?"

Jonas said nothing. He just stared down into the mahogany case as if he were looking through a window into another world.

"His former area of expertise is the Renaissance," Verity told her father quietly as she watched Jonas. "But apparently he has a broad range of knowledge on the subject of arms and armor. Well, Jonas?"

He looked up then, his gaze trapping hers. The glittering gold of his eyes made her catch her breath. She sensed a battle going on behind that gaze; perhaps a battle between ghosts. She couldn't tell if Jonas was furious or desperate or excited or eager, or if his new mood was a dangerous combination of all of those emotions. She knew only that there was a wildness in him in that moment that defied description. Verity swallowed uneasily, wondering what had been unleashed inside him. Already she regretted her impulsive demand.

"Jonas?" she whispered with uncertainty.

"You don't know what you're asking," he said, his voice raw and harsh. "But maybe this is as good a time as any for both of us to find out."

He reached into the case and lifted out one of the pistols.

The instant his hand closed around it, Verity experienced a sudden, overwhelming sensation of being pursued. A ripple of terror went through her. Her palms grew damp and her heart began to beat too quickly, as though she were preparing to run for her life.

That was exactly what she wanted to do. Like a doe fleeing the hunter's hounds, she wanted to whirl and run. The nameless fear gripped her. The walls of the cabin seemed to close in around her, curving, elongating, taking on the shape of a dark tunnel.

Someone was in that tunnel with her. She couldn't see him yet, but she knew he was hunting her. Soon he would reach out for her. If he caught her she would never escape.

Her whole future would be altered if the hunter in the dark corridor found her.

Verity stood frozen in the center of the room, desperately trying to understand what was happening to her.

Panic attack, she thought frantically. The abrupt onset of an irrational fear that triggered the ancient fight-or-flight mechanism in the human body. She'd never had one, but she had heard about them. She knew other women who had experienced them. The attacks struck without warning, leaving the victim shaking with an anxiety that had no known source. Stress was sometimes blamed. Perhaps Jonas was right. Maybe she had been working too hard lately.

In her mind she turned a corner in the tunnel taking shape and started to run. There was no end to the corridor; no light ahead. But she ran regardless, because anything was safer than staying to confront the hunter who pursued her. Already she could feel him coming closer, hands reaching for her.

"Don't run from me. You belong to me. Don't run."

The words echoed in her mind, part command and part plea. She thought she should be able to recognize that voice. It was rough, male, and full of power. And it only made her want to flee faster through the corridor. She had to get out of there.

Then, without any warning, the curving walls and the sense of being pursued disintegrated. Verity was abruptly, violently aware of Jonas, who stood perfectly still beside her. He was no longer holding one of the pistols. He had returned it to the case. But he was looking at her with his strange golden eyes. There was a raw, unleashed hunger in that gaze. It was both undeniably sexual and much more, indefinable and dangerous and compelling.

The room around Verity looked exactly as it had a moment ago. Nothing had changed, although she was dazed. Something felt terribly, horribly different. In a way she couldn't explain, she sensed that her world would never be quite the same again.

"The gun is genuine," Jonas said in a voice that sounded unnaturally calm. "As Verity told you, my field is the Renaissance, but I know enough about old weapons to tell you that you've got a very valuable set of pistols there. Take care of them, Emerson. They're worth a great deal of money."

"I guess my daughter was right," Emerson said cheerfully. "Luck follows the virtuous. Now all I have to do is figure out how to turn these pistols into cash. Well, it's been a long day. What do you say we all hit the sack? I could use a night's sleep, and Verity here looks a little washed out. What's the matter, Red? Haven't you been getting enough sleep lately?"

"She works too hard and she doesn't eat properly," Jonas said. His eyes never left her face. "Come on, Verity, I'll walk you back to your cabin."

She wanted to refuse. The panic attack, or whatever it was, seemed to have vanished with as little warning as that with which it had materialized, but a lingering uneasiness remained.

Some part of her was almost certain that Jonas Quarrel was the source of her uneasiness. Yet, when he took her hand and led her outside into the night, Verity followed without protest.

Chapter
Five

"*A*re you all right?" Jonas asked quietly. His fingers closed around Verity's hand as he guided her through the trees along the barely visible path that led to her cabin.

"Of course," Verity mumbled, taking deep breaths of the crisp night air. Jonas's grip felt strong and reassuring. He seemed to be communicating some of his quiet strength to her. Verity tried to drink it into herself without being too obvious about it. "Why shouldn't I be all right?" She concentrated on the familiar sights and sounds of the night around her.

Everything was utterly normal here at Sequence Springs. The wind rustled in the trees. Scattered lights gleamed along the shoreline. The glow from her cabin window was warm and welcoming. Now and then the distant sound of an automobile engine rumbled briefly, then faded.

Everything was normal. She was normal. She was just fine.

"Your father was right," Jonas said slowly. "You looked a little washed out back there in the cabin. Sure you're okay?"

"I told you, I'm fine. Just a little tired, that's all. Having Dad show up out of the blue is always a bit disconcerting."

79

She felt defensive. Damned if she was going to admit to this man that she had suffered a momentary hallucination tonight.

"Take it easy," Jonas said soothingly. He released her hand and put his arm around her shoulders.

Verity found herself nestled closely against his side. The warm, heavy, oddly comforting weight of his arm around her sparked mixed emotions. On one hand, she was still aware of an inexplicable uneasiness. A part of her insisted on irrationally associating Jonas with the fear she had known a few minutes ago. But another, equally primitive and very feminine part of her was convinced that the masculine power in Jonas offered safety from those same terrors. In desperation, she tried to make normal conversation.

"It figures my father's only here because he's in trouble. If it isn't one thing, it's another. Now he's got a loan shark after him. Are you sure about those dueling pistols?" she asked.

"Sure about them being genuine? Yes, I'm sure."

She glanced up at him, curious and perplexed. "How can you be certain without doing some sort of tests?"

Jonas shrugged, the action somehow pulling her more tightly against him. "I've seen a lot of old guns. I know what old steel looks like. I know what old craftsmanship looks like. And I know what a dueling pistol feels like."

"What it feels like? What do you mean?"

He was staring straight ahead at the light in her cabin. "It's hard to explain. A good dueler feels right in the hand. The aim is true. Point it and it's aimed. You can sense it. In a real duel there's no time to line up the target in the gun's sights. All you can do is point the weapon in the general direction of the target. Dueling pistols are usually fairly heavy, too. They're designed so that in the grip of a very nervous man the aim is less likely to be affected by a jerky trigger finger."

Verity shivered. "Makes sense. I can imagine how nervous I would be if I were standing on a so-called field of honor at dawn waiting for someone to give the signal to fire."

Moonlight glinted briefly off Jonas's bleak smile. "The feeling goes beyond nervous, believe me. It's similar to the sensation you get when you hold a rapier with an unblunted tip and face a man who's holding another one just like it. Talk about life on the edge."

"You really were an expert on old weapons at one time, weren't you?"

"Yes. Feel better now?"

"I told you, I feel just fine. Perfect. Peachy keen," she retorted, irritated by the concern in his voice, even as she longed to indulge herself in his unexpected solicitude. "Why do you keep harping on how I feel?"

He stopped in the middle of the path and tugged her around to face him. His hands slid under the lapels of her coat. The moonlight and the night washed away the gold in his eyes, leaving colorless, gleaming gems that seemed to see past all her defenses into the depths of her soul. A faint echo of the panic she had experienced earlier shot through Verity. She caught her breath, half-preparing to run.

Jonas's hands tightened on the lapels and he held her still. "Relax," he ordered quietly. "It's over for now."

"What's over?" she whispered, searching his moonlit gaze for answers to questions she did not know how to ask.

"Nothing. Never mind." He groaned and pulled her closer. "Verity, you're safe with me. I swear you're safe. Please don't run from me. I'll take care of you. I swear it."

She stared at him, stunned by the intensity of his words. "Jonas, please, I don't know what's going on here."

"Yes, you do. You're not a child. You're a woman and you're attracted to me. I've seen it in your eyes. I can make you want me, honey. Really want me. I knew it when I kissed you in the spa." His voice was low, caressing, mesmerizing. "God knows, I want you. Let me have you. Give yourself to me. Let me show you how good it can be between us. Verity, I *need* you. Now. Tonight. I've waited as long as I can."

In that moment she believed him. He wasn't the only one who seemed to have the power to look into souls tonight. She was looking at him but she was also looking into him in a way she could not explain. She knew only that when he did battle with his silent ghosts, the struggle was not unlike what she had gone through dealing with the strange, amorphous fear that had swamped her earlier.

She did not comprehend the nature of Jonas's ghosts or of the battle being waged, but Verity knew with a woman's certainty that he spoke nothing less than the truth when he said he needed her tonight. She could feel the driving sensual force in him and knew it was focused totally on her.

And, with a small sigh, she acknowledged to herself that she needed him, too. She wanted him to drive away the memories of the dread she had felt a while ago, even though a part of her insisted on connecting him with that same panic. It didn't make sense in any logical fashion, but it made incontrovertible sense to the deeply hidden primal part of her nature. She and Jonas belonged together tonight. They needed each other.

For Verity the sensation was unique. She had never before felt this kind of need for a man.

The sighs of the breeze-ruffled pines haunted the night as Verity stood facing Jonas. Another shiver went through her but this one was not generated by cold or fear. This quickening of her senses was linked only to the man whose strong, elegant hands still gripped the lapels of her coat.

The intuitive realization that had come to her the first time he kissed her returned to her now in an overwhelming wave. *This was the right man; the one she had been waiting for.*

Instinctively she moved closer, seeking the warmth of Jonas's body and simultaneously pushing aside the feminine caution that had kept her safe from a man's demands for twenty-eight years. She rested her head on his shoulder, silently giving him the answer he sought. Jonas shuddered heavily and wrapped his arms around her.

"Yes," he rasped. "Oh, Christ, Verity, yes."

Then his mouth closed over hers, hot, hungry, filled with restless urgency.

This kiss was unlike the one in the spa pool. That one had only hinted at the passion that lay buried in the man. This time Verity found herself inundated with a resonating need unlike anything she had ever before experienced. It swamped her senses the way the unnamed fear had overtaken her earlier in her father's cabin.

But this time she felt no more than a fleeting desire to run. Her need to stay and sample the maelstrom of passion overcame twenty-eight years of wariness and caution. She surrendered to the moment, feeling her senses come alive with a new kind of sensitivity. Excitement swept through her.

But above all there was a driving need to answer the demand radiating from Jonas. Verity knew that she might have been able to resist the lure of passion, but the need to give Jonas what he wanted so desperately tonight was irresistible. She had never been needed like this. She had never wanted a man like this. Her head was spinning with the glittering lures held out before her in shining array. Heedlessly she reached to take hold of the priceless jewel of passion. Her arms went around Jonas's neck and she plunged her fingertips into the darkness of his hair.

"Verity," he groaned. "Sweet tyrant. I'm going to learn all your secrets tonight. Every last one of them. No more games."

His hands tightened around her, forcing her closer until she could feel the hard outline of his aroused manhood. The rough fabric of his jeans was taut across his groin. He moved against her, making her tremble in response.

"You feel so damn good," he muttered thickly. He nuzzled the sensitive place behind her ear and then he found the lobe with his teeth, sampling her with exquisite care. Verity moaned and locked her arms more urgently around him. "So soft. I'm half out of my mind with wanting you. I need to be inside you. I need to feel you wrapped around me." He released her slightly and started urgently along the path.

Verity stumbled along beside him, her footsteps made awkward by the combination of Jonas's tight hold and by her own shimmering sense of anticipation.

When they reached the cabin door, Jonas fumbled briefly with the unlocked door and then they were inside. The pleasant warmth and light enveloped them.

Verity stood blinking in the glare of the light until Jonas reached out and flipped the wall switch. Instantly the room was plunged into darkness.

"We don't need the light," he said.

She looked up at him and realized he was right. She could see all she needed to see of him. Almost too much, in fact. There was enough moonlight filtering through the cabin windows to reveal the starkly aroused expression on his harsh face and the burning heat in his eyes. Maybe it was better to view him in the soft glow of the moon rather than the more revealing glare of artificial light. Verity wasn't sure she could take the full impact of what she would see. For an instant she knew a jolt of fear once more.

"Jonas, I . . ."

"Hush," he said, kissing her back into silence. "I've told you I'll take care of you. You'll be safe with me."

She wondered why he was so determined to promise safety but there was no opportunity to ask. Jonas was already untying the sash of her coat and unbuttoning the oversized buttons.

"I knew it," he muttered as the coat fell to the floor. There was satisfaction in his voice. "I knew you were wearing your nightgown. I sat there watching you sip that vodka and I got hard just thinking about what you had on under that coat. Did you come to see me tonight intending to stay with me until morning, sweetheart?" He touched his tongue to the corner of her mouth. "Were you going to seduce me after you had apologized?"

She shook her head violently. "No. I was only going to say I was sorry for yelling at you. I never meant to stay."

"Don't say that," he said, indulgent amusement in every word. "You don't know for certain what you wanted. You don't even know your own secrets."

"And you think you do?" she challenged softly.

"I can only guess at some of them." His fingers worked the tiny buttons of her flannel nightgown until he had it open to her breasts. When he brushed against the gentle swell of her softness he sighed hungrily.

For a few seconds Jonas teased both of them by exploring the curves that were partially exposed and then he grew impatient. His fingers slipped inside the gown to cup her completely. He held her gently captive in the warm palm of his hand and his thumb flicked over one velvet nipple. There was an instant, uncontrollable response. Verity caught her breath and her nails sank into the cotton of Jonas's shirt, finding his hard, muscled flesh underneath.

"Go ahead and use your claws on me, vixen," he said, the words rough with his desire. "I don't mind carrying your mark. I think I was meant to bear it."

"Jonas, sometimes I don't understand you."

"You will soon enough. Don't think about the future, sweetheart. Just think about the here and now. It's all we need tonight."

He shoved the gown down over her hips, letting it fall into a pool at her feet. His gaze roved over her as she stood nude before him.

His hands followed the trail of his gaze, scorching her skin as he explored the small valley between her breasts and the curve of her waist. Then his fingers went lower, tangling lightly in the dark red curls at the juncture of her thighs. The heat in him assailed her, summoning forth a torrent of damp fire between her legs. When his fingertips brushed through that liquid fire, Verity thought she would collapse. All the strength seemed to be gone from her limbs.

"Jonas, I can hardly stand."

"I know. I feel the same way. You don't know what you're doing to me. You're so wet and hot. Why the hell did we wait this long?"

Verity gave a small, shaky laugh and clung to his shoulders. "We haven't waited long at all. Jonas, we hardly know each other."

"Not true." His fingers glided around to her hips. He squeezed her gently and then he picked her up and carried her down the short hall to her small bedroom. "I know you better than you think and soon you're going to know all you need to know about me."

He put her down in the center of the small bed and his hands went to the buttons of his shirt. He stripped the garment off with ruthless energy while he stepped out of his low boots, and he tugged at the button of his jeans. He yanked the pants off along with his briefs and a moment later he was standing naked beside the bed.

Verity looked up at him, her eyes full of feminine wonder. The shadows in the room concealed the details of his arousal but gave hints of the broad planes of his shoulders and chest. Silhouetted against the pale glow of the window he seemed very large and very male. "You're strong," she murmured, trailing questing fingertips along his taut thigh. "Strong and hard."

"Harder than I've ever been in my life," he agreed with a groan as he came down beside her on the bed. "I feel like I'm going to explode. I need to be inside you more than I need my next breath. Open for me, honey. Let me touch you."

She felt his hands on the insides of her thighs, prying apart her legs. Verity was suddenly aware of her own vulnerability. Things were going much too fast, she realized. She needed a little time.

"Wait," she begged as he anchored her resisting leg with his own heavy thigh and began to explore her with increasing intimacy. "Please, Jonas. Not so fast."

He leaned over her and kissed one peaked breast. "But

you're ready for me, sweetheart." His fingertips found the tiny bud of desire that lay sheltered in the curls below her waist. When he stroked it lightly, Verity gasped and lifted herself against his hand. "You see?" he said with soft satisfaction. "You're more than ready. My hand is damp from touching you. You're slick and moist and welcoming. Honey, I can't wait. Don't ask me to go slowly tonight. I'm desperate for you."

She closed her eyes as her body responded to his touch. Behind her lids she expected to see some fantasy generated by the fever of desire pulsing through her. But what she saw was an endless dark corridor. Once more she was running from an unseen pursuer and once more she was convinced that pursuer had eyes of ancient gold.

Verity froze and frantically lifted her lashes, willing the vision to pass. "Jonas, I'm scared."

"Not of me. You can't be frightened of me." He raised his head and looked down at her as he felt the new rigidity in her body. "I won't let you be scared of me."

"Wait, please, I need to think. I can't get something out of my head. Something that happened earlier when you picked up the gun. It's been bothering me and I want to . . ."

He interrupted her with a harsh exclamation. "Don't think about that now. Think about me. Think about us. I'm going to make you forget what happened earlier. Look at me, Verity. Open your eyes, dammit, and *look at me.*"

He loomed over her, parting her legs with his own, caging her within his hands, blocking out the moonlight. Verity looked up at him, her whole world suddenly narrowed down to her tiny bedroom and the man who dominated it.

Once more the fierce sensual need swept through her. She did want him. This *was* the right man. There was no need to fear Jonas.

Verity was poised on a sharp blade of desire. She could not stay teetering on the brink for long. The tension was too great. It would tear her apart. She must either pull back now, this instant, or she must hurl herself forward into the darkness.

"Hold on to me, sweetheart," Jonas whispered, the words raw. "Just put your arms around me and hold on to me. Take me inside you. We'll both be safe then."

She wanted to tell him again that she did not understand but instead she clung to him. She held him tightly, passionately aware of the strength in him, wanting that strength for herself. When he slid one hand under her buttocks, lifting her, she gripped him so fiercely that she knew she must be leaving marks with her nails.

Jonas sucked in his breath under the impact of the small punishment Verity was delivering and then he pushed himself against her. She felt the thick, broad head of his shaft probing the opening to her body and once more she tried to think clearly for a few seconds. He needed to know that this was new to her. He needed to know he should go slowly now.

"Jonas, listen to me. I want to tell you something."

"You can tell me later," he promised, and then he surged heavily into her.

Verity lost her breath for a few frantic seconds. When she regained it she cried out a soft, wordless protest.

She was totally unprepared for the size of him and the suddenness with which he had penetrated her. She was not naïve. She had thought she had a fairly good idea of what to expect when she made love for the first time. But this burning, stretched, invaded sensation was definitely not it.

It was Jonas's turn to freeze as Verity's body clenched in protest around him and her nails dug angrily into his skin. "Verity?" he got out thickly. "Verity, what the hell is going on?"

She had anticipated a feeling of fullness, perhaps a little initial discomfort until her body adjusted to the new experience. But this incredible, painful tightness was too much. Verity pushed at Jonas's broad shoulders.

"That's enough," she gasped. "Stop it, Jonas. Now." She

was accustomed to giving him orders and she expected to be obeyed.

But Jonas didn't move. His face was a mask of iron control, but he didn't move. "Honey, I'm sorry. I didn't know. I didn't realize. Dammit, it's too late now. Just relax. Take it easy. You're too tense. You're hurting yourself."

"I am not hurting myself," she said between set teeth as she continued to shove at him. "You're the one who's hurting me. Get off. I told you you were going too fast, but you wouldn't listen. Men. You're all so sure you know what you're doing."

"You didn't tell me *why* you wanted me to slow down," he defended himself. He was vibrating with tension as he fought to hold himself unmoving within her and at the same time keep her pinned carefully beneath him. The muscles of his back and thighs were as contoured steel. His forehead was damp.

"I didn't know a simple request for gentlemanly restraint required a detailed explanation!"

"Verity, calm down. It's too late. I made a mess of things. I'll apologize later, I swear. But it's too late to stop now. You're okay, sweetheart. Just stop fighting yourself and me, too. Let yourself relax. It's going to be all right. It's going to be so damn good. You'll see. You're going to want me as much as I want you. I know there's passion in you." His lips were warm and soothing on her throat. Then he kissed the curve of her shoulder. "Please, honey. Let yourself relax."

The desperation in his words got through to her. Verity breathed deeply, trying to rally her scattered senses. There was nothing really wrong with her, she decided objectively. It was infuriating to hear him say it, but logically she knew Jonas was right. She would undoubtedly be much more comfortable if she let herself relax.

What was happening wasn't Jonas's fault, she reminded herself grimly as she slowly retracted her nails from his shoulder. She always took responsibility for her own actions and there was no denying she had wanted this lovemaking.

She had been longing to throw herself into bed with Jonas since he had kissed her in the spa; perhaps even before that. Maybe from the first time she'd seen him. She couldn't blame him if she stumbled her first time out of the gate. Deliberately she tried to unclench her strained muscles.

"That's it. You're doing great. You're going to be doing a whole lot better in a few minutes, believe me." Jonas muttered encouragement as she stopped trying to shove him off of her. His hands were clamped around her arms, his body still taut as he dropped more reassuring kisses across her breasts and into the hollow of her shoulder.

Verity licked her dry lips. "Maybe . . . maybe we're not physically compatible. You feel much too large and I don't seem to be feeling whatever it is I'm supposed to be feeling. Maybe we both made a mistake."

He made a small, husky sound that was part laugh and part groan. "No mistake. You're perfect for me. Trust me. Just hang on and trust me."

He slid his hand down her side to her hip and then he wedged one tapered finger between their bodies. Verity twisted slightly as he found the tiny nubbin of desire. When he began to tease it gently, she sighed and twisted again, arching upward against his hand. Pleasure began to replace the too-tight, too-stretched, too-invaded feeling.

"Better?" he whispered as she moved beneath him.

"I may survive after all." She flexed her fingers on his shoulders but this time she didn't dig her nails into him. Experimentally she lifted her hips and felt him move an inch or so within her. The sensation was interesting, she decided. She tried it again.

Jonas sucked in his breath. "I'm glad you think you'll survive. I'm not sure I will."

He began to move carefully within her as her body unclenched and began to turn soft around him. Slowly, with exquisite care, he measured the length of her feminine sheath, filling her to the hilt and then withdrawing slightly.

"Oh, Christ, Verity. You're so warm and tight," he grated. "I've never felt anything like this. So perfect."

"Jonas?" She sighed his name in a half-spoken question as a tingling, liquid heat began deep inside her.

"Honey, I'm trying to take this slow and easy but I don't think I can last much longer. I'm going out of my mind." He drew a savage breath and removed his hand from between their bodies. Then he gripped her with sudden fierceness, driving himself into her with increasing urgency.

The tingling feeling increased. Verity tightened herself around Jonas, seeking more of the delightful sensation. Instinctively she wrapped her legs around his hard hips and her lower body strained to hold him within her.

"Verity."

She felt Jonas lose what was left of his self-control. With one last agonized groan, he surged deeply into her and went rigid. His muffled shout of satisfaction filled the room.

Time hung suspended for a few moments before Jonas sagged heavily on top of Verity, his head on her breasts.

For a long time Verity lay trapped beneath his weight, her hands moving on his back, unconsciously stroking him as she would a cat. She looked up at the ceiling and smiled vaguely to herself. She knew enough to realize that things hadn't gone perfectly. She had missed out on something important, but she felt strangely contented nonetheless. There was a sweet satisfaction and pleasure in knowing that Jonas had been satisfied. And common sense warned her that first times for anything seldom went exactly right. Practice made perfect, and she was determined to practice.

Jonas was silent for a long moment, apparently enjoying the soothing feel of her hand. Then, with a low, lazy sigh, he eased himself out of her and rolled to one side. He gathered her against him and kissed her ear.

"You should have told me this was going to be new for you," he chided gently.

"The subject never arose. I didn't expect everything to

happen so quickly. I thought I'd have weeks, maybe months to get to know you and be sure."

"Really? Do you think I could have waited even a few more days, let alone weeks or months?" He squeezed her rounded buttock. "Don't you know what you've been doing to me ever since I first saw you?"

Verity smiled dreamily against his chest. "What have I been doing to you?"

"Driving me wild. Verity, you're twenty-eight years old. Why in hell did you wait this long to go to bed with a man?"

She shrugged unconcernedly. "Haven't you heard? There's a man shortage."

"Don't give me that bull. Why, Verity?"

"It never seemed right before," she said with simple honesty.

He pulled away so that he could see her face. His eyes searched her expression. "And it felt right with me?"

"Mmm." She tried to snuggle closer, hungry for the warmth of him.

But Jonas continued to hold her where she was, his face intent. "Honey, I want you to know you won't regret it."

"Good. I never did believe in useless regrets. When do we do it again?"

He laughed, the sound deep and husky in the darkness. "I should have known you'd be a tyrant in bed as well as out of it. Serves me right, I guess." He tangled his fingers in the jumbled mass of her hair. "You know, you remind me of someone."

"A former girlfriend?" Verity was not pleased.

Jonas shook his head. "Nope. Not a former girlfriend. It'll come to me one of these days."

"And in the meantime?" she asked invitingly. She wriggled her toes along his leg.

"I'll be damned. I've created a monster." Jonas's grin was wicked as he released her with a proprietary slap on her rear and climbed out of bed. "Stay where you are."

"Where are you going?"

"I'll be right back," he promised, disappearing into the small bathroom.

Verity saw the light come on behind the half-closed door and heard water running in the sink. Idly she stretched beneath the sheet, taking inventory of the tiny aches and pains that were the silent protest of formerly unused muscles. She felt languid and happy, eager to explore the wonderful feeling of closeness she had just discovered with Jonas.

She felt as though she had opened the door to a whole new world tonight; a realm in which her relationship with Jonas governed everything. It was as if her life were being realigned along a new axis.

During the short time she had known him he had dominated her thoughts, intrigued her, compelled her to learn more about him. Tonight he had taken her into the uncharted waters of physical sensation, and she had navigated by hanging on to him. In that moment Verity knew she never wanted to let go of Jonas Quarrel. The intuitive knowledge that he had wanted her and needed her filled her with unlimited delight.

She wondered if this was what it meant to be falling in love. Somehow the notion didn't seem nearly as anxiety-provoking as it once had.

Verity leaned over the edge of the bed and eyed the heap of clothes Jonas had left there. He had been impatient for her, she reflected happily, so impatient that he had left his pants and his shirt in a tangled pile.

Enjoying a novel feeling of domesticity, Verity sat up and reached down to pick up Jonas's clothes. She would fold them neatly and stack them on the chair.

As she picked up the jeans, the earring she had lost two months ago in a Mexican alley fell out of the pocket with a tiny, tinkling clatter. She recognized it instantly when it rolled into the shaft of light that crept out from under the bathroom door.

Verity stared down at the golden circlet and her new, bright, sensually warm world began fading around her. Her fingers clenched around the jeans in her hand as she tried to understand what was happening.

There was no sound from the bathroom doorway, but the pattern of light shifted on the floor and Verity looked up to see Jonas watching her. He had a damp washcloth in one hand. His eyes followed hers to the golden earring on the floor. The relaxed, satisfied expression he had worn on the way into the bathroom was gone.

Verity stared up at him, asking silent questions with her eyes.

Jonas exhaled a deep sigh and walked slowly to the bed.

"It's a long story," he said.

Chapter Six

*H*e had been careless. Stupid and careless. Too late Jonas realized he'd been so hungry for Verity when he'd emerged from the psychic corridor that he hadn't even stopped to think about the earring in his pocket or the risks it presented if she discovered it. It had been all he could do just to maintain some semblance of superficial calm when he walked her back to her cabin. When he finally had gotten her into bed, the urgency of his desire had blinded him to everything, including her obvious lack of experience, until it was too late.

Not that it would have made any difference in the final outcome if he had known she was a virgin. He'd been consumed with his need to possess her and she had welcomed him. That was more than enough. He was damned if he would feel guilty on top of everything else.

But he hadn't expected the violent sexual arousal that had accompanied this latest trip into the dangerous corridor in his mind. He'd never had that particular problem before after making the connection with an ancient object of violence. True, he'd nearly killed a man the last time he'd gone into the corridor, but he hadn't come back out wanting to throw himself on the nearest woman.

The physical arousal he'd experienced this time must have had some direct link with discovering that Verity too could enter the corridor. The sense of possessiveness he felt toward her now was almost overpowering. He wanted to shout his triumph and exultation to the stars. The indescribable relief at having found her was enough make him lightheaded.

But there was no way to explain it to her yet. She wouldn't believe him; wouldn't understand the truth. He had only the vaguest comprehension of it himself. How could he tell her that she was the key to controlling his talent?

"I don't understand." Verity looked down at the earring again. "I just don't understand how you could have that earring."

Jonas sat down slowly beside her on the bed, afraid that if he made any fast moves he might panic her.

"I was the other man in the alley the night good old Pedro tried to rape you. I was the one whose face you didn't see. You never even stopped to look at me. You just turned and ran."

Verity looked dumbfounded. "You found my earring and followed me here to Sequence Springs?"

"It wasn't easy. Took me two months."

"But why? It doesn't make any sense."

He tried a smile. It came out crooked. "Do you believe in love at first sight?"

"No," she retorted flatly. "And I don't believe in Prince Charming, either. Men don't follow a woman a couple of thousand miles because they happened to find her shoe or her earring. Besides, you couldn't possibly have gotten a good look at me that night."

Jonas thought back to that evening in Mexico. He could still hear the raucous calls of the cantina's patrons as they caught sight of the redheaded gringa in their midst. "I saw your red hair in the light of the cantina as you stood in the doorway looking for your father. I saw your face and the color of your eyes. I'd never seen eyes that shade of green before."

"Where were you?"

"I was on the street outside, watching you." No point in explaining that he had followed her from the cantina down the street where she had stopped previously. She would only ask other questions that would be even harder to answer.

"Jonas, this doesn't make any sense. Are you trying to tell me that because of a brief glimpse and a broken earring, you tracked me down here in Sequence Springs? You expect me to believe that?"

The washcloth grew cold in Jonas's hand. He looked down at it. He had intended to use the cloth to bathe away the pungent, sticky residue of their lovemaking. He had thought Verity might appreciate the warm bath. He had also wanted to soothe the tender female flesh he had taken with a lot of heat but not much finesse. Something told him Verity would not welcome such intimacy now. He put the cold, damp cloth on the table beside the bed.

"I followed you, Verity, because I had to," he said simply. "I wanted to see you again. After all, I'd saved you from Pedro. Is it so strange I would want to find out more about you? You ran from that alley as if all the demons in hell were at your heels."

"I thought you were just another would-be rapist."

He watched her profile. "Well, now you know I'm not, don't you?"

She pulled the sheet around herself, withdrawing from him. "I'm not so sure. Maybe you're just more subtle than Pedro."

Anger flared in him. He caught her shoulders and forced her to face him. "That's a hell of a thing to say. You know damned good and well that what just happened between us wasn't rape. Don't you dare accuse me of that. When I left the bed a few minutes ago, you were practically begging me to rush back and make love to you again."

She flinched, her eyes faltering beneath his momentary fury. "You're right," she said grudgingly. "It wasn't rape. But it wasn't love, either. So why are you here, Jonas? Why did you follow me and go to work for me and then take me to bed?"

She would never believe the real story in its entirety. All he could do was stick by the bare bones of the tale. "I told you the truth. I wanted to see you again. If you'd stuck around that alley until I'd finished with Pedro, I would have introduced myself then. But you ran. So I followed."

She edged away from him. "Jonas, don't hand me that kind of line. Men don't do things like that."

He shrugged. "I did."

He watched her chew on that undeniable fact. Then something flickered in her eyes and she astonished him with her next leap of logic. "Does this have anything to do with my father, by any chance? Are you here because of him? Do you work for that sleazeball who's after him to repay the gambling debt? So help me God, Jonas, if you followed me and used me to get at him, I swear I'll slit your throat."

Jonas was startled at her deduction. "No, I don't work for anyone but you. I knew nothing about your father's problems until he told us both about them tonight. That's the truth, Verity. The only reason I came to Sequence Springs was to get to know you better. Can you blame me? I saved you down in Mexico and you didn't even stick around long enough to thank me. A man can weave a lot of fantasies about a woman he rescues. Human nature. Male nature. And there was nothing to keep me in Mexico. I was free to follow you and learn more about you, so I did just that."

She eyed him warily. "A true drifter. You just go where your fancy takes you, is that it?"

He gritted his back teeth but kept his voice casual. "That's it."

"I'm not sure I believe you, Jonas. You're making me very nervous."

Jonas kept a tight rein on his self-control. "I'm sorry, Verity. I guess my following you out of Mexico doesn't strike you as a romantic gesture, does it? Four hundred years ago someone would have written a ballad about it."

"Times change," she informed him. "Maybe women today are a little more savvy than they were back then."

"Times change," he agreed. "Human nature doesn't. If you'd been born four hundred years ago you would have been the same arrogant, stubborn, infuriating little shrew you are today."

She paled and Jonas instantly flayed himself mentally for his loss of temper. She had been through a lot tonight and she had every right to her suspicions.

"If you feel that way about me, I'm surprised you were so eager to go to bed with me," Verity whispered.

He swore softly and reached out, capturing her before she could slide away. Deliberately he overcame her brief struggles and pinned her close against him, his face in her hair.

"I'm sorry, honey. I didn't mean that. I should have kept my damn mouth shut."

He could smell himself on her, Jonas realized as he pulled her close. The acrid scent combined with the lingering fragrance of her feminine arousal made him pulsatingly conscious of the claim he had staked tonight. He could not yet explain to Verity the mental bond that linked them or why he needed her to preserve his sanity. She wouldn't believe him, let alone understand what he was trying to say. All he could do was reinforce the physical and emotional bonds he had forged tonight. And there were definitely such bonds between them whether she wanted to admit it or not. She would never have gone to bed with him if she hadn't wanted him very badly.

Hell, he told himself encouragingly, the woman had waited twenty-eight years to go to bed with a man. Surely she must have felt something very powerful for him.

"Jonas, I feel like I've been through a wringer. I don't know what to think." Her voice was muffled against his chest.

He clenched his hands in the wonderful fire of her hair. "I know, honey. I didn't handle this very well. I should have told you who I was right from the start. But you wouldn't

have believed me then, either. In fact, you probably would
have been even more suspicious of me if I'd shown up on
your doorstep and announced I'd followed you from Mexico. I didn't know how to play it, so I tried to keep things
low-key. I wanted us to get to know each other. Was that so
wrong?"

"No, I suppose not, but I still don't know what to believe.
It's all very strange."

"It will look a lot less strange in the morning," he assured
her. "I promise. You're just shook up now because you've
been through a brand-new experience tonight and you're still
coming to terms with it." The new sexual experience was
only part of the package, he thought. Wait until she realized
that she hadn't been hallucinating earlier when she'd entered
that psychic corridor. But he'd leave that for another time.

"Does it take a lot to come to terms with the experience of
going to bed with someone?" she demanded tartly, sounding
more like her old self.

Jonas winced. "I didn't exactly make your first time a
fantasy come true, did I? I was in a rush and I was clumsy.
It's been a long, long time since I've been to bed with a
woman, and maybe I . . . Never mind. Let's just say I'm
aware I made a hash of things."

Her head came up so quickly Jonas almost got his chin
cracked. Her eyes appeared very wide and deep and feminine in the darkness.

"Jonas, you mustn't think that. I thought your lovemaking
was very," she paused, obviously searching for the right
word, "interesting," she finished quite earnestly.

"Interesting?" Jonas stared at her, chagrined, and then his
sense of humor kicked in. He hugged her fiercely for a few
seconds. "That's my Verity. Honest to the core. Interesting,
huh? Thanks, boss. You really know how to bolster the old
male ego."

"But, Jonas," she went on hesitantly.

"What is it, sweetheart?"

"I really don't understand the rest of this. It's very hard

for me to believe you actually followed me all this way just because you caught a glimpse of me that night outside the cantina. Men just don't do things like that in this day and age, regardless of what they might have done four hundred years ago in the Renaissance. And this business of having my father show up unexpectedly is unsettling, too. I want some time to think about everything."

Jonas stilled. He didn't like the idea of giving Verity a lot of time to think. On the other hand, he didn't see what else he could do under the circumstances. "We'll talk more in the morning," he temporized. He found her breast beneath the sheet she insisted upon clutching. When he touched her nipple he felt it harden instantly. "Plenty of time in the morning," he muttered, his voice growing thicker as his body flamed into awareness. She was so soft and sweet, he thought. And she belonged to him now. So damn sexy. He'd really lucked out. For the first time in five years, he had finally lucked out.

"Jonas . . ."

"I'll do it right this time," he vowed. "We'll take it easy. Lots of time. No rush. I swear I won't hurt you. You'll see. This time it's going to be so good between us."

"Jonas, I think you should leave now."

He blinked, dazed. "Leave?"

She pushed herself away from him and stood up with the sheet twisted modestly around her. "I can't figure out what's going on here. I need time to think. I told you that."

"Save your thinking for tomorrow, sweetheart," he tried persuasively.

She smiled grimly in the shadows. "That's a typically male piece of advice. I think I've already done enough tonight without thinking about it first. I need some time to myself. Good night, Jonas."

"Fifteen minutes ago, you were begging me to make love to you again," he reminded her bluntly.

"That was fifteen minutes ago. I've changed my mind. It's a woman's right. I want you to leave, Jonas."

"Verity, this is crazy. You can't kick me out now."

She tilted her head curiously. Verity ran her own life. She was not accustomed to the notion that she could not run it the way she wished. "Why not?"

He shot to his feet, running a hand through his hair in exasperation. "Why not? Dammit, nothing has changed. You want me and I want you. We've already made love once. There's no reason we shouldn't spend the night together." He was rock hard and ready for her. More than anything else on the face of the earth he wanted to lay her down and sheath himself in her again.

But she was busy throwing him out.

"Good night, Jonas." She walked to the door and opened it. The sheet trailed behind her like a royal train. Once again it occurred to him that when she was at her most haughty, Verity reminded him vaguely of someone else.

"Dammit, Verity..." But it was useless to argue with her. He could see that now. Reluctantly he yanked on his pants, aware that he had lost this round. As he picked up his shirt the earring tinkled again. He reached down and scooped it up off the floor and dropped it into his pocket. "This is stupid." He tried one last, weak excuse: "It's not fair to make me face your father alone. He's going to have a good idea of what happened here tonight. What am I supposed to say to him?"

Verity smiled her first real smile since she had found the earring. It was a smile of glittering secret amusement. "My father will be thrilled. He's been worrying for the past five years that I'm gay."

Jonas discovered he was on the edge of losing his temper all over again. The little tyrant was baiting him now. "He's a father. Somehow, I'm not so sure he'll be all that delighted to know I've just screwed his precious virgin daughter."

"Ex-virgin," she stated proudly, as if taking personal credit for the transformation.

What remained of Jonas's temper went up in smoke. As usual when he got very angry, his voice got very quiet. He showed his adversary a lot of teeth in a savage smile. "Ex-virgin is right," he said. "Thanks to me. Remember that, lady. You didn't manage your new status all by yourself. You needed me to do the job. Having done it very thoroughly, I intend to claim a reward. I deserve it."

He stalked to the door and out into the night before Verity could respond to the harsh words. The door was slammed shut behind him with enough force to echo through the trees.

His red-haired tyrant was angry.

Well, so was he, Jonas thought vengefully. Things had started out smoothly enough this evening, but they had wound up disastrously. The fact that he had no one to blame but himself did not alleviate his mood one bit.

The lights were off in the cabin when he reached it. He opened the door and saw the dark shape on the bed. So much for flipping a coin to see who got the sleeping bag. Possession was nine-tenths of the law.

There was no sound from Emerson Ames. Jonas was grateful. He didn't feel like making explanations for his prolonged absence. Emerson was no fool.

Jonas unrolled the old, musty-smelling sleeping bag he had found in a closet and stripped off his clothes. He was sliding into the bag when Emerson's sleepy voice came from the direction of the bed.

"You're back earlier than I expected. What happened? Did my daughter kick you out of bed?"

Jonas swallowed an oath and decided to evade the question. "Your daughter reminds me of someone, Emerson."

"Yeah, I know. I've often thought the same thing."

"Yeah?" Jonas was intrigued in spite of himself. The elusive comparison had been haunting him for some time.

"Sure. I finally figured it out a few years ago. Think about it. It'll come to you. Small, red-haired, sharp-tongued, acts like she's royalty, especially around men. Smart as a whip and just as dangerous. Picture her in a white lace ruff."

"Christ. The young Elizabeth the First."

"You've got it," Emerson said smoothly. "Watch out you don't follow in the Earl of Essex's shoes."

Jonas remembered how England's great Renaissance queen had sent Essex, a former court favorite, to the headsman. "It's not my head I worry about when I'm around your daughter," he told Emerson bluntly.

Ames chuckled. "I know. It's your balls you've got to protect. A word of advice, pal. Old Liz the First could take care of herself. If nothing else, I like to think I've taught my daughter to do the same."

"You did a good job," Jonas grumbled. "Maybe too good a job."

"Had to. When she's doing her Elizabeth the First routine, she's damn near invincible. But when she smiles . . ."

"I see what you mean," Jonas said quietly. He folded his hands behind his head and stared up into the darkness. Verity's smile was a double-edged sword. It could bring out a man's latent gallant instincts, if he had any. It could make him long to prove himself worthy of her. But it could also tempt another kind of man to reach out and vandalize the alluring promise of sweet chastity and integrity. Verity's smile made her vulnerable in ways she didn't even dream.

"Good night, Quarrel. Whoever gets up first makes the coffee."

Emerson rolled over and went back to sleep. Jonas stayed awake for a long time. When he finally fell asleep, his dreams were far from pleasant. He spent most of the night trying to catch Verity as she ran ahead of him down an endless corridor.

Verity woke very early the next morning and found it impossible to go back to sleep. It was going to be a long day.

When she slid slowly out of bed she discovered that all the small aches she had noticed after Jonas's lovemaking had intensified during the night. Her inner thighs felt as if she had been riding a horse. The thought amused her briefly as she made her way into the shower.

The idea of putting a saddle and bridle on Jonas Quarrel was more than mildly humorous; it was downright interesting.

She felt better after the shower, but still not up to her normal morning standards. A glance at the clock told her that she had plenty of time before she had to go to work. Verity decided to head for the spa. What she really needed was a good, long soak in one of the hot mineral baths. She also needed some time to think. At this hour of the morning the baths would be nearly empty. Laura and Rick wouldn't mind her using the facilities.

Verity dressed in her jeans and an old shirt, snagged her terry robe out of the closet, and headed for the Sequence Springs Spa.

The morning was cool and crisp and invigorating. By noon Sequence Springs would be pleasantly warm. In the distance the white-walled resort building gleamed in the bright sunlight. The lake was as still and reflective as a mirror. Here and there a small boat dented the perfect surface. A surreptitious glance toward the other cabin revealed no signs of life.

Typical of a man to be able to have no trouble sleeping after a night spent making love to a woman and then traumatizing her with wild tales of lost earrings.

Verity's mouth tightened as she replayed the night's events. She still felt dazed. Last night she had known a sense of certainty when she gave herself to Jonas. This morning she did not understand where that certainty had sprung from but she still felt it. She could not figure out why she was sure he was the man she had been waiting for all these years. The man had undoubtedly lied to her from the moment he appeared on her doorstep. Jonas's tale was simply too crazy to be believed.

On the other hand, it was impossible to accept the conclusion that she had waited all this time to give herself to a man she could not trust. She had always prided herself on having a reliable sense of intuition. She could not have been that wrong about Jonas Quarrel.

Once again she reviewed his story. Men in this day and age didn't set out on such quixotic quests, she told herself for the thousandth time. But she couldn't think of any other explanation for Jonas's actions, unless she had been right when she suspected some link with her father's gambling debt. That possibility was frightening. She grappled with it the rest of the way to the spa.

The blue and white tiled bathing room that housed the women's spa was, as Verity had expected, almost empty. Caitlin Evanger was lounging naked in one of the bubbling pools. Another woman hovered near the edge with a stack of towels.

"Hello," Caitlin said pleasantly. "Another early riser, I see. Come and join me, Verity. We have the place to ourselves. I don't believe you've met Tavi Monahan." Caitlin's sleek, gilded head turned slightly as she smiled briefly at the other woman. "Tavi is my friend and companion. She takes excellent care of me. I don't know what I'd do without her. Tavi, this is Verity Ames, the owner of the restaurant I told you about."

Verity smiled. "Nice to meet you, Tavi."

Tavi nodded politely in greeting. "Miss Ames." Her voice was gentle and calm, her eyes oddly serene.

Tavi's hair was dark brown with the faintest hint of silver at the temples. She wore it parted in the middle and pulled back into a simple, classic twist. There was a quiet elegance about her, Verity thought. She wore a pair of brown well-cut slacks and a cream-colored pullover that went well with her olive complexion and dark, veiled eyes. Those eyes, Verity decided, were eyes of a woman who could hold an infinite number of secrets.

"What got you out of bed so early, Verity?" Caitlin inquired politely. "Or do you always get up at the crack of dawn as I do?"

"I'm an early riser but generally not this early." Verity

smiled again as she started toward one of the changing rooms. She wondered if Caitlin noticed any outward change in her, then chastised herself for the juvenile notion.

Halfway to the slatted booth she remembered she had forgotten to bring her bathing suit. She stopped.

"Something wrong?" Caitlin asked.

Verity cleared her throat. "No. I'll be right back." She went determinedly toward the booth. Considering what had happened last night, it was probably high time she learned to lead a more daring lifestyle. The thought made her grin. She stepped into the booth, took off all her clothes, and returned to the pool wearing only a towel and a smile.

She tried to appear nonchalant as she walked back to the pool. This sense of awkwardness about displaying herself was the price she paid for never having attended high school gym classes, Verity decided ruefully. But she was determined to get over it.

She dropped her towel at the edge of the pool and stepped into the warm, foaming water. The mineral scent filled her nostrils. It felt very therapeutic. Just what she needed. Verity sighed and lounged back on the underwater seat.

"It's a sign of anxiety, you know," Caitlin remarked from the other side of the pool.

Verity arched her eyebrows. "What is?"

"Waking up too early and being unable to get back to sleep. It can be very disturbing." Caitlin leaned her head against a towel Tavi had placed on the edge of the pool. She closed her eyes. "I have endured the problem for years. Night after night."

"I'm sorry." Verity wasn't sure what to say. She felt a sudden welling of compassion for this strange woman. She sensed painful depths in her and wished she could offer comfort. "Have you, uh, seen a doctor?"

Caitlin's eyes opened again and she looked at Verity with cold amusement. "There is no need to consult a therapist. I know exactly what is wrong with me. I'm aware of the source of the anxiety."

"I see." Jonas wasn't the only one with ghosts in his eyes, Verity thought.

Caitlin lifted a hand out of the water in a dismissive gesture and then allowed it to drop back under the surface. "It's not all bad, you know. I do some of my best work in the dawn hours. Isn't that right, Tavi?"

"Yes, Caitlin." Tavi's voice was soft as she spoke to her employer. There was a trace of sadness in the words, but Caitlin seemed oblivious to it. Tavi stood motionless, holding the stack of towels. "Some of your best paintings have been completed just before dawn. But I'm not sure that the money you have made from them has been worth the price you've paid to finish them."

Caitlin grimaced. "One of the reasons I have employed Tavi all these years is that she is unrelentingly honest with me. Honesty is a rare trait in this world."

Verity thought of Jonas. "It's nice to be able to trust the people one hires," she said grimly.

Caitlin gave her a speculative glance. "Are you having problems with your new employee, Mr. Quarrel?"

The temptation to confide in another woman almost overcame Verity. Caitlin was holding out the lure of mutual feminine understanding at a time when Verity badly needed some. She deeply appreciated the offer, but she managed, barely, to restrain herself. This was between her and Jonas. "No, not really. He's a good worker. I can't complain about his dishwashing skills and he's good with the customers. His background is a little unusual, though."

"An interesting man. He really was quite brilliant in his field, you know. I'll never forget that lecture I heard him give at Vincent, and that was just a routine classroom talk. He had the whole room in the palm of his hand, even those of us who had no real interest in Renaissance warfare. You could almost see the blood and guts and treachery. He had such a passion and a knowledge of the subject that you could even believe he might actually have lived the life of a *condottiere*."

"A Renaissance mercenary soldier?" Verity was suddenly fascinated. "Jonas reminds you of one?" She remembered that the bustling Italian cities of the time had squabbled constantly. The great families who governed Florence, Venice, and the other city-states had figured out quickly that it was easier and more economical to hire freelance generals with private armies to fight their endless wars than to rely on hometown loyalty and enthusiasm from the citizens. There was never any lack of work for an able-bodied mercenary during the Italian Renaissance.

Caitlin shrugged, her full breasts rising and falling magnificently under the water. "As I said, the man had a passion for his subject. It showed."

The man had other kinds of passion too, Verity thought. She would remember the impact of his passion on her all her life. "I wonder how well Jonas would have taken orders from a Medici or a Borgia," Verity mused.

"The *condottieri* were an independent lot, as I recall. They took orders when it suited them and ignored them when there was a better deal being offered elsewhere."

Verity nodded as bits and pieces of history came back to her. "True. They were definitely entrepreneurs, weren't they? They worked for whoever paid the best. Yesterday's foe was tomorrow's client. They were mercenaries to the core. Some of them became very powerful, too, as I recall. And wealthy. A few even became heads of state."

Caitlin gave her a wry glance. "Whereupon they instantly elevated themselves to the status of gentlemen by investing heavily in art. It was a great era for artists. Great strides were made in technique. Lots of work was available. Everyone from ex-mercenaries and upwardly mobile bankers to popes was busy commissioning statues and portraits. The Italian cities of the Renaissance must have been fascinating, their homes, streets, and public places filled with art."

Verity chuckled. "It was during the Renaissance that the whole modern concept of collecting and investing in art originated. A fact for which everyone making a living in art today is no doubt grateful."

"Extremely grateful. But some collectors today are every bit as ruthless as collectors were back then."

Verity laughed and found herself relaxing at last. Caitlin was just what she needed this morning. After the disconcerting events of the previous evening, it was good to sit here in the pool and talk to another woman. Women needed other women, and in Caitlin, Verity discovered she was finding a friend.

"I meant what I said last night, Caitlin. I admire your work tremendously. Did you always know you wanted to paint?"

"I dabbled in paint and ceramics and a few other areas during my teen years," Caitlin said, focusing on the heaving water around her. "But I didn't commit myself to painting until I was in my early twenties. That's what it takes to be successful, you know. A true commitment. It's rather like entering a convent, I suppose. Without a sense of dedication, there's little chance of becoming a success. Art is a harsh taskmaster."

"I understand. But I'm curious. What made you realize you were ready to commit yourself to such a demanding career?"

Caitlin's smile didn't even touch her eyes. The only thing that filled that cloudy gaze was distant pain. "You could say that something happened that gave me a new perspective on life."

Verity sensed she was probing too closely, but her curiosity and growing sense of friendship drove her to push just a little. "The car accident?" she asked gently.

Caitlin looked momentarily surprised, as if her mind had been on another catastrophe altogether. "Yes, the accident had a great deal to do with it. I spent nearly two years in and out of hospitals. That sort of thing tends to realign one's priorities." Smoothly she reversed the conversation. "What about you, Verity? When did you know you wanted to open your own restaurant?"

Verity thought about it. "I'm not sure. Somewhere along the line I must have made some mental connection between having a kitchen of one's own and having a home. It's hard to explain. I guess I began to associate cooking with roots and a sense of permanency."

Tavi did not participate in the conversation as it jumped from the Renaissance to gourmet food and went on to an analysis of a recent film that was making news. Verity made a few attempts to include the quiet woman but Tavi merely smiled politely and ignored them. Tavi's dark eyes rarely left her employer and Verity couldn't help noticing the concern reflected in them. Caitlin had more than a paid companion in Tavi, she also had a loyal friend, whether she knew it or not.

When Caitlin signaled at last that she had had enough of the pool, Tavi moved forward instantly to assist her. She helped the blond artist out of the water, handed her the ebony cane, and quickly dried her.

Verity caught a glimpse of Caitlin's withered leg and looked away as Tavi adjusted the terrycloth robe.

"It's all right," Caitlin said calmly. "It happened a long time ago."

"It must have been terrible for you," Verity said quietly.

Caitlin shrugged as Tavi fastened the brace. "They told me in the hospital that I was lucky to be alive. But everyone has a different definition of luck. I enjoyed our chat this morning, Verity. I shall look forward to another meal or two at the No Bull. Perhaps we could have tea together one afternoon?"

Verity nodded happily, again enjoying the pleasant sense of a dawning friendship. It was like that sometimes between two women. Sometimes you just clicked with another person and the friendship sprang into life almost immediately. In this case her sense of compassion was a factor, too. She had the odd feeling that Caitlin needed her friendship. "I'd like that. Good morning, Caitlin. Tavi. I'll see you both later."

Tavi gave her a strange, assessing glance and then turned to escort her employer from the baths. There was a distinct tenderness in the grip she had on Caitlin's arm and in the way her head was bent toward the other woman.

Verity watched them leave and then decided that she'd indulged herself enough for one day. There was work to be done and sooner or later a man to be faced. She rose from the pool and picked up her towel.

From now on she was going to bathe nude in the spa pools. Much more relaxing. Verity grinned to herself at the thought. Obviously her night of licentiousness and unmitigated debauchery had thoroughly corrupted her.

Upstairs in the suite Caitlin had rented, Tavi served tea and yogurt from a room service tray that had been ordered earlier.

Caitlin sat in the white wicker chair near the window and looked out over the lake as she sipped her unsweetened tea.

"Verity Ames is the key, Tavi. I'm certain of it. Everything hinges on her."

"Perhaps," Tavi agreed doubtfully. She poured tea for herself and watched the other woman's profile as Caitlin stared at the water. There was so much strength in Caitlin, but it was warped and twisted toward only one goal. Tavi was at a loss as to how to alter the direction of her headlong flight toward revenge. Sometimes all you could do was be there for someone. Sometimes there was simply nothing else that could be done.

Tavi had been Caitlin's only friend for five years, ever since the day she had gone to work for a lonely, isolated artist who needed friendship and love far more than she needed a housekeeper/companion. Tavi had seen past the hard surface to the woman beneath it, the woman who lived with constant pain.

"No, I'm sure of it. She's an unexpected bonus. I had no idea we'd find someone like her when we located Quarrel.

It's going to make everything infinitely easier. I'm already beginning to get the germ of an idea."

"The more people involved, the more dangerous this whole thing will get," Tavi pointed out.

"True, but I can see no way of manipulating Quarrel without a lever. He's too free, too independent. Originally I considered simply paying him to do the job, but I know now that wouldn't work. He'd tell me to get lost. There's nothing I can offer him or use to coerce him."

"Except Verity?"

"Except Verity. He wants her, Tavi. That was crystal clear last night. The man is as possessive as hell. I saw it in his eyes. In fact, I would be willing to bet that he made love to her last night. There was something about her this morning that was not there last evening. I suspect Quarrel staked his claim in bed."

"It could all be a figment of your imagination." Tavi's cup clattered on its saucer. She finished her tea with trembling fingers. "You've been living with your schemes and plans for so long that you might be fooling yourself into thinking you can actually turn them into reality."

Caitlin's frown was sharp as she snapped her head around to glare at her companion. "I found him, didn't I? I located Quarrel after all this time. You didn't think I'd get that far, but I did."

Tavi nodded reluctantly, saying nothing.

Caitlin relaxed and turned back to the view. "I knew that when I found him I would need some leverage to persuade him to play his role. Verity Ames is that leverage. I know she is."

"Just because she's sleeping with him, you think you can use her to manipulate him?"

"It's not a casual affair," Caitlin rasped. "You didn't see the look in his eyes last night. I did. There's no telling how long he will want her. A man's attention span is apt to be quite short. But for the moment he's captivated by her, and while he's in that state he will be easy to maneuver."

"Why?"

"Because there is a streak of wildness in him," Caitlin stated. "Most of the time he has it under control, but when it appears, he is vulnerable. I saw it the day he gave that lecture at Vincent and I saw it later when he nearly killed a man."

"Wonderful. Now we're dealing with a crazy man."

Caitlin shook her head. "No, far from it. I've read the reports on him. He's definitely not crazy. In fact, he has great strength of mind, otherwise he wouldn't have survived his talent this long."

"Caitlin, you don't know that. You can't be certain. You're taking a huge risk."

"What do I have to lose?"

"You know the answer to that as well as I do. You've told me yourself that if you go through with this you'll never paint again. And if you stop painting I think you might decide to do something very drastic."

"You're being morbid."

"How would you describe your view?" Tavi demanded tightly. "You've lived for years with no other goals but revenge and your art. If you satisfy your lust for vengeance and simultaneously cease painting, what will you have left?"

"It won't matter. The only thing that matters is sending Damon Kincaid into hell in a fitting style. I will compose his exit from this earth as I would compose a painting." Caitlin's smile was without pity. "Quarrel is the man who can carry out the task for me. He will be my mercenary executioner. He will be the man who makes the punishment fit the crime."

"What if he finds out he's been used?"

"It won't matter. Nothing will matter after Kincaid is dead. Ah, Tavi, it's all working out so beautifully. Kincaid fancies himself a modern-day Borgia. He thinks he has hidden his old lusts well beneath a slick, sophisticated surface, but I know all about them and I can exploit them. Soon he will learn what it is to be the victim. Do you know something, Tavi? That conversation I had with Verity about Renaissance mercenaries was prophetic. Jonas Quarrel is going to play the role of *condottiere* for me."

"The most important thing to a *condottiere* was getting paid."

Caitlin laughed. It was a low, harsh sound that made Tavi close her eyes. "He'll get Verity. That will have to be enough for him."

Chapter Seven

V*erity* was in her office going through a pile of receipts when she heard footsteps in the hallway that led to the kitchen. She recognized them instantly.

"Hello, Dad. Had breakfast?"

Emerson Ames appeared in the doorway. "In a manner of speaking. Quarrel puts together a mean cup of coffee. Went great with the three-day-old doughnuts he had in the cupboard."

Verity made a face. "That man has made no effort to learn anything about good nutrition even though I have given him one lecture after another on the subject."

Emerson grinned widely behind his graying red beard. "I'll just bet you have. You always were damn good at giving lectures and advice even when you were a little kid."

"We all have our talents," Verity retorted dryly. "The real burden I have to bear is knowing I'm so good at giving lectures and advice and having so few people pay attention to me."

"Meaning people like me and Quarrel. Don't worry, Red. We pay attention. It's just that we don't always do as we're told."

"It can be extremely frustrating," Verity said with a rueful smile.

"Think of it as a challenge. What are you working on there?"

"I was just doing a little bookkeeping. I was about to take a break and make myself some tea. Want some?"

"Sounds good. I need something to wash away the sludge Quarrel fixed for me. I think I'm getting older, Red. Coffee like that wouldn't even have made me blink ten years ago."

"It's not a question of getting older," Verity said brusquely, "it's a matter of finally gaining some common sense."

"I shall resist common sense with my last breath," Emerson declared in ringing tones.

Verity glanced at him in quick assessment. Her father appeared as hale and hearty as ever. The thought of him losing any of his vitality and zest for life was a disturbing one. She was mature enough to recognize the inevitable processes of life, but another part of her resisted the idea that they should apply to Emerson Ames.

There were times when her father's blithe, here-today, gone-tomorrow attitude drove her nuts, but she had instinctively relied on his strength for years. Perhaps it was inevitable that fathers defined masculinity for their daughters. Verity knew only that she had never met another man who had that same inner core of male energy and power as her father had.

Except Jonas Quarrel.

She pushed aside that unsettling thought and strode out of the office. Emerson ambled after her as she walked into the kitchen of the No Bull Cafe.

"Where's Jonas?" Verity asked, not looking up from her tea preparations.

"When I left the cabin a while ago he was reading. Machiavelli, I think. The man has interesting tastes." Emerson opened a cupboard door experimentally. "Got anything edible in here?"

"There are some sesame seed crackers in that carton in the

corner and some dried prunes, too, I think." Verity poured out hot water. "He's due here at work in forty-five minutes."

"Who? Machiavelli?"

"Very funny. I meant Jonas."

"I'm sure he'll show up on time." Emerson munched a cracker. His eyes gleamed. "He wouldn't dare be late to work. I get the feeling this job is important to him."

"Washing dishes is quite a comedown for a man who was once headed for the top of his profession," Verity grumbled.

"Depends on your point of view. Where did you find him, Verity?"

"I didn't find him. He found me. Didn't he tell you?" Verity demanded grimly. "I finally got the whole story last night. He was the other man in the alley down in Mexico. The one who pulled that damned Pedro off of me. I didn't hang around to say thanks. Jonas claims he tracked me down so that my little oversight could be corrected. I left one of my earrings behind in that alley. Jonas returned it last night."

"I see."

"Well, I'm glad you do, because I don't." Verity peered at her father as she sipped her tea. Emerson might be an irresponsible rogue who had turned his back on his literary talent in favor of indulging himself in the wilder side of life, but no one had ever said he was stupid. "Dad, tell me something. Do you really believe any man would follow a woman two thousand miles just to return an earring?"

One bushy red-gray brow climbed. "Correct me if I'm wrong, Red, but I got the feeling Quarrel did more than return an earring last night."

Verity flushed, in spite of herself. "Don't look at me with so much prurient interest. We both know I'm not the type to bore you with girlish confessions. Tell me what you really think about Jonas."

"So you value your old man's opinion on some things, after all, hmmm?"

"You know very well I value your opinion on a lot of things," Verity said tartly. "I'll say one thing for the lifestyle you chose, you've picked up some useful pointers on human nature and motivations."

"Praise at last from my prudish, conservative, disapproving daughter. You astonish me, Red."

"I asked a straightforward question."

Emerson grinned. "I've hardly had a chance to get to know the man, but I'll tell you one thing. If he succeeds in helping me sell those dueling pistols for enough cash to get Yarington off my back, your Jonas is going to be my best buddy for life."

Verity frowned. "Jonas is going to help you sell them?"

"Claims he knows some private collectors who will gladly pay top dollar and not ask too many questions about where those pistols came from. Says he met a few during the days he was holding down a respectable job as a college professor. Seems he was asked to authenticate certain items being considered for purchase by people who didn't care where the items came from as long as they were genuine."

"Dad, are those pistols *stolen?*"

Emerson chuckled. "Calm down. I've told you before, frowning in shock like that will eventually give you wrinkles. They're not stolen. At least, not by me. My old friend gave them to me free and clear. You remember Lehigh down in Rio?"

Verity groaned. "Lehigh's the one who gave them to you? But where did he get them?" Samuel Lehigh was an engaging eighty-year-old charmer with a very vague past.

"That's the part that gets a bit sticky, I'm afraid. I'm not sure how Lehigh acquired them and I was too much of a gentleman to ask. Let's just say it would be simpler if, when I turn around and sell them myself, my buyer is as discreet as I am."

"Oh, hell."

"Take it easy, Verity. If those pistols were stolen, it happened a very long time ago. They've been in Lehigh's possession for years. I'm sure of that much. And now that Jonas is sure that they're the genuine article, I'm all set. All we need is a buyer."

"And Jonas has promised to put you in touch with one. Interesting. I can see that any opinions I get from you regarding Jonas are going to be somewhat biased," Verity said with a sigh.

Her father eyed her for a short moment. "You know better than that, Red." He took a large swallow of tea. The teasing light went out of his eyes and was replaced by something far more dangerous. "I'd have slit his throat when he walked back into the cabin last night if I really thought Quarrel was dangerous to you."

Verity gave him a weak smile. "Is that right?"

"Sure." Emerson's eyes brightened again. "Fair's fair, after all. He nearly gutted me earlier when I broke into the place."

"He *what?*"

Emerson made a soothing gesture. "Relax, Red. It was just a simple case of mistaken identity. It was late when I arrived and I didn't want to wake you to get the key. So I tried the door and then one of the windows to see if I could jimmy it open. When I came through the window, Quarrel was waiting with a knife in his hand. I knew right then and there, you'd finally shown some intelligence when it came to your hiring practices. From what I've seen of your previous employees, none of them could have handled a scene like that with what Papa Hemingway liked to call grace under pressure."

"Oh, my God, one of you could have been killed." Verity was momentarily stricken as the implications sank in. She choked on her tea.

She had seen her father cornered once after a bar brawl by a combatant who had been dissatisfied with the official outcome of the fight. In the middle of a moonlit, waterfront street the man had gone after Emerson with a knife. Verity had been with her father at the time. Emerson had come out of the short, savage duel with only a few scrapes. His younger opponent had been badly cut. Verity had never forgotten the color of blood illuminated by moonlight. It was black.

Emerson patted his daughter on the back, the affectionate blows causing her to stagger slightly. "Hey, take it easy, Red. Neither Quarrel nor I got upset about it, so don't you get in a tizzy. Although I'll admit it's nice to see you still have a little faith in your old man's ability to take care of himself. But like I said, the little scene last night was just a slight case of mistaken identity. We soon cleared it up."

"How reassuring." Verity shook her head. "Dad, you are absolutely incorrigible." She paused, nibbling on her lower lip as she studied him. He smiled at her, unrepentant but full of a father's love. She put down her teacup and stepped forward impulsively to wrap her arms around Emerson's waist. He felt as strong and sturdy as he always had.

She had taken that strength for granted ever since the day the two of them stood in a hospital room beside her mother's bed, clasping the limp fingers of a dying woman they both loved with all their hearts. Amanda Ames had been the victim of a drunk driver. Verity had learned that day when the terrible news came that the universe could no longer be counted upon to play fair. Her father, who had known that truth all along, had helped her accept it in his own assertive way.

"You take care of our little girl, Emerson," Amanda Ames had ordered gently.

"I'll do better than that," Emerson had promised. "I'll teach her to take care of herself. She'll be okay, my love. I swear it."

Amanda had nodded. "I know," she had whispered. "I know. I can trust you to take care of her. I love you both very much, you know. Don't spend too much time grieving. Life is for living. You've always been very good at living, Emerson. Teach Verity to be good at it, too."

Amanda had closed her eyes for the last time then and Verity had learned an important lesson about men. It was all right for a strong man to cry. She and her father had shed their tears together and then Emerson had taken Verity to the Caribbean.

"We both need a change of scene," he had explained as he bought two tickets to Antigua. "Let's go sit on a beach somewhere and think for a while. Guess we'd better take along a few books. Don't know when you'll get back to school."

"You better write a note to my teacher," Verity had said, ever mindful of the proprieties, even at the age of eight.

"Nah, we won't bother your teacher with this. She'll only get upset and so will everyone else at your silly school. The thing about bureaucracies, Red, is that they tend to get upset over all the little piddling details and ignore the really big, important things."

Verity had never been enrolled in a formal school again. Emerson had laughed about it more than once during the years that followed. "Just think," he had told her, "you may be the only kid born in North America who doesn't have to go through the torture of putting on a school play."

"And you're saved the torture of having to sit through one," Verity had retorted shrewdly. She was twelve at the time and starting to hone her sharp tongue.

Emerson had roared with laughter. "I also am saved from having to perjure myself writing excuse notes for the principal's office. I always dreaded having to write those things. Your mother made me do one every time I took you out of school to go to the zoo or the museum or the race track. She said if I was going to be the cause of your missing so much school, I had to assume the responsibility of thinking up the goddamned excuses. Talk about creative writing!"

Standing in her kitchen, her arms around her father, Verity's mind skipped laserlike over a thousand small scenes from her youth.

Through countless hotel rooms, beachside cottages, and boardinghouses, her father's strength and love of life had always been reassuring constants. In his own way, Emerson had always been there when she needed him. He had been there during the long, lonely nights when she had cried for her mother. It was he who had explained the facts of life to her in a blunt, straightforward fashion. And it was he who had given her the defenses she would need against the more predatory members of his sex. He had taught her to take care of herself in all the ways that counted. And he had loved her. Verity remembered that and blinked rapidly, clearing a suspicious dampness from her eyes along with all the footloose memories.

"Dad," she asked, listening to him chew the last bite of a sesame seed cracker. "Are you really in trouble with this Yarington character?"

"Worrying about your old man, Red?" He patted her shoulder again with his big paw of a hand. "Don't fret. I've been in worse situations. This one is under control. If your friend Quarrel comes through for me, I'll be free and clear of Mr. Reginald C. Yarington, international loan shark, soon enough."

Verity stepped back out of his arms, scanning his face for reassurance. She was about to ask another question when the back door of the cafe opened and Jonas strolled into the kitchen. He smiled blandly at Verity, looking for all the world as if he had only a vague recollection of how he had spent the previous evening. She scowled at him. If he couldn't look like a man who had been recently overpowered by passion, the least he could do was have the grace to appear mildly apologetic about that passion.

"Am I late?" he asked easily, seeing her frown.

"No, you're not late," she was forced to admit. "You can start rinsing spinach for the salads I'm going to do for lunch." She winced at the edge to her words. If this situation was to remain bearable, she would have to demonstrate some graciousness. The only alternative was to fire Jonas on the spot. She decided he would probably sue on grounds of sexual discrimination if she tried that.

"You see what I have to put up with for minimum wage?" Jonas appealed to Emerson.

Emerson gave Jonas a commiserating look as he helped himself to another cracker. "I assume the tips must be good or you wouldn't stick around to take this kind of abuse," he murmured meaningfully.

Jonas grinned and looked straight at Verity. "The tips," he agreed, "are excellent."

"That does it," Verity announced. "If you two are going to hang around you can both start rinsing spinach. I won't tolerate loafers and freeloaders." She went to the refrigerator, opened it, and pulled out several large bunches of spinach. "Here, show me that God put men on earth for some useful purpose after all." She tossed one of the spinach bundles at Jonas.

"Anything you say, boss." Jonas fielded the spinach with casual expertise. "Come on, Emerson. Give me a hand. You owe me for taking the bed last night."

"Sure, why not?" Emerson rolled up his sleeves and turned on the water. "Won't be the first time I've played kitchen helper. Verity always puts me to work when I show up."

"It's good for you," Verity said briskly as she busied herself preparing pasta for a chilled salad. "Builds character."

"Hah. I haven't worried about building character since I wrote *Juxtaposition*," her father retorted. "I learned then it was a distinctly painful and unrewarding process." He held spinach leaves under the running water and gave Jonas a speculative glance. "Ever read it, Quarrel?"

"*Juxtaposition*? I read it. Everyone on campus was reading it ten years ago. It was hot for a few months."

"What did you think of it?"

Jonas unwrapped the thin wire that bound a bunch of spinach. "It's been ten years, Emerson."

"Don't hedge, man. Tell me what you thought."

Verity waited expectantly, spoon poised over a steaming

kettle of pasta shells. "It was a fantastic book, wasn't it, Jonas?" she said encouragingly.

Jonas gave her a wary glance and then said to Emerson, "You want the truth?"

"Yup."

Jonas paused again. "Well, like I said, it's been a while. But I seem to recall being very impressed at the time."

Verity was pleased. "What impressed you about it?" she prodded.

Jonas shrugged and dumped a pile of spinach into a colander. "I remember thinking that Emerson Ames, whoever he was, was nothing less than brilliant. He'd found the perfect formula for putting on the entire literary establishment. He'd written a book that had it all: lots of painful, maudlin introspection, a neurotic hero who liked to wallow in guilt and anxiety, a generous sprinkling of cynicism that passed for insight, a dash of psychodrama, and a meandering, plotless tale that ended somewhere in the middle of a sentence. I knew by the end of the first page that New York was going to love it, and because New York loved it, everyone who had any claim to being a member of the literati was going to fall all over himself praising the book. I remember telling myself when I finished that Emerson Ames had balls. Not to mention chutzpah."

Emerson was laughing so hard by the time Jonas finished that he could hardly stand. He leaned his elbows on the sink and roared until his eyes grew moist. "Jesus, Red," he gasped, "you waited so long I thought you were planning to enter a convent, but I got to admit that when you finally picked a man for yourself, you did all right. I must have brought you up right, after all. Congratulations, kid. Not only can he use a knife, he's got some brains. A damn rare combination in this day and age."

Verity lifted her eyes helplessly toward the ceiling. "You'd think I'd have the sense to know when I'm outnumbered," she mumbled as the kettle of pasta boiled over onto the stovetop.

* * *

The day went surprisingly smoothly after that. The No Bull Cafe got busy around eleven-thirty, which took Verity's mind off the problems she was having dealing with the men in her life. She ran the kitchen with a firm, competent hand, giving orders to Emerson and Jonas, greeting her guests, organizing the cooking. She was in her element.

By the time the No Bull closed for the afternoon, she felt much better. There was nothing like taking charge of a situation to restore a woman's self-confidence. As she totaled up the noon profits and prepared to make a trip to the bank, she told herself she could even deal with the shaky beginning to her first love affair.

"Going into town with the loot?" Jonas asked, wiping his hands on a towel as he finished the dishes.

"That's right."

"I'll ride shotgun with you. I want to pick up some more beer."

Verity tried to keep her pleasure from showing. This would be the first time she would be alone with Jonas all day. "All right, you can come as long as you don't buy any junk food to go with the beer."

Jonas tossed aside the towel. "Honey, you know you can't drink beer without junk food. The two go together in a very delicate chemical process. It would be foolish to interfere. No telling what harm might be done. Let's go."

The day was sunny and warm, the kind of fall day that would help ensure a good harvest for the nearby wineries. The road from the lake front into the town of Sequence Springs passed through a stand of trees and then through a wide meadow. Jonas reached out and took Verity's hand as they walked along the roadside. His fingers tightened around hers.

"Okay, Verity," he said calmly, "let's have it."

She glanced up in surprise. "Have what?"

"The morning-after postmortem."

"Oh." She thought about it. "Is a postmortem necessary?"

He raised one brow. "Not as far as I'm concerned, but I thought it was de rigueur from the female point of view."

"You've had to endure a lot of postmortems?" she demanded.

"Ouch. Don't get snappish on me. The answer to your question is no, I haven't had to endure a lot of them. Not for quite a while. You want to know the truth? It's been one hell of a long time since I've been with a woman. Contrary to popular female opinion, a man does get to a stage in his life when he realizes he can abstain for extended periods of time without committing hara-kiri. Or maybe he just gets to the point where he finds it's easier to do without than go through the postmortems." He paused and then said a little roughly, "I'm sorry I was clumsy with you last night."

"You weren't clumsy," Verity snapped. "I've already told you that. I doubt if you could be clumsy if you tried. Things got a bit rushed, that's all. Everything was going beautifully until I found that earring."

"Finding it scared you, didn't it?" He stopped and pulled her into his arms beside the deserted road. The warm sun beat down on both of them as he caught her questioning face between his palms. "I'm sorry about that, too, Verity. The last thing I want to do is frighten you. Let's just give ourselves some time, okay?"

"Time?"

"Isn't that what you were asking for last night? Time to get to know each other? We've got lots of time, sweetheart. I made up my mind this morning to back off. You don't have to be afraid I'm going to show up on your doorstep every night trying to talk you back into bed. I won't rush you again."

Verity smiled tremulously. "Dad said he saw you reading Machiavelli this morning. Is this new strategy a result of a refresher course in the sneaky uses of power and politics?"

"Are you admitting I've got some power over you, sneaky or otherwise?"

"Not for a minute."

He smiled but his eyes were serious and intent. "You're important to me, Verity. I don't want to screw things up between us by pushing you too hard. Just give me a chance. I give you my word I'll take it easy for a while. I want you to trust me."

She thought about the earring that had fallen out of his pocket last night. Then she thought about all the things she had learned about men from watching her father over the years.

There were very few males in the world who would take a romantic gesture as far as Jonas had taken it when he traced her out of Mexico.

A man who followed his own whims, a man who had absorbed the spirit and philosophy of a bygone age, a man who could quote Renaissance love poetry might be one of the select few who would think it perfectly normal to follow a woman a couple of thousand miles, carrying her lost earring.

Verity touched Jonas's wrists on either side of her face. She could feel the corded strength in them, a compelling contrast to the astonishing sensitivity of his elegant hands. "You're important to me, too, Jonas. I don't know how or why, but you are very important to me."

He drew a deep breath and pulled her close for a quick, hard kiss. "Then we'll take it from there. And we'll take it slow. Everything's going to be all right, little tyrant."

Caitlin Evanger showed up for dinner that night accompanied by Tavi. They came alone. Verity wasn't surprised, after the conversation she'd had with Laura Griswald that afternoon.

"She's a fascinating woman, I'll admit," Laura had said, "but it was something of a strain trying to entertain her. Rick said he'll take a garden variety yuppie any day before he'll take another artist out to dinner. You and Caitlin seemed to hit it off well, though."

"I like her," Verity had admitted. "And I admire her tremendously. She's a woman who's made it on her own. She's talented and hardworking. And, for some reason, I feel a little sorry for her."

"I know what you mean. I think she's more than hardworking and talented," Laura said thoughtfully. "I think she's driven. There's something strange about her, Verity."

"Maybe all true artists are driven. Maybe that's what makes them able to produce art," Verity had suggested. "Maybe that's what men such as my father and Jonas lack, a sense of drive."

"And maybe you're luckier than you know," Laura had said. "I think it would be very difficult to live with someone who was obsessed."

"You think Caitlin Evanger is obsessed with her art?"

"She's obsessed with something. I can see it in her eyes. Oops, there's the other line. I've got to run. See you later, Verity."

Verity had hung up and sat for a few minutes thinking of Caitlin Evanger's eyes. Laura had a point. There was something unsettling about Caitlin's compelling gaze. More ghosts. But that knowledge only made Verity feel a greater sense of compassion.

Caitlin and Tavi both ordered the fresh pea soup with mint and the vegetable pilaf. Caitlin selected a bottle of wine, and Emerson, who was helping out as a waiter, served it with a flourish. Caitlin nodded austerely to him when he finally poured but she did not seem overly impressed by the dramatics.

"Jesus," Emerson complained as he came back to the kitchen. "Talk about the original iceberg. Brrr."

Jonas's mouth twisted wryly. "Better you than me. I had to put up with her last night."

"Cut it out, both of you," Verity ordered. "You just don't understand her, that's all."

"Yeah?" Her father gave her a sour look. "Well, it's your turn. She's asking for you."

Verity smiled loftily. "She probably wants to tell me how much she enjoyed the pilaf."

"I wouldn't count on it," Jonas cautioned. "She probably wants to tell you she's going to report you to the health authorities because she found a fly in her soup."

"Professional restaurateurs do not appreciate that sort of low humor, Jonas." Verity moved to stride past him into the dining room, aware that Jonas and her father were exchanging grins over her head. The male-bonding bit was getting a bit thick, she decided.

But she should have expected Jonas and her father to get along well. They were, after all, two of a kind.

"How was everything, Caitlin?" Verity asked as she came to a halt beside the table. A quick glance showed that both women had eaten most of their meal. A reassuring sign. As usual when anyone showed obvious evidence of having enjoyed her cooking, Verity was pleased.

"It was an excellent meal, Verity. In your own way, you are very much a creative artist. I hope you realize it."

Verity couldn't squelch another little burst of pleasure. "Thanks, Caitlin, I'm glad you enjoyed it. How much longer will you be staying?"

"Only one more day. I had planned to stay through the weekend, but I find that's impossible now. I wanted to see you this evening because I would like to invite you to come and visit me next Monday. You could spend the night and drive back Tuesday morning in plenty of time to open the restaurant for lunch. My home is over on the coast, about an hour and a half away from here. What do you say?"

An invitation to visit Caitlin Evanger was the last thing Verity had expected. She was so startled, she had to pause to gather her thoughts. "Caitlin, that's very nice of you. Monday?"

"The No Bull is closed on Monday, isn't it?"

"Well, yes, but I hadn't planned . . ."

Caitlin smiled at her, a strangely pleading smile. "I'll understand if you can't get away. But I was hoping you might make it. I will admit I don't have a great many friends. I count you as one of them, however, and I would like to get to know you better. Women such as us need our female friends, don't you think?"

Verity found herself returning the smile. "You're absolutely right, Caitlin. Women such as us need our friendships." There was absolutely no reason on earth why she couldn't take a day off and drive over to the coast to visit Caitlin. Besides, it would be interesting to see a real artist's home and studio. *Why not?* Verity thought silently. Aloud, she said, "I would love to stay with you on Monday." She pulled out a chair at the table and sat down. "You'll have to give me your address and directions."

"Tavi has them for you, don't you, Tavi?"

Tavi nodded silently and reached into a small satchel she had brought with her.

Standing in the kitchen doorway, Jonas watched the small scene at Caitlin Evanger's table. He couldn't overhear the conversation, but when Verity pulled out a chair and sat down, Jonas made an exclamation of disgust and turned back to wipe down a counter.

"Trouble out in the dining room?" Emerson asked. He popped the top off a can of beer and leaned back against a counter.

"Probably," Jonas said dryly. "Verity just sat down to chat with her good pal Caitlin the Ice Lady. I don't know what Verity sees in that woman. From the look of things, Evanger is making a real effort to turn Verity into her best friend."

"Maybe they both figure they have a lot in common," Emerson mused. "They're two strong-willed, intelligent, independent women who have built careers for themselves. I can see where they might have a lot to talk about."

Jonas shot him a cold glance. "Verity is not one damn bit like that icicle of an artist. She doesn't really have anything in common with Evanger, she just thinks she does. She's got a bad case of hero-worship."

"As long as Verity believes she has something in common

with Evanger, she *does* have something in common with her," Emerson pointed out reasonably. "The reality of a situation is never as important as the individual's perception of that reality. You know that."

"The hell with it. I'm not in the mood for a lecture on the differences between reality and perception." Jonas tossed aside the cloth he had been using and went back to lean in the doorway. He folded his arms and broodingly watched the three women at the table. The restaurant was empty now except for Verity, Caitlin, and the quiet woman who accompanied the artist.

"What do you think they're discussing so intently?" Emerson asked, coming up behind Jonas.

"Beats me, but I don't like it. Verity looks too damn interested in whatever Evanger is saying."

"Worried?"

"I just don't like it," Jonas said stubbornly. "Evanger's a bad influence on Verity."

Emerson chuckled. "Verity's been thinking for herself for a long time. First thing I taught her was to ask critical questions. It's the first thing they should teach kids in school, but of course they don't. Don't worry. My daughter isn't easily influenced by anyone or anything."

"You raised an interesting daughter, Emerson. She's as stubborn and independent as a Missouri mule."

"All the more reason for you to stop worrying about Caitlin Evanger's influence."

"But every little mule has its blind spot. Verity has a mind of her own, but she's also got a streak of naïveté. She's something of an innocent in spite of all those sharp thorns she's developed to protect herself. Verity's blind spot might be Caitlin Evanger. I can see the problem now. Evanger's a couple of years older than Verity; a woman who has lived up to her potential, at least in Verity's eyes. Verity's real big on living up to one's potential."

"I know." Emerson sipped his beer. "Easy to see why Verity admires Caitlin."

Jonas straightened. "I think it's time I put a stop to this."

"Good luck," Emerson murmured behind him.

Jonas strode out into the dining room and stopped at the table. All three women looked at him as if he'd just dropped in from another planet. He looked pointedly down at Verity.

"Time to close out the till," he said.

Verity smiled cheerfully. "I'll take care of it later, Jonas. Go on home with Dad if you're ready to leave."

So much for plan A, Jonas thought grimly. *Time to drop back to plan B.* This one required more subtlety. It was based on the principle of "if you can't beat 'em, join 'em." He noticed the piece of paper in front of Verity.

"What's the map for?" he asked.

"I'm going to visit Caitlin on Monday. Tavi just finished drawing me a little map so I can find the house."

Jonas felt something clench in his stomach. He shot a glance at Evanger, who just looked back at him with her cold, expressionless eyes. "Is that right?" he asked softly. "How are you going to manage the time away from the No Bull?"

"It won't be a problem," Verity assured him. "I'll be back in plenty of time on Tuesday to open for lunch."

Jonas tried a last ditch effort. "I thought you and I might drive up into the wine country next Monday."

Verity raised her eyebrows, clearly surprised. Jonas couldn't blame her. He was a little surprised himself. He hadn't planned anything at all for next Monday until approximately sixty seconds ago.

"Maybe next week," Verity temporized politely.

It was Caitlin Evanger who stepped in to resolve the situation. "Why don't you come with Verity, Mr. Quarrel?" she suggested smoothly. "You could drive over to the coast with her and see some of the wine country en route. I have plenty of room at my home for both of you."

Verity smiled enthusiastically. "That's very kind of you, Caitlin." She rounded on Jonas. "Isn't it? Do you want to come with me on Monday?"

Jonas sorted through his limited set of options and then met Caitlin Evanger's eyes. "Sure," he said coolly. "Why not?"

Much later that night Tavi sat on the edge of Caitlin Evanger's bed, massaging her employer's ruined leg with firm, tender hands.

"So it worked," Tavi observed with a sigh.

"I told you it would." Caitlin adjusted herself on the pillows and sipped the glass of brandy she routinely used to help put herself to sleep. "I knew Quarrel would never allow Verity to visit me by herself. Not if there was an alternative. He doesn't like me and he likes even less the fact that Verity and I are on friendly terms. But he knew tonight that he couldn't stop her from spending the night at my home. He chose the only alternative he had."

"The only alternative you offered," Tavi clarified, her fingers working deeply into the atrophied muscles.

"I've told you, Tavi, that as soon as I saw the way he looked at Verity, I knew she was the key to manipulating him. The plan I've been putting together is almost complete."

"Now you'll have a chance to test him with the rapier."

"I have to be certain. I have to know for sure that he still has the talent and that he can be made to use it when the time comes." Caitlin shifted again on the pillows. "That's enough massage for tonight."

Tavi halted and looked at Caitlin in surprise. "You said your leg was hurting badly this evening."

"It is. But the pain is good, Tavi." Caitlin smiled her humorless smile. "Don't you see? I use it to keep my attention trained on what I'm going to do. There is nothing like pain to focus one's mind. Planning an execution takes a certain amount of fortitude, I've discovered."

Chapter
Eight

The nearest signs of human habitation were several miles away as Verity and Jonas drove through the tiny village indicated on Tavi's map. They glided past a small general store and gas station, a post office, and a handful of gray, weathered cottages. A scattering of unprosperous-looking fishing boats sat huddled in the microscopic harbor waiting for a tide that never seemed to arrive.

Verity, who had been in a relentlessly cheerful mood since she and Jonas had set out from Sequence Springs, found the village charmingly picturesque.

"I should have brought my camera," she exclaimed, enchanted by the fishing boats. "Isn't that a lovely scene?"

Jonas was distinctly unimpressed. "The whole place looks like it's ready for the morgue."

Verity's good mood slipped. She had been tolerating his brusque, unenthusiastic comments most of the way from Sequence Springs, but enough was enough. "I don't know why you bothered to come along," she snapped. "It's obvious you aren't enjoying yourself."

He took his steady gaze off the narrow, curving road long enough to give her a direct look. "I didn't come along with the intention of enjoying myself."

"Then why did you insist on coming along?"

"I didn't have much choice. I couldn't talk you out of it, remember?"

"I remember," Verity muttered, "but that doesn't explain why you felt you had to come with me."

"I didn't want you making the trip alone." His voice was vaguely defensive.

"I've got news for you, Jonas," Verity assured him in growing exasperation, "I'm a big girl and I've been traveling all by myself for ages."

"I've already had a sample of the kind of trouble you get into when you're traveling by yourself. I saw you in action down in Mexico, remember?"

Verity was about to tell him what she thought of his lousy logic but something stopped her. "Jonas," she finally said more gently, "why did you feel you had to accompany me today? The real reason."

He startled her with the blunt honesty of his response. "I don't know. Something to do with Caitlin Evanger. The woman gives me the chills. I didn't want you driving over here and staying with her alone. End of subject. Find another topic of conversation."

Jonas had made it clear several times during the weekend that he wasn't looking forward to visiting Caitlin Evanger, which had only reinforced Verity's determination to make the trip. She had fully expected that at the last minute he would tell her to go by herself. But he hadn't.

On Monday morning, Jonas had resignedly thrown a few things into his duffel bag, tossed the bag into Verity's car, and then climbed into the front seat and held out his hands for the keys.

Verity had toyed with the idea of telling him to stay behind and go fishing with her father. But in the end, eager to be on her way, she'd handed him the keys.

Now, as they drove the winding road that led to Caitlin's house, she wondered if she had made a wise decision. Jonas showed every sign of putting a real damper on the occasion.

But what really bothered her was his illogical insistence on accompanying her. He couldn't explain it even to his own satisfaction, let alone to hers.

Ghosts, Verity thought suddenly. Jonas was having problems with his private ghosts again. She wondered what she had to do with those ghosts.

Then they saw the house. It was huge, dour, and astonishingly ugly, clinging like a large, faceted-eyed insect to the edge of the cliff, defying the frothing white sea that surged relentlessly below. It wasn't until one got close to it that it became clear the insect-eye effect was created by the oddly designed windows that bulged outward.

"That house looks like some do-it-yourselfer went crazy with a bunch of concrete and steel left over from some other do-it-yourself project that failed," Jonas commented. He halted Verity's compact at the side of the road for a better look.

"I think it's an example of some architect's idea of modern art," Verity suggested. "It's not quite what I expected. It doesn't look like the sort of place that would appeal to Caitlin."

"Oh, I don't know," Jonas said laconically. "I think it suits her just fine. All that concrete and steel compliments her personality perfectly, if you want my opinion."

"When I want your opinion, I'll ask for it." Verity surveyed the gloomy, windswept scene. The day had been warm and bright back in Sequence Springs, but here along the ocean the sky was overcast. The sea looked like hammered gray metal stretching out to the horizon. A glance over the edge of the cliffs revealed that it was a long way down to the water.

Definitely not a California surfing beach, Verity thought. Anyone foolish enough to try riding those waves would find himself beaten to a pulp against the rocks at the base of the cliffs. The dark, wild setting represented the flip side of the state's brilliant sun-and-sand image.

"Seen enough?" Jonas asked as he restarted the car. "We

can always go back to town and phone her to say we can't make it today."

"Don't be ridiculous. I'm looking forward to visiting Caitlin."

"I don't know what you see in the woman." Jonas glanced over his shoulder to check traffic, then swung the wheel of the car. "She gives me the creeps."

"I'll tell you what I see in her," Verity said quietly. "I see a strong, lonely woman in need of friendship. Why shouldn't I be her friend? After all, Caitlin and I have a few things in common."

"You *what?*" The car whipped around a curve in an arc that was a little too tight. Jonas corrected the maneuver with a disgusted oath. "Are you out of your tiny little mind? You've got nothing in common with Caitlin Evanger. Nothing at all."

Verity leaned back into her corner. "I'm not so sure. Oh, I'll admit I don't have her artistic talent. My skills are a lot more mundane. But there is something about her and the way she lives that has a familiar feel to it. Have you ever had a glimpse of the future and discovered that it looked familiar?"

"No." The single word was clipped as Jonas concentrated on the narrow road. "Only the past."

Verity wrinkled her nose in a question. "What do you mean by that?"

Jonas stifled a soft curse. "Nothing much. Just that I guess it's possible to say the past has a familiar feel. After all, it exists. Has existed. It has tentacles that reach into the present. We're all victims of it. But it makes no sense to say the same about the future."

"I think it does. I look at Caitlin and I see the woman I may be in another couple of years. Minus the artistic genius, of course. She has carved out a space for herself and she occupies it completely. She's strong. I know she employs Tavi to handle the day-to-day problems of life, but you always have a sense that Caitlin would do just fine without Tavi if it was necessary."

"Verity, Evanger is one cold fish. Trust me. A man knows that kind of woman when he sees one."

Verity shrugged. "You see that because she makes it clear she has no need for a man. What's wrong with that? It gives her a kind of freedom that many women will never know. She's not dependent on a man for anything, least of all her own happiness. She takes care of herself and finds satisfaction in doing so. I should think you would admire a woman like Caitlin. She's the kind of woman who would never make demands on a man. She would never try to tie him down or turn him into something he's not. In short, the perfect female."

"Don't put words in my mouth, Verity. It's obvious you've got a bad case of hero-worship, but don't try to drag me into the congregation."

"It's not a question of hero-worship. I like her. I think she needs friends and I have no objection to being her friend. That's all there is to it." Verity smiled wryly and stared out the window. "Maybe we'd better change the subject."

"Maybe we'd better, since you're not making much sense."

"Jonas, I'm warning you, if you don't behave yourself I'm going to fire you on the spot."

"Yes, your majesty."

She opted not to respond to that piece of provocation. Jonas had been in an unreadable mood ever since he had told her he had decided to give her time.

It was very thoughtful of him, Verity had decided. The problem was, she was coming to the conclusion that she didn't really want any more time. With a man such as Jonas, a woman had to accept the fact that she wouldn't have him around for long. It was beginning to occur to Verity that it was a shame to waste what time she did have with him. Like her father, he would take off one of these days. And it was, after all, her father who had taught her to enjoy what life offered when it was offered because there were never any guarantees.

She developed a queasy feeling in the pit of her stomach every time she thought of how much Jonas and Emerson had in common. Several times a day she told herself it was better if the brief affair she had begun with Jonas was nipped in the bud. The last thing she needed in her life was a relationship with a man who shared none of her own values.

On the other hand, given her advancing age and future prospects, surely she had a right to at least one interesting sexual fling, she decided wryly.

"Well, here we are," Jonas announced as he parked the car in a wide, graveled drive. "I don't see anyone rushing out to greet us. Maybe no one's home."

"Don't sound so hopeful." Verity opened her door and got out. The wind off the sea whipped her hair into an instant tangle. The jeans and plaid shirt she had put on that morning in Sequence Springs were not proof against the crisp, snapping breeze, so she reached into the backseat for the bright yellow windbreaker she had brought along.

As she fastened her jacket, the door slammed on the other side of the car. Jonas stood, one arm resting casually on the roof of the car while he eyed the forbidding structure in front of him.

"One half-expects someone named Igor to open the door," he said dryly.

Before Verity could respond, Tavi Monahan opened the wide, gray door. She stood at the top of the concrete steps leading up to the house and looked at them with an unreadable expression.

"Caitlin will be pleased to know you're here," Tavi said very quietly. Tavi herself looked a little less than pleased. Verity thought there was a sense of anxiety beneath that serene, elegant facade.

"I'm glad somebody is pleased," Jonas muttered as he pulled his duffel bag and Verity's small suitcase from the backseat.

Once again, Verity decided to pretend she hadn't overheard the crack. Sometimes the only thing a woman could do with someone like Jonas was ignore him.

They followed Tavi down a hallway paved in gray and black stone. Everything in the house seemed to have been finished in gray and black. Verity silently decided that Jonas was right. Some designer had gotten a little carried away with the theme of concrete and steel. The unusual windows at the front of the house that had looked so much like insect eyes from a distance allowed light in on three levels.

Caitlin's home was large and as untraditional inside as it was out. The floor plan of the three-story home did not seem to follow any familiar pattern. A steel-banistered staircase connected the various levels, but the rooms Verity saw as she followed Tavi to the top floor seemed strangely shaped. Walls curved and assumed odd angles.

There was a second, narrower staircase that connected the levels from some point at the rear of the house.

Tavi opened a door in the center of a long, battleship-gray corridor and revealed a granite-colored room that had a wall of angled glass on the ocean side. A huge four-poster bed dominated the room, but it was unlike any four-poster Verity had ever seen before. Instead of being fashioned from heavy oak or mahogany, it was metal. The four posts were stark, monolithic pillars pushing toward the ceiling. A gray and black quilt covered the bed.

"What an interesting room," Verity said with forced enthusiasm.

A quick, sardonically amused glance from Jonas reminded her for some reason that *interesting* was the way she had described his lovemaking. She knew from the expression in his eyes that he was remembering the word and the previous context in which she had used it. Verity was annoyed to feel herself turning pink.

Tavi spoke up. "You have the room at the end of the hall, Mr. Quarrel. I will show you to it. Caitlin will be waiting for both of you downstairs."

"Just a minute," Jonas said as he caught sight of an old rapier hanging on the wall near the bed. He walked a few steps closer to the blade and stood studying it silently. He made no move to touch it.

Verity followed his glance and saw the long, delicately tapered sword mounted on a metal plaque. The thin, sharply pointed weapon had an elaborately gilded hilt with what appeared to be small, finger-sized rings built onto it.

"Is that an antique sword?" she asked curiously, aware of his sudden fascination with the weapon.

"A rapier. Mid-eighteen hundreds, I'd say. Or a hell of a good reproduction." Jonas swung around to confront Tavi. "Does your boss collect or is this just for decoration?"

Tavi glanced at the blade without much interest. "The rapier was here when Caitlin bought the house a few years ago. There is another one in your bedroom. The former owner was apparently a collector. When he died, the place was sold as is by the heirs. They had little interest in the house or anything in it. As far as I know, the rapiers are genuine, not reproductions, but I can't be certain. There's one in every bedroom. Caitlin has never had them appraised."

Jonas nodded and looked at Verity. "I'll drop my bag in my room and meet you back here in a few minutes." He spoke with authority.

"Yes, Jonas," she said with mocking obedience. "Anything you say." Two could play at the sarcasm game, she decided.

Caitlin was waiting for them on the first floor in a long rain-colored room that faced the ocean. She had been standing at the window, staring out to sea. As they walked into the room she turned, her ebony cane in hand. Her eyes went first to Jonas but it was Verity she greeted.

"Thank you for coming, Verity."

There was more than simple graciousness in the words. There was a hint of relief, as if Caitlin had been more than a little anxious about their arrival. A wave of sympathy went through Verity. She went forward with a warm smile and gave her hostess a quick, friendly, woman-to-woman hug.

"Thanks for having us, Caitlin. What a fabulous view. You seem to have this entire stretch of coast to yourself."

"I prefer to work without distractions. This house, ugly as it is, serves my purpose." Caitlin gestured her guests to a low, padded bench covered in gray silk. "Please have a seat. Tavi is getting lunch ready. I have instructed her to prepare a vegetarian menu while you're here."

Verity chuckled. "That was thoughtful of you. I hope it won't mean a lot of extra work for her. I'm very good at making a meal off all the goodies that usually get served around a slab of beef. I'm not a fussy eater, believe me."

"Just don't try to import hamburgers and french fries from a local fast food joint," Jonas advised. "You'll never hear the end of it." He didn't take the seat Caitlin had indicated. Instead he walked to the window to examine the view.

Verity glared at his back but he seemed unaware of the censuring look. "Jonas has a peculiar sense of humor," she warned Caitlin.

"I'll remember that," Caitlin said. "Perhaps after lunch you and Jonas would like to take a walk along the cliffs. There's a storm heading our way. It should be here by to-night. The cliff views are quite spectacular when a storm is moving inland from the sea. You must exercise caution, however. The former owner had a fence installed but it's since collapsed in a few places. I haven't had it repaired. There's a path down to the beach at the far end of the cliffs."

"I'd like a walk later," Verity said, thinking she could use the opportunity to tell Jonas once again to behave himself. For all the good it would do. "Where is your studio, Caitlin?"

"On the top floor. I'll take you upstairs and show you while we wait for Tavi to prepare lunch. That is, if you'd like to see it?"

"Very much. I've never seen the studio of a working artist."

"Come with me, then."

Caitlin climbed the stairs with a slow, stately tread, using her cane to steady her braced leg. As she made the ascent to the top floor of the house, she explained that she had bought her home three years earlier.

"When it came on the market the heirs were not exactly swamped with offers," she explained. "The views are great, but most of the people who could afford this kind of location and this size house were put off by the architecture."

"It is unusual," Verity noted cautiously.

"No need to be polite. It's cold and ugly," Caitlin said calmly. "I understand the former owner suited it perfectly."

It was Jonas who picked up on that. He was climbing the stairs behind Verity. "Who was the former owner?"

Caitlin paused, one hand on the steel banister. She glanced back over her shoulder. "I'm told his name was Sandquist. From all accounts he was a very successful businessman who kept this place for a weekend retreat. He died here one weekend and it was several days before anyone thought to come looking. They found the body on the beach. He had apparently fallen from the top of the cliffs. The circumstances of his death were the kind they call suspicious in detective novels. At least, the locals liked to call them suspicious. There was some talk about murder but nothing ever came of it. The real estate agent assured me the authorities never pursued the investigation very far. Apparently they were satisfied."

"Who started the rumors of murder?" Jonas asked curiously.

"A few of the people in that little town down the road. The real estate saleswoman who showed me the place said that the villagers liked to think this house had been the scene of wild orgies and sadistic rituals. Sandquist used to throw parties here for his friends, apparently. None of the locals was ever invited, so of course they invented a lot of tales about what went on at the gatherings. When Sandquist died, it was no great surprise that the villagers assumed some of the festivities had gotten a little too wild. Who knows? Maybe it's the truth. It doesn't matter now."

Verity grinned. "No ghosts hanging around?"

Caitlin started up the next flight of stairs. "We all have a few ghosts cluttering up our lives, Verity. Some of us have more than others. But I've never seen the ghost of the former owner here in this house."

"Why should you?" Jonas asked blandly. "It would be busy haunting the cliffs where Sandquist died."

Verity shot him a repressive glare.

The studio at the top of the stairs occupied an entire corner of the house. The bulging, faceted windows allowed light from two sides into the stark, bare room. It was the first room Verity had seen that was not painted gray. Caitlin's studio was white from floor to ceiling.

There were several canvases stacked facing the walls, most quite large. An easel, a huge table decorated with several years' worth of spattered paint, and some artist's tools sat in the middle of the white floor. One large canvas, much bigger than the others and draped in a sheet, was tilted inward against one wall.

"Is that the painting you're currently working on?" Verity inquired, indicating the large canvas.

"*Bloodlust* is done," Caitlin said, her voice perfectly neutral. "I finished it a few months ago. I'm preparing to sell it at an auction. Until then, I'm not letting anyone look at it."

"An auction?" Verity eyed the draped canvas, wondering what was underneath. "Will it be conducted by a San Francisco auction house?"

"No," Caitlin stated firmly. "I will conduct the auction myself, here, in this house. Only a certain, select group will be invited to bid on *Bloodlust*."

"Are you planning on holding the auction soon?" Verity's curiosity was definitely aroused, although she wasn't certain why.

"Yes," Caitlin said. "Soon." Her eyes went to Jonas, who was glancing around the white room with idle interest. "Shall we go downstairs? Tavi will be ready with lunch."

Much later that night Tavi went through the ritual of preparing her employer for bed. She removed Caitlin's robe and the brace on her leg and poured a snifter of brandy.

"He might not touch it," Tavi warned. "He didn't touch the rapier in her room earlier today. He didn't take hold of the one in his own room when I showed him into it. Maybe he won't try to touch it at all."

"He won't be able to resist handling it, however briefly," Caitlin said with grave certainty. "It's perfect for him. It's from the right era, the right historical context, and it's genuine. What's more, although you and I can't feel it, it must be carrying a whole freight load of heavy, screaming emotions. All the vibrations associated with rape and death. How can he not take it in his hands, at least for a moment or two? That rapier will draw him like a magnet. And when he does take it down from the wall to examine it, we'll know for certain that he still has the touch. He's bound to show some reaction." She looked at the small television screen on a table near the bed. "The camera is working well."

The television screen held a black and white image of a long, tapered rapier mounted on the wall of a bedroom.

Tavi nodded reluctantly. "I set it up this morning and double-checked it while Quarrel and Ames walked along the cliffs this afternoon. If Quarrel takes hold of the rapier and it has any obvious effect on him, we'll be able to observe it. Unless, of course, he picks up the rapier after he's turned out the lights, in which case the camera will be blind."

"He's not likely to look at such a valuable item in the dark," Caitlin scoffed. "He'll have the lights on when he checks it out."

"You're sure you'll be able to tell if he responds to the rapier?" Tavi asked doubtfully. "I don't see . . ."

"I'll know," Caitlin said. "I'm sure of it. I saw what happens to him when he picks up anything that carries a strong emotional charge."

"I'm not sure if I believe in this strange talent you say he has."

"Psychometry?" Caitlin sipped her brandy, her eyes steady on the unwavering image on the television screen. "Believe in it, Tavi. It's for real. It caused him to nearly kill a man five years ago."

Tavi frowned. "If you say so, Caitlin. If you're right and the rapier has a strong effect on him, what's to keep him from going crazy the way he did the last time? He might kill us all in our beds."

Caitlin shook her head. "No, we'll be safe enough as long as the present time context is considerably different from the historical context in which the rapier was used. The lab reports are clear on that score."

"What do you expect him to do tonight?"

"He'll probably try touching the rapier for a moment or two because his curiosity will get the better of him. He'll drop it quickly when it becomes too much for him. That was the way he dealt with objects during the testing sessions I observed at Vincent." Caitlin stared at the television screen. "I wonder what goes on in his mind when he touches an old object and senses its past vibrations. I wonder what he actually sees."

Tavi shivered and said nothing as she began to massage Caitlin's weak leg. She wasn't sure what to believe, but she knew that there was little chance of changing her dear, tormented friend's mind. Caitlin had to have her vengeance. On the television screen the black and white image remained unchanged.

Jonas glanced at his watch and tossed aside the book he had been reading. It was a collection of Lorenzo de' Medici's poems, which he had borrowed from Emerson Ames's library. Jonas had brought the book along on the trip with some vague notion of brushing up his own love poetry. He had decided to take lessons from a master.

Lorenzo had been a true Renaissance man: a connoisseur of art, an astute banker, a politician, scholar, and poet. In addition, he could handle a sword, as he had proven the day he fought his way to safety after an assassination attempt in a church.

The man had also had a bawdy sense of humor. Jonas savored one of the light carnival songs Lorenzo had penned for a holiday procession. It was a paean to Bacchus, desire, and dance. Wine, women, and song. But underneath the bright lyrics was a subtle warning that life was short and it was foolish to postpone pleasure and happiness. Lorenzo must have had a few premonitions. He had died at the age of forty-three.

Jonas reflected briefly on the sobering thought of just how close he himself was getting to forty-three. He had wasted a lot of years running from something he still didn't understand, let alone know how to control. Some would say he had taken Lorenzo's advice and opted for life's pleasures during the past five years, but he knew better.

He got up out of the steel and gray-leather armchair and walked to the window. He had taken off his shirt and boots earlier and now wore only his jeans. He had planned to go straight to bed but that had proved impossible. The room was filled with a disturbing influence that made him restless and uneasy.

Jonas didn't like the room, the house, or the whole situation. Its sense of wrongness was stronger than ever. Everything about Caitlin Evanger set off his internal alarm signals. He only wished he could make Verity understand his feelings, but she was hell-bent on being Caitlin's friend. He stared out into the darkness and wondered again how much that woman knew about his past.

The damn room was really getting to him. It didn't take any great intuition to guess the immediate source of his problem tonight. Jonas had known what the trouble was right from the start. It was that rapier hanging on the wall. The thing was packed with resonance. He had been trying to ignore the weapon for the past hour.

At the window, he focused his thoughts on himself. He had put off his future long enough. Now that he had found Verity he knew he was on the brink of coming to terms with that future as well as with his past.

The storm that had been gathering out at sea all afternoon had just struck an hour ago and was now in full regalia. Rain hammered the bulbous windows and the wind screamed as it lashed the cliffs. Jonas thought fleetingly about Caitlin's story of the death of the house's previous owner. Then he wondered if Verity was lying awake in bed listening to the storm and thinking about Sandquist's ghost.

There were times when she would look at Jonas in a certain way that gave him the eerie feeling that she saw more than he intended her to see.

His mind leaped from that disquieting thought to the memory of the night he had made love to her. He had been so desperate for her after handling the dueling pistol. After chasing her down the endless corridor in his mind, he had been unable to resist catching her for real and pinning her safely beneath him.

His body tightened with the tension of gathering desire as he tormented himself with the recollection of what it was like to make love to Verity. He had lost himself in her softness that night. He wanted nothing more than to lose himself that way again. It was taking all his self-control these days to live up to his promise to take things slowly. He could still feel the sweet pressure of her legs and the sharp edges of her nails as she clung to him. She had been so tight and hot and sweetly, innocently sensual.

Jonas still marveled that she had waited all these years to experience the mysteries of passion. Then he grimaced wryly at the memory of his haste and clumsiness. In one very important way, he acknowledged, Verity was still waiting to experience the mysteries of passion. She had not

found the ultimate satisfaction in his arms that first time and
had kicked him out of bed before he could give it a second
try.

They had been dancing around each other ever since; a
frustrating, precariously balanced pattern of advance and retreat that was bound to explode sooner or later. Jonas hoped
it would be sooner. His body ached to possess again the fire
in Verity.

He turned away from the window, grimly aware of his
aroused state. Just the thought of Verity lying naked in his
arms was enough to put him in this condition. It was ludi-
crous. At his age he should have a hell of a lot more self-
control. Maybe a cold shower would help.

At least the dull ache of desire had one positive side effect, he reflected as he walked past the shadowed rapier: it
helped take his mind off the weapon. He stepped into the
stainless steel bathroom and flipped on the light.

The cold-water treatment would be excruciating but probably fairly effective. It should help him gain some control
over his rampaging hormones. At this rate Verity was going
to drive him crazy. The little tyrant probably didn't even
realize what she was doing to him. He wondered how much
more time he could afford to give her before he lost his
sanity.

He had his hands on the buttons of his jeans, and was
wishing they were on the fastenings of Verity's pants, when
he became dizzyingly aware of the rapier.

For an instant a series of violent emotions flitted through
his brain. *Fury, lust, fear.*

No doubt about it, the pull of the thing was getting
stronger. The remnants of the past that still clung to the steel
of the rapier were powerful. Too powerful. He knew he had
better stop trying to fight them.

Jonas stalked across the room to examine the weapon.
Proximity was a factor, he knew. The closer he was to an
object carrying the residue of old violence, the more he was

affected by it. It would help if he got the rapier out of the room. He decided to store it in a closet overnight.

He went to the wall, aware of the increasing level of his awareness as he approached the old metal. No doubt about it, the thing was genuine. He was willing to bet the steel had been forged in Milan. No reproduction would be screaming silently at him the way this thing was. It was from the era to which he was most psychically vulnerable.

Jonas reached up and tentatively took hold of the edges of the plaque. He didn't dare touch the rapier itself. It was generating too much emotional energy.

He lifted the plaque from the wall and started toward the closet, thinking that if Verity saw him now she would be certain he was crazy. A part of Jonas secretly wondered if he really was crazy.

He was halfway across the room when he realized he'd made a terrible miscalculation. He was in big trouble.

His fingers were well clear of the steel, but Jonas reeled under a wave of powerful emotions that had been generated four hundred years in the past. He was suddenly in the endless corridor. It was already coalescing around him and he knew that the spectral tentacles of old feelings would be waiting. And they would find him soon, seeking with a rampaging hunger. Instinctively he fought the compulsion to fling himself heedlessly down the psychic tunnel. That way lay madness. He had always known that. There was no way to outrun the snakelike ribbons of old hate and lust and vengeance.

Sweat dampened his forehead and trickled down his sides in tiny rivulets. Jonas hung on to the remnants of his consciousness with all his willpower. He staggered and lost his balance, going down on one knee.

He had to get rid of the blade. He had to drop the metal plaque on which the rapier was mounted.

It was so simple. All he had to do was drop the damn thing.

Jonas struggled to relax his grip. But the pull of the rapier was far more violent and compelling than he had expected. Under assault, he sensed with grim shock that it had never been worse than this except that day in the lab when he'd almost killed a man.

Few things he had ever touched had hit him this hard. Tonight he was going to lose himself in the dark corridor. He was going to be overwhelmed by the past. It would either kill him or drive him out of his mind.

He had been a fool to touch the plaque. He should have guessed how powerful the rapier on it was. But it had been so long since he had experimented with an object from his prime time period that he had almost forgotten how strong the past could be. Perhaps he had grown overconfident because of his experience with the dueling pistols the other night.

Or perhaps that subtle confidence had started growing in him the day he had found Verity.

Jonas shook his head, groping for the reason why he had gotten away with handling the pistols.

He remembered picking up one of the guns and simultaneously reaching for Verity in his mind. She had been there, running ahead of him down the corridor. He had chased her. He hadn't been able to touch her but had gotten close enough to learn that she exerted as much pull on him as the gun itself. What's more, the twisting ribbons of emotion were drawn to her. She could chain them.

Verity.

If he could touch her now, Jonas knew, he stood a chance of escaping the compulsion of the rapier. He had to get to Verity.

Jonas struggled to his feet. The effort sent him reeling against the bed, where the metal plaque was jarred from his grasp and hit the floor with a sharp thud. The rapier bounced free, clattering.

Before Jonas could get out of the way, the weapon rolled twice and came to a halt against his bare foot.

Fury rippled through him. Raw, murderous, overwhelming fury. *He would kill the man who had tried to rape his lady.* He would see the bastard's blood soaking into the tiles of the palazzo before the light of the new day dawned.

Jonas reached down and scooped up the rapier. He had to get to Verity. His red-haired lady was in mortal jeopardy. He had to get to her and kill the man who threatened her.

Chapter Nine

V*erity* was hovering on the edge of a dream when the door to her bedroom opened with a crash. She struggled up out of sleep, wondering vaguely if the storm had smashed one of the insect-eye windows. Sitting up against the pillows, she blinked sleep out of her eyes.

Although the room was in darkness, she noticed a patch of lighter gray where the door should have been. It was then she realized that the door was open and she was looking out into the shadowed hall. Before she had time to wonder how the door had been flung back on its hinges, she saw the figure of a man looming in the opening. She could barely make out the object he held in his right hand. Then it came to her.

A rapier.

She tried to scream but in that instant the man moved into the room, gliding forward in a fencer's crouch. Lightning crackled outside the window, briefly illuminating his lean, powerful figure and the menacing shape of the naked blade he held. She knew then who it was. Stunned shock ricocheted through her.

"Jonas."

The figure jerked at the sound of his name as if one of the

bolts of lightning had struck him. She saw him shake his head as if to clear it and then he came toward her soundlessly to stop at the foot of the bed. While she saw the blade gripped firmly in his hand, it was not pointed at her. Verity scrambled backward until she was crouched against the wall.

"Jonas, for God's sake, what's wrong?" The words were hoarse with fear and tension.

"Touch me." Jonas's voice was so raw it was almost unrecognizable. *"Touch me."*

He was in the grip of some terrible nightmare, Verity thought. As long as he held the rapier, she didn't dare get near him. Caught up in his fevered dream, he might easily mistake her for some imagined foe. He held the rapier as if he knew how to use it, even in a nightmare. Warily she edged over to the side of the bed.

It was then she realized that there was something wrong with the room. It seemed to be curving around her, cutting her off from reality. A new fear washed over her.

"Jonas, wake up. Do you hear me? Wake up!"

He tracked her sidling movements with eyes that burned in the darkness. "Verity, touch me. Hold me or I'll never make it. *Touch me."*

She wanted to run but the desperation in his voice forbade it. Verity got to her feet beside the bed, her nightgown tangling with her legs. She took a deep breath, searching for the words that might bring Jonas out of his delirium.

He took a step closer to her and she realized that now he was much too close. She was trapped.

The room finished its bizarre twisting movement and she was back in that terrible corridor she had found herself in the night Jonas had picked up the dueling pistol.

"Verity, don't run from me."

She heard the words in her mind, echoing down the tunnel from a great distance. They sent panic through her. She knew now for certain that it was Jonas who was hunting her in that dark, endless corridor. In her mind she tried to flee but her legs would barely move. It was like running through quicksand. She was in a waking nightmare of her own.

"Hold me. Hold me or I'm lost."

The words were a fierce command and a poignant plea. It was the plea that touched her soul. Verity came to a shaky halt in the corridor and turned helplessly to confront the man who pursued her. She could not run from that desperate demand.

For a shattering instant she couldn't see him. The tunnel was dark and yet there was shape and form to it. She was aware of Jonas's presence, aware of him closing the gap between them, but she could not yet identify him. Something moved in the shadows and once more Verity wanted to flee. Every instinct warned her to turn and run.

"No. Don't run from me. I need you. Help me."

Verity gasped for air as if she had been running for her life. And then she took a step forward in the bedroom. Simultaneously she was moving again in the corridor; making her way toward the voice that had called out to her. Shadows swirled mistily around her. She was afraid to look at them too closely.

Lightning crackled again and a fierce, hot whiteness temporarily lit the room. Verity, dazed, saw two realities at once, the room where she had been sleeping and the inside of the dark corridor. Jonas still held the rapier there in the bedroom but he was holding out one hand to Verity. His lightning-lit face was a mask of savage intensity.

Verity saw the hunger, desperate hope, and violent command in his eyes before the white glare faded. She hesitated no longer. She didn't know what was wrong but she knew beyond a shadow of a doubt that Jonas needed her.

She broke free of her paralysis and hurled herself across the room into his arms. She came up against his hard, bare chest with enough impact to send a shudder through him. He brought his left arm around her in a rough, near-violent embrace.

"Verity."

In the corridor in her mind, she simultaneously found Jonas in the shadows and reached for him. His outstretched hand touched hers. Ribbons of violent color, black, bloody, some the shade of steel, roared out of the tunnel's darkness and whirled around her as if drawn to her. She had the impression they wanted to cling to Jonas but were sidetracked by her presence.

Verity tried to scream and couldn't.

"It's all right," Jonas said there in the corridor. "They can't hurt you. You have power over them. You draw them and hold them. You can chain them for me; you're my anchor."

She didn't understand anything he was saying but in the bedroom the rapier clattered to the floor at her feet and Jonas's other hand closed convulsively around Verity.

The curving walls of the corridor vanished.

Another deep shudder went through Jonas. Verity wrapped her arms around him and held on as if he might somehow slip away from her. She heard the sound of his deep, heaving breaths and felt his face as he buried it in her hair.

"Verity. *Verity.*" Jonas was holding on to her as if she were his lifeline. His body was hard and fiercely aroused. "You don't know . . . you can't even guess what it means— what you did. You held on to those things and you held me here." His hands moved over her as if he were trying to assure himself that she was real. He dropped a thousand urgent little kisses into her hair, on her temple, down her throat. Hot, equally urgent words poured over her in a mixture of triumph and relief. "If only you knew what you just did. Dammit to hell, honey, I can't explain. . . . Not now. Not yet. I need you. God, how I need you."

"Jonas, please, tell me what happened." She raised her head and cradled his hard face between her palms as she tried to steady him long enough to get an explanation out of him. "What was going on just then?"

"Later," he breathed, kissing her forcefully back into silence. "Later. Everything later. I swear. Right now I need you. I have to have you. I'm on fire for you. Put your hands on me. Feel me. Feel how much I want you. I'm going to explode."

He caught hold of one of her wrists and pushed her hand down to where his jeans were stretched taut over a heavy erection. Verity flinched at the heat in him. She tried to free her hand but he held it where he wanted it, groaning thickly as she cradled him.

The fighter's tension that had gripped Jonas when he entered her bedroom earlier had transformed itself into violent sexual desire. Verity could feel the change in him. She realized with a shock that the two emotions seething within him were not unrelated. The knowledge alarmed her, but before she could deal with it Jonas picked her up and tossed her lightly onto the bed. Then he yanked at the fastening of his jeans. A moment later he was naked, fully aroused and ready. His expression in the shadows was taut and intent. Muscles rippled smoothly across his shoulders as he came toward her.

Verity sucked in her breath as he lowered himself quickly to the bed and sprawled heavily on top of her. His need for her was as irresistible as the tide. She was suddenly pulsing with her own feminine desire.

His legs tangled with hers and his hands pushed up the hem of her nightgown until the material bunched around her waist.

"I want you," Jonas rasped. "I want you so damn much. I have to have you. You belong to me."

She was catching fire under his touch. His urgency was now hers. Verity twisted beneath him, responding recklessly to the relentless emotions that were driving Jonas. She was swamped with a cascade of feelings that ran the gamut from fearful excitement to an aching desire for surrender. She felt wild and free and chained all at once.

"Yes," she cried out softly as his palm closed over her

dampening female flesh. She arched against his possessive touch and clutched at his shoulders. "Yes, Jonas."

He muttered a hoarse response, the words unintelligible as he shoved a knee between her legs and cradled himself in the warm space there. He bent his head to kiss the satin skin of her thigh, teeth grazing her with exquisite care.

He yanked at her nightgown, trying to jerk it off completely. Verity raised herself on one elbow to free the thin fabric, but before she could maneuver the gown over her head there was a sharp, rending sound. The delicate material parted under Jonas's urgent grip.

The sound broke through her dazed excitement. Verity gasped. She went still.

"No. Don't think about it. Not yet," Jonas said huskily, pulling the offending gown free and tossing it aside. "Don't worry about it. Think about us. Hold on to me, Verity. Put your hands on me and hold on to me the way you did in the corridor."

She stared up at him, suddenly frightened. She was frozen beneath him. "Jonas, I don't understand any of this."

He swore in soft despair. Then he closed his eyes and set his teeth, struggling for mastery of himself. Verity could feel the rigid control he was exerting. Every inch of him was rock hard with muscle tension. He breathed deeply. For a timeless moment neither of them moved. Then Jonas's eyes flicked open and she saw the smoldering fire he had managed to partially bank.

"You don't have to be afraid," he said in a dark, hoarse voice. "I'm not going to hurt you."

Her fear began to dissolve. Verity's fingertips stroked his shoulder in an unconsciously soothing pattern. "I know," she whispered. And she did. She did not have any reason to fear Jonas. What she feared was the unknown that seemed to dwell within him.

Deliberately he lifted himself slightly away from her. His eyes locked with hers, telling her silently of his need as his hand slid warmly down the length of her, caressing her breasts and then the small curve of her stomach. His fingers were trembling with sensual tension when they touched the inside of her thigh. But he was in control now. He repeated his full-length stroke.

Verity couldn't look away from him. His eyes never left hers. He held her trapped with the knowledge of his need as surely as he held her trapped in his arms. He continued his slow, sensual stroking.

"Touch me again," he begged thickly. "Please, Verity."

Tentatively she obeyed, trailing her fingers through the curling hair on his chest and down toward the crisp thicket that framed his manhood. She held her breath for an instant as she touched him intimately and Jonas groaned. He bent his head and found her nipple with his tongue. The delicate nub hardened quickly and he sucked it gently between his teeth.

Verity caught her breath, then she sighed and began to relax. Her legs parted willingly this time for Jonas's gentle prodding.

"Harder," he coaxed when she began to tease him with her fingertips. He pushed himself more heavily into her hand, dampening her palm with the evidence of his arousal.

Verity touched him more firmly, wondering at the steel in him.

"That's it," he breathed. Then he began touching her with equal intimacy. His strong, blunt fingers circled the small, pouting opening between her legs until it began to flower. "That's it," he muttered again as he felt her body readying itself for him. "Ah, honey, you're so wet and hot. You feel so good. So perfect. No need to be afraid. No need, I swear it."

Verity trembled as her excitement bloomed quickly once more. She moved restlessly, opening herself further to his touch. He kissed her deeply as he slid one finger a short distance inside her damp channel. The erotic movement of his tongue echoed the motion of his stroking finger. The combination was wildly, unbearably thrilling.

Now it was Verity who was overcome with urgent desire. It swamped her as Jonas continued to caress her. The last of her fears vanished in the white hot heat of passion and she lifted herself against him in silent, feminine demand.

Jonas needed no further urging. He was hard and ready. She reached for him the way she had reached for him in the dark tunnel.

And he came to her, his lips raining fire on her breasts, his muscled hips pushing apart her soft thighs until his heavy shaft was poised against her body. He reached down to part her softness with long, sensitive fingers that trembled and then he drove himself into her, sheathing himself to the hilt with a shuddering groan.

The impact of his sensual invasion sent a convulsive tremor through Verity. There was no real pain this time, but, just as she had the first time, she felt too tight and too stretched. She felt invaded.

She was still too new at this, she decided. Either that or Jonas was simply too big for her. All the small, delicate muscles in her lower body felt strained to the limit. She cried out, half in passion and half in protest, only to have the soft sound cut off by Jonas's mouth.

"Stay with me," Jonas muttered thickly against her lips. "Don't leave me alone. Not now. Stay with me. Hold me."

Verity opened her eyes, her breath coming quickly as her body slowly began to adjust around him. Maybe he wasn't too large, after all. Maybe he was just right for her. Jonas's fingers tightened on her shoulders and she looked up to find him staring down at her with molten eyes. He started to move within her, establishing a throbbing rhythm that radiated out to every nerve ending in Verity's body.

She felt a strange tingling, clenching sensation begin deep within her as Jonas withdrew himself almost completely and then surged back into her. She could feel the whole, heavy length of him as he opened her small passage and occupied the soft, feminine territory. The sense of being pinned and invaded gave way to a spiraling sense of wanting that was new to her. She clung to him and felt herself tightening around him, seeking something she couldn't quite identify.

"That's it, honey," Jonas grated, shuddering powerfully. His urgent words poured over her, coaxing, beseeching, commanding. "That's the way. Give yourself to me. Let me have everything. God, I can feel you holding on to me like you'll never let me go. So hot, so tight. You're going to squeeze me dry. Let me get all the way inside. All the way. I don't want to think of anything else except how good you feel. . . ."

Verity's shivering, violent climax took her by surprise. She had not known what to expect, but when it washed through her she knew exactly what it was. She seized it eagerly with all her might and gave herself up to it and the man who had inspired it.

"Jonas."

"Oh, yes. Christ, yes. Yes. *Yes*." He shuddered heavily once more and then froze for an instant, eyes closed, face taut as he pumped out his own release.

And then there was only silence.

Verity came slowly back to herself, aware first of the storm that still beat against the windows and then of the weight of the man who sprawled on top of her. She lay quietly for a long moment, listening to his deep breathing while she enjoyed the lingering, relaxed contentment that pulsed within her.

So that was what it was all about. She smiled up at the ceiling and wriggled her toes. Then another jagged shaft of lightning lit the room and she saw the rapier lying on the floor. Memory returned in a rush.

The blade appeared wet in the platinum glare of the lightning, as if it had been dampened with fresh blood. The too-white light disappeared, plunging the room into merciful shadow. Verity's sense of peace and satisfaction shriveled.

"Jonas?" She touched his shoulder. "Jonas, are you awake?"

"I'm awake." He made no move to lift his head from her breast. She felt his warm breath on her nipple.

"Are you . . . are you all right?"

"I'm fine. Thanks to you." He yawned.

"Wait a minute," Verity said, her tone sharpening. "Don't you dare go to sleep on me, Jonas. I want to talk to you."

"In the morning."

She slapped his shoulder lightly, reprovingly. He groaned in response.

"No, not in the morning," Verity said firmly. "Now. What in the world happened to you tonight? What made you bring that sword in here? Did you have a nightmare?"

Jonas didn't react for so long that Verity began to fear he'd gone to sleep after all. But finally he sighed heavily and shifted himself reluctantly to lie on his back beside her. He had one arm over his eyes.

"You could call it that," he said quietly.

"Jonas . . ."

He took his arm away from his eyes and propped himself up on his elbow so that he could look down at her. His expression was remote and wary but his gaze seemed brilliant in the shadows. *Florentine gold.*

"It's a long story, Verity. Are you sure you want to hear it tonight?"

"I most certainly do want to hear it tonight," she declared firmly, pulling herself up against the pillows. "I want to know what happened. Do you have a lot of bad dreams?"

"Not if I'm careful," he drawled wryly and sat up on the edge of the bed. "And believe me, I've been very careful for the past five years." He got to his feet and paced to the window, where he stood looking out into the blackness of the storm. "You're not going to understand or believe any of this, Verity. You'll think I'm crazy. Sometimes I think I'm crazy."

"Try me."

He shook his head. "I'd rather wait awhile. I'd rather let you get to know me better so that you can trust me."

"I have to know what's going on, Jonas. For better or worse, we seem to have started something. If I'm going to sleep with you, even occasionally, I must have some answers."

His mouth crooked wryly. "So demanding. What a little despot you are, honey."

"I have a right to know more about you, Jonas," she insisted with grave dignity.

"I suppose that's true. Well, we might as well get this over with as quickly as possible. You're probably going to come unglued when you hear what I have to say."

"It takes a lot to make me come unglued," she stated with calm pride. "My father gave me a practical sort of education, remember? I've lived in a lot of places and I've seen a lot of things. I may have been a virgin when you met me, but I have definitely not led a sheltered life. Dad doesn't believe in sheltering people."

Jonas braced one hand against the steel windowsill and nodded. "Having met your father, I'm inclined to believe you. All right, here goes. Have you ever heard of something called psychometry?"

Verity was silent for a moment. This wasn't what she had expected to hear. She had thought there would be some long explanation about nightmares and the reason behind them. She had been prepared to listen to a tale of real-life terror that still haunted Jonas.

"You mean the psychic thing?" she finally asked cautiously. "That claim that some people can touch an object and sense stuff about its history?"

"Yeah." He ran a hand through his hair. "The psychic thing. I've got the ability, Verity. In spades. You accused me once of walking away from my talent, but I swear the ability I have is no talent. It's a curse."

Verity frowned, turning the concept over in her mind. She had never paid much attention to the so-called paranormal. She had always considered such things a matter of fad. Fads came and went. They might be interesting, but that was no reason to take them seriously. Jonas was the last person she would have thought would believe in psychic powers. It was disconcerting to find out that he did.

"What makes you think you have a gift for psychometry?" she asked cautiously.

"I don't think I've got it," he rasped, "I know it."

"Please, Jonas, don't snap at me. I'm trying to understand."

He muttered something and sighed. "I know. Verity, I don't have any good, easy, simple way of explaining this."

"When did you first begin to think you might have this, uh, ability with psychometry?" she probed gently.

"You don't have to treat me as if you think I suffer from delusions. I started wondering if there was something wrong with me during my junior year in college. It was no big deal at first. Just a flicker of awareness when I handled something that was very old or had a lot of violence associated with it."

"Something like an old rapier?"

He nodded grimly. "I hadn't been exposed to museums or collections of old objects much when I was growing up. In my neighborhood you worried more about the present than the past. My mother raised me by herself after Dad split. She worked as a secretary and money was always short. As a result, I grew up focusing on the present and the immediate future. The big questions in life revolved around matters such as whether the power company was going to turn off the lights if the electric bill went unpaid another month."

"I know what you mean," Verity said with sudden, unexpected empathy. "That kind of lifestyle tends to focus one's attention on the here and now, all right. Dad never worried too much about money. Not that there was ever enough of it around to worry, except when he sold *Juxtaposition*. Even that went pretty fast, as I recall. When I was growing up I was always the one who had to figure out how to put the landlady off for another month or so."

Jonas gave her a brief, wry smile. "I'm not surprised. That explains some of your current problems."

That annoyed her. "I don't have any current problems except the one I'm trying to figure out at the moment, which is what happened to you tonight."

He held up a hand. "Sorry. As I was saying, I don't know whether my gift, as you call it, was something that I always had and it just hadn't had a chance to come into full bloom because of a lack of stimulus or whether it was a naturally late-developing ability. That question was one of many the guys in white lab coats were trying to answer at Vincent College."

That interested Verity. Maybe there was more than Jonas's imagination involved here. "You were tested?"

"Over and over again. Some eccentric alumnus of Vincent, a guy named Elihu Wright, gave a huge endowment to the college and stipulated it had to be used for psychic research. The trustees were horrified but they weren't about to turn down cold, hard cash. At any rate, research flourished for a while. Where there's money, there's never a lack of researchers ready and willing to spend it, no matter how bizarre the subject matter. While it lasted, Vincent's Department of Paranormal Research was the best equipped in the nation. But then, there wasn't much competition."

"While it lasted?"

Jonas's mouth twisted sardonically. "I heard they dissolved it a couple of years ago. Wright died and the college was losing other sources of funding because too many people thought any school that was wasting money on paranormal research must be a flaky sort of institution. All in all, I guess the trustees decided to junk the project. No loss, as far as I'm concerned. Those researchers were a bunch of ghouls."

"Go on," Verity said when he stopped talking for a long moment.

"The problem with the testing I was undergoing was that it seemed to be directly influencing the development of whatever ability I had," Jonas said at last. "I got picked for the test program because I showed a few vague traces of psychometric ability. By the time I got out of the program I had a full-blown talent."

"How did you get chosen as a subject?"

"The researchers routinely tested all students and faculty, looking for subjects who showed hints of paranormal talent. I agreed to be tested because I was curious, myself. As I said, in the beginning, all I could do was pick up a faint sense of awareness when I was given something to touch that had a violent history and that dated from an era to which I'm attuned. But as the testing continued, my ability got stronger."

"You think the testing process was honing it and developing it?"

"That was the only explanation anyone could think of. It caused quite a furor in the department. I started getting nervous because I could feel something very strange was starting to happen every time I ran through a test. But no one cared about my concerns. Every researcher in sight wanted a piece of me. I was the most important thing to hit the lab since they'd bought their first bunch of white mice. As things progressed I had about as much say in the research being done on me as the mice did."

"That would have irritated me severely," Verity avowed feelingly.

"I was irritated, all right. In fact, I raised hell a few times. But I always came back for more. I couldn't resist. I started losing sleep and missing meals and classes. My social life was almost nonexistent. I admit that at that point, I was as fascinated as everyone else was. I wanted to know what was going on. More than that, I wanted to learn how to master this weird ability I had. Hell, it was part of me. I had a vested interest in finding out what it was all about."

"What do you mean, master it?"

"You have to understand, Verity. The stronger my gift or curse or whatever you want to call it got, the less control I had over it. It began to feel as if the past was just waiting out there beyond a fragile barrier."

"Waiting?"

"Waiting to pounce on me or swamp me or possess me. I sensed that all it needed was an access route, a way through the barrier."

"Do you get this reaction from just any old object?"

"No. I have a special affinity for a period that ranges from the fourteenth to the sixteenth century."

"The height of the Renaissance," Verity mused.

Jonas shrugged. "Objects from that era hold the strongest attraction for me. I suppose I was always attracted to that time period. Hell, I chose it as a major in college and then concentrated on it in grad school for some reason. There was nothing in my upbringing that predisposed me to be intrigued by that time period. But the talent, whatever it is, isn't limited to that time zone. I could sense the authenticity of those dueling pistols of your father's, for instance, and they're nearly two centuries younger. But anything out of the prime time zone feels a lot weaker and has a lot less impact on me. I can handle my reactions to objects from other historical periods. It's only stuff from the Renaissance that's really dangerous."

"Can you sense things about contemporary objects?" Verity asked, deeply curious despite her doubts.

"The eighteenth century is about my limit. I've never had any particular sensations from modern objects. Thank God."

"Why do you say that?"

"Just think of how many objects there are lying around today that I'm liable to run into that might trigger the talent. Guns, knives, cars that had been in accidents, you name it. The list is endless. The object has to have been associated with violence, but that limitation still covers a lot of territory."

"Yes, I can see that."

"The testing got more dangerous. More and more often it

seemed that every time I picked up an object that carried a load of old, violent emotion, I was carving out an access route, making it stronger and more defined. For a long while I was arrogant enough to think I could control it and whatever tried to come through it. But gradually I realized I was in danger of being completely overwhelmed. And if that happened . . ." He broke off abruptly. "One day it did happen."

Verity watched him for a moment. Whatever the reality of the situation, there was no doubt that Jonas believed everything he was telling her. Something had gone very wrong back at Vincent College; something that had shaped the past five years of his life.

"You say you were in danger of being overwhelmed. What would that mean to you?" she asked quietly. Unwillingly she remembered the corridor in her mind. "Did it feel as if something or someone was trying to suck you back into the past?"

Jonas closed his eyes and leaned his forehead against the arm he had braced on the edge of the window. "No. It wasn't like that. It was as if the forces I tapped in to in the past were trying to use me as a conduit into the present. I had the feeling that if I lost control, I would be lost, too; swamped by the emotions associated with whatever object I happened to be holding at the moment. It would be like being possessed or something. Maybe like losing my soul. Dammit, I told you this was going to be hard to explain."

"I'm listening, Jonas."

"Sure. But you're not believing any of it, are you? Thinking of having me fitted for a straitjacket?"

"At the moment, I'm reserving judgment. One of the many things I learned at my father's knee was not to jump to intellectual conclusions about things I don't understand. Tell me how you responded when you realized you might be losing control over your psychometric ability."

He lifted his head and stared at her, his gaze hard and

steady. "I started testing myself, touching objects that had the most powerful attraction for me, pushing myself and whatever was trying to get through me into the present. I fought back whenever I felt in danger of being over-whelmed. I made some progress, but that progress turned out to be a two-edged sword. I got to the point where I could control the talent when dealing with things that weren't too saturated with violence. But if I picked up something soaked in old blood or hate or anger, the emotions generated around the object seemed stronger than ever. I finally realized that I might be able to fight back but the cost was high. Sooner or later the battle would cost me my life or, worse, my sanity. Then one day I nearly killed a lab technician."

"Oh, my God, Jonas." Verity's fingers tightened around the sheet. "You almost killed someone during a test?"

He nodded, saying nothing.

"Tell me about it," she pressed.

He exhaled slowly. "I had started doing work for some museums and private collectors. Word had spread from Vincent that I had the touch, as everyone called it. What's more, there was a rapidly accumulating pile of laboratory proof to back up the claim that I could verify the authenticity of a variety of old objects. People who worried about that kind of thing started checking with me for a second opinion when they had doubts about an item in their collection or about something they were considering for purchase. Then one day someone set up an experiment with a fifteenth century Italian sword. The researchers had a theory."

"What kind of theory?"

"One of them thought that if the present was made to resemble a scene from the past—a context that suited the sword in this case—the connection between me and the past might be more direct. With a little help from the drama department, some whiz fixed up a setting that resembled a street in a Renaissance town. It wasn't hard to do. They just used some stuff borrowed from a production of *Romeo and Juliet*."

"What happened?"

"I stepped onto the set, picked up the sword, and before I could take another breath I was swamped with the emotions of someone else."

"Who?"

"All I know was that he lived in Florence during the time of Lorenzo de' Medici and his name was Giovanni. I only got a glimpse of him. Sometimes there are . . . pictures, *images* in the corridor. He was in a street fight. Not an uncommon occurrence in those days. He was in the act of killing a man. I could feel all the emotions he must have been generating a few hundred years ago when he fought for his life with the sword I was holding."

"You could sense all this?" Verity questioned.

"I was literally awash with everything he had felt in those minutes when he thought he was probably going to die. All the fury and the desperation and the adrenaline poured through me as if I were the one caught in the fight. I was holding the sword he had held. I looked around the set and saw a dark, rainy street in Florence. In my mind the lab techs around me were converted into a bunch of would-be assassins and they were closing in on me. I reacted instinctively when one of them came at me with a hypodermic needle. I saw it as poison about to be delivered on the tip of a sword."

"You went for one of the lab techs thinking he was a fifteenth-century assassin," Verity concluded softly. She was awed by the realization that Jonas believed every word he was saying. Whatever had happened in that lab at Vincent College, one thing was certain: Jonas really had tried to kill someone. "Good lord, Jonas. Did you hurt him?"

"I almost gutted him. You could do that with a broadsword, you know. It's not like a rapier, where all the attack is done with the point. Fifteenth-century swords made bigger messes than sixteenth-century rapiers."

"Jonas, stop it. Did you kill him?"

Jonas hesitated. "No."

"He got out of the way in time?"

"No. He got hurt. Badly hurt. But before I could finish him off someone got close enough to jab me with another needle. I turned on him and nearly got him before the drug took effect. When I came to, I was tied to a hospital bed and everyone was looking at me with a kind of excited horror. I'll never forget those expressions. I was completely out of it for nearly two days, they told me later. They don't know how far out of it I really was. Only I knew I had nearly lost my mind in the struggle to control whatever had reached from Giovanni to me. I had the feeling that if I'd actually killed that lab tech, whatever was invading me would have taken over completely. When I recovered I knew I couldn't take any more chances. I also knew those damn scientists couldn't wait to get me back into the lab."

"So you walked away from everything connected with the experience at Vincent."

"I didn't just walk, Verity. I ran. For my life. For five long years."

"What do I have to do with all this, Jonas?" It took courage to ask the question. She realized she was frightened of his answer.

He looked at her, his face harsh. "Don't you understand? You're the reason I've stopped running."

"Me?" She stared at him in confusion.

"I knew the night I found your earring in that alley down in Mexico that you were some kind of key for me. You were connected to me somehow. There was a possibility that you were the only means to control things in that corridor that I was ever likely to get in this lifetime. Until I met you, I wasn't even sure there was such a thing as controlling what happened inside. But with you, I think I can start exploring that corridor again."

Verity sat perfectly still, mesmerized by the intensity of his expression. "Jonas, what are you saying?"

"That with you I have a chance of dealing with this curse that's been laid on me. You're the lifeline that I can hang on to when the past tries to rip through me into the present. With you I think I can control my psychometric ability."

Chapter
Ten

*V*erity was subdued and thoughtful the next morning as she descended the steel staircase to meet her hostess for breakfast. She was also feeling washed out and tense, an unsettling combination. The events of the night had kept her awake until nearly four in the morning and it was only seven now.

Jonas had not spent the remainder of the night in her room. He certainly would have done so, given the slightest encouragement, but Verity had not encouraged him. She needed time to think. His lovemaking seemed to have that effect on her, she acknowledged wryly.

It was beginning to look as if every time she made love with Jonas, she needed time and space afterward in which to recover. Why couldn't the man have been a normal, sex-crazed male looking for an easy, no-strings-attached affair? Things would have been much simpler in that event. She'd had some practice keeping such men at bay.

Jonas had left the rapier behind in her bedroom, though. He had told her bluntly that if he picked it up he would be in the same situation as he had been in last night when he charged through her door.

"I'm sure you don't want that," he had said dryly, taking his dismissal with bad grace.

"No," Verity had agreed with alacrity, "I don't want that. We'll put it back where it belongs tomorrow."

"You can hang it back up on the wall," he had told her without much interest, "or throw it over a cliff. Hell, I don't care what you do with it. I won't be spending another night here, so it doesn't matter where the rapier winds up."

He had stood for a moment in the doorway of her bedroom as she prepared to close it in his face. His gaze was brooding and watchful as he looked down at her.

"I see a pattern developing here. I'm not sure I like it. Are you always going to kick me out after I've made love to you?"

"Are you always going to spring a surprise on me after we've gone to bed together?" she had countered aggressively. "Last time it was that earring in your pocket. This time you liven things up by admitting you're only interested in me because you think I'm some kind of anchor for whatever it is that happens to you when you pick up old swords."

"Don't put words in my mouth, Verity." He reached for her, his hands closing around her shoulders. "I wanted you the first time I saw you standing in that cantina doorway. The light was in your hair and you had on one of those breezy little Mexican dresses and you looked sweet and sexy as hell. I followed you initially because I wondered what a fire-haired little gringa with jeweled eyes was doing going from cantina to cantina. I figured if you were just looking for some fun on the wild side of Mexico, you might as well have it with me. Considering what Pedro had in mind for you, you're damn lucky I was attracted enough to follow you that night."

"Maybe any woman who attracts you physically can act as the key you say you need," Verity said seriously. She wondered if he was telling the truth about his initial attraction. It wasn't much consolation, but it was better than nothing, she supposed.

He shook his head impatiently at her suggestion. "That's not so. I just wish it were that easy. If it were true, I would have found out by now. Verity, listen to me. I know this has all come as a shock. We need to talk some more. I need to explain some things to you."

She softened then, touching his hard jaw with her fingertips. "Jonas," she said earnestly, "I believe you when you say you've got a problem. I'm not sure I believe in your psychometric ability, but I know you believe it and I accept that. But for some reason you've fixated on me as a solution to your problem. I'm not sure what that means, but it might be dangerous for both of us. Perhaps you should seek professional help."

"Christ, don't tell me to get counseling. I don't need therapy! I gave that a whirl back at Vincent when I first began to think I might go crazy. It was useless. I'm not suffering from delusions or psychoses. I'm suffering from an excess of reality, past and present. You haven't understood a word I've said tonight, have you?" He dropped his hands and gave her a small push back into her room. "Go ahead and go back to your lonely bed. I hope you enjoy your solitude. But I'm willing to bet it won't be nearly as satisfying as the way I made you feel a while ago when you were shivering in my arms."

"Getting a little egotistical, aren't we?"

"You've had a taste of the real thing now, lady, and you're going to want more. You are one hot little number. You've been locked away in ice all these years but I've melted that ice. The next time you want to feel as good as you did when I was inside you, just remember I'm the man who can make it happen. You need me for that, if nothing else. Sweet dreams, your majesty."

He had turned and stalked off down the corridor, leaving Verity more confused and wary than she had ever been before in her life.

No one really believed in psychometry.

And no one except the most sheltered and naïve of innocents believed in finding true love with a man who was wrong for her on every count.

On her way downstairs Verity reminded herself forcefully that she never had been sheltered, nor was she naïve. She had no excuses for the daydreams she hadn't even begun to acknowledge until recently. Whatever she had with Jonas amounted to nothing more than an affair that probably wouldn't last through the winter.

The odds were that Jonas would grow restless and hit the road long before spring. Or she would lose her temper with him one time too many and wind up kicking him out for good. Either way, once he was gone she would never see him again.

A sobering thought. The man might be difficult, crazy, and haunted by ghosts, but he was her first lover. It was depressing to think she had waited all these years for a wacko to sweep her off her feet and into bed. That probably said something about her own flawed judgment, Verity decided gloomily.

At least now she knew the source of the ghosts in his eyes.

As she entered the gray-on-gray dining room she found Caitlin waiting for her at the far end of the granite table. Verity decided she did not care for the table. With its unrelenting near-black surface and its wide, heavy base, the thing reminded her entirely too much of someone's idea of a witch's altar.

Caitlin was pouring coffee from a silver pot when Verity walked into the room. She turned her scarred face to looked at her guest, her eyes searching for answers to questions that remained unasked.

"Good morning, Verity. I hope you slept well. Did the storm disturb you? We get some violent ones this time of year."

"Storms don't bother me." That much was true. "That coffee looks good."

"Help yourself. Tavi is busy in the kitchen. I take it Jonas is not up and about yet?"

Verity concentrated on pouring her coffee. "I didn't stop by his room to see if he was in motion."

"I see." There was silence for a moment and then Caitlin said quietly, "It was kind of you to come for a visit, Verity. I want you to know how much I appreciate your company. I feel that in a short time we have become rather close. Is that presumptuous of me?"

Verity's head came up sharply at the diffident tone in Caitlin's voice. "Not in the least. I feel exactly the same way. I've enjoyed the visit thoroughly and I hope you'll be able to come back to Sequence Springs soon. I don't have a second bedroom, but Laura can always make room at the spa."

"That would be nice." Caitlin started to say something else but broke off, her eyes going to the doorway behind Verity. "There you are, Jonas. I was wondering if you would want to sleep in."

Verity turned to glance at Jonas, who strolled into the room with his usual negligent grace. He always looked so calm and at ease on the mornings after. It wasn't fair. He took the seat beside Verity and reached for the coffeepot. She thought she saw some evidence of exhaustion around his eyes but she couldn't be certain. Probably wishful thinking on her part.

"Good morning, Verity," he said politely.

"Good morning, Jonas."

They might have been the most casual and polite of acquaintances, Verity thought in annoyance.

"I was just about to tell Verity about some plans I've made regarding the sale of *Bloodlust*," Caitlin said smoothly as Tavi walked into the room carrying a platter of eggs and fruit.

"Is that right?" Jonas did not appear overly interested. He was concentrating on his coffee, treating it as if it were an expensive drug.

Verity tried to cover up Jonas's lack of social grace. "What plans, Caitlin?"

"I believe I mentioned that I will be conducting a bidding session for the painting."

Verity nodded. "I remember. You said you were going to handle the auction yourself."

"That's right. This is a very special sale for me, you see. *Bloodlust* is the last painting I plan to do."

"The last one?" Verity was shocked. "Caitlin, you can't stop painting. It's your life. You have a great talent and you're in your prime. Why on earth would you want to stop?"

Caitlin smiled fleetingly but her eyes were on Jonas. He was watching her speculatively. "I have my reasons."

"Like instantly driving up the prices of all your works by making it clear there will be no more?" Jonas asked sardonically. "Not a bad move, Caitlin. It would cause a flurry of interest in the art world."

"Jonas, for heaven's sake," Verity hissed.

Caitlin waved a dismissing hand. "He's right. Financially, it will be an interesting move. I still have several unsold paintings left. Their value will probably triple when word gets out that *Bloodlust* is my final work."

"And *Bloodlust* itself should go for a fortune." Jonas dug into the eggs Tavi had put in front of him.

"I fully intend to get as much as I possibly can for it," Caitlin agreed calmly. "I also plan to make my auction a major event. I have always kept my distance from the art world but I would like to leave it with a bang. There has always been a certain amount of curiosity about me among art patrons. I have never allowed myself to be photographed, never mingled socially. Call it a whim, but I want to exit with an event that will not only satisfy that curiosity but will be remembered for a time."

Verity looked down as Tavi placed a plate in front of her. She noticed that the woman's fingers were trembling. As she looked up, she caught a tight, pinched, almost desperate look on Tavi's face. Then it was gone. Tavi moved on toward Caitlin's end of the table.

"What are you planning to do to make your auction special?" Verity asked uneasily.

Caitlin took another sip of coffee. "I have been giving the matter much thought. Jonas, you're the one who gave me the final inspiration. In three weeks I'm going to hold a Renaissance costume ball here in my home. I'm going to recreate a sixteenth century court setting as closely as possible. We will eat, drink, and converse as any wealthy gathering would have done back at the height of the Renaissance. The ball will be held on Sunday evening. On Monday I will conduct the auction. What do you think?"

"I think," Jonas said, "that it sounds like a hell of a lot of work."

"Oh, it will be, but Tavi and I have little else to do. The preparations should be amusing. We have already started the research."

"It sounds magnificent," Verity said thoughtfully. "But it'll cost a lot of money to organize something like that." She didn't say aloud that the idea was far less appealing today than it might have been yesterday. After last night, Verity was not feeling a great deal of interest in the Renaissance. But then, it wasn't her party.

"Money is not a problem," Caitlin said easily. "I have the freedom to indulge myself. And I'm glad you like my whimsical little notion, because I would very much like for you and Jonas to attend."

"No, thanks," Jonas said mildly. "Sounds too rich for my blood. And Verity has to run the No Bull Cafe on Sunday evenings."

"In three weeks we'll start closing on Sundays," Verity pointed out, annoyed at the way he had answered for her.

"I believe Laura Griswald mentioned your winter routine," Caitlin murmured.

Verity sighed. "It sounds fantastic, but I'm afraid Jonas is right. You'll be entertaining people who are accustomed to moving in the social stratosphere. I'd feel out of it, Caitlin. You can understand that. Besides, what you're planning is going to be basically a business affair. You don't need me. I'll come for a visit afterward."

Caitlin leaned forward, her cool fingers touching Verity's hand. Her eyes were deep and filled with urgency. "Please, Verity. I want you to come. It's important to me. I have no other close friends to invite except Tavi and yourself. The others who will be coming will all be strangers who will be indulging me out of a morbid curiosity. I would like to have you there as my friend. I'll pay for the rental of your costumes and I'll cover all your other expenses."

"Caitlin, that's not necessary," Verity interrupted quickly, flicking a glance at Jonas. She could see the disapproval in him and she felt momentarily trapped between two opposing forces. For an instant she had the unsettling sensation that she was merely a pawn being tossed back and forth between these two. But that was ridiculous.

"Humor me, Verity. I'm going to need you when I sell *Bloodlust*."

A dish clattered loudly as Tavi moved away from the table. Jonas said nothing but Verity could feel his aggressive anger. She knew he wanted nothing to do with Caitlin's Renaissance ball or the aftermath.

Well, he didn't have to attend, Verity rationalized as she gave in to the appeal she saw in Caitlin's face. She knew then that, for whatever reason, Caitlin needed her.

"All right," Verity said finally. "If you really want me there, I'll be there."

Caitlin closed her eyes and nodded in relieved satisfaction. "Thank you." She turned to Jonas. "What about you, Jonas? Will you escort your employer?"

Verity hastened to get Jonas off the hook. "I don't think this is going to be Jonas's idea of a fun time," she said lightly. "I'm sure he'd rather go fishing with my father."

"It's definitely not my idea of a fun time," Jonas agreed

harshly. "But if Verity insists on attending, I'll come with her."

Caitlin looked satisfied. More than satisfied, Verity decided with sudden perception. She looked almost triumphant.

Two hours later Verity was still trying to work through her astonishment over Jonas's willingness to accompany her to Caitlin's party. She got into the passenger seat of her compact while he tossed their bags onto the backseat and slid behind the wheel. She waved at Caitlin and Tavi, framed in the open doorway of the steel-gray house. Tavi did not wave or smile back. Caitlin lifted one hand in farewell and turned to go inside.

"All right, Jonas, let's have it. Why are you going to come with me to Caitlin's party?"

"For the same reason I came with you on this stupid little jaunt. I don't want you driving over here alone. I don't trust that woman. She wants something from you, Verity."

"Friendship."

Jonas shook his head with great certainty. "Caitlin Evanger doesn't need anyone's friendship."

"We all need friends, Jonas," Verity said gently. "Just because she gives the impression of great self-sufficiency, that doesn't mean Caitlin's an exception."

"She's got good old Tavi."

Verity frowned, thinking about that. "You know, now that you mention it, I don't quite understand that relationship. I know Tavi is a paid companion, but I get the feeling she's very attached to Caitlin. Did you notice how nervous she was this morning when she served breakfast? She was very tense."

"Maybe she had a bad night." Jonas was not concerned about Tavi. "Forget those two, Verity. I want to talk about us."

"What about us?" she asked warily.

"Now that you've had a few hours to think about what I

told you last night, do you still think I'm crazy?" he asked
bluntly.

"I never said you were crazy," she muttered defensively.

"You might not have said it, but don't try telling me the
thought hasn't crossed your mind. Dammit, Verity, tell me
the truth. Are you afraid of me?"

The question took her by surprise. She thought about it.
"No, I'm not afraid of you," she finally said honestly. "I just
don't understand what's going on."

He shot her a searching glance. "I'll take what I can get
for the moment. It's enough that you don't think I'm going
to turn into a werewolf some night when the moon is full. In
the meantime, will you help me?"

Her head came around in surprise. "Help you do what?"

"I want to conduct some tests," he said tersely. "I want to
see how far my control extends now that I've got you to hold
on to. We can use those dueling pistols of your dad's to start.
I only touched one long enough the other night to get a sense
of its authenticity. As soon as I felt the emotions attached to
it, I dropped it. But not before I felt you in that corridor with
me. You were in that corridor again last night, honey. I saw
you. You touched me."

Verity gave a start. Shock widened her eyes. "What corridor?" Her breathless demand gave her away.

Jonas smiled briefly and ferociously. "I wondered if it
would translate into your mind with the same imagery. Apparently it does. Interesting."

"Jonas, please . . ." The plea drifted to a halt. Verity didn't
know what to ask for. She swallowed, her mouth going dry.
Until now she had been certain the corridor was merely a
quirk of her imagination.

"I'm talking about a long, maybe an endless tunnel. A
corridor that seems to stretch forward and backward into
infinity. If there is such a thing as infinity," he added
thoughtfully. "Personally, I'm not so sure there is. At least
not on the continuum that links time and space. Maybe there
are other continuums that are truly infinite. Or maybe each

universe is finite but the potential for the creation of universes is infinite. Or maybe time isn't on a continuum at all. Maybe it's more like a foggy sea surrounding us. Or there could be millions of time continuums all existing simultaneously. . . ."

"Jonas, you're losing me rapidly," Verity said with a quiet desperation.

"No, I'm not. You told me yourself you had an excellent education. You just don't want to hear what I'm going to say. But you're going to listen, Verity." The ancient gold of his eyes burned for an instant. "There's not much else you can do. After all, like it or not, you're trapped in this car with a crazy man who just happens to be your lover."

Verity flinched. His sardonic remark was far too close to what she had been thinking earlier that morning as she descended the steel staircase. If Jonas was getting to know her well enough to second-guess her thoughts, she was in real trouble. "I never said you were crazy and two nights of sex does not automatically make you my lover. At this point you don't qualify as anything more than an occasional bed partner."

"Your *only* occasional bed partner." His long fingers tightened on the wheel. "Tell me something, Verity. Are you using me?"

"Using you! What a thing to say! If anyone's using someone in this relationship of ours, it's you."

"I'm not so sure about that. I've been wondering why, after twenty-eight years of sleeping alone, you suddenly decided to let me into your bed."

"I didn't exactly let you into bed," she pointed out carefully. "You sort of muscled your way in."

"Bullshit. You let me in. You wanted me there. Don't you dare imply there was any rape involved, Verity Ames, or so help me, I'll turn you over my knee."

"Threats now, Jonas?" she asked in taunting, liquid tones.

"You bet your sweet little ass. Now answer my question.

Are you using me? I have a right to know just what the basis of this relationship is."

His arrogance was breathtaking. "Don't be absurd. How would I be using you?"

"As an experiment," he said succinctly.

"An experiment!"

"Sure. I've been the subject of enough experiments in my life to know a setup when I see one. It makes a nasty kind of sense. After all, you're looking at thirty on the horizon and there's no relationship in sight. Hell, there's not even a man in sight for a weekend fling. You were a little too picky for a little too long, I guess. Either that or you flayed every man in sight with that sharp tongue. Whatever the reason, you find yourself alone facing spinsterhood. You're a naturally passionate woman who's denied herself an outlet for her sensual needs for too long. You begin to wonder if you'll ever experience sex or have a genuine affair. It's only natural that you might be getting desperate as you see an important aspect of life passing you by."

Verity was incensed. Her hands closed into small fists. "I am not desperate. I may be picky but I am not desperate."

"What woman wouldn't be desperate in your situation?"

"You egotistical, chauvinistic bastard!"

"I'm just trying to get at the truth. I want to know if you decided to experiment with me. I want to know if you're using me to get a taste of what you've been missing all these years. After all, I'm convenient, there's an attraction between us, and I'm willing. What's more, the relationship probably feels safe to you because you think that ultimately you're in control of it. Hell, I work for you. How much more in control could you get? You can always fire me if I start boring you in bed.

> *"My lady thinks she will command the dance*
> *She calls the tune and dictates every measure.*
> *I tread the steps, ensnared with every beat,*
> *While she sips the rich dark wine of pleasure."*

Verity wrinkled her nose. "Another rough translation of some Renaissance poem?"

"Yeah. Some courtier's humble ode to his beloved who kept him dancing on the end of her string. Translating poetry is not my forte, but you get the point. I'm like the poor courtier who ended up dancing to his beloved's tune."

"Somehow, I don't see you playing the humble courtier, Jonas. If you do occasionally, it's for your own purposes. If we're going to use Renaissance imagery, I would have to say you're more of a *condottiere* who's busy with his own schemes and plans while he pretends to be working for a client."

Jonas's mouth tightened. "You haven't answered my question."

"About whether I'm using you? Experimenting on you? Never mind. It will give you something to think about while I'm wondering why I'm allowing a crazy man to continue washing dishes for me."

There was a frozen silence from the other side of the car and then Jonas asked in a too-neutral voice, "Do you really think I'm off my rocker?"

Verity caught her lower lip between her teeth and gnawed painfully for a moment. "No," she said finally, thinking of what she had seen in his golden eyes.

She had seen humor in that gaze as well as intelligence, passion, and anger. She had never seen anything that made her wonder if he was mentally unstable. She had never sensed anything in him that made her think he was dangerously out of control.

"Thanks for that much, at any rate."

"Tell me about this . . . this corridor," she ordered tightly.

His expression gentled as he looked at her. Jonas took one hand off the wheel long enough to squeeze her clenched fingers. His touch was warm and comforting. "Don't be afraid, honey. Whenever you're in the corridor, I'll be there with you. What can scare the living hell out of someone is finding himself alone there, not knowing what's ahead or behind."

Verity looked at him with wide, uncertain eyes. "You see yourself in a corridor whenever you go into one of your trances or whatever you call the condition you were in last night?"

Jonas nodded once. "A long, dark tunnel, like a tube that connects the past and the present. I didn't know if, when you joined me there, you would see the same thing, but apparently you do. That should help, Verity. It gives us a point of reference. The experience is similar enough for both of us that we should be able to share certain aspects of it."

Verity searched frantically for some logical explanation. "Maybe you're telepathic or something. Maybe that corridor is a construction you've invented in your own mind and you can somehow make me see it, too. Maybe this has nothing to do with psychometry."

"You're telling me it would be easier for you to accept telepathy than psychometry?"

"Well, there are a lot of instances of people believing they've seen or heard things that they couldn't have sensed in any normal way." Verity picked her way painfully through the words. "I don't know, Jonas. As dumb as it sounds, I think it's easier to believe in some form of telepathy than in psychometry. When you talk about psychometry, you're talking about the forces of the past. To be honest, that gives me the creeps."

He smiled wryly. "Compared to that, telepathy looks normal, right?"

"More acceptable, maybe," she admitted. "Were you ever tested for that while you were at Vincent College?"

"Yeah. Sorry to disappoint you. I showed absolutely no trace of telepathic ability, not even after the psychometry started getting so strong."

Verity sat in silence, trying to come to terms with a host of strange concepts. "You really believe everything you're telling me, don't you?"

"It's almost killed me, Verity, or worse. And it almost made me kill another man. Yeah, I believe it. I've been forced to accept the reality of it."

"And now that you've got me to hold on to, you want to test yourself and see if the talent is more controllable, is that it?"

"Yes. I wasn't going to rush you. To be honest, I didn't know how to go about explaining the whole thing. But last night you were exposed to everything, so there's no point pretending any longer."

Verity sighed. "By all means, Jonas, let's stop the pretense."

He flexed his fingers on the wheel and glanced over at her. His lashes hooded his narrowed eyes. "You'll help me run some tests?"

She must be the crazy one in the car, Verity decided. "All right. I know I'll probably live to regret this, but good help is hard to get. I don't want to have to advertise for another dishwasher. I'll let you run some experiments with me, if that's what you want."

"Gracious as ever, little tyrant."

But when she looked over at him, she saw that he was grinning.

Tavi poured more coffee for her employer and carried it to where Caitlin sat staring out the window. "Do you really think you can control his actions the night of the ball?" she asked.

"You saw the way the rapier affected him last night."

"What we saw was a man who almost collapsed. When he did manage to pull himself together he went charging out of the room as if he intended to murder someone. I think he was close to being out of control, Caitlin. You said he was not a danger as long as the current context did not resemble the past associated with that rapier."

"His reaction was a little stronger than I expected," Caitlin admitted. "But he eventually did control himself."

"You're lucky he didn't put that blade into Verity's throat. Or yours, for that matter. He looked crazed when he picked it up." Tavi stood beside Caitlin and stared stonily out to sea.

Caitlin shook her head. "It doesn't work that way. Believe me, I know what I'm talking about. I studied all the research reports. Every last one of them. I know more about Quarrel than he knows about himself."

"You're sure that you can get him to kill Kincaid for you?"

"Very sure. He's been tuned to that particular rapier now, you see. The next time he touches it, he'll fall far more quickly under its spell. That's the way it works. Once the connection has been established between him and a certain event or emotion from the past, especially the Renaissance era, it gets easier and easier to reconnect. On the night of the ball I will see to it that the present will strongly resemble the past."

"He'll use the same rapier on Kincaid that was used on you," Tavi concluded with deep, knowing compassion.

"Yes." Caitlin's face was a frozen mask. The scar was white against the cream of her skin.

"Your plan hinges on Kincaid trying to seduce Verity. What makes you so certain Kincaid will find Verity sexually interesting?"

Caitlin looked at her companion in surprise. "After all these years of studying him, I know Kincaid's habits very well. He'll be bored and looking for sexual entertainment on the night of the ball. I have made it clear that his invitation is for one, only. He won't be bringing any female companion with him. Verity will appeal to him. She's just the type to bring out the evil in his nature. In addition, I'm counting on this house, looking exactly as it did that night all those years ago, to inspire some memories in the man."

"The kind of memories that will incite his lust?"

"Inciting lust in Kincaid is never difficult. It's his nature to always be on the lookout for victims. I will see to it that

Verity will look like a victim. Dressed in a Renaissance gown with her hair pulled into one of the classic styles, I think she will be quite striking. In addition, there is a rather charming aura of innocence about her, don't you think? That should be the frosting on the cake as far as Kincaid is concerned. He won't be able to resist the opportunity of despoiling something that is cleaner and more innocent than himself."

"Verity is no innocent. She's sleeping with Quarrel," Tavi pointed out quickly.

Caitlin smiled. "Innocence is not just a matter of virginity, Tavi. You should know that. It's a thing of the spirit. Verity's spirit is still bright and clean. It shows in her eyes and in her smile. I'm sure that's why Quarrel hangs around her. To a man with a spirit as haunted as his must be, she would be a compelling creature. In a different way, Kincaid will find her equally fascinating."

"I don't like it, Caitlin. I don't like any of it. This plan you've constructed is too complex, too dangerous. It's not too late to cancel everything. We can put all the vengeance behind us and get on with our lives." Tavi spoke with the desperation of a woman making one last stand against a terrible future. "Please think this through one more time, I beg you."

"I have thought of little else since the night Kincaid raped me, Tavi. Believe me, I have done all the thinking necessary. The way I have chosen will bring me justice and satisfaction and maybe peace. It is the only way that will. When this is over, everyone will call it a great tragedy. They'll say Quarrel was mentally unstable, that he must have gone crazy. No one will connect the killing with me. Only you and I and Kincaid will know that justice has finally been done."

"In killing Kincaid, I fear you will kill yourself, Caitlin," Tavi said. "It's not worth it."

"You're wrong," Caitlin said calmly. "It will be worth it."

Chapter
Eleven

*D*amon Marcus Kincaid picked up the exquisitely crafted stiletto and caressed it with a lover's hands. Kincaid's assistant, a man of carefully cultivated colorlessness, watched respectfully.

Although he was silent, Hatch was secretly awed by the breathtaking resemblance between his boss and the small dagger. Kincaid, Hatch knew, would treat the stiletto with infinitely more care and consideration than he would ever offer another human being. Hatch suspected at times that his employer wasn't all that fond of his fellow human beings. Those strong, tapering fingers moving over the dagger should have belonged to an artist, someone who had the soul of a creator. The only thing Kincaid created was more money and power. Kincaid would have made a terrific Borgia.

Hatch knew better than to inquire too deeply into the recent history of the stiletto. It was rumored that Kincaid had connections into a shadowy world whose members frequently went far beyond the limits of normal business practices. There was some clout to be had from working for a man who wielded such power, but it was safer not to look into the shadows around him.

Hatch was getting quietly concerned about those shadows, however. Kincaid paid well, but money wasn't everything. There were other potential employers in San Francisco. He had already started looking. Quietly, of course.

"Lovely, isn't it?" Kincaid said, admiring the object as if it were a woman he was thinking of bedding. "Early sixteen hundreds. Beautifully crafted. Did you know that in one form of Italian swordplay the stiletto was used in conjunction with a rapier? The stiletto was for parrying and the rapier for thrusting, you see."

"It sounds like it would have been a difficult skill to acquire," Hatch volunteered neutrally.

"It was. The dual style required a great deal of training. But then, the men of the time had ample motivation. Just going to church was a dangerous business. Assassination was a national pastime in Italy during the Renaissance. Rather like kidnapping today, I imagine."

"I see." Hatch winced at his own banal words. But he could hardly say that he thought his employer looked a little too enthusiastic about such murderous pastimes.

Every so often Hatch caught a glimpse of something in Kincaid's eyes that made him very uneasy. It was nothing he could define, but Hatch knew instinctively that whatever it was, it went beyond the acceptable levels of the kind of cutthroat enthusiasm associated with the American way of business. If he'd been forced to put a name to what it was he sometimes sensed in Kincaid, Hatch would have labeled it lust. But it was a lust Hatch did not understand. The secret lust that Kincaid harbored was neither gay nor straight in orientation. Hatch suspected it wasn't sexual at all but something far less wholesome.

"The stiletto is interesting. Italian, you said?" Hatch asked politely.

Kincaid's head came up and Hatch found himself staring into those soulless, unreadable eyes. It was always an unnerving experience, even for Hatch, who, having worked for

Kincaid for two years, knew he should be accustomed to the jolt.

Damon Kincaid was nearing forty but his body was in excellent shape; lithe, thin, and strong. It was the kind of body that could have belonged to either a professional dancer or an expert fencer.

Anyone who assumed that Kincaid was a dancer was either dumb as a brick or blind. Kincaid preferred physical activities that had a lethal edge to them. Fencing, not dancing, was one of his passions. A stuffed dummy used for practice was suspended in the corner of the office. It looked like a dead man swinging from the end of a rope.

Even without the strong, lithe build, Kincaid would have been a striking man. He was tall, with features that would have suited some Renaissance sculptor's idea of a natural nobleman: strong-boned and austere yet refined. His eyes were the only unsettling elements in the physical landscape of his face. They were an indeterminate shade between blue and gray and frequently appeared silver.

What made the eyes unsettling was that they rarely reflected any emotion except that occasional hint of unnatural lust that Hatch had glimpsed once in a while. Kincaid's gaze was strangely superficial; completely unreadable and never illuminating. Hatch had learned to use other cues in his employer's personality to help predict and interpret Kincaid's responses. It wasn't an easy task and Hatch had been wrong more than once. Right now he groaned inwardly, wondering if he hadn't appeared sufficiently impressed by the four-hundred-year-old stiletto.

"Yes, it's Italian," Kincaid said, but he did not berate his assistant for failing to perceive the true beauty of the object. Instead he put the old weapon down on a marble table and walked across the office to take the high-backed leather chair behind the inlaid mahogany desk. The desk had no file drawers. That single fact instantly told a visitor just how powerful Damon Kincaid was. He ran his corporate empire with an aristocrat's disdain for the niceties of modern business.

The office was empty of furniture, except for Kincaid's elegant desk and thronelike chair. Anyone who was shown into the room was forced to stand while he conducted his business. It ensured that Kincaid retained the psychological edge. As the only one who could sit down, he was clearly the most important man present at all times. Hatch was forced to admire his boss's intuitive understanding of human nature.

Kincaid, himself, was unreadable but he had an uncanny ability to assess others and figure out how to use them. It was a talent that served him well in business.

The floor of the office was polished marble. There was no rug to soften the impact of the cold, hard, brilliant finish of the stone. On the walls hung a variety of swords, rapiers, and daggers dating from the fourteenth to the nineteenth century. Walking through Kincaid's door was rather like walking into an ancient armory.

The only object hanging in the office that was not overtly lethal in nature was a Caitlin Evanger painting. Hatch disliked Evanger's work, even though he freely admitted he was fascinated by it. A lot of people were. Kincaid was an avid collector, however, and seemed to be entranced by the disturbing style and ferocious images that characterized Evanger's work.

Hatch resisted the urge to shift restlessly while he waited for Kincaid to make his wishes clear. He stood, placid and politely expectant, as Kincaid swiveled around in the chair to examine the view of San Francisco far below.

"You have this week's report on Evanger?" Kincaid asked, his eyes narrowed as he studied the Bay.

"Yes, sir. The investigative agency has maintained the round-the-clock surveillance you ordered when you first heard the rumors about Evanger getting ready to sell her final painting." He glanced at some papers in his hand, although he already knew the information cold. He never showed up unprepared in Kincaid's office. "According to their report, Evanger and her companion returned from the health spa before the weekend. The only other incident of any significance is the fact that they entertained on Monday evening. Their guests arrived that afternoon and left the next morning."

"Evanger had guests?" Kincaid's voice was as close to sharp as it ever got. "That is, indeed, significant. The original background report I commissioned from that agency mentioned the fact that she seldom, if ever, entertained. It confirmed she was very reclusive. She's never even granted an interview."

"I remember." Hatch glanced at his notes. "Her guests were two people she met while she was at the health spa, a local restaurant owner named Verity Ames and her employee, Jonas Quarrel. The report speculates that Quarrel and Ames may be sleeping together. That part is unconfirmed. It sounds fairly unimportant, Mr. Kincaid. Ames is just barely making a living and Quarrel is nothing more than a dishwasher/waiter. Not the sort of people who would be investing in expensive art. I don't think you have to worry about them."

"You never know, Hatch. Artists are, by nature, unpredictable and eccentric. Given the little information the agency could dig up on Evanger, we have to assume she's more unpredictable and eccentric than most artists. Evanger might have taken it into her head to let these two see the painting. It's not inconceivable that they are interested in *Bloodlust*. Maybe one of them has a rich daddy who could loan the money to buy it."

Hatch decided it was time to pull his small rabbit out of the hat. "The report goes on to say that Evanger placed a phone call to her agent this morning to announce just how she will go about selling *Bloodlust*."

Kincaid didn't move but there was no doubt that Hatch had his full attention. "At an auction?"

"A private auction, according to the agency. She's going to conduct the bidding herself in her own home."

"When? Who's invited?" The questions were rapped out like gunshots.

"That part was a little unclear." Hatch frowned over the report. "Apparently she's going to have a party. A send-off for herself as she prepares to leave her career behind, I suppose. A number of people involved in the art world will be there, but only a handful of people will be asked to return after the party to bid on *Bloodlust*."

"I must be on that guest list, Hatch. More important, I must be on that list of bidders. See to it. I want that painting."

Hatch nodded, foreseeing no difficulty. Any artist, regardless of how eccentric, would be delighted to know that Damon Marcus Kincaid was interested in bidding on a painting. If Kincaid was interested, the price was practically guaranteed to go very high. When Kincaid wanted something, he got it, regardless of what he had to pay for it. If this Evanger woman had any brains she would jump at the chance of having Kincaid among the bidders. After that, her only problem would be to make sure there were enough other wealthy, determined would-be buyers present to ensure a lively auction.

"I'll contact Evanger's San Francisco gallery immediately," Hatch told his employer.

"You do that. Now."

Hatch's mouth tightened, although he was used to the tone of absolute command. "I'll get back to you soon, Mr. Kincaid." He let himself out of the office with his usual sense of relief. So far Hatch had stayed afloat in the dangerous waters that surrounded the shark, but a man had to keep an eye on the beast at all times. It was too easy to start looking like shark food.

Kincaid turned back to the window as the door closed behind his assistant.

That damned ugly monstrosity of a house seemed fated to

reappear time and again in his life. It was almost uncanny. Coincidences, he was forced to acknowledge, apparently did happen now and then but he instinctively found them disturbing.

He let his mind drift back to the first time he had seen the place. That had been back when he was much younger and a little drunk with the power he was starting to accumulate. The house had belonged to Sandquist, who had been as close a friend as Kincaid had ever had. After Sandquist's demise, Kincaid had been careful not to cultivate any more close friends. They were too dangerous.

But in those days, Kincaid had been excited to learn that Sandquist shared a taste for the exotic when it came to sex. Neither man was cursed with any strong inhibitions or moral limits and the two of them had gone out of their way to construct a very interesting retreat at the house on the cliffs. It had proven easy enough to lure carefully chosen women to the house for the extravagant, thrilling orgies Sandquist had a talent for organizing. Drugs and money and the threat of violence had generally ensured silence from the victims, most of whom came from the streets.

There had been only one exception, a woman who might have gone to the police if she had been allowed to do so. It had been a mistake to take Susan Connelly to the house. But Kincaid had been unable to resist. She had been perfect: beautiful, naïve, innocent, and wildly in love with him. Kincaid still got an erection whenever he thought about the methodical way in which he had stripped sweet Susan of her beauty, her naïveté, her innocence, and her passion. It had been a glorious night but a potentially dangerous one.

Kincaid had come to his senses later and realized he had to get rid of this particular victim. A car accident on a lonely stretch of coastal highway had taken care of the problem. The woman had died in the accident. Always a thorough man, Kincaid had checked the obituaries to be certain she had not survived.

That experience had brought home to him that it was

probably time to put a halt to the exotic weekends. He was moving up in the business world, busy with a balancing act that required creating a respectable facade while he cemented underground connections enabling him to operate in the shadows of legitimate business. Kincaid told Sandquist there could be no more weekends.

Sandquist had accepted his friend's decision, saying he understood. The two had gone their own ways until three years ago. Kincaid still remembered the gut-wrenching shock he had experienced when he received the blackmail message from Sandquist. Now, looking back on it, Kincaid could only pity the naïveté of his younger self. He had never guessed that Sandquist had filmed some of the violent orgies. There had been carefully hidden cameras in every bedroom.

There had been only one solution, of course. Kincaid had once again entered the house on the cliffs. Sandquist had stupidly failed to install new security systems. The ones in place were the same ones that had protected the house earlier during the days of the weekend orgies. Kincaid remembered the systems well and bypassed them easily.

He found Sandquist in the big corner room on the third floor. Sandquist, sunk in a foggy world induced by pills and booze, was so far lost in his dreamland that he didn't even recognize his intended blackmail victim. Kincaid had simply led him downstairs and pushed him over the cliffs.

The murder had been declared an accident brought on by an overdose of drugs. Very tragic. Who would have thought Sandquist had a drug problem? But then, drugs were so prevalent these days at every level of society.

Kincaid had walked out of the cliff house that night certain that he had seen the last of the place.

He hadn't even been aware that the house had been sold until recently, when he heard the rumors in the art world that Caitlin Evanger was making plans to put her self-declared final painting up for sale.

Kincaid already owned three Evanger pictures, although he hadn't bought them just as an investment. Something about the repressed violence in them and the artist's grim, surreal view of reality appealed to him. It matched his own in some indefinable way.

Word of a final Evanger painting had spread like wildfire among collectors. When the rumors had reached Kincaid, he paid attention. He wanted that painting. Dispassionately he wondered if Evanger had flaked out and decided to set the scene for an elaborate, headline-grabbing suicide.

Damon didn't particularly care if the woman killed herself after selling her last work. In fact, it would be better if she did. It would ensure that she didn't change her mind and start to paint again.

Evanger's suicide would go a long way toward protecting Kincaid's investment in her art. He smiled faintly at the thought. One way or another, when this was all over and he owned *Bloodlust*, he would have to make sure Caitlin Evanger did indeed kill herself.

But the first priority was to make certain he was on the guest list for what promised to be a most exclusive auction.

Once again Damon Kincaid would be entering the ugly house above the sea.

Maybe this time when he finished his business there he would see that the place was destroyed. It had appeared too many times already in his life. He could do without a fourth time.

Kincaid swung back to his desk and touched a button on a small console. His secretary's cultured voice answered at once.

"Yes, Mr. Kincaid?"

"Get Hatch."

"Yes, Mr. Kincaid."

Hatch answered at once. "Yes, Mr. Kincaid?"

"When you've finished getting me on the Evanger bidders' list, I want you to get in touch with that investigation agency again. I want them to run a background check on that restaurant owner and her lover with the dishpan hands. Find out whatever you can and get back to me as soon as possible."

"Yes, Mr. Kincaid."

Kincaid sat back in his chair with a sense of satisfaction. Unlike some executives, he liked to employ "yes" men and women. It made no sense to hire people who might think too much for themselves.

Verity finished off the yogurt dipping sauce with a touch of curry and put the glass bowl containing the mixture into the refrigerator next to the beer her father and Jonas had stored there. The flavors in the sauce would be perfectly blended by tonight when it was brought out to be served with fresh vegetables at the evening meal.

Verity had been in a flurry of activity all day, ever since she and Jonas returned from Caitlin's. They had arrived home at ten, just in time for the mad rush to get ready for lunch. There had been no letup for her since then.

She wiped her hands and glanced around the kitchen. The restaurant had been closed since two o'clock and she had been working steadily and alone for nearly two hours. It was now almost four and she decided she deserved a break. Everyone else in the vicinity seemed already to have taken one. She hadn't seen anything of her father or Jonas since shortly after two. They had departed together with one of the six-packs from the refrigerator.

Neither man had bothered to ask Verity whether she minded them storing their beer in her commercial-sized refrigerator. She had simply opened the door and found the six-packs piled inside. It was very annoying but she decided it wasn't worth orchestrating a battle over the matter. She had other things on her mind.

Verity stepped out onto the back porch of the little restaurant and stretched luxuriously. The afternoon sun was warm on her shoulders as she considered her options. She could grab a can of fruit juice and walk down to the lake, or she could go visit Laura, who would be enjoying the lull before check-in time.

Or she could go hunt up Jonas and see if he really meant what he'd said about trying to test the bizarre psychic power he claimed to have.

She shoved her hands into the back pockets of her jeans and started up the path to the small cabin that her father and Jonas were sharing. As she walked through the trees she spotted both men lounging in the sun on the steps of the deck that lined the front of the cottage. They each held a can of beer, and the remainder of a six-pack was chilling in a bucket of ice between them. An open bag of potato chips was sitting upright on the step. Verity shook her head in mild disgust as she approached.

"It's obvious neither one of you will ever have a big problem adjusting to retirement," she remarked as she reached them. "Some men can't handle it, you know. They die or go crazy when they no longer have a regular nine-to-five job. The shock of being without work for the first time in their lives is too much for them. It's good to know you two won't ever get too dependent on that kind of routine."

Jonas leaned back against a railing post, one jeaned leg resting on the step below the one on which he sat. His other leg was stretched indolently out along the redwood boards. He ate a chip, tipped the beer can to his mouth, and emptied it with obvious pleasure before he spoke.

"Practice, practice, practice. Right, Emerson?"

"Damn right," Emerson agreed from the opposite side of the steps. He smiled blandly at his daughter. "Sit down, Red. If you promise not to lecture us on the virtues of employment, we might let you have a can of beer and a handful of chips."

Verity raised her eyes briefly toward the heavens and surrendered. "It's a deal. I'm too tired to try whipping either of you into shape today."

Jonas patted the step below him. "That's good news. Have a seat. I'll even open the beer for you."

"Always the gentleman." But she accepted the cold, wet can with some gratitude. For some reason, she didn't have the energy to lecture today.

Jonas leaned back against the post again and looked at Emerson. "Where the hell did she get such a heavy dose of the old-fashioned work ethic, anyway?"

"Don't look at me," Emerson said. "It didn't come from my side of the family."

Verity wrinkled her nose at both men, choosing to ignore the deliberate provocation. Sometimes a woman had to rise above the generally primitive sense of humor frequently favored by the male of the species.

The three of them sat in companionable silence for a few minutes, absorbing the faint sound of the murmuring trees and the sight of the lake in sunshine. Neither Jonas nor Emerson seemed inclined to start a conversation so Verity waited until she'd fortified herself with a few swallows of beer before she took the initiative.

"Well, Jonas, have you told Dad about the test you want to run with the pistols?"

Jonas shrugged. "I told him."

Verity looked at her father. "What do you think, Dad?"

Emerson rubbed the back of his neck. "About what?"

"About this psychometry business," she said bluntly, not looking at Jonas. "Do you believe in it?"

"Red, I believe in a lot of things I can't see or taste or touch. Things like black holes in the heart of the universe, and the Theory of Relativity. I'm willing to keep an open mind toward this psychic stuff. If Jonas says he's got some kind of talent for it, I'm willing to wait and see."

"Do you know anything about psychometry?" Verity demanded.

Emerson raised a heavy brow. "I know that any really good collector, antique dealer, or museum director will tell you he's heard stories of people in his line of work who just seem to 'know' when an object is genuine. It's usually passed off as some kind of intuition based on extensive experience, a gut feel for what's real and what's not. But who knows? It could be the rudiments of psychometry. And if it is, it makes sense to think that a few people might have been born with more than just some rudimentary talent. A few might have gotten the full-blown power. Like I said, I'm keeping an open mind. What about you?"

Verity glanced at Jonas, who had his dark head resting against the post. His eyes were closed and he seemed not to be paying any attention to the conversation.

"I'm keeping an open mind, too," Verity said.

Jonas spoke without opening his eyes. "If you believe that, Emerson, I've got some oceanfront property down in Arizona I'd like to sell you."

Emerson chuckled. "I guess we'll find out a little more about all this when you two run this test, huh? If nothing else, it should be amusing. I always enjoy a good party trick."

"Did Jonas tell you that the last time he practiced his party trick someone almost got killed?" Verity sensed Jonas's sudden, deep stillness.

"Just a lab tech, from what I hear." Emerson was unconcerned. "In this day and age lab techs are as common as hite mice. What's one more or less?"

"Dad!"

Emerson grinned. "Just teasing, Red." He reached for a fresh can of beer. "When are you planning to do your stuff, Jonas? I want to be around. Wouldn't want anything to happen to those pistols."

"The pistols will be safe enough," Jonas said calmly.

"Do I get the same guarantee about Verity?" Emerson asked blandly.

"Verity will be perfectly safe," Jonas said quietly.

"Of course I'll be safe," she tossed back, irritated. "What can possibly happen to me, even if Jonas is right about having this weird power?"

Jonas opened one eye and regarded her thoughtfully. "I'll tell you what might happen to you, little tyrant. One of these days I'm going to catch you in that corridor and I might not let you go again. When we're in that corridor, I'm the one in charge. You work for me there."

Verity swallowed too much beer and nearly choked. By the time she had recovered, Jonas and Emerson had casually decided when to run the test.

"Tonight after Verity closes the restaurant will be a good time," Jonas said. "She's usually exhausted after the evening cleanup. With any luck she'll be too tired to fight me when I try to make the connection."

Verity shot him a quick, repressive glare. He was talking about a psychic connection, but it struck her for the first time that the only occasions she had ever actually wound up in bed with Jonas were after she had seen him in that mysterious corridor.

She spent the rest of the evening wondering if there was some link between the psychic events Jonas claimed to experience and his passion afterward.

It was an unsettling thought.

The No Bull Cafe closed a half-hour early on Tuesday night. Business had been light during the evening and Jonas and Emerson got the cleanup work done in record time. Verity found herself loitering behind them, double-checking lists and going over small details she already knew by heart.

"Ready, Verity?"

She jumped as Jonas approached her from behind. She glanced back over her shoulder and met his steady gaze. "I guess so. As ready as I'll ever be."

His expression hardened slightly. "You don't have to look as though I've just invited you to a funeral. This will only take a few minutes. When it's over maybe I'll have some answers to some questions I've been living with for a long time."

Verity's resentment flickered and died. Jonas believed in this mysterious talent he claimed he had. Right or wrong, it was eating at him and had been for years. Apparently it had shaped a good portion of his adult life. She couldn't deny him her help in this small test.

Impulsively she reached out and took his hand. "Okay, let's go see what happens."

Jonas's eyes lightened and his strong fingers clamped fiercely around hers. "Thanks, Verity. One of these days I'll repay you for the favor, I promise."

"Forget it. Consider it a job perk. Given the low wages I pay, I suppose you deserve one or two." Such as sleeping with the boss and playing strange psychic games with her. "Ready, Dad?"

Emerson, who was leaning against a counter, his arms folded across his broad chest, nodded briefly. Teeth flashed somewhere in his beard. "Let's go see what happens."

They locked the restaurant and walked along the path to the small cabin. When they filed inside and closed the door, Emerson reached under the sagging bed to pull out the pistol case. He opened it and set it down on a table. Verity thought the old guns looked sinister in the harsh light of the ancient bulb overhead. But then, she always thought guns of any kind or any age appeared sinister and quite repugnant.

"What do we do next, Jonas?" she asked calmly.

"You don't have to do anything except sit down in that chair and try not to fight me or run from me." He indicated one of the straight-back chairs at the table.

Verity frowned as she slipped onto the seat. "I'm not going to fight you. I agreed to do this, remember?"

He nodded, sitting down across from her. "I know, but your instincts may take a different viewpoint when they sense what's happening. On the other two occasions when I tried to connect with you in that corridor, you were terrified."

It was disturbing to know that his memories of that mental corridor were as sharp as her own. They really had shared some sort of mental imagery. He even knew she had tried to run from him. Somehow he really had been there with her. It was the last thing Verity wanted to admit. Surely there was some rational explanation. If push came to shove, she would vote for a diagnosis of mental telepathy before she agreed with the verdict of psychometry, she decided.

Telepathy was bad enough but somehow psychometry was even more difficult to accept.

"Let's just get this over with," she said between set teeth.

Jonas gave her a grim glance before reaching across the table for her hand. "Yes, ma'am," he said dryly.

Emerson hovered. "Where do you want me in all this?" he asked.

Jonas looked up at him, his expression thoughtful. "Just stand nearby. If, uh, anything looks like it might get out of control, take the pistol away from me. Once I'm no longer in contact with the gun, the reaction will stop."

Emerson's eyes narrowed. "You going to go crazy on us, Jonas?"

Jonas smiled faintly. "I'll be okay. I've got Verity. Don't worry. I've already touched these pistols briefly and their impact isn't too bad."

"What do you mean, their impact isn't too bad?" Verity demanded.

"I mean I didn't sense any death associated with them," Jonas explained impatiently.

Verity shuddered. "Oh. Well, that's encouraging. I guess I'm ready."

"Such enthusiasm." But Jonas hesitated no longer. He reached into the case and picked up one of the pistols.

Jonas felt a faint, glittering flicker of awareness and closed his eyes. He felt the eerie sensation of suddenly having to share his place in time and space with something else that didn't quite belong there. The cabin walls began to curve around him.

This was not going to be nearly as intense an experience as handling the rapier had been. But then, he had already known that. The pistol dated from a later time period. Its effect was bound to be less dramatic.

The grip of the gun was warm and solid in his hand. He felt a damp sheen of sweat break out on his forehead.

The tunnel continued to form in his mind.

He started moving along the corridor, aware of the tendrils of old emotion that seemed to be pulling him toward one end. He ignored them for the moment, concentrating on finding Verity first before he tried to deal with the sensations of the past. He could sense her presence somewhere up ahead in the misty shadows that drifted in the endless corridor. With the sure sense of her presence came the feeling of being safely linked to his primary reality.

Something flickered in the darkness ahead. Exultation gripped Jonas. She was there. He caught a tantalizing glimpse of her standing very still, poised to flee but not yet giving in to the fear. Jonas gave her full marks for being in control of herself. The little tyrant was one gutsy lady.

But then, he had always known that. She'd been putting up one hell of a fight when he'd pulled Pedro off of her in that Mexican alley.

Jonas continued moving forward in the corridor. He took his time, concentrating on the feeling of being in control. On previous occasions when he entered the corridor he had always been forced to deal with the immediate impact of emotions and images that were waiting to swamp him. Entering the corridor had always meant going into battle. But not tonight. A vast relief and a sense of satisfaction poured through Jonas. There was no doubt that Verity's presence strengthened him in some way.

Verity's presence made it possible to tame the flickering ghosts of the past.

He would connect with Verity in the corridor and then he would turn to confront the ghosts.

Jonas pushed his way through the last of the shadows and found Verity waiting for him. She stood braced, her hands in small, determined fists at her sides. The feeling of being anchored grew stronger. A part of Jonas had the freedom now to make some observations.

One of the things he noticed was that he and Verity both appeared to be dressed exactly as they had been all evening. Apparently the mental images they constructed in their minds reflected current reality outside the corridor. The main difference was that inside the tunnel they each moved independently. In current time/space, neither one got up from the table, but inside the corridor each had full capability of movement.

Jonas saw the wariness in Verity's eyes and tried a reassuring smile. He came to a halt in front of her, not touching her in the corridor.

"Hi," he said, wondering if she would break and run.

"Hi, yourself," Verity tore her gaze from his face and glanced around. "So this is it, huh?"

"This is it. Think of it as a tunnel through the sea. Instead of being surrounded by water, we're surrounded by time. We're immersed in it."

Verity hugged herself and nervously rubbed her upper arms. "And you think that some bits and pieces of time enter this corridor?"

"When I handle an object that carries a strong load of emotion from the time frame I seem sensitive to, those emotions seep into the corridor. It's as if they're trying to relink with the object itself through me. It's hard to explain, Verity, but it's real."

"There's another explanation," she said defensively.

"What's that?"

"We might both be going crazy."

Jonas shook his head. "Believe me, I've considered that possibility. But we're not going crazy. Come with me. I want to see what happens when we face the emotional junk connected with the pistol." He held out his hand.

Verity hesitated and then gave him her hand. He circled her wrist and tugged her gently down the corridor. He felt her flinch, but she made no protest. She was going to go through with this, just as she had promised. Jonas felt a wealth of gratitude and admiration well up in him.

They didn't have to go far in the corridor to find what Jonas sought. They hadn't gone more than a few steps into the swirling mists when the colorful, snaking tendrils appeared and began to curl hungrily around them.

The multicolored ribbons headed first toward Jonas like a pack of dogs cornering a fox. But then something happened. They slowed, veered aside, and slowly turned toward Verity.

"Jonas? What's happening?" Verity shifted anxiously as the multicolored manifestations swirled around her. She batted at them with a free hand.

"They won't hurt you. You're not sensitive to them in the same way I am. But for some reason you're a magnet for them. Your presence frees me, Verity. Together we're a lot stronger than they are. Feel anything?"

"No," she said quickly and then changed her mind. "Yes. I don't know. It's weird, Jonas."

"I know. Don't worry about it. I'm the main contact."

"What's it like for you?" she asked in hushed tones.

Jonas concentrated, enjoying for the first time the glorious sensation of really being in control of what he was facing. This wasn't a firefight, for once. He didn't have to battle these twisting, writhing things; he could handle them. This time he was the dominant force in the corridor.

Slowly he reached out with his free hand and touched one of the tendrils, a golden streamer that pulsed invitingly. The moment he made deliberate contact with it, it freed itself from the tangle surrounding it and leaped to coil around his arm.

Adrenaline pumped through Jonas's veins. And then a new sense of awareness. It was someone else's sense of awareness, not his own. He was standing on a grassy field at dawn, dressed in polished Hessian boots and pale fawn trousers. He was in his shirtsleeves. A manservant standing near the carriage held his green frock coat and black felt hat. There was a pistol in Jonas's fist. The same pistol he was holding in the cabin.

A short distance away another man, similarly attired, held the mate to the weapon Jonas had. Both men were waiting for a signal from the man who stood between them. Somewhere in the distance a horse stamped and blew in the cold dawn air. Harness metal rattled. A few men stood at the side, observing. One of them was Jonas's second, the man who had made the formal arrangements for this morning's confrontation.

Jonas was aware of fear but it was held at bay by the surge of cold anger and adrenaline pumping through him. His only goal this morning was to draw blood from the man who had insulted Amanda. He would teach the bastard a lesson.

The signal came. Jonas lifted his pistol in a smooth, sure motion. But even as he did so, he knew somehow that the action wasn't his. He was still an observer. His opponent's hand also swept upward. But Jonas was already tightening his finger on the trigger of the heavy pistol, confident of the gun's sure aim.

Then, without any warning, Verity screamed and yanked at his arm. For an instant all the images blurred. Jonas was both the man on the grassy field and the observer in the corridor. Furious at the distraction, Jonas tried to jerk free of Verity's compelling grip. But she clung to him, yelling at him.

"Stop it! Do you hear me? Stop it this instant. I won't have this foolishness carried any further." She grabbed the golden ribbon and pulled it free. It slithered back into the tangle at her feet.

Jonas blinked at the upper-class English accent. His eyes widened.

"Amanda?"

"No, I'm not Amanda. I'm Verity. Come with me. We're getting out of here."

He turned back, seeing the images of the dawn-lit scene already fading rapidly.

Disoriented, Jonas whirled to face Verity. She was pulling at his arm and shouting commands.

"I said come with me, dammit." The English accent was

gone. The voice was once again Verity's. "We're getting out of here."

"Honey, it's okay." Jonas tried to soothe her but she was already tugging him back down the corridor. "Everything's under control. It's all right. Just calm down, Verity. I want to do some exploring."

"How do we get out of this corridor?" she demanded.

Jonas became aware of the pistol in his hand. He opened his fingers and dropped it.

The corridor vanished at once. Jonas was again facing Verity across the small table.

It didn't surprise him to realize that he was sexually aroused. Having experienced the same after-effects on the previous two occasions when he had encountered Verity in the corridor, he was expecting it. The only difference this time was that the desire to pull Verity down onto the nearest bed, strip her, and bury himself in her was stronger than ever. Sweat trickled down the side of his face.

"Well," Emerson said, looking from one taut face to the other, "how was the minivacation?"

"We almost lost our traveler's checks," Verity said in a grim voice.

Chapter Twelve

Jonas could feel the tension radiating from Verity as he walked back with her to her cottage. It had a heightening effect on his already simmering desire. But he was determined to control himself tonight. Verity had had a traumatic experience this evening. The decent thing to do was to give her time to adjust. She was bound to want to talk it all out.

He told himself that if he was a gentleman he wouldn't try to push her into bed tonight the way he had the last two times. He ought to show some respect for the effects of the experience on her. Tonight was a night to be spent soothing, gentling, and reassuring her. Jonas was determined to be gallant even if it took every ounce of willpower he possessed.

There was no doubt that Verity needed some soothing. He could almost see her nerve endings glowing in the dark. He wasn't sure he could explain to her just why it was so important to him that he start testing himself, start seeing how far his talent could stretch. He wasn't even certain he could explain it to himself. But he knew a strong sense of urgency, one he had felt ever since that morning when he awakened in Caitlin Evanger's ugly house.

"Poor tyrant," he said softly. "It really got to you, didn't it?"

"Of course it got to me. What did you expect?" she snapped.

He winced. "Not quite what happened, I'll admit."

"What does that mean?" She peered up at him in the darkness.

Jonas paused, searching for words. "Verity, when I found your earring in that alley I knew there was something special about you. I knew you were more than a woman I wanted to take to bed. But I can't really describe what I felt when I touched that earring. Just a sense of certainty. A sense that you were somehow important to me. I knew I had to find you and discover what it meant. I had never had that feeling about anyone else in my life."

"In other words you fell for my brain, not my body?"

He squeezed her hand a bit too tightly in retaliation. "Spare me the sarcasm tonight. I'm trying to explain things to you. At any rate, when I found you again, nothing really became any clearer until the night I tried picking up the pistol with you standing next to me. I hadn't stepped into that corridor for years but I recognized it instantly. I also realized something else. All of a sudden I wasn't alone in that tunnel in my mind. You were there. It was the first time I had ever had anyone else with me."

"Not even when you were testing your ability at Vincent?"

He shook his head. "No. Until I met you I had no idea it was even possible to take anyone with me into that corridor. I had always found myself alone in there, and believe me, that damn tunnel has got to be the loneliest place in space or time."

"I can believe it." Verity's fingers tightened comfortingly through his. "My God, I can believe it."

Jonas felt the gentle warmth in her touch and smiled to himself. He was supposed to be the one doing the comforting tonight. Underneath all those prickly thorns there was a decidedly soft, empathic streak in his flame-haired tyrant. Knowing that made him feel more protective and possessive than ever. No wonder Emerson had felt obliged to give her as many self-defense mechanisms as possible. She would never admit it, but Verity needed protection in this hard, cold world.

"That first time I found you in the corridor with me I reached for you and you ran," Jonas explained slowly. "I dropped the pistol and that was the end of it. I still wasn't sure what it meant, but I knew I had to find out."

"And the next time you found me there?" she prompted.

"When it happened last night at Evanger's house, things were a lot more serious."

"Because that rapier was from the era you're so attuned to?"

He nodded. "It's a much more dangerous time zone for me and I was really caught up in it last night. I made a mistake. I took a chance and I paid for it. I knew I had to get to you before I was completely overwhelmed by the forces that were attached to the rapier."

"So you came traipsing down the hall to my room."

"I went after you because I sensed you could keep me from being swamped. I was right. At first you ran, but at the last moment you stopped and turned around and came to me. Once you were with me I was back in command of myself. It was close but we got through it together. Last night I had my proof. Tonight was a controlled exploratory trip. Now I'm convinced. With you around, I can learn to control my trips into the corridor. Do you have any idea what that means to me, Verity?"

"I'm not sure I want to know," she retorted gloomily.

He ignored that. "The rapier I had last night, or anything else from that era, is not a good test object because it's too powerful. The pistols were much easier to experiment with. They're infinitely more manageable."

"Hah. Manageable my foot. Two men were getting ready to kill each other in that corridor. I couldn't see very well, the image was all broken up like an Impressionist painting, but I got the overall picture."

"I've never seen such a clear image in that corridor," Jonas mused. "But then I've never had the luxury of taking my time and studying what was going on around me. Every other time I've gone in, I've been moving fast, trying to avoid too much contact with those twisting streamer things. It was interesting to be able to stop for once and look around."

"What would have happened if that other man had fired?"

Jonas shrugged. "Nothing. What could have happened? It's like watching a movie. The images never last more than a few seconds."

"I'm not so sure that the images are harmless. I got the impression you were somehow being drawn into one of the men holding a gun. Does that make sense?"

"In a way, I guess. I was feeling what he was feeling. I knew things he knew, such as why he was fighting the duel. But there was no danger. I wasn't him. He wasn't me."

"I was frightened, Jonas. I thought that if the other man fired, you might actually be killed."

Jonas stopped short in the middle of the path. "What the hell are you saying?"

"I can't explain it. I just had this fleeting feeling that you were in as much danger as the man who was holding the pistol in that image. That's why I started yelling about getting out of the corridor. You called me Amanda and dropped the pistol and the next thing I knew we were out of there." She shivered. "You shouldn't have touched that golden ribbon."

Jonas felt a prickle of cold sweat. He banished the queasy feeling at once. "Verity, your imagination got away with you. Perfectly understandable. After all, that was the first time you were ever caught up in one of those corridor situations. You don't realize how easily corridor reality gets mixed up with present-time reality. Don't worry about it. We were both safe."

"I'm not so sure about that."

"Trust me," he said. "I've had a lot more experience in that corridor than you've had. It can be dangerous. In the past I've worried about being swamped by the lingering emotions of someone who lived in the past, but tonight I felt totally in control. Damn, it felt good." A joyous relief that could no longer be suppressed made him laugh out loud. "It was a fantastic sensation, Verity. Incredible. For the first time I was in command in that corridor. I knew I didn't have to worry about fighting off any garbage from the past. I was stronger than anything the residue off that pistol could throw at me. Dammit to hell, what a feeling of freedom. After all these years, I finally feel free, and I owe it all to you, lady."

"If you want to pay your debt, take me to bed," she said fiercely.

Jonas was so startled that for an instant he could only stare down at her in amazement. "What?" he finally got out.

Her eyes were deep, mysterious pools in the shadows as she looked up at him. "Take me to bed. Now. Right this minute."

"Wouldn't you rather talk some more? You had a hell of an experience tonight. Maybe you'd rather we discussed it. I can answer some of your questions. Not all of them, but a few. You must have thousands, considering what you've been through."

"You're not listening to me. The questions can wait. I want to make love first. Right away."

"Uh, sure. You bet. My pleasure. I've been thinking along those lines myself. I mean, I've been wondering if you would be willing, but I thought I ought to give you a little time to . . ." He broke off, certain he had turned into a gibbering idiot. "Lady, sometimes you really take me by surprise."

She put her arms around his neck and pressed close. He could feel the firm roundness of her small breasts against him as she rose onto her toes and forcefully pulled his head down to hers. He could feel her nipples hardening beneath the pullover she wore.

"When did you stop wearing a bra?" he demanded.

"Never mind that. Kiss me," she urged passionately.

Jonas caught his breath, aware of the hot rush of blood in his veins. "Your wish is my command," he tried to say with a small, mockingly gallant smile, but he never finished the sentence.

Verity was assaulting his mouth while she pressed her body against him. Her lips were hot and demanding on his. When she thrust her small tongue between his teeth, Jonas's already aroused body kicked into high gear. He was suddenly throbbing with desire, as frantic for Verity as she was for him. The knowledge that she wanted him with such demanding urgency had much the same effect as pouring gasoline on open flames. Jonas nearly exploded.

But Verity seemed to be a couple of steps ahead of him. She was already in flames. Jonas was dazed by the hunger in her. She was all over him, peeling open his jacket and yanking at the buttons of his shirt, entwining her leg around his and arching her lower body into his thighs. Jonas groaned as the blaze of his passion mingled with hers. When her small, eager hand slipped down to his waist and stopped to unfasten his jeans, he came back to his senses long enough to free his mouth.

"It's cold out here. Let's get to your cabin," he ordered tersely.

She blinked as if trying to clear her head for an instant and then she gave up the effort. "No," she said, her fingers back at work on his jeans. "Here. Right now. Right here. I can't wait. I want you, Jonas. I want you so much. I've got to have you. You must make love to me."

"Believe me, I will. As soon as we get inside where it's warm." He groaned, fighting for enough self-control to get both of them off the path and into the privacy of the cabin. When she refused to cooperate, he lost what was left of his patience. He captured her wrists and held them behind her back.

She twisted, trying to free herself so that she could get at him again. "Let me touch you," she begged. "Please let me touch you. I want to feel you. I want to hold you in my hands and watch you get big and hard and heavy and then I want to take you inside me. Deep inside me. I want to feel every inch of you. I want to drain you. Please, Jonas."

"Woman, you're going to make me come right here in the middle of the path if you keep on talking like that. *Let's go.*" He scooped her up into his arms and almost ran to the cabin. He was on fire and so was she. The heat in her was beating at him. The night was clear and cold but Jonas felt as if he were holding a small furnace in his arms.

Verity gave up struggling and concentrated on clinging to him as he carried her. Her fingertips were tiny daggers sliding under the collar of his jacket and sinking into his shoulders. Her mouth was glued to his.

"The door," Jonas rasped when they reached it. "Open it, Verity."

With a soft, impatient moan, she did as he ordered and reached down to open the door. A second later they were inside. Jonas kicked the door shut behind him and started down the short hallway to Verity's small bedroom. He could hardly wait now.

He barely made it. For a moment he was sure that he was going to collapse under Verity's compelling touch and wind up making love to her on the hardwood floor. He managed to fall heavily onto the bed, instead. Her fingers went straight to his jeans to resume the task they had begun outside.

"Oh, yes, baby," he muttered, fumbling desperately with her sweater. "Anything you want, honey. Take anything you damn well want. It's all yours. And I'm going to have all of you in return. I'm going to get so deep inside you, you'll think I'm a part of you."

He freed her breasts just as she succeeded in opening his

jeans. His throbbing manhood leaped into her hands, pushing against her palm and thrusting between her fingers with blind hunger. Verity's nails scored him lightly, then glided over the sensitive, velvety soft head. Jonas sucked in his breath, fighting to keep himself from climaxing then and there.

"Hell, Verity."

"Is it?" she asked breathlessly.

"No, no, no." He groaned and leaned down to close his teeth lightly around one of her tight little nipples. "More like heaven. You're so damn hot tonight."

She slid her fingers down his shaft and continued further below. She cupped him, squeezing a little too hard.

"Jesus Christ, take it easy, honey," he gasped, torn between excruciating pain and excruciating desire. He grabbed her hand and pulled it slightly away from its target. "Easy does it."

She frowned. "I'm sorry. I didn't mean to hurt you."

"It's okay, it's okay," he said quickly. "You just need a little practice,that's all." He pushed her hand back into position, already missing her touch. "Try it again."

She did, this time with such exquisite sensitivity that Jonas was sure he would never get enough of her.

"Better?" she whispered.

"Perfect." He moved his hand down her body to the waistband of her jeans and quickly unzipped them. "Lift that sweet little tail far enough off the bed so I can get these damn jeans off you."

She did as instructed. Jonas made certain her silky panties came off along with the jeans. She didn't wait for his coaxing touch on her thighs. Her denims had barely hit the floor before she was raising one knee and parting her legs. The scent of her arousal made Jonas's head swim.

The feminine invitation was irresistible. Jonas's fingers clamped around her silken thighs, pushing them wider apart so that he could have free access to the treasure awaiting him. He parted the soft folds with his thumb and forefinger.

Verity moaned softly and Jonas's fingers were instantly bathed in spicy dew. He slowly probed the tight, secret corridor, groaning with anticipation as he felt her clench around him.

"You're so tight and hot," he breathed in awe. He was dazed with her excitement. She was wild for him. Her moisture coated his whole hand. He used a second finger to open her wider, and his lower body tightened unmercifully as he felt her small muscles close fiercely around his two fingers. Deliberately he stroked deeply into the velvet sheath. Then he slowly withdrew to the entrance. Verity twisted beneath his touch, clutching at him. Her soft cries were an erotic cross between a siren's compelling demand and a woman's sweet surrender. They vibrated through Jonas, making him tremble with his own demanding need.

He stroked his fingers into her again, this time using his thumb to tease the small, rigid little bud at the juncture of her legs. She arched frantically, trying to pull him to her.

"*Jonas*. Love me. Take me now. I want you inside me now. Hurry. I'm going crazy."

He lowered his head to where her tiny passion bud, swollen and throbbing, snuggled into dark red curls. He curled his tongue around it and was rewarded with Verity's desperate cry of need. She grabbed his head and tried to hold him to her, offering herself to him with uninhibited passion.

Jonas reveled in the response he had provoked. A heady sense of masculine power made him tantalize her again instead of moving to satisfy her. He loved having Verity like this, full of sweet, demanding surrender. He had never had a woman respond so completely to him. It was enough to give a man delusions of grandeur.

"In a minute," he promised, sliding one finger down beneath her hips to trace the dark velvet furrow between her clenched buttocks. "I'll take you completely, honey. I won't leave any part of you untouched, I promise. I'm going to go deep inside you. So deep you won't ever be able to forget me."

Verity gasped and pushed at his shoulders. Unprepared for the surprise move, Jonas found himself on his back. Before he could reassert himself, Verity scrambled on top of him, straddling him the way she would a stallion. He realized she was going to take matters into her own hands and he laughed triumphantly at her overwhelming excitement.

"Okay, honey, I get the message. Just let me get these jeans off and I'll take care of everything."

But Verity ignored him. She reached down to where his shaft sprang eagerly from the unbuttoned denims and grasped him. Then she lowered herself, trying to force him into her.

Jonas groaned in frustration as she fumbled awkwardly. His desperate manhood collided with her thigh. "I'll help you," he growled, reaching down between her legs. He found her damp, tight opening with one hand and guided himself quickly to the entrance with the other. "Now," he ordered, his voice thick. "Take me into you now. Show me what you want to do to me."

Verity's fingers splayed wide on his chest and her head tipped back as she slowly started to ease herself down onto him. He barely survived the torture. He knew he wouldn't last more than a few seconds once he was inside her.

He dug his fingers into her round derriere and forced her to complete the union. She gasped as he invaded her fully. She rose and fell twice, three times, and then her nails sank deep into his skin as she cried out and convulsed around him.

"Sweet hell," Jonas whispered, and then he exploded with white-hot violence.

The questions came later. Much later. Jonas lay with one arm around a drowsing Verity and stared at the shadow pattern on the ceiling.

A wise man did not look a gift horse in the mouth, he told himself. He was fortunate to find himself in the middle of a torrid affair with a woman who wanted him so much she had practically raped him tonight. He had made love to her on only three occasions but she seemed to have become addicted to it. Theoretically, he should be thanking his lucky stars that he was the man who had awakened the sleeping tigress, and who was now in a position to enjoy the pleasures of tiger taming.

But Jonas was experiencing an inexplicable uneasiness. He had never trusted much in luck. He was a believer in the iceberg theory of the universe: never take anything at face value. Regardless of what showed on the surface, you could bet there remained a lot of unexplained territory underneath.

Now as he lay physically satiated beside Verity he found himself questioning what had not been evident during the passionate interlude that had just taken place. He was grateful for the experience, but he had to wonder just what had prompted it.

She had responded to him as if she had just taken a potent aphrodisiac. She had come out of that psychic corridor this time as aroused and ready for sex as he was. Possibly even more so.

"Mmm." Verity shifted against him, stretching like a contented cat. She opened her eyes and smiled dreamily up at him. "Hello."

He turned on his side and propped himself on one elbow, trying to read her expression. "How do you feel?"

"Wonderful. How about you?"

"Drained," he admitted wryly. "You take a lot out of a man, boss."

"Don't worry about it." She patted his shoulder and yawned hugely. "You've got a lot of resources to call upon in emergencies." She glanced at the clock. "Good grief. Look at the time."

"If you're getting ready to kick me out again, forget it. I want to talk to you tonight, Verity."

She raised her eyebrows. "About what?"

"Let's start with sex," he suggested, feeling mildly aggressive.

"I thought we just finished with it."

"Save the cute remarks. I want to know what turned you on so completely tonight."

She smiled slyly and tapped one finger against his lower lip. "That should be obvious. Feel free to take full credit."

"I'd like to, but something tells me there was a little more involved than just my great charm and large muscles."

Her smile slipped and her eyes turned speculative. "I know what you mean. I had the same impression the last two times you made love to me. There is a pattern here, isn't there?"

He frowned at her, confused. "What are you talking about?"

She shrugged, the action causing her nipples to push against the sheet. "I'm talking about the fact that the only times you've ever made love to me were after a trip into that damn corridor. It seems to have a distinct effect on your libido. You haven't shown any interest in me outside of those two occasions, unless you count that kiss in the spa."

Jonas was stunned. "Are you telling me that your libido got overcharged tonight due to that test we ran?"

She shifted her gaze toward the ceiling and pretended to yawn. "This is going to be one unusual affair if it turns out the only time we get sexually excited is after a trip into the corridor."

Rage flared in Jonas. "I told you I wanted you that first night down in Mexico. I wanted you that night we kissed in the spa. And I've wanted you every night in between."

"Really? Then how come we only wind up in bed on the nights you play psychic time voyager?" she asked quietly.

"Probably because those are the times when my self-control is at its weakest," Jonas grated. "The rest of the time I've tried to take things easy and not push you. Don't you understand? Going into the corridor doesn't by itself make me horny. I never got a hard-on during all those tests at Vincent. My physical reaction is connected with you, not the psychometry."

"Is that right?" She looked dubious.

"Damn right. What about you? What was it that got you so excited tonight?"

"Relief, I suppose," she said with a sigh.

"Relief at getting through the test?"

She shook her head on the pillow. "No. Relief that you didn't get shot inside that corridor." The wary, teasing tone was gone from her voice. Verity's expression was very serious as she stared up at the ceiling. "I thought you were going to get killed in there. When we got out, all I wanted to do was throw myself on top of you and reassure myself that we were both all right."

Jonas pondered her answer. "I told you, I wasn't in any danger."

"I know what you told me."

He drummed his fingers impatiently on her sheet-covered thigh. "You're saying you jumped on me out of a sense of relief after what we'd gone through in the tunnel?"

"Something like that. I'm not sure I can explain it completely."

"And you've been assuming I get turned on enough to take you to bed only after I've been into the corridor?" he persisted, wanting to get the facts straight before he decided what to do next. "You think this affair of ours is dependent on frequent use of my psychometry?"

"Well, it does appear that way, doesn't it? Be honest, Jonas. You've admitted that the only reason you followed me out of Mexico was because of my connection to your talent. You wouldn't have hunted me down if you thought the only thing you'd missed that night was a good lay."

"I ought to take a belt to your sweet ass, lady. Talk about jumping to conclusions." Jonas was infuriated by the fact that part of what she said was absolutely true. He had come after her because of the mystery. And he had made love to her only on the occasions when he'd made a trip into the corridor.

"Don't yell at me, Jonas. I'm just stating facts." She

smiled wistfully and touched his cheek. "I don't want to argue. Not tonight. I'm much too glad to have you here safe. Let's forget about the facts and all the reasons we got together and just enjoy being together. You'll go away one of these days and I want to be able to say I took full advantage of my first love affair. After all, given the statistics, I may never have another one."

Anger mixed with a sudden flare of guilt. "Why do you say I'll go away?"

"Men like you always move on. You're like Dad. You don't really want responsibility or long-term commitment. Don't worry. I knew that going into this affair. I had my eyes wide open. Besides, I'm not looking for marriage anyway. I've told you that, so relax. I'm planning on growing into a bossy, independent, tyrannical old lady. A real shrew. But at least I won't be an old maid."

"Verity, this is getting all mixed up. I don't think I like being written off as useless in the long run. And I don't like your assumption that I'm staying here only because of your ability to anchor me when I go into that corridor. Maybe I did follow you initially because of the mystery surrounding you, but there are other factors involved now. This isn't a simple situation for either of us. Don't try to make it simple by pigeonholing me or our relationship. And don't get the idea you can use me as a stud for a while and then discard me when it suits you."

"I don't want to argue. Not tonight, Jonas." Verity slid her leg between his knees. Her skin was creamy smooth against his tough, hairy flesh. Her fingertips drew a small pattern on his thigh. Jonas groaned and swore softly as his body reacted instantly. "Show me you want me now," she whispered. "Prove to me you don't have to make another trip into that corridor to work up a desire for me."

Jonas leaned over her, trapping her teasing legs with his own. He was already hard again. He tested himself against her thigh, letting her know that he was more than ready.

"I already knew you were hell to work for," he muttered

against her mouth. "Now it looks like you're going to be equally demanding in bed. Lucky for you I'm so easygoing, good-natured, and willing to please."

"I've always heard opposites attract."

Kincaid looked up impatiently as Hatch walked into the elegantly bare office.

"Well?" Kincaid asked.

"I've got the initial background report on both Ames and Quarrel. Ames is not particularly interesting. Nothing more than what she seems, a woman running a little cafe in a small town. But Quarrel is a bit more unusual. He's got a Ph.D. in history and until five years ago he had a reputation as a consultant for museums and collectors."

Kincaid frowned. "What kind of consultant?"

"He was frequently asked to verify the authenticity of certain items being considered for purchase. Seems he had what some people call the 'touch.' He was never proved wrong. But five years ago he walked away from his teaching job and his consulting work and started drifting. He's held odd jobs every place from Tahiti to Mexico. Now he's washing dishes and waiting tables for Ames."

Kincaid sat silently for a moment, letting the information sink in. "A dishwasher with a background in museum consulting who has somehow gotten himself invited to Caitlin Evanger's home. Very interesting."

"The investigator made some inquiries at the spa near the restaurant. Ames is good friends with the owners. The investigator got the impression that Evanger is Ames's friend and that it was she who got the invitation to visit. Apparently Ames just decided to take Quarrel along for the ride." Hatch shrugged. "The report says it's almost certain he's her lover."

"Were Ames and Evanger friends before Quarrel appeared on the scene?"

Hatch glanced hurriedly through the report. "No, sir. Doesn't look that way."

"Quite a coincidence that a reclusive artist who has few known social contacts suddenly becomes close friends with a little cafe operator who just happens to have a lover who's got a background in consulting for museums and collectors."

"There's more, sir."

"Finish it." Kincaid swung around to face the view from his window.

Hatch cleared his throat. "It seems that Jonas Quarrel has let it be known in certain circles that he is acting as an agent for an unidentified party who wishes to sell a very valuable set of antique dueling pistols."

Kincaid steepled his hands. "Has he contacted any museums?"

"No. The investigation report says it's all being handled on the quiet. This is to be a very private sale."

Kincaid considered. "I want to talk to this Jonas Quarrel myself. I need an opportunity to size him up. He may be perfectly harmless. But we have to consider the fact that he is close to Evanger, who has a history of not letting anyone from the art world get close to her. We must also consider the possibility that he is somehow involved in the sale of *Bloodlust*."

Hatch frowned. "How?"

Kincaid shrugged. "I don't know. The most likely scenario is that he's representing an interested bidder who prefers to remain anonymous. If so, that bidder, whoever he is, obviously has special status—otherwise his agent, Quarrel, would not be paying private visits to a woman who never invites people to her home. I want to know what I'm facing. I can deal with financial competition, but if there's something more involved, I need to know about it in advance. I'll be able to tell a great deal about Quarrel if I can meet him. I might be able to figure out where he fits in to the picture."

"I understand," Hatch said calmly. He did not like Kincaid, but could not doubt the man's ability to assess the motives and weaknesses of others. That skill was one of the many that had brought Kincaid this far. "What do you want me to do?"

"Let's try the easy way first. Advise him discreetly that you've heard rumors of the availability of the pistols and that you represent a collector who's interested in them. Let him know that money is no object and that your collector certainly won't ask any awkward questions concerning the provenance of the pistols. See if he takes the bait. If he does, invite him to see me here in my office."

"Yes, sir." Hatch nodded to Kincaid's back in the same formal, polite way he would have nodded if Kincaid had been facing him. Habits were habits, and the ones Hatch had cultivated had kept him employed for quite a while.

Chapter Thirteen

O_n the following Monday morning Verity stood on the busy San Francisco sidewalk and examined the entrance to the tower of glass soaring into the sky above her. "You'd think that in a state that had a definite earthquake problem there would be laws against building big glass buildings."

"Since when has California worried much about earthquakes? Only tourists worry about quakes." Jonas adjusted the package under his arm and gave Verity a gentle push toward the revolving door. "Come on. Let's see if this Kincaid guy is going to get the privilege of delivering your poor old father from the clutches of a loan shark."

"And after we take care of Dad's business we get to shop for the gown I'm going to wear to Caitlin's party," Verity reminded him firmly.

"Hey, lay off. I've already surrendered on that count, remember? I've accepted the fact that I can't talk you out of that dumb Renaissance ball and I've promised we'll hit the costume shops for a gown today. What more do you want from me?"

Verity smiled sunnily. "Gracious, was I whining?"

"You never whine, Verity. You just nag." Jonas came to a

halt in front of a bank of black and gold elevators and scanned the list of businesses housed in the glass tower. "Here we go. Top floor. The man must be doing all right, just like his representative implied."

"Maybe we should have brought Dad along," Verity said. "This is his deal, after all."

"Take my word for it. The person with the item for sale is the last one who should handle the negotiations. Your father knows that. That's why he turned the whole thing over to me. Now stop displaying your appalling lack of faith in my business abilities and get ready to smile sweetly."

"Sweetly?" Verity practiced a sugary smile. "What's my role in all this supposed to be?"

Jonas gave her an arrogant grin full of male challenge in response to the saccharine one she was bestowing on him. "You, my dear, have nothing more to do than play my fluff-brained but sexy redheaded girlfriend who insisted on coming with me today. All you have to do is remember to smile frequently."

"What a thrill." Verity stepped into the elevator.

"Believe me, when this Kincaid character sees that smile, it'll be a case of instant trust. He'll know we're not trying to pull anything shady with the pistols. One look at you and he'd never believe you could be associated with anything underhanded or sneaky."

"Do you always date fluff-brained, sexy redheads with sincere smiles?"

"You're my first," he assured her as the elevator door closed. "Definitely one of a kind."

"It's nice to be appreciated."

They stood in silence as the elevator rose. Verity stole a glance at herself in the mirrored wall. She was wearing her one good suit, a striking black and white number with a full jacket and a very narrow skirt. She hadn't worn high heels in ages and the black pumps were already beginning to pinch. Jonas was wearing a five-year-old jacket and slacks he had been packing around for no apparent reason.

"Actually," Verity said, studying the dark suit that fitted his lean figure quite well, "that outfit doesn't look five years out-of-date. Fortunately for you, men's styles don't change too much."

Jonas fingered a lapel and glanced down. "Believe it or not, I occasionally find a use for this suit. Sooner or later a man needs something to wear to a funeral."

"Or a wedding," Verity retorted.

Jonas gave her a mild look. "I haven't attended a single wedding in the past five years."

"A cheerful thought." Verity lapsed back into silence, practicing her fluff-brained pose. The banter with Jonas was typical of the way they had been communicating for the past few days. There was a wary, sparring quality to their relationship that disappeared only when they were locked in the mortal combat of passion or the equally compelling forces generated inside the time corridor.

She had made two more trips into that corridor with him since the first one. Jonas had been eager to use the pistols as a catalyst. Too eager, as far as Verity was concerned. She still did not understand what happened to her when she accompanied him and she wasn't certain she wanted to understand. Jonas had kept both trips short, but there was no doubt that he was very determined to explore the control he now had over his talent. In fact, he seemed driven to explore that control. That worried Verity.

The passion in their relationship was growing more powerful, too. Ever since the night Jonas had run his first so-called test, he had made it abundantly clear that he did not need a jaunt into the psychic corridor to get an erection.

Verity winced, thinking about the way she had spent the past few nights. She supposed she had unintentionally challenged him, and now Jonas was out to prove he could be insatiable with little or no provocation.

He was certainly doing a good job of it. Verity sometimes wondered how much longer she would hold up under his relentless demands. But she always found herself responding, even when he roused her from a sound sleep as he had at three this morning. She had awakened curled on her side, her hips nestled into his warmth, and discovered that he was sliding into her already moist channel from the rear. Her small protest had been replaced by a gasp of excitement as her body quickly responded to his. Jonas had chuckled deeply, the sound replete with satisfaction as he felt her immediate reaction. One thing was for certain, she was managing to keep his ego stroked and well fed.

Afterward he had left. He always left around three in the morning to return to the cabin he shared with her father. Verity never asked him to stay. She wasn't quite certain why, but she had a hunch it probably had something to do with the fundamental uncertainty surrounding their relationship. Not letting Jonas spend the whole night with her was a way of keeping him at a slight distance emotionally.

They had not discussed the future of their relationship. Things continued normally at the restaurant and Emerson watched with a benign eye as Jonas openly staked a man's claim on Verity. The older man never even commented on the fact that Jonas routinely returned to the smaller cottage around three in the morning. He seemed to accept that his daughter had taken a lover.

Verity supposed her father figured that at her age it was much too late to get out a shotgun.

The elevator doors opened onto a sophisticated lobby occupied by a sleek-looking dark-haired receptionist and several pieces of expensive furniture of contemporary Italian design.

"May I help you?" the receptionist asked politely, her dark eyes on Jonas.

"Jonas Quarrel and Verity Ames. We're here to see Mr. Kincaid," Jonas said easily. "We have an appointment."

"Of course, Mr. Quarrel." The woman's voice was warm honey. "You may go right in. Mr. Kincaid is expecting you. His secretary will show you the way."

Another sleek-looking woman, this one a blonde, walked

into the room. She greeted the visitors in a finishing-school accent. Verity surreptitiously examined the designer suits both the receptionist and Kincaid's secretary wore and decided that pink-collar work must pay better than restaurant work. She'd better be careful or Jonas might decide to try office work. It was a cinch either of the women in Kincaid's office would be happy to welcome him into their ranks. They'd probably welcome him into a few other places, too.

It occurred to Verity that she might be jealous. The knowledge made her feel extremely fluff-brained. She remembered the smile that went with the image just as Kincaid's secretary showed them through a heavy paneled door.

"Miss Ames and Mr. Quarrel, sir." The secretary excused herself with a polite nod at Jonas.

Verity noticed two things very quickly about Kincaid's office. One was the stuffed dummy suspended from the ceiling, which looked like a dead body; the second was the Caitlin Evanger painting on the wall. It was one of Caitlin's most violent works, a picture of a woman struggling to swim through a bloody sea. Verity stifled a small shiver. The pain in Caitlin's work never failed to touch her.

Then she turned her smile on the astonishingly good-looking man who rose to greet them. He appeared to be about Jonas's age—somewhere in his late thirties—and he was built along similar lines. There was the same lean, vital quality captured in a tall, strong-shouldered, narrow-hipped frame.

But the similarities ended there. Not only was Damon Kincaid technically better-looking than Jonas, but he radiated the kind of power associated with great financial success. His burnished blond hair was cut with the precision achieved only by stylists who charged the equivalent of a meal at a Union Square restaurant. Kincaid's silvery gray suit was Italian, cut to emphasize his sleek build. His shoes were handmade, and the scrap of blood-red cloth in his breast pocket was silk. It was embroidered with a tiny *K*.

"Miss Ames." Kincaid inclined his head with a gallant

grace that somehow conveyed masculine admiration without in any way suggesting a come-on. He stared down into her smiling face for a few seconds longer than necessary, as if intrigued by something he saw there. Then he turned to Jonas. "Mr. Quarrel. Thank you very much for making the trip here today. I was very sorry to put you to the trouble, but when my assistant, Hatch, informed me that you were planning to come into the city to see other potential buyers, I couldn't resist the request that you stop by my office."

"No problem," Jonas said, casually laying his package down on the one piece of furniture in the room, Kincaid's desk. "My client wishes to make the best possible deal, and your man Hatch implied you could afford what we've got to offer."

"Money is not an issue," Kincaid said coolly. "Authenticity and condition are, however."

"The pistols are in excellent condition," Jonas assured him, beginning to unwrap the package. "Windham and Smyth flintlocks. Original case. Probably 1795 or so. Definitely a pair of duelers. You'll know as soon as you hold one." Jonas paused just a fraction of a second as he lifted the lid of the mahogany case. "If you know dueling pistols, that is."

"As you can see from what's on my wall, my chief area of interest is swords, but I also have some duelers at home and I'm familiar with them." Kincaid examined the contents of the case and then reached inside to lift out one of the guns. "Excellent grip. Good, heavy pistols." His gaze slid from the gun to Jonas. "You're certain of their authenticity?"

"Absolutely."

"What can you offer as proof?"

"I'm not at liberty to discuss the collector who owned them last, but I can tell you that the pistols belonged to a prestigious British family for a hundred and seventy-five years before they came into the hands of the last collector. They were carried to the scene of a duel between a member of that family and another man shortly before 1800."

Verity shuddered and went to stand by the window.

Kincaid appeared more interested. "An actual duel? What was the outcome?" He gazed down at the steel barrel of the pistol he was holding as if it were made of diamonds.

Jonas glanced at Verity's profile as he answered the question. "No shots were fired. The duel was halted when the cause of the challenge interrupted the affair and put a stop to it."

For some reason Verity happened to turn her head at that moment and caught the expression on Kincaid's face. She could have sworn he looked disappointed.

"You say the cause of the duel interrupted things?" Kincaid murmured. "A woman, I presume?"

"Her name was Amanda," Jonas said calmly.

"I see." Kincaid picked up the second pistol. "Well, the fact that they've never been fired reduces their value to me. I prefer arms that have been used as they were intended to be used. A personal quirk, I'm afraid."

"I understand." Jonas held out the case so that Kincaid could replace the pistol.

Kincaid's brows came together over his aristocratic nose, but he surrendered the weapon. "That doesn't mean I don't intend to make an offer. I would like to have them properly appraised."

Jonas smiled blandly. "As I said, you're welcome to have your own expert examine them, but I can't make another trip here to your office. I intend to close a deal as soon as possible and I have three other potential buyers to see today. The other three are experts themselves and won't have to waste time hiring someone to check out the pistols. I'm sure you understand. However, if I don't reach an agreement with one of those three today, feel free to contact me again and set up a time to have your man look over the guns."

The subtle insult had its effect. Kincaid clearly did not like the implication that he was not enough of an expert to reach his own decision. But he covered his reaction with cool poise. "I'll consider that. Keep me informed about the outcome of your negotiations today." He deliberately turned away from Jonas and walked over to stand beside Verity at the window. "Lovely view, isn't it, Miss Ames?"

"Very." She practiced her smile and noticed that Damon Kincaid seemed quite fascinated by it. Maybe she ought to use it on more men more often. "You're lucky to have this office, Mr. Kincaid. If I had it, I don't think I'd get much work done. The view is too much of a distraction."

"You get accustomed to it," he assured her with a smile. "It's easy to become accustomed to beauty. Too easy, perhaps. Eventually one finds that a superficially beautiful view or pistol or woman needs more than simple attractiveness to hold a man's attention."

Verity looked up at him. "The pistols are beautiful in their own way, but because they've never been used for their intended purpose, they lack a certain element of interest for you."

Kincaid smiled approvingly. "You are very perceptive, Miss Ames. That is exactly the case." He indicated the swords and rapiers on the walls. "These weapons all have histories. I do not collect ceremonial or dress swords, only those that I have reason to believe were used by the men who carried them." He glanced at Jonas. "Do you know anything about swords, Mr. Quarrel, or is your expertise limited to pistols?"

Jonas's eyes were cold and unreadable as he took in the sight of Damon Kincaid standing very close to Verity. "I know a little about swords." He flicked a glance toward a long, tapered rapier on the wall nearest him. "Enough to know that the dagger hanging next to that Italian rapier is a reproduction."

"A reproduction!" Kincaid's suave poise was momentarily shattered. He recovered quickly, however. "You must be mistaken. I bought that dagger from a very reliable source. It's late sixteenth century."

Jonas raised his brows and strolled over to take a closer look. "Mind if I handle it?"

Kincaid hesitated, then shrugged. "Go ahead."

Verity realized she was holding her breath. She wondered if Jonas was going to test himself again. She knew he was eager to explore his new command of his talent, but this wasn't the time or place for such experiments. However, she couldn't think of any way to stop him. She braced herself for the impact of finding herself in the long corridor.

Then she remembered that he had claimed the dagger was a fake. If it was a reproduction, she told herself in relief, it shouldn't have any effect on him. She relaxed again.

Jonas took the dagger down from the wall. Verity trembled as a flickering image of the psychic tunnel slithered in and out of her mind. It didn't take a firm, solid shape the way it had the last time she had seen it. It was as if this part of the corridor were not as completely constructed; as if it were somehow *newer*.

There was a brief impression of Jonas's presence but she couldn't see him. She was turning around to look at him when a hazy image appeared in the corridor behind her. Thinking it might be Jonas, she hurried toward it. She did not like being alone in this psychic tunnel.

She was almost on top of the image before it crystallized briefly into a scene of an old-fashioned, formal dining room. There was a man seated in an ornate armchair at the far end of an inlaid table. He was clutching at his heart, a stricken expression on his aging, florid face. He seemed to be staring past her toward someone who was not present.

Heart attack, Verity thought, instinctively moving forward. But even as she watched the man pitched forward, the upper half of his body sprawling across a plate of what appeared to be linguini with prawns.

It was then that Verity saw the blood. It welled from the man's chest, mingling with the linguini and turning the white cream sauce a sickly shade of red.

Verity halted in shock. No one bled like that from a heart attack. Her mind whirled as fear and a terrible sensation of violence swirled around her. Writhing tendrils of emotion leaped from the image and dived toward her.

Verity turned to run and collided with Jonas. He grabbed her wrist, his eyes narrow and grim as he looked at the flickering, fading scene behind her.

"It's okay," he said roughly. "It's okay, honey. I'm releasing the dagger. We're out of here."

An instant later the half-formed corridor and the dying man at the dinner table popped out of existence in Verity's mind. She opened her eyes and nearly lost her balance. Automatically she reached out to steady herself and found herself grabbing Damon Kincaid's arm.

"I beg your pardon?" Kincaid, who had been watching Jonas with close attention, glanced down at Verity's hand on his arm. "Something wrong, Miss Ames?"

"No, nothing." She took a deep breath and tried another of the smiles Jonas had instructed her to apply. "I just felt a bit dizzy for a moment. I haven't eaten today. Time for lunch." She let go of Kincaid's expensive jacket sleeve. Across the room, Jonas had restored the dagger to the wall. He was watching her with a furious glint in his eyes as she freed their host's arm.

Kincaid glanced at the thin gold and steel watch on his wrist. "You're right," he said jovially. "It is almost lunchtime. I would be pleased if the two of you would allow me to take you out to a meal as a thank-you for bringing the duelers here to my office." He looked at Verity, not Jonas, for an acceptance of his invitation.

Verity, still reorienting herself, looked at Jonas for guidance. She didn't want to kill a potential deal by making the wrong choice here.

Jonas took immediate command of the situation.

"No, thanks," he said coldly. "Verity and I have to be on our way. We've got a lot to do today. Are you ready, Verity?"

"Yes, Jonas," she said meekly, trying out the sweet smile

again. She was curious to see if it had any direct effect on him the way it seemed to have had on Kincaid.

"Let's go." He closed the mahogany pistol case and started for the door. He appeared to be totally unaware of Verity's fluff-brained smile.

"Just a moment," Kincaid said as they reached the door. "You didn't give me your final verdict on the dagger. Still think it's a phony now that you've had a chance to handle it?"

"It's not sixteenth century," Jonas said from the doorway. "More like 1955. Excellent work, but definitely a reproduction."

Kincaid's mouth hardened. "You must be mistaken."

Jonas shrugged. "Suit yourself." He started to close the door and then paused one last time. "If I were you, though, I'd be careful about dealing with whoever sold that dagger to you."

"Why do you say that?"

"For one thing, he sold you a reproduction. For another, I get the feeling his acquisition technique is a little crude."

"What the devil are you talking about?" Kincaid looked furious.

"Forget it. Probably just some minor professional jealousy on my part. After all, he got a fortune out of you for a fake and I couldn't even sell you a genuine set of pistols. Goodbye, Mr. Kincaid."

Kincaid stared at the door as it closed. He was torn between rage and a deep sense of danger. He stabbed the intercom on his desk.

"Get Hatch in here."

"Yes, Mr. Kincaid."

Hatch appeared almost immediately, his colorless eyes blandly inquiring. "Yes, sir?"

"Get hold of Gelkirk. I want him here in one hour."

"The appraiser? I'll call him immediately."

William Gelkirk scuttled nervously into Kincaid's office forty-five minutes later. He was a rotund little man with a fringe of hair surrounding a bald head and small eyes that looked out at the world through thick lenses. Kincaid found him irritating, fussy, and boring, but there was no doubt that Gelkirk was one of the finest authorities on sixteenth-century armor on the West Coast. He had appraised a few items for Kincaid in the past, but Kincaid had not consulted him about the dagger.

Kincaid had been very certain of the dagger's authenticity. After all, he had removed it himself from the vault the night he had calmly shot Henry Wilcox dead. The police had declared the incident a random act of violence since nothing seemed to be missing from Wilcox's Beverly Hills mansion. No one had known about the dagger. Wilcox had only recently acquired it and not yet insured it.

Wilcox had been so proud of the dagger, Kincaid remembered. The first time he had displayed it was to a fellow collector whom he knew would appreciate it. Kincaid had taken one look at it, considered its untraceability, and decided he appreciated the weapon far more than Wilcox did. He made his decision and acted on it immediately. He used Wilcox's personal gun, the one the older man kept in his desk drawer to protect himself in the event of a break-in.

The police were always warning people that weapons kept in the home were far more likely to be used against the owners than in self-defense. In this case, they were right, as usual.

Kincaid no longer did his own acquisition work. He now had the kind of contacts that enabled him to contract out that sort of thing. But back in his younger days he had been much more impetuous.

He forced a reassuring smile as he handed the dagger to Gelkirk. "It was very kind of you to come on such short notice. I'm extremely anxious for your opinion on this dagger. For years I assumed it was the genuine article, sixteenth century, Italian. But recently someone put some doubts in my head. If you would be so good as to give me your opinion? The usual rates, of course."

Gelkirk nodded eagerly and took the dagger. He peered at the ornately fashioned grip and then carried it to the window to examine the steel blade in sunlight.

"I'd have to run some tests to be certain, but my first impression is that this is not sixteenth century. It just isn't heavy enough. They had good steel in those days, legendary steel, but it wasn't this light. My guess is that the blade, at least, is modern. Would you like me to take it back to my shop and check it more thoroughly?"

Kincaid contained his fury behind a facade of rueful gratitude. "No, I don't think that will be necessary. I may follow up later to see just how badly I've been had, but in the meantime I'll take your word for it. This experience will teach me always to get a second opinion before I buy. Thank you, Mr. Gelkirk. My secretary will issue you a check for your services and call you a cab."

Gelkirk beamed. "Anytime, Mr. Kincaid. Anytime. I'm always pleased to be of service to a dedicated collector such as yourself. And don't feel too bad about the dagger. It really is an excellent reproduction. A lot of experts wouldn't have been suspicious."

"I'll take what comfort I can from that," Kincaid said dryly, holding the door for Gelkirk. He waited impatiently for the little man to walk through and then closed it with a carefully controlled slam.

"Goddammit."

He took three long strides across the marble floor and snatched up the brass-plated telephone. The number he dialed was unlisted. It was answered on the second ring by a man's voice that confirmed the number but offered no greeting.

"This is Kincaid. I want to talk to Tresslar."

The male receptionist did not respond verbally. He simply made the connection. A few minutes later a low-pitched voice with a thick southern accent answered.

"Yeah?"

"Tresslar?"

"You got it."

Kincaid winced at the accent. "I have a job for your firm. Do you have someone available?"

"Sure. I always have a man available. Rates have gone up some since we last worked for you, though."

"That's not a problem as long as I get reliable service."

"You got it."

Kincaid described Jonas and the location of the restaurant in Sequence Springs. "His name is Quarrel. Jonas Quarrel. I want it to look like the work of a small-time thief who got scared and used his gun on his victim. That sort of thing happens all the time these days. The police can only investigate so far before they give up and wait for the thief to try his luck again."

"You got it."

Kincaid wondered how many more times he could deal with Tresslar before the accent got to him. "The money will be deposited to your account under the same arrangements as last time. Half up front. Half when the job is done."

"How soon you want this done?"

"As soon as possible. This week, in fact."

"You got it." Tresslar hung up the phone.

Kincaid gritted his teeth and hung up his receiver. Then he stalked to the window.

There was no doubt about it. Quarrel had to be eliminated. He was turning into a major question mark. It appeared that he did indeed have the "touch." And he was somehow involved with Caitlin Evanger. According to Hatch, he had been invited to the exclusive little get-together being held in two weeks at the house on the cliffs.

Quarrel could easily be representing a mysterious collector who wanted *Bloodlust*. But that wasn't the reason Kincaid wanted him dead. Kincaid was confident he could compete financially against almost anyone. He had had Quarrel investigated only because he wanted to know in advance exactly what he would be up against. But now there was something more involved. Kincaid's instincts were aroused at last.

Kincaid wanted Quarrel dead because he had seen the look on Quarrel's face when he held the dagger in his hand. For just a moment Quarrel's cool, sardonic expression had been replaced with another. It was an expression of sudden, jarring recognition. It was as if Quarrel had somehow *known* the blade at once, not just as a fake but for what it was, the cause of a murder.

And then there had been that parting crack at the door about the ethics of the "dealer" who had sold Kincaid the dagger.

Kincaid watched the sailboats on the Bay and drummed his neatly manicured fingers on the glass.

Whoever Quarrel was, it was plain he knew too much. There was no question about it. Kincaid didn't understand how or why, but he didn't question his instincts. He had survived on those instincts for years and he trusted them implicitly. Better to be safe than sorry.

There were too many factors coming together lately, he reflected. Coincidence was acceptable up to a point, but one too many made a man nervous. The appearance of Quarrel, with his mysterious ability, was too much to swallow in addition to this business of having to go back to the house on the cliffs. Something dangerous was afoot. The more Kincaid thought about it, the more everything seemed to be slowly focusing around Jonas Quarrel.

It was very disquieting that Quarrel had picked out that single dagger from all the blades on the wall. It gave Kincaid a strange, hunted feeling.

Rumors stayed alive for years in the world of collecting. Eventually some of them became legends. Kincaid did not like the notion that his dagger might be the basis of some unfortunate rumors that led back to him.

It was definitely time to get rid of Jonas Quarrel.

And when he was finished with Quarrel, Kincaid decided,

he just might make it a point to get to know the little redhead better. Something about her smile had revived the old thrilling lust, the kind he had once indulged in Sandquist's house on the cliffs. He hadn't been able to luxuriate in that side of his nature for a long while.

Chapter Fourteen

A deal for the dueling pistols was made with one Phillip J. Haggerty late Monday afternoon. Jonas presented the buyer's check to Emerson Ames on Tuesday morning when he and Verity arrived back in Sequence Springs. Emerson kissed the check.

"I do believe you've saved my hind end, Jonas, old pal," Emerson chortled. "Here, have a beer and tell me all about it."

They were standing in Verity's kitchen as she tried to set up for the luncheon crowd. Verity's hands were full with a stack of stainless steel salad-mixing bowls. She glared at both men as she was forced to maneuver sideways to get around them. "Jonas can't have a beer now. He has to help me with lunch."

"Don't pay any attention to her." Jonas popped the top off the can and tipped back his head to take a long, thirsty swallow. "The Tuesday lunch crowd is the lightest of the week. She just needs something to complain about. You know how it is. Besides, I can wash dishes just as well drunk as sober."

Her father chuckled richly, but Verity felt herself flushing as Jonas proceeded to give Emerson the tale of their visit to the city. She turned away to take a potato and pea salad out of the refrigerator. Normally she responded to Jonas's cracks about her shrewishness with equanimity, but today, she discovered, his words hurt. Maybe she really was turning into a mean-spirited, fussy spinster.

Or maybe she was frequently sharp with Jonas because a part of her was trying to protect herself from the uncertain future she saw awaiting her. It was easier and far safer to yell at Jonas than to let herself fall in love with him.

But Verity was very much afraid her tactics weren't working. She was scared to death that she had already fallen in love with Jonas. That knowledge seemed only to whet the edge of her tongue.

Jonas finished the tale of their trip to San Francisco, elaborating cheerfully on his brilliant handling of the negotiations.

"So that was that," he concluded triumphantly. "After getting the price up another three thousand, I accepted Haggerty's offer. After that, Verity and I went shopping for costumes for that damned Renaissance ball Evanger's planning. Verity went crazy in the costume store, by the way. I had to forcibly restrain her at times. You should have seen the gown she wanted to rent. Scarlet and gold, and it was cut to her navel."

"It was a beautiful gown. And very authentic. They wore lots of low-cut gowns during the Renaissance," Verity defended herself as she added stone-ground mustard to her potato and pea salad.

"Who's the authority on the Renaissance around here, anyway?" Jonas retorted. "That dress you wanted looked like it was designed for an expensive call girl."

"I wanted to go as a Renaissance courtesan."

Jonas smiled grimly. "Be grateful I didn't rent the nun's outfit for you."

Verity raised her eyebrows as she looked at her father. "He was in a terrible mood when we went into the costume shop, even though he'd made that great deal for the pistols.

He'd been annoyed with me ever since we left Kincaid's office."

"She kept smiling at the bastard," Jonas muttered.

"I was only following orders. Your orders, Jonas," Verity said pointedly. "You're the one who told me to smile at the man, remember? I was supposed to play the part of a fluff-brained redhead."

"You didn't have to go overboard, dammit. He was looking at you the way a shark looks at a swimmer's feet."

Emerson held up a palm, seeking peace. "Children, children, that's enough squabbling for now. This is too grand a day to ruin with bickering. Save your fighting for later."

"Good idea," Verity said. "I'm too busy to fight now anyway. But you haven't heard the whole story of our little adventure, Dad. Jonas didn't tell you that he tested himself again on a dagger that was hanging on the wall of Kincaid's office."

Emerson cocked a bushy brow. "Is that right? Same thing as when you handled the gun? A mental image in a long corridor?"

"The corridor seemed different this time," Verity answered. "Vaguer, somehow. Less clear and defined. But there was a scene in it. A horrible one. It was an image of a man sprawled on a dinner table. Blood all over the linguini."

Jonas studied the small print on his beer can. "I've been thinking about the lack of definition in the corridor itself," he said slowly. "I wonder if it's got something to do with the fact that the dagger and the scene we encountered were only a few years old. Maybe the psychic energy they generate is still coalescing and shaping itself. The thing is, I shouldn't have been able to pick up on anything that recent."

"Did you know the dagger was twentieth century when you asked Kincaid to let you handle it?" Verity asked.

Jonas nodded. "I was almost certain it was a reproduction. There was something about the look of the steel. The instant I touched it I knew it was contemporary, but at the same time it was giving off vibrations like crazy." He shook his head. "I don't understand it, unless . . ."

Verity bit her lip. "Unless what?"

He gave her a disturbingly direct look. "Unless being around you is having the same effect all that testing back at Vincent College did."

"You mean your talent might be getting stronger?" Verity asked uneasily.

"Yeah."

There was silence in the kitchen as they both considered the ramifications of that. Emerson looked curiously from one to the other. "Trouble?"

"Jonas considers his ability a mixed blessing," Verity explained quietly. "But at least up until now it's been limited to a certain era of the past. If he's getting stronger in terms of range, he's going to run into more and more objects that will trigger his trips into the corridor."

"I get it," Emerson drawled. "Could get to be a real nuisance, couldn't it?"

"To put it mildly," Jonas agreed. "Damn." He crumpled the beer can in his hand. "I could have done without this added complication."

Verity felt a cold chill. She was the cause of this "added complication" in his life. Her fingers clenched tightly around the bowl in her hand. Jonas had been drawn to her originally because of her connection with his psychic ability. Maybe that was the very thing that would drive him away from her.

"The psychometry still seems to be limited to objects associated strongly with violence, though," Jonas said thoughtfully. "I'm not picking up on just any old emotion, thank God."

"What do you think that scene in the corridor was all about?" Emerson asked curiously.

"I don't know," Jonas said. "That's the problem with these corridor scenes. I never get more than a few seconds of information. It's like looking at a few frames on a reel of film. Probably the frames that show the single most violent moment associated with the object I'm holding. It's the one image that's most clearly captured, for some reason. Sometimes I feel like I'm part of the image. I know what's going on around me for those few seconds. But other times, it's like looking at a photograph of people I don't know. That's the way it was yesterday."

"Don't you have any theories about why that dagger elicited that particular image of a man bleeding into a plate of linguini?" Emerson persisted.

Jonas shrugged. "If I had to hazard a guess, I'd say we were probably looking at the former owner of the dagger at the moment when he lost possession of it to someone else. Or we could have been looking at someone who had just been stabbed with it."

Verity was startled. "That's funny. For some reason, I assumed the man had been shot."

Jonas gave her a thoughtful glance. "Did you? It's possible."

Emerson shook his head. "This is incredible. I didn't know what to think the night you tried that first test with the pistols and I still don't. I tell myself I have an open mind, but Christ, this is stretching the limits of it, I'll tell you. You do realize how bizarre this whole thing is, don't you?"

"It's been pointed out to me," Jonas said dryly.

Emerson shook his head. "It's one thing to think you might have a touch of psychic talent. Hell, lots of people are convinced they've had a psychic experience of one kind or another. Telepathy, a bit of precognition, whatever. It's damn common, in fact. But this business of both of you seeing the same images in some mental corridor is downright spooky. I'd swear you were both lying except that I know my daughter too well. Verity doesn't lie. And I don't think you'd bother with this kind of elaborate fiction, Jonas. Too much work involved."

"That's the truth." Jonas spoke with great feeling. He tossed his crunched beer can into a trash basket in the corner. "But if you think this whole thing is weird, imagine what it's like for me. I've been assuming for years that I'm the only one on the face of the planet who sees these damned visions when I'm handling old junk." He looked at Verity, his eyes molten gold. "It's one hell of a relief to find someone who can share the experience with me. At least I can be relatively certain that if I'm slowly going insane, I'm not going there alone."

Emerson looked at both of them. "Neither of you is crazy and neither of you is a liar. We're stuck with the only other conclusion—there really is some kind of mental weirdness going on between the two of you. Tell me more about the guy who was bleeding into the linguini."

"There's not much to tell," Verity said. "I had just turned around and spotted the image when Jonas came up behind me and said we were getting out of there."

"But he was definitely connected with the dagger?"

"Probably," Jonas said slowly. "I've always had the impression that the people who show up in the corridor images are directly connected with the object I'm holding at the time. But I don't always understand the connection."

Verity wiped her hands on her apron. "The clothes the man was wearing looked a little out-of-date. Maybe ten or fifteen years old."

"You were very observant," Jonas remarked, eyeing her curiously. "You didn't mention the age of his clothes when we talked this over last night. Did you notice anything else?"

"No, except maybe a feeling that the guy knew who it was who had just killed him. The poor man looked so astonished, as if he wasn't expecting anything like that to happen. Almost as if the other person was a friend."

"I think you're right," Jonas said reflectively. "Although I guess it's equally possible a stranger walked into the room and shot him. A man caught unawares like that could have the same expression of astonishment on his face."

"What about Kincaid?" Emerson asked shrewdly. "Do you think he knows anything about the history of the dagger on his wall?"

Jonas lifted one shoulder in a negligent gesture. "Who knows? He thought the dagger was a genuine sixteenth-century piece, I do know that. He was furious when I told him it was a reproduction. He probably paid a fortune for it. But most collectors like him don't ask too many questions about the recent past of an object they want to buy. The less they know, the better, as far as they're concerned. If someone shot and killed a man to get hold of that dagger and sell it at huge profit to a fanatic collector like himself, Kincaid wouldn't want to know about it. Just as Haggerty didn't push too hard to know the recent history of those pistols. It was enough for him that they were genuine."

"I can understand that line of thinking, although I've always thought it was better to be informed than take a chance on being hung out to dry. Ignorance is not bliss. But I guess we can assume that Kincaid doesn't know too much about the dagger," Emerson concluded.

"He didn't even know it was fake," Verity scoffed. She shoved a pan of pasta into Jonas's hand. "Here, put this on the counter behind you."

He looked down at the pile of naked, steaming noodles. "What is it?"

"Linguini. I was going to make a red sauce for it, but for some reason I changed my mind this morning. I'm going to make a nice green pesto sauce instead."

Much later that evening Verity did something she hadn't done since her affair with Jonas had fully blossomed. She left Jonas and her father playing chess in her father's cabin, grabbed her terrycloth robe, and headed for the peace and solitude of the empty spa. Both men were concentrating so hard on their game that they barely noticed her departure.

The blue and white tiled room was empty, as it always was at this time of night. Verity left most of the lights off, turning on only the few she needed to find her way to her favorite pool. She stripped off her jeans and blouse and slid nude into the pool.

When she was submerged to her neck, Verity leaned back and contemplated the recent chain of events. She had found a lover, discovered a rather useless psychic talent, and become friends with a famous artist, all in the space of a few short weeks. The quiet, orderly lifestyle she had painstakingly created for herself in the past few years had been severely altered.

The question was, how much of it would last and for how long? The psychic talent was connected to the lover who would undoubtedly go away one of these days, and the famous artist was on the point of giving up her brilliant career. Compared to everything else going on around Verity, her restaurant business looked stable.

Verity decided not to dwell on the psychic connection she shared with Jonas. It was too disturbing, too fraught with unanswerable questions. Tonight she preferred to deal with hard facts.

The first hard fact that came to mind involved herself. She closed her eyes and wondered if she really was turning into a shrew. That led to the question of how long any man would hang around such a woman.

It was easier to wonder about that than about how long a man would hang around a woman who was causing his weird psychic ability to get stronger and more weird.

"You are not, by any chance, sitting naked in that pool because you knew I'd be along after a while, are you?"

Jonas's indulgent voice, sounding unabashedly hopeful, took Verity by surprise. Her eyes snapped open. Instantly she was violently aware of her nudity. Considering all the nights she had spent with Jonas, her flushed reaction was ridiculous. With any luck he would attribute the pinkness in her cheeks to the heat of the mineral water.

"I thought you were playing chess with Dad," Verity said quickly.

"I was playing chess with him until he won. My mind was wandering. We've scheduled a rematch for tomorrow night. I went looking for you and discovered you were not tied up in a red bow and waiting in bed for me." Jonas came to a halt at the edge of the pool and began unfastening the buttons of his blue work shirt with lazy intent.

"When have you ever found me wearing a red bow and waiting in bed for you?"

His grin was wickedly knowing. "Never, but a man can fantasize, can't he?" His eyes moved over her body, most of it quite visible in the crystal-clear water. "Don't worry, finding you this way is just as good."

Verity stirred and glanced toward the entrance of the spa room. "What if Laura shows up again the way she did the last time we were here together?"

"I doubt she'll be terribly surprised at what she finds." Jonas tossed his shirt aside. His long fingers went to work unbuttoning his jeans.

Verity watched, half-mesmerized by the sexy sight of Jonas undressing. He took his time about it, revealing his strong shoulders and flat stomach first. The hair on his chest seemed to offer an open invitation for her fingers to scamper through it. When he stepped out of his jeans he was already partially aroused.

Verity cleared her throat. "Are you practicing to be a striptease artist?"

He slanted her a laconic smile and moved into the water. "I don't believe in teasing you, little tyrant. What you see is what you get." He spread his arms out along the edge of the pool and leaned back, savoring the hot water. "Damn, this feels good."

Verity held her breath for a few seconds and then rushed into the question that was hovering in her mind: "Do you really think I'm a petty tyrant?"

"Little, not petty. There is nothing petty about you, honey. But there are a few little things I could mention." He half-opened one eye, obviously prepared to turn the conversation into sexy channels.

"Jonas, I'm serious," Verity said urgently. "You think I'm a shrew, don't you?"

"It's part of your charm," he assured her blandly.

Verity got angry. "No, it's not part of my charm. You're always pointing it out and making rude remarks about it. And now there's this other thing about your talent getting more bothersome. Let's face it, Jonas, I'm not your kind of woman."

"Oh, hell." He closed his eye again. "I get the feeling someone is spoiling for a fight tonight, and it's not me."

"I'm not looking for a fight. I just want to clarify a few things."

"Such as?"

"Such as why you're hanging around."

"I'm hanging around because I need the job and I have discovered that sleeping with you is like sleeping with a cactus. Once a man gets past the thorns, the fruit is very sweet."

"If that's supposed to thrill me, you're in for a surprise. I don't like being compared to a cactus," Verity muttered, feeling put upon. She was prepared for an intense, in-depth, thoroughgoing discussion of their relationship, but Jonas was in a bantering mood.

He put his hand on her shoulder and pulled her against his side. "Hey, what is this?" he asked gently. "We're supposed to be relaxing after a long, hard day."

"I'd like us to be honest with each other, Jonas. You find me a shrew and a tyrant. You say I'm sarcastic. I don't pay well. Furthermore, we're complete opposites in a lot of ways. We don't even share similar nutritional habits. There is nothing between us but sex and your weird psychic talent."

"I've got news for you, honey. That's a lot to have between us. More than I've ever had with any other woman." He lifted his dark lashes again and examined her intense expression. "And it's more than you've ever had with any other man."

Verity leaned back against his arm. "Maybe we're just using each other. You need me to explore your psychic abilities and I need you to give me a taste of what passion is all about."

"Even if that's all there is to this relationship of ours," Jonas said roughly, "it's enough for now. Verity, you're going to drive yourself nuts if you dwell on this too much. Just relax and go with the flow."

"That's good advice for someone like you who's lived by that principle for years. But I'm different, Jonas."

"I know," he said wryly. "You're going to spend an enormous amount of time and energy dissecting our relationship, examining it inside and out, and generally working yourself up about something that should just be taken one day at a time. It's your nature to try to label and organize things."

"You're right," she agreed. "Maybe we'd better change the subject. When's Dad going to pay off that shark?"

"Reginald C. Yarington? In a couple of days. As soon as Haggerty's check clears, I imagine."

"I hope Dad doesn't get so excited by the prospect of having all that money in his hands that he rushes out and places a few bets at the track instead of paying off the shark," Verity said worriedly.

"Don't worry, I'm certain Emerson will pay off his loan. He really does think of a gambling debt as a debt of honor, you know. He also assures me that Yarington is not a man to be trifled with. Emerson doesn't want to have to spend the next few years looking over his shoulder."

Verity shuddered. "Dad and I owe you for this, Jonas," she said very seriously. "You helped us a lot by handling the sale of those pistols. Neither of us would have known how to go about contacting big-time private collectors and we wouldn't have been sure of what to ask for the guns."

His hand tightened abruptly on her bare shoulder. "Let's get something straight, Verity. Your dad may feel he owes me a favor or two, but you don't owe me anything. Got that?"

She was startled by the harshness of his voice and the fierceness of his grip. "But, Jonas, we do owe you, and even though you think I'm a shrew, I want you to know that I always pay my debts."

"Shut up, Verity," he said gently. "There is no debt between us, and if you bring up the matter one more time I may do something rash. And for the record, I don't mind taming the occasional shrew. A man needs a challenge once in a while. *Ouch!*" He doubled over, clutching at his ribs as Verity landed a quick punch.

"Just how many shrews have you tamed?" she asked a little too sweetly.

"You're the first," he admitted, still holding his ribs. "And at this rate, you may be the last. One shrew per lifetime may be the limit for any man."

Satisfied, Verity settled back against his arm. Her mood had suddenly lightened, she discovered. On to other topics of conversation. "What are you going to do now that you've started exploring your talent again, Jonas? Go back to teaching history? Or work for a museum?"

"I don't want to go back to teaching. I've been away from it too long. One thing I discovered during the past five years is that I don't miss grading exams or lecturing to a classroom full of students who're more concerned with the development of their sex lives than with the contrast between Renaissance humanism and Renaissance military philosophy. To put it simply, teaching sucks. But it has crossed my mind that I could go back to making a few bucks doing consulting work. It pays well, doesn't demand a lot of time, and it's interesting."

"You said something earlier today about getting stronger," Verity said slowly. "Do you think you'll get to the point where one of these days you won't need me to anchor you when you enter that corridor?"

Jonas sighed. "I don't know. I just don't know, Verity. I've got as many questions as you have about what happens between us when we enter that corridor."

They sat in silence for a few minutes. Verity turned Jonas's words over in her mind. He was right, she was dwelling on the relationship far too much. Verity wondered if Caitlin Evanger had ever found herself involved with a man to the point where she spent a great deal of time and energy fretting about the relationship.

"What are you thinking about?" Jonas asked whimsically.

"I was thinking about Caitlin; wondering if she ever had a great love in her life."

"I doubt it," Jonas said with flat certainty. "I can't see her loving anything but her art, and she's apparently planning to abandon that."

"I think there's a lot more to her than you can see," Verity said earnestly. "I wouldn't be surprised if she went through some great trauma at some point in the past. Something other than the car accident, I mean. Perhaps she was badly hurt emotionally. No one withdraws from the world the way she has without a good reason."

"Some people are born cold-blooded, Verity. Take my word for it. I've met men who can kill with as little concern as they apply to eating breakfast." He paused. "Kincaid's cold."

Verity glanced at him in astonishment. "What makes you say that?"

"Something in his eyes when he looked at you. Don't tell me: you found him warm, charming, and attractive, right?"

She thought about it. "To tell you the truth, I didn't know quite how to take him."

"He'd take you in a hot second if he thought he could get you into bed."

Verity nearly choked. *"What?* Are you serious, Jonas?" She was shocked. "I'm not his type at all."

"Yes, you are," Jonas said thoughtfully. "A man like Kincaid has a lot of types, and one of them would be the bright-eyed, fresh, wholesome type. Just the type to cleanse the palate after a surfeit of sophistication and glamour. You don't know how perpetually innocent you look, honey. There's a genuineness about you that makes a man think you'd hold nothing back if he could just get you into bed. If

I hadn't been around, I have a hunch Kincaid might have tried to seduce you. If you were still a virgin and he had known it, I would probably have had to use that dagger on him to keep him away from you. Not because he had fallen for one Verity Ames on sight, but because he's the kind of creep who gets off on the idea of seducing virgins. Hell, the main reason I pulled that stunt with the dagger was that I wanted to get his attention off you. I knew that for him, the idea that he might have been conned would be a whole lot more important than any woman."

Verity was stunned. She stared at Jonas, open-mouthed in astonishment. "Do you really believe that Damon was attracted to me?"

"Don't look so dumbfounded. I'm a man. Give me some credit for being able to judge the members of my own species. And like I said, it wasn't you, the person, that attracted him; it was you, the sweetly smiling innocent, he wanted."

"Dammit, I am not an innocent!" She frowned fiercely and touched the tip of her nose. "Maybe it's the freckles that give people that impression."

Jonas chuckled indulgently, bent his head, and kissed her parted lips with quick, hard possessiveness. "I find it very reassuring to know we're highly unlikely to ever run into Damon Kincaid again. The truth is, I'm glad you live here at Sequence Springs, where the population of available males is, according to your friend Laura, as limited as hen's teeth."

Verity shook her head in amazement. "Well, I'll be darned. Damon Kincaid. Who would have thought . . . ?"

"Don't get any ideas," Jonas interrupted dryly. "I can see I should have kept my mouth shut. Now I suppose your female ego will be inflated to triple its normal large size. I should have known better than to do anything to stroke it."

Verity smiled brilliantly and nuzzled close to Jonas. "Actually, there are other portions of my anatomy that I wouldn't mind having stroked."

Jonas smiled slowly, a sexy grin. "Is that right? You must tell me exactly where, my sweet, in great detail."

Verity forced back a blush. She still wasn't accustomed to all the freewheeling, sensual nuances of Jonas's lovemaking. "You already know where," she said, her lips against his chest.

His arm closed around her and he lifted her onto his thighs. "I want the words, honey. I love it when you talk dirty."

"Pervert."

"You love it," he said confidently.

Not only that, Verity thought wistfully, *I think I love you, too. What am I going to do when you leave, Jonas?* But she didn't say those words. Instead, when she felt his hand part her legs under the water, she gave him the words he wanted to hear. Words that begged, promised, cajoled, and pleaded. Jonas drank them from her lips while his hand moved in precise response to her every command.

When she tried to wriggle around so that he could enter her, Jonas held her still.

"Not so fast, love. Verity is the spice of life," he said. "I'm going to show you just how spicy you can be." Then his long fingers moved inside her, probing the narrow, warm passage until she was shuddering in his arms. Her legs tightened around his hand and he laughed softly.

"So hot," he whispered as he leaned down to kiss one nipple that projected above the surface of the water. "Clean, hot, honest fire. Burn for me, baby."

And she did, until she was a trembling, twisting wanton in his arms, a woman who craved the man who could do such things to her. When he thrust his tongue into her mouth and simultaneously thrust two fingers deeply, slowly into her body, Verity cried out. He held her tightly as she convulsed delightfully in his arms.

"Now we'll go back to your cabin and I'll get my turn," he announced, heaving himself up out of the water with Verity cradled against his chest.

She looked down as he set her on her feet and reached for their clothing. His iron-hard manhood appeared ready to explode. Dreamily she put out a hand to cup him with soft fingers.

"I'll never make it back to your place if you keep that up," he warned in a husky voice.

Verity smiled at him and continued to stroke him gently. Jonas took one look at her smile and groaned in surrender.

"I guess we can always go back to the cabin later," he muttered.

He put her down on top of the pile of clothing, parted her legs with hands that trembled with passion, and thrust himself heavily into her warmth. Verity tightened herself around him, drawing him into her until he was lost.

A long while later Jonas slid out of Verity's bed and pulled on his jeans and boots. He hooked his shirt over one shoulder and turned to take one last look at Verity, who woke up long enough to smile sleepily.

"Good night, Jonas."

"Good night," he muttered and let himself out of her cottage. It was cold outside. He shrugged into the shirt but didn't bother to button it. He would be inside again soon enough.

He remembered what Emerson had said a few nights ago when Jonas had tried to let himself silently into the cabin.

"All that racket. Night after night. Why the hell don't you just move in with her?" Emerson had complained in a muffled voice.

"I haven't received an invitation," Jonas had growled back.

Tonight her small but persistent act of independence bothered him more than ever. He sensed that by sending him away each night she was somehow trying to preserve the fiction that he was only a casual, part-time lover to her, not someone to whom she had committed herself, body and soul.

Jonas walked quickly down the short path through the trees to the other cabin. The stars were almost hidden by the canopy of dark branches overhead. The lake was a black mirror silvered with moonlight. Jonas saw that Emerson had left on the old, weak porch light. He paced toward the small yellow beacon, his mind on Verity's body and soul. He had to admit that his thoughts were probably weighted more toward her body, which he had thoroughly enjoyed tonight, than they were toward her soul.

She was so incredibly responsive. He'd never felt anything like the way he felt when she tightened her legs around him and pulled him to her.

Jonas was wondering what to do about the erection he was developing when he caught the faint movement out of the corner of his eye.

It was nothing more than a shadow that merged almost immediately with the right-side wall of Emerson's cottage. Too high off the ground to be a stray dog hunting for open garbage cans. Too motionless now to be anything but a man. No tree branch would be so still.

Jonas did not break his stride. The last thing he wanted to do was broadcast the news that he had been warned. The front door would be unlocked—Emerson would have left it open for him—but Jonas could hardly approach it now.

He kept moving toward the cottage but then suddenly veered to the left, using the trees as shelter. The back of the cottage, where the window with the broken lock was, would be shrouded in darkness, unlike the front door, which was lit with the pale glow of the porch light. As he moved, Jonas kept every available object between him and the shadow.

He walked behind Emerson's rented Buick, stayed to the left of his own Jeep, and put a few richly branched trees between himself and the cottage.

Jonas made it to the shelter of the left side of the cottage and halted. If the intruder was simply a vagrant who had been nosing around, he would probably choose this moment to flee into the trees, unseen. However, if he had more interesting intentions, he might wait until Jonas was in the cottage before making his move.

Jonas found the open window and raised it quickly. It squeaked with protest. The sound echoed loudly in the night. Emerson stirred on the bed as Jonas swung one leg over the sill.

"Coming through the window is a good way to get your throat slit. Ask me, I know."

"Emerson," Jonas whispered, "I think we've got company outside."

"No shit?" Emerson sat up, fully alert. "Where?"

Jonas explained, keeping his voice low. "If he's going to invite himself inside, he'll probably use a window. If he's already checked the place out, he'll know this one has a broken lock."

Emerson rolled out of bed wearing only his briefs. "Should be simple enough. There's two of us and one of him." He went to stand in the shadows to the left of the window, moving with surprising quiet for a man his size.

Jonas went over to his duffel bag, unzipped it, and slipped his knife out of its sheath. He was heading toward the opposite side of the window when the front door slammed open without any preliminary scratching at the lock. The intruder must have tested it earlier and found it unlocked.

Almost simultaneously light splashed the room from the overhead bulb as the man in the doorway hit the switch. He crouched there in a gunman's stance. He was dressed in a camouflage shirt and dark pants. There was a death's-head grin on his all-American farmboy face.

The .357 magnum in his hand did not look like it had come off the farm. It looked very big-city. It also appeared that its owner knew how to use it. The gun was pointed at Emerson, who did not so much as blink an eye. As if he suddenly realized that there were two people in the cabin, the intruder started to jerk the barrel around toward Jonas.

But Jonas's knife was already in the air, sailing toward its target with the eagerness of a lover. The gunman's finger spasmed on the trigger as the blade hit home.

Chapter Fifteen

The sound of the gunshot brought Verity awake with an adrenaline rush. She sat up in bed as if she had been struck and listened to the awful silence that followed the shot.

Perhaps she had dreamed the crack of the gun. There were other explanations. A car might have backfired.

But Verity was a woman with a well-rounded education. She had heard the brutal roar of a gun before.

She scrambled out of bed and raced to the window, wishing Jonas had spent the night with her. A sickening thought followed on the heels of that vain wish. The shot could easily have come from the cottage. She realized with a start that the lights were on in the other cabin.

Verity grabbed her jeans and yanked them on, stuffed her feet into a pair of loafers, and reached for a blouse as she passed the closet. By the time she opened the front door she was almost dressed.

Fastening buttons frantically, she raced out into the night, heading toward the cottage at a dead run. Jonas and her father, the two most important people in the world to her, were in that cabin and something was terribly wrong.

Verity rushed along the path, the crisp night air stinging

her cheeks. As she neared the cabin she saw that the front door stood wide open. A triangle of light poured out into the darkness, revealing the crouched figure of a man. He was bending over a man who was lying crumpled and unmoving on the threshold.

"Jonas!"

Jonas glanced up and in the glare of the cabin's overhead bulb his face was a cold, dangerous mask carved in stone. The man on the floor groaned but did not open his eyes. The plain, frighteningly utilitarian handle of a knife protruded from the folds of his camouflage shirt. A dark, slowly spreading stain circled the area around the point where the blade had entered his body just below the left shoulder.

"It's all right, Verity," Jonas said in what was probably supposed to be a soothing voice. "Emerson is fine."

Emerson stepped into the light and said reassuringly, "All in one piece, thanks to Jonas here. This is one very handy dishwasher you've hired, Red. Maybe you ought to give him a raise."

Verity flicked a glance at her father, assuring herself that he was telling the truth about his condition. Then her attention went back to Jonas. She eyed him searchingly. "What about you?"

He appeared mildly surprised by her inquiry. "I'm fine. But it's time to call the law and an ambulance. Since there's no phone in this cabin, Verity, you're elected to run back to your place and make the call."

"What about him?" Verity swallowed silently and stared down at the man on the floor. He appeared to be about her age. His light brown hair was cut so short that it looked almost a parody of a military cut. The camouflage shirt, heavy boots, and web belt could have been a costume if it weren't for the blood and the gun lying on the floor in the corner.

"The bleeding's under control as long as I leave the knife where it is. I'll let the medics remove it." Jonas's narrowed eyes went over the man's ashen face. He leaned across and put two fingers against the carotid artery. "He's going into shock. Better get moving, Verity, or we'll lose him, and if we lose him we won't ever get any answers out of him."

Verity closed her eyes and sucked in a deep, steadying breath. "I'll be right back." She whirled and started to run back the way she had come.

"Verity?"

She paused, turning back. "What is it, Jonas?"

"Right now, all we know is that this joker tried to break in to the cabin. Probably thought it was an empty tourist cottage. When he found it occupied, he panicked and used his gun. Don't volunteer any more information than that to whoever takes the call."

"What other information is there?" she demanded with asperity.

Emerson chuckled. "That's the ticket, Red. Just play innocent. You're good at that."

"For God's sake, what are you two talking about? What's going on here?"

"We'll discuss it later," Jonas promised.

Verity longed to dig in her heels until she had some answers but somehow she didn't think the tactic would work. For the moment Jonas was in charge and Emerson was backing him. A stranger was slowly bleeding to death on the floor. That left her without a lot of options. The situation confirmed her long-held opinion that it was never a good idea to put men in charge of anything.

It seemed a very long while before things settled back to a state resembling normal. By the time the sheriff's men had left and the unconscious man had been taken away on a stretcher, Verity had finally figured out what Jonas and Emerson had concluded earlier.

Scowling, she paced the small cabin, her arms folded under her breasts. Jonas and Emerson lounged at the table. There was a glass of straight vodka in front of each of them. Both tracked Verity's restless progress with hooded expressions. They looked as if they half-expected her to go up in flames in front of them at any moment.

"Let me get this straight," Verity said coldly. "You think the man who broke in here tonight was sent by that loan shark you're dealing with, Dad?"

"There's a distinct possibility Yarington sent him," Emerson said blandly.

Jonas thoughtfully tapped one finger on the scarred wooden table. "Except for one thing: sharks don't normally kill the client who's just a little late in paying. What's the point? You can't collect from a dead man."

Emerson shrugged. "He probably wasn't sent to kill me. He probably had orders to impress me with a display of mayhem."

"Why the gun?" Verity snapped.

"A man who makes his living as a collection agent for a loan shark doesn't run around unarmed," Jonas pointed out dryly. "The gun was probably for effect. But when he realized there were two people in the cabin he panicked. He didn't know what he was up against, so he decided to shoot first and ask questions later."

Verity shook her head despairingly. "Why didn't you say something about this to the deputies? Why let them think the man was just some unknown thief? What will happen when the guy wakes up and starts talking?"

Jonas rubbed the back of his neck with a weary gesture. "Probably not much. Why should he say anything? His boss has undoubtedly issued standing orders to his collection agents about what to do if they get picked up, and those orders probably cover such issues as keeping their mouths shut until a lawyer arrives to take over."

Verity glared at her father. "And I suppose you don't want to say anything because it will open up a can of worms. You'll have to explain about the gambling debt, the man who gave you the pistols, the deal that was made for the pistols, which, it just occurs to me, did not include California State sales tax, and heaven knows what else."

Emerson sighed. "Like you said, Red, a can of worms. I can handle it if it's necessary, but I'd just as soon not go into all the fine nuances of the thing if it can be avoided."

Verity came to a halt and confronted both men with her hands planted on her hips. "This is an inexcusable debacle. You both realize that, don't you? It's crazy and it's stupid and it's dangerous. Not to mention shady to the point of being illegal. And none of it would have happened, Dad, if you'd had the common sense to avoid a piece of lowlife like that damn loan shark Yarington."

"I know, Red." Emerson gave her a woeful-eyed spaniel look that didn't fool Verity for a minute.

She swung her attention to Jonas. "As for you, do you have any idea what could have happened here tonight? You and my father might both have been killed. Instead, you nearly killed a man, and there you sit, calm as can be, drinking vodka and acting as if nothing out of the ordinary has occurred."

Jonas shifted uneasily in his chair. "Now take it easy, honey. I know you're a little upset about all this. . . ."

"A little upset? You and my father nearly get blown away by some hit man who works for a mobster, I find you with your knife stuck in a man's chest, you make me a party to the deception you're perpetrating on the authorities, and then you have the nerve to tell me not to get upset? Are you out of your mind, Jonas, or just totally insensitive?"

"Now, Red," Emerson began soothingly.

"Don't you 'now, Red' me," Verity hissed. "I've had as much as I can take for one evening. While the two of you celebrate your machismo, I'm going home to see if I can get any sleep at all before morning. Unlike certain members of the assembled company, I have a legitimate business to run and I need my rest. The two of you go right ahead and enjoy your vodka. I'm sure you have a lot to hash over. You've certainly got enough in common to keep a conversation going for the rest of the night." She spun around and slammed the cabin door behind her.

There was a long silence in the small cottage after Verity's noisy departure. Jonas stared broodingly at the closed door, his fingers locked around the small glass of vodka. On the other side of the table Emerson sighed again and took a healthy swallow of his drink, draining the glass in the process. He reached for the bottle.

"She always did have a bit of a temper," Emerson said apologetically. "Tends to be assertive."

"I've noticed."

"My fault. I raised her to speak her mind." He brightened. "Don't worry about it," he advised more cheerfully. "She'll calm down and come around. She always does. You'll see."

"Wishful thinking," Jonas said. "Did you see the look on her face when she saw my knife in that jerk's chest? She looked like she'd seen a ghost."

"Verity doesn't approve of violence," Emerson explained carefully. "Maybe I accidentally exposed her to a little too much of the rough side of life while she was growing up. I tried to protect her from the really bad stuff, but you know how it is in some of the more interesting places around the world. And besides, I didn't want to be overprotective. She witnessed her share of barroom brawls and once or twice a knifing."

"She says I'm like you," Jonas said.

"Well, hell, that's a dumb comparison. I don't even have a master's degree, let alone a Ph.D."

"I don't think that's quite what she meant."

Emerson nodded gloomily. "I was afraid of that. She thinks you've got the same wanderlust I've got, doesn't she?"

"Among other things," Jonas agreed dryly. "She also thinks I'm irresponsible, unreliable, and incapable of long-term commitment. She thinks the only reason I'm here is because I want to explore the effect she has on my psychic abilities."

"So why does she let you hang around her cabin until

three in the morning?" Emerson demanded shrewdly, obviously striving to make a point in spite of the vodka.

Jonas tipped his glass and poured the last of his drink down his throat. "Damned if I can figure it out. I guess she thinks I'm hell on wheels in bed. We have to face the possibility that your sweet, innocent, puritanical, prissy little daughter is using me for cheap thrills, Emerson."

"I don't have to face that possibility," Emerson corrected. "You do. Good luck. In the meantime, I guess I'd better get cracking on getting that money wired to Mr. Reginald C. Yarington before he does anything else rash."

Jonas shook off his gloom and tried to focus on more practical matters. "Just how late are you on that tab, Emerson?"

"Not more than a few weeks. Hell, Yarington knows I'm good for it eventually. Wasn't any need to send some knee-crusher after me."

"Wonder how he found you."

"The crusher?" Emerson considered that. "Good question. I must have left more of a trail than I thought. Not inconceivable that someone who knows me and who also knows Yarington told him about my daughter, and he may have tracked her down to see if I was hiding out with her."

"Not inconceivable," Jonas agreed. "All the same, when you send the money to Yarington maybe you'd better verify that the guy who imposed upon our hospitality this evening was really a representative of the Yarington Savings and Loan Association."

"I'll do that. Maybe that fat deputy who took notes earlier this evening will get something out of our visitor."

"I doubt it. The guy who came through that door with such a flourish is obviously into heavy drama. That camouflage shirt looked like it came out of a catalog aimed at the well-dressed-mercenary market. He'll consider silence a noble virtue. And I don't think the Sequence Springs sheriff's department has had a lot of experience breaking down professionals. My guess is it will be a while before anyone gets him to talk."

"That's assuming he survives the night."

"Yeah," Jonas said. "That's assuming he survives. Be just my luck to have him croak. Verity would probably hold me personally accountable." It was bad enough that he had been responsible for all that blood that had soaked the guy's shirt. Jonas didn't want to think about what Verity might say or do if it turned out that he had killed him.

"You've got a point there. My daughter has witnessed violence before in her life but she doesn't tolerate it well. Behind that sharp tongue she's a sensitive little creature. Too empathic and too sympathetic for her own good. It's what makes her prone to the dangers of naïveté. Takes after her mother in that respect."

The initial shock of the evening's events had worn off by midmorning, but Verity was still tense and filled with a vague anger as she headed for the No Bull Cafe. She sought solace in the kitchen, throwing herself into the preparations for lunch. When Jonas warily walked in around eleven, she was ready for him.

She was determined to be nonchalant and matter-of-fact about last night's events. She could be just as cool as either Jonas or her father.

"You're here on time. Good. You can chop these carrots. Do a careful job, Jonas. I want them neat. When you're finished with that you can unpack the shipment of soy sauce that arrived a few minutes ago."

"Yes, ma'am." He went to work without another word.

Verity watched him out of the corner of her eyes for a few minutes, waiting for him to say something about the previous night. But Jonas worked in silence, peeling carrots and slicing them into neat little circles as if he wasn't worried about anything else in the world. Eventually Verity couldn't stand it any longer. She cleared her throat warningly.

"Any word on the condition of that man who attacked Dad last night?"

"He's alive." Jonas didn't offer any more.

"That's a relief." Verity frowned. "Well? Has he said anything to the authorities?"

"Not that I know of."

A wave of angry frustration washed though her, momentarily driving out her determination to be serenely casual about the situation. Jonas's attitude of remote calm was too much. "Dammit, he could have killed both of you!" she said through her teeth. "He had a gun. A big one, in case you didn't notice. All you had was a knife. I could have knocked on the cabin door this morning and found both you and Dad dead on the floor. Dammit to hell, Jonas!"

"Take it easy, Verity. Everything turned out all right."

She wanted to scream at him that there was no way she could take anything like this easily, but at the last second Verity regained her self-control. She instantly regretted the temporary loss of it. She would be calm about this if it killed her.

"If you've finished the carrots you can put them into that bowl. I've got to make some salad dressing." She picked up the bottle of extra virgin olive oil.

Jonas glanced at her but said nothing about her abrupt shift in attitude. It was as if he didn't know quite how to handle her as she skipped from one mood to the other. Verity took what satisfaction she could from that.

She took further satisfaction from the way both Jonas and her father tiptoed around her for the rest of the day. Neither man seemed inclined to risk setting free her short temper. They took orders meekly, carried them out swiftly, and generally kept out of her way.

Verity felt more shrewish and tyrannical than ever.

When the No Bull closed for the night, she headed for the mineral baths at the resort. Jonas and Emerson turned down the path to their cottage with little more than a polite goodnight. Verity glanced back over her shoulder a couple of times, wistfully wishing that Jonas had said something about joining her in the spa. But it was obvious he had other plans for the evening. Another chess game, probably.

She could hardly blame him, she told herself. After all, she hadn't been very encouraging all day. The man had a right to suspect she wanted to be alone tonight. But the truth was that she didn't want to be alone. For better or worse, she was getting accustomed to having Jonas Quarrel around in the evenings.

With a barely stifled groan of frustration, Verity let herself into the empty spa room and undressed. She had rarely needed the therapy of the pools as much as she did tonight, she reflected as she slipped into the hot, aromatic water. Her love life was a disaster, some gunman had nearly killed Jonas and her father, and she had spent the day sniping at the two people she loved.

At least Jonas hadn't been turned into a killer by the whole thing. She didn't waste any sympathy on the man he had downed with his knife, but she was grateful that Jonas wouldn't have to add one more ghost to his collection. He had enough phantoms in his eyes.

She leaned back against the tile, closed her eyes, and sent out a silent apology to Jonas. Depressingly confident that she was not the least bit telepathic, she added a mental call for him to join her in the baths. It would be so much easier to use passion rather than words as a means of smoothing over the awkwardness between them. She was not good at apologizing to men like her father or Jonas who seemed inclined to get themselves into trouble. They hardly qualified as innocent victims in this world; therefore, she felt a strong tendency to lecture them on their flaws.

No, she told herself, she definitely did not owe Jonas or Emerson an apology for her short temper today. Both men were far too much at ease with violence. They didn't need to be coddled or encouraged in that direction.

Half an hour later, Verity realized Jonas wasn't going to

show. So much for her poor powers of telepathy. She would become a prune if she stayed in the spa any longer.

Slowly she got out of the pool, dried herself, and dressed in her jeans and shirt. She left her hair pinned up in a shower of curls clustered at the top of her head. Then she let herself out of the spa and started back toward her cabin.

The lights in her father's cottage were still on, she noticed as she neared her place. The chess game must be a night-long marathon.

For a long moment she stood on the path, trying to make up her mind. Going over to the other cottage would probably look like an act of feminine weakness on her part. Men such as Emerson and Jonas would be quick to pounce on any sign of weakness.

But she had nearly lost both of them last night and the knowledge would send chills through her for a long time to come.

Verity made up her mind. Flinging her damp towel over her shoulder, she strode up the path to the cottage. Her brusque knock was met with a slurred response.

"Enter at your own risk," Emerson called.

Verity winced. Her father sounded as if he'd had one too many vodkas. When she opened the door and stepped hesitantly inside, she saw that she was right. Nor was her father the only one who had made inroads into the new bottle of vodka that Emerson must have purchased that afternoon. Jonas was sprawled on a chair, his legs stretched out in front of him, his dark hair falling forward over one eye.

The remains of an unfinished chess game sat on a table.

Jonas's golden eyes glittered at her between narrowed lids as she entered. He lifted his glass in mocking salute.

> *"Behold, my lady doth appear,*
> *a noble goddess, fair and wise.*
> *She doth fill the room with beauty*
> *and a warmth which lasts until*

*You see the shrew who looks at you
from the depths of blue-green eyes."*

"What are you two celebrating?" Verity asked mildly.

"Got the money wired to Yarington this afternoon," Emerson announced. "We're celebrating the fact that no one else is going to show up on our front door step with a mini-howitzer this evening."

"That's a reassuring piece of news." Verity peered at Jonas. "Are you very drunk?"

"If I'm not, I will be soon. I'm working hard on the project. You should be proud of me, little tyrant. You're always giving me lectures telling me how I should apply myself and stick with something until I'm successful. I've decided to take your advice. Tonight I am applying myself. I'm going to get successfully drunk and prove to you that I have what it takes to reach a worthy goal." He tipped the vodka bottle over his glass and replenished his drink. "Emerson, being the good buddy that he is, has promised to help and encourage me in my endeavor."

"Least I could do," Emerson said with a modest shrug. "You being the guy who saved my ass and all."

"To the fine art of saving asses." Jonas raised his glass in another salute. "A potential career path for me."

Verity smiled wryly at him. "I think you've had enough, Jonas." Her tone was gentle.

He glared at her. "What makes you any kind of judge? I'll bet you've never been thoroughly drunk in your entire prudish life. I'll bet it sickens and disgusts you to see a man drinking like this, doesn't it? I'll bet you just can't wait to slam that door on this whole nauseating scene and scurry back to your own little bed where I'll bet no man has ever spent an entire night. Hell, I *know* no man has ever spent an entire night there. I'm the world's leading authority on your sex life, aren't I?"

"If you say so." Verity walked across the room to stand in

front of him. A smile flirted at the edges of her mouth. "I really do think you've had enough, Jonas."

"Yeah?" He gave her a belligerent look. "Shows how much you know. I haven't even started."

She reached down and took the glass from him. She'd expected a struggle and was surprised when he released it at once. Without a word she set the glass down on the table and took hold of his hand.

"Come with me," Verity said softly.

Jonas blinked owlishly and obediently got to his feet. He was remarkably steady, considering the amount of vodka he had imbibed. "Where are we going, boss?"

"Home to my place." She kissed her father's cheek. "Good night, Dad. I'll see you in the morning. Be sure to lock the front door tonight."

"I'll do that. Make sure Slick, there, has his key. I don't want to have to get out of bed at three in the morning to let him into the cabin." Emerson's eyes twinkled.

"Don't worry," Verity said. "He won't be needing his key tonight."

"I won't?" A slow, remarkably cheerful grin curved Jonas's hard mouth.

"No," Verity confirmed steadily. "You won't. You're undoubtedly going to pass out when I get you home and you probably won't wake up until morning."

"Your faith in my ability to hold my liquor does wonders for my ego," Jonas managed dryly.

"If you don't like what I do to your ego, you're free to stay here. I can always go home alone."

His fingers, which had been lying docilely within hers, abruptly moved to clamp around her wrist like a manacle. "I'm ready to go when you are. Night, Emerson."

Emerson raised his glass. "Good night, Jonas. Been a pleasure drinking with you."

Verity wasn't quite certain who led whom back to her cabin. There was no doubt, however, that Jonas was more than willing. When she got him inside the warm cottage and closed the door, he exhaled in deep satisfaction and began unbuttoning his shirt.

"Let's go to bed, honey," he said, starting down the hall.

"I'll be right there," Verity promised as she moved around the room turning out lights.

When she finally went down the hall to her room she was not altogether surprised to find Jonas naked under the quilt. He was sound asleep.

He stirred slightly when she slipped into bed beside him but he didn't awaken. His arm went around her in a possessive manner and his breath was slow and steady in her hair.

Verity thought she would be awake for a long while thinking about Jonas and herself and their unresolved relationship. It was certainly a subject that provided a good basis for insomnia.

But instead she fell asleep within minutes.

Jonas awoke around three in the morning with the vague notion that he was supposed to get up and go somewhere. He had gotten into the habit lately of going someplace at three in the morning. It took him a minute to remember where that place was.

Then he felt Verity stir beside him and recalled that tonight he could stay right where he was. Verity had brought him home and Jonas distinctly remembered her telling her father that he would be passed out for the night.

Jonas was not fool enough to wake Verity in order to find out if she'd meant what she'd implied. He had learned long ago not to question the bits and pieces of occasional good luck that sometimes fell into his path. He took what he could get in that line and gave thanks.

Jonas was about to turn on his side and pull Verity closer when he became aware of his parched mouth. Too much vodka. He reluctantly got out of bed without disturbing his sleeping partner and padded into the kitchen to get a drink of water.

On his way back to the bedroom he wondered once more why Yarington would have sent someone to kill the goose that laid the golden eggs. It didn't make any sense.

In spite of the discussion he'd had earlier with Emerson, Jonas was still not convinced that the gunman had burst into the cabin intending only to terrorize his victim. The .357 had been aimed and was about to be fired before the man realized there was someone else in the room. Not the actions of a professional knee-crusher.

Jonas put the disturbing thought aside for later consideration as he slid back into bed. He reached for Verity, easing her into the curve of his body until her soft, rounded buttocks were cradled against his thighs. He intended to wallow in the luxury of being able to cuddle all night with her. After spending the entire day enduring her displeasure, it was a blessed relief to be able to hold her like this. She was sound asleep, but that didn't matter. He'd been listening to her give orders all day long. There were occasions when silence was golden around Verity. This was one of them.

He was congratulating himself on her present state when Verity wriggled a little. Somehow she managed to shift her position so that his manhood was lodged in the soft cleft of her derriere.

"Jonas?"

"I knew it was too good to last," he murmured, nuzzling her neck.

"What was too good to last?"

"Never mind. Go back to sleep, Verity. We'll talk in the morning."

"About what?" she asked with a yawn.

"About whether or not you issued me an invitation tonight."

"You mean whether or not I'm inviting you to sleep here on a regular basis?"

"Are you?" He was being gently squeezed between her buttocks and could feel himself getting very hard.

"Do you want to move in with me, Jonas?"

He groaned. "Yes."

"I guess we could try it for a while," Verity said slowly. "I don't know how long it can last, though. We'll probably be at each other's throats within a couple of days."

"Ever the optimist, aren't you? Personally, I give us at least a week." He stroked himself in the warm furrow and felt Verity stir again. Jonas leaned over and brushed his mouth across hers. "Hell, maybe two weeks if you intend to apologize the way you did tonight every time you lose your temper with me."

"I did not apologize!"

"A matter of interpretation," he assured her and deepened the kiss so that she could not argue.

Damon Kincaid scowled at the view outside his office window. Behind him on the desk lay a list of the guests who had been invited to bid on *Bloodlust*. Kincaid had studied each of the half-dozen names very carefully. Jonas Quarrel's name was not on it.

Strange. Kincaid knew all the names on that list and he knew all of them did their own bidding.

If Tresslar's discreet mercenary agency had done its job properly two nights ago, Kincaid wouldn't have been bothered with Quarrel now. But things had gone wrong; disturbingly wrong.

The report of failure had arrived a few minutes earlier, delivered by Tresslar in that annoying hick accent. Kincaid had been furious.

"Is your man alive?" he'd demanded.

"He's alive."

"How much does he know?"

"The only thing he had was a description and location of his target. He does not know why the contract was issued or who issued it. I assure you our safety precautions are all in place and functioning. You are in no danger."

"What happens to that idiot you hired to take care of Quarrel?"

"As I said, he knows nothing of importance. He's on his own. It was part of our arrangement. My guess is he'll tell the authorities he was merely looking for an empty cabin in which to spend a cold night and was startled to find it occupied. He thought he was being attacked. He panicked and tried to protect himself. As I said, it's his problem. My agency is out of it and so are you. We are both protected by my precautions."

"What about the down payment I gave you?"

"You have two options. We will be happy to refund your money, or you can give us the go-ahead to conclude the contract, in which case, I myself will do the job this time. We like satisfied customers."

Kincaid had given that consideration. "I believe I'll have you finish the contract, but this time we'll do it my way. I want to give the instructions. I will be actively involved and I will be in charge in the field. Don't worry, I don't need to see your face. You'll be working at night and out-of-doors. You can wear a ski mask or something."

There had been a long pause on the other end of the line. "It'll cost you a lot more to do it that way."

"Never mind the cost. Can you guarantee the job this time?"

"You got it." The phone was replaced on the other end of the line.

Kincaid reran the conversation several times in his head and then reran his own blossoming plans. After a moment he got up and went to the wall to take down a handsome rapier. Dropping into fencer's crouch, he made a few quick feints before sliding skillfully into a long, deadly thrust that buried the blade in the stuffed dummy.

He was looking forward to the night he would be spending at the house. It was a long time since he'd had an excuse to do his own dirty work. But an old lust that he'd kept under control for a long time was stirring deep within him.

There had been little problem satisfying his superficial sexual needs in the past few years. Women were drawn to power and money the way moths were drawn to flames. But he'd been forced to suppress this other need, obliged to dampen and conceal it in the darkest part of himself.

The prospect of personal involvement in violence was enough to draw aside the veil that had covered this other lust for far too long. He discovered that the dark, thrilling passion was still there within him, as strong as it had ever been. Now that he had awakened it once more, it would not be hidden again until it had been satisfied.

Kincaid thrust the rapier into the helpless dummy again and felt the sensual tension that pulsed in his groin.

Chapter
Sixteen

The sea appeared deceptively calm from the windows of Caitlin Evanger's house. Verity stood in the bedroom she had been assigned, the same one she'd had last time, and gazed down at the cliffs. She noticed that from this angle she could see the broken safety fence where it sagged precariously at the edge. Caitlin really ought to get that fixed.

Verity wondered what the view was like from Jonas's window and smiled to herself as she recalled the annoyance in his eyes when he discovered he'd been given a separate bedroom.

Moving into Verity's Sequence Springs cottage had wrought an interesting change in the man. Jonas had become fiercely territorial in the past few days.

Verity was still trying to decide how to adjust to this new, possessive side of her dishwasher-waitperson-handyman. She was also trying to decide how to deal with her reaction to having a lover under her roof. Her emotions were still jumbled in some ways, but diamond bright in others. She spent a lot of time warning herself that the situation was temporary at best and that she shouldn't allow herself to invest too much emotion in the man or the situation.

Jonas had a talent for reading the past but he obviously preferred to ignore his own future.

But Jonas showed no signs of wanting to leave Sequence Springs yet, and the more settled in he got, the more Verity began to think in terms of permanence. She was wondering what would happen if Jonas ever found another woman with whom he could "anchor" himself, when the door opened almost silently behind her. Verity spun around at the faint creak and saw who stood there.

"Oh, hello, Tavi. You took me by surprise." Verity summoned up a bright smile. She got no response. "I was just admiring the view."

Tavi looked at her with unhappy, anxious eyes. "I want to talk to you."

"Of course. Have a seat." Verity indicated a black leather chair.

Tavi ignored it. Her hands twisted together as she spoke. "What's going to happen here is wrong, but I don't know how to stop it. I have done a great deal of thinking about it and I have come to the conclusion that only you can do something about it. You're the key, just as Caitlin says. That's why I want to talk to you."

Verity stared at her. "I don't understand what you're talking about, Tavi. Does this have something to do with Caitlin's decision to sell *Bloodlust*?"

"It has everything to do with it," Tavi whispered fiercely. "She must not sell it. It will be the end of everything. I think it will kill her."

"Oh, Tavi, no." Verity sighed and sank down onto the chair Tavi had ignored. "I was afraid of something like this. The morning she told me of her plans, I wondered why she was so obsessed with selling this one last painting and then not painting again. Do you think she means to kill herself?"

"I don't think she has thought about anything, including life or death, after the sale of the damned painting." Tavi looked at her pleadingly. "You could stop this whole thing."

Verity jerked her eyes up in astonishment. "I could stop

it? What on earth are you talking about? What could I possibly do to stop her from selling *Bloodlust*?"

"You could take your lover and leave and never come back," Tavi whispered.

Verity recoiled from the plea in the other woman's eyes. "What good would that do?" she managed to ask in a reasonably steady voice.

"If you leave she will be forced to cancel all her wild plans."

"Tavi, be reasonable. There's nothing to stop her from carrying out the auction without me. At least if I'm here, I'll be able to talk to her afterward. We'll know then just how much the sale is going to affect her. You must see there's no point in forcing me to leave. I can't do anything for her if I'm not around."

"It all hinges on you," Tavi rasped. "Can't you see? Why do you think she invited you here? You and that man who watches you as if you were gold he must protect at all costs. You don't really think that under normal circumstances Caitlin would have made friends with someone like yourself? She has no friends except me. She has seduced you in ways you don't even comprehend. But your lover knows. I can tell by the way he acts around her. He knows she's dangerous to you but he doesn't know what to do about it. Only you can do something about it. Take him and leave. Now."

"Tavi, I don't understand any of this. You're not talking rationally. What is it you think Caitlin wants to do to me?"

The door opened again before Tavi could respond. Jonas stood on the threshold scowling at both women. Tavi glanced at him, turned, and walked swiftly out of the room. Jonas watched her go and then shut the door behind her.

"What was that all about?" he asked, raising dark eyebrows as he scanned the bedroom.

"I don't know," Verity admitted. "I think Tavi might be slightly unbalanced, Jonas. She was acting very strange. The one thing that was clear is that she's concerned for Caitlin.

She worries about what Caitlin's going to do after she sells the painting."

"So what?" Jonas began to prowl the room. "You're worried about Caitlin, too. Hell, everyone seems to be worried sick about the poor, eccentric artist who's obsessed with selling one last painting. Let me tell you something, honey. Evanger is no fool and she's no innocent eccentric. She's got something up her sleeve. I can feel it. If you had any sense you'd see it."

"Is that right? What do you think she's up to?" Verity snapped, irritated.

He shrugged his graceful, courtier's shrug. "Who knows? It's probably got something to do with jacking up the price of *Bloodlust* until it's high enough to keep her in cocaine for the rest of her life."

"Jonas! That's enough. I don't want to hear you say anything like that again. Caitlin is no druggie and you know it."

"How do I know it?" He stopped by the bed and stood staring at it with great intensity. "I'll tell you something else I don't like. I don't like the way she's split us up tonight."

"We're guests in her home and we're not married," Verity said stonily. "It's only natural she'd give us separate rooms. We had separate rooms last time."

"This time it's different between us. You should have told her to put us together," he insisted, his attention still on the bed. "Hell, we're lovers now. It's official. We're even living together."

"We've been living together for all of a few days. That hardly constitutes a long-term relationship," Verity pointed out dryly. "Be reasonable, Jonas. It would have been embarrassing for me to ask to have you moved into my room, especially when all the arrangements have been made for us to have separate rooms."

"You're embarrassed about having me for a lover?"

Verity pleaded silently with the heavens for forbearance. "That's not what I meant and you know it. It's one of those social situations, Jonas. One does the polite thing. There are still certain proprieties, even in this day and age. One doesn't contradict the sleeping arrangements provided by one's hostess. Can't you understand that?"

"Don't lock your door tonight."

She eyed him warily. "Why not?"

"Because after the party I'm going to sneak down the hall and slip into this room. The same way I did the last time we were here," he added with satisfaction.

"You didn't exactly come tippy-toeing down the hall last time. You showed up half-naked with a big sword in one hand. When the lightning lit the room I thought I was about to be stabbed to death by a madman."

"You have an overactive imagination."

"Hah. You're the last person on the face of this earth who should be lecturing someone else about an active imagination. Jonas, why are you staring at that bed?"

"I don't know. Something about it is . . ." he broke off, searching for the word. "Disturbing."

"Now who's showing signs of an overactive imagination? What do you mean, disturbing?"

"It's disturbing in the same sense the dagger in Kincaid's office was disturbing. I've never picked up vibrations from modern stuff until I met you, Verity. But things seem to be changing. First the dagger and now this bed."

Verity froze. "The bed? You're picking up a sensation from the bed? Something that leads to that damned corridor? I thought you only responded to weapons."

"Or something that has a close association with violence. Anything can be used as a weapon or have an association with violence," he explained absently.

"But a bed?"

"Let's see what happens."

Belatedly Verity's alarm bell started ringing. "Wait! Jonas, I don't think this is a good idea. Maybe you'd better not touch it."

But she was too late. He had already curved his fingers around the steel bedpost and the instant he touched the metal, Verity was disconcerted to find herself inside a fuzzy version of the now-familiar psychic corridor.

"*Jonas.*"

"I'm here." He came up behind her in the corridor and his hand closed over her shoulder. "Look."

He spun her around and Verity found herself staring at an insubstantial dream image of the bed. It floated in the corridor, vague and indistinct. But in this image the bed was wildly rumpled. The sheets were bloodstained and the nude figure of a woman was lying obscenely spread-eagled across the mattress. There was blood between the woman's legs and in her dark hair. She had her head turned away. The woman appeared to be either dead or unconscious.

Verity reacted with more horror than she had felt toward any of the other images she had encountered in the corridor. She was paralyzed with it. She knew without further examination that she was staring at the scene of a violent rape. Even as she watched, savage red emotions unfurled from under the bed and twisted blindly toward Jonas.

They got sidetracked when they sensed Verity's presence and reluctantly swerved to curl around her feet in obedience to the invisible pull she had on them.

Verity cried out and found some control over her muscles, enough to enable her to flee. She whirled to run, afraid she would vomit before she could get out of the corridor. Her stomach was churning.

"Jonas, help me. *Help me.*" It was the first time she had ever called out to him. Always before he was the one who had demanded help in the corridor. He caught hold of her, his fingers like iron on her shoulders.

"I'm here, Verity." He held her tightly, refusing to let her flee. "It's all right. Everything's under control. I want to see if I can handle a couple of those ribbons. I've definitely been getting stronger lately and I may be at a point where I can manage some of the emotions instead of being overwhelmed by them. Should be an interesting experiment."

Verity was frantic with her horror. She grabbed the front

of his shirt with two small fists and shouted in his face, "No. Absolutely not. Get us out of here. Now."

Something of her terror must have gotten through to him. He looked down at her and in real time he released his hold on the bedpost.

An instant later they were both standing safely in the bedroom. Verity was trembling so badly she had to sit down. Automatically she started to sink onto the bed and then she remembered the scene she had just witnessed. She jumped up again and went across the room to the chair, taking deep breaths to steady herself.

"Oh, God, Jonas, that was the worst one yet," she whispered. Her hands twisted together in her lap. She tried to still them between her jeaned legs.

Jonas went over to stand beside her, his hand moving soothingly in her hair. "Maybe it was bad for you because there was a woman in it," he suggested. "You've never seen a woman in one of those images before."

Verity shook her head desperately. "It wasn't just that there was a woman. It was the fact that I know her."

"What?" Jonas's hand stopped making gentling movements in her hair. He caught her chin and lifted her face so that he could look at her. "You think you know her? Verity, I've never seen anyone I know in those images."

"Since you've only recently started seeing contemporary images, that's hardly surprising," she muttered.

"Well? Don't keep me in suspense. Who is she? Or should I say who was she?"

"I'm not sure. There was just something about her I recognized. I just had a feeling I knew her, that's all."

"Honey," he said gently. "I don't think that's possible. She may have resembled someone you've met at some point in your life, but that's all."

Verity surged to her feet. "I know what I saw. Jonas, this is awful. How can I sleep here tonight? I won't be able to close my eyes without seeing that horrible picture of that poor woman. She'd been raped. She might have been dead. I couldn't tell for sure. I can't possibly sleep in this room."

"That problem is easily solved," he said firmly. "You'll sleep with me. Now come on. Get your jacket. We're going for a walk down on the beach. It will clear your head. Exercise is good for stress."

For once she was grateful to have Jonas take charge. Verity didn't argue. She got her jacket and meekly allowed him to lead her down to the sea. On the way down the steep trail that led to the beach she decided he was right. She would be the one sneaking down the hall tonight. The hell with social niceties. She was not going to sleep alone in that terrible bed.

"Jonas?"

"Yes."

"Remember what Caitlin said about her house having once had a reputation for wild orgies?"

"I remember."

"Everyone has a different definition of what constitutes an orgy. It's easy to see where the locals might have exaggerated things for the sake of a good story."

"True," Jonas agreed neutrally.

"But now I wonder."

"Yes."

Neither of them said anything else for a long time.

Verity could not get either the rape scene or Tavi's demands out of her mind after lunch. Caitlin seemed not to notice her guest's uneasiness. Throughout the midday meal, which was served by a grimly silent Tavi, the artist talked incessantly about her plans for the evening and about the auction she intended to hold the next day.

Lunch was served in an alcove off the kitchen because the rest of the bottom floor of the house had been taken over by caterers and decorators. Caitlin was sparing no expense to recreate her Renaissance salon scene in the huge room that fronted the house on the ground floor.

Verity covertly studied her friend's too-brilliant eyes while she ate. As she listened to the unrelenting excitement in Caitlin's voice, she wondered for the first time if Jonas might have been right when he implied that the woman was into drugs. Verity had never seen Caitlin like this. She was simmering with a barely restrained tension. Her movements were too quick at times and she radiated a strange, hungry sense of anticipation.

Verity sliced into a ripe, red tomato on her plate, watched the juice run, and thought of vampires preparing to feed.

"I have specifically told all the guests to arrive after seven this evening," Caitlin was saying. "No one will be admitted without an authentic-looking costume. The six people who will bid on the painting are the only exception. They will be staying the night in the house and they have been given permission to arrive a bit earlier, if they wish. The bedrooms have all been prepared. One thing this ugly old house has is plenty of bedrooms. Sandquist must have had an active social life."

"I'll be glad to help Tavi with the buffet," Verity said quickly. The silent woman gave her a sharp glance but said nothing.

"That's very kind of you, but Tavi and the caterers can manage things," Caitlin said, dismissing the matter. "By seven you will be in your costume, Verity, playing the part of a lady of the court. I wouldn't want to see you spill mustard down the front of your gown. Did you have any trouble finding something suitable?"

Verity shook her head. "Jonas helped me choose a gown. Nothing like having an expert to call on."

Caitlin looked at Jonas who, as usual, was not participating wholeheartedly in the conversation. "Yes, I imagine his advice would have been invaluable. For all their fine brocades and velvets and satins, though, the women of the Renaissance had very little freedom, did they, Jonas? They were still, by and large, victims. The best they could hope for was a marriage based on business or political ties, or perhaps a place in a convent. If they lacked the protection of a strong family, they were vulnerable to any man who wanted to use them. Not a good era for women, but then, what time period has been good for us? All women are potentially victims and all men are potentially dangerous to us. Some men are more superficially civilized about it than others, but sooner or later they find ways to use us, don't they, Verity?"

The uncomfortable thought that Jones had sought her out with the sole purpose of using her to anchor his psychic talent flickered through Verity's mind. Her head came up and she saw Jonas looking at her, his gold eyes blazing with anger. Neither of them was telepathic but Verity knew they didn't need any psychic ability to communicate silently in that moment. Jonas knew what she was thinking and she was equally aware of his frustrated fury. She turned to Caitlin.

"I have a hunch that women use men just as much as men use women," Verity said calmly.

"Ah, but there is a distinct difference in that women, even women who are good at using men, seldom resort to violence, do they?"

It was then that Verity decided she wanted an advance peek at *Bloodlust*. Something was happening here in this ugly house, something that was going to culminate in the sale of the painting tomorrow. She was suddenly consumed with curiosity about Caitlin's last work.

She waited until after Tavi had cleared away the luncheon plates before saying politely, "I hope no one minds if I take a nap? I'd like to rest up for this evening."

"By all means." Caitlin nodded. "I think I will do the same. Jonas, will you be able to amuse yourself for a few hours?"

Jonas's eyes were on Verity and again she knew what he was thinking even though she couldn't read his mind. He was wondering how the hell she was going to nap in that terrible bed.

"I have a phone call to make. After that I think I'll take another walk on the beach. I'll see you both later," he said.

In the end, it was easy to sneak upstairs to the white-on-white studio. Verity simply waited until Caitlin had retired to her own room, ascertained that Tavi was busy in the kitchen, and made sure Jonas was on the phone in his bedroom. Then she hurried up the steel staircase.

The door to the white room was unlocked. Verity slipped inside and shut it behind her. She stood for a moment, surveying the stacked canvases, easels, and odds and ends that comprised an artist's working materials, and then she walked purposefully to the large shrouded canvas on the other side of the room.

At the last moment she hesitated, her hand on the sheet. She was uncomfortably aware that she had no right to do what she was about to do. But too many disturbing nuances were in the air, and Caitlin's whole future seemed to be linked to whatever was on this canvas.

Verity's mouth tightened as she made up her mind and yanked aside the white sheet.

A dark nightmare of intense, violent colors met her shocked gaze. The picture was a fiercely abstract version of the rape scene Verity had glimpsed that morning in Jonas's psychic corridor. There was one horrifying difference. In Caitlin's painting the rapist was still present. He stood over his victim, his body that of a demon, his eyes windows into hell. There was a rapier in his hand.

Verity shuddered and grasped the edge of the steel frame more tightly in order to steady herself. She recognized the woman on the bed now. The features were highly abstract and the hair was a different color, but the still-bleeding scar on the cheek was all too familiar. Verity knew it was a younger version of Caitlin Evanger.

The man with the grotesque body and the view into hell was Damon Marcus Kincaid.

"So you've discovered my little secret," Caitlin said behind her. "Not a pretty picture, is it?" she added mockingly. "I like to think that good art is not pretty."

Verity swung around to face her. Caitlin's eyes were still

too bright and her expression too intense but she didn't look quite as hyper as she had earlier. Slowly Verity redraped the canvas, buying time in which to compose herself.

"No, Caitlin. It's not a pretty picture. That's you on that awful bed, isn't it?"

"It's me."

"Oh, Caitlin." Verity found no words. Sometimes there were no words. Impulsively she walked forward and put her arms around the taller woman, hugging her in the way women have always hugged each other when they sought to give consolation for great grief. "Caitlin, Caitlin, I'm so sorry."

Caitlin stood unmoving and unresponsive. "Don't feel sorry for me, Verity. I will have my revenge. And then it will all be over."

Verity released her and stood back, searching Caitlin's taut, ravaged face. "Revenge against Kincaid? He's the man in that painting, isn't he?"

Kincaid's name startled Caitlin. "You know Damon Kincaid?" she gasped.

"He's a collector of old weapons, among other things," Verity explained slowly, not wanting to say too much about the pistols. "Jonas had business dealings with him a few days ago."

Caitlin's expression was frozen with shock. "Business dealings?"

"Jonas brokered a sale of some old guns he had authenticated. It was nothing, really. We weren't in Kincaid's office for more than a few minutes. Kincaid didn't buy the guns and Jonas sold them to another collector."

Caitlin closed her eyes. "The world of high-flying collectors such as Kincaid is a small one, I'll grant you. But the odds of Kincaid coincidentally running into you and Quarrel must be staggeringly high. I can't believe it." Her eyes snapped open. "Quarrel knows Kincaid?"

Verity shook her head quickly. "Jonas doesn't know Kincaid any better than I do. I told you, we were only in his office a few minutes while he looked at the pistols. It's just a ghastly coincidence, Caitlin. As you said, the world of big-time collecting is a small one. When Jonas started fishing around for someone who would be interested in the pistols, who lived within a reasonable radius of Sequence Springs, and who could afford them, he came up with a very short list."

"I can't believe it was a coincidence that Kincaid was on that list." Caitlin leaned heavily on her cane as she moved slowly toward the window. "My God, is it going to come apart now after all my planning?"

Verity watched her. "Tell me what this is all about, Caitlin. I must know what is going on here. Surely you can see I have a right to know. Tavi tried to tell me this morning that I was involved. She said that if I left and took Jonas with me, everything would change. What did she mean by that?"

"Tavi hopes to protect me from carrying out my vengeance. But nothing can stop me now, Verity. Not even the fact that Kincaid may have become suspicious. His ego will keep him from behaving cautiously. The man thinks he is all-powerful. He will be certain he can take care of himself. Even if he wonders what is going on, he will still come here tonight and I will have him."

"Tell me about him, Caitlin," Verity said softly.

"You saw the painting."

"He raped you? Cut you with that rapier? Here in this house? In that bedroom you've assigned to me?"

"He and Sandquist. They took turns. They tied me to that bed and they played terrible men's games until I was unconscious. They hurt me, Verity. I thought they were going to kill me."

Verity shivered. "My God, Caitlin."

"When I woke up, I was in a motel room a few miles from here. They must have gotten nervous when I passed out and decided to get me out of the house in case I did something awkward like die on them. Or maybe they were just through with me and and wanted to get me out of sight. After all, I was no longer very pretty after they had finished with me. All I know is that I woke up alone." Caitlin turned her proud head to look at Verity. "From the moment I awoke until now, I have dreamed of revenge. I was cheated once when Sandquist got drunk and fell to his death. I will not be cheated again. Kincaid was the worst of the two. He was the one who got Sandquist high on drugs and then orchestrated the rape. It was he who used the rapier on me. I will have my vengeance tomorrow."

Verity stood very still. "How, Caitlin?"

Caitlin's smile was a terrible thing to see. "I know Kincaid very well in some ways. I know he will be consumed with the desire to own *Bloodlust*. He always gets what he wants. But this time he will not only be denied the object of his desire when I sell the painting to someone else, he will be forced to endure the shock of having it unveiled in front of the other bidders. They will recognize him instantly. No matter what he says or does after that, everyone in the elite world in which he moves will know he is the rapist in Caitlin Evanger's last painting. It will taint him for the rest of his life. Especially when everyone realizes I was the victim."

Verity sucked in her breath, a deep wariness overshadowing her compassion. "Where do I fit in to all this? What about Jonas?"

"In the beginning I did not care one way or another if Quarrel was around," Caitlin said with a slight shrug. "I wanted you here with me because you are my friend. I need both you and Tavi with me when I pull the cover off that painting tomorrow. But perhaps it's just as well Quarrel will be here along with the other bidders. Kincaid is, after all, potentially dangerous. He enjoys hurting people. He has a lust for it that is sexual, I think. In him, the lust for sex is closely related to the lust for violence. It must have been hard on him controlling himself all these years while he made a success of himself in the business world."

"You expect Jonas to act as a bodyguard?" Verity asked incredulously.

"No, of course not," Caitlin assured her. "I just think that there is some safety in numbers."

"You think Kincaid will go nuts when he sees that painting?"

"I don't know what he will do. I doubt he'll lose his self-control, but you never can tell. I have already suffered at his hands once. I do not intend to do so again." Caitlin shuddered. "I would kill myself before I let him touch me again."

"Tell me something, Caitlin. After you have carried out your vengeance, do you intend to kill yourself?" Verity asked calmly.

Caitlin looked away toward the sea. "I don't think about anything beyond what will happen tomorrow. But if it's any concern to you, you might keep in mind that I did not kill myself after what happened here in this house all those years ago. I'm not likely to kill myself after taking revenge."

"How old were you, Caitlin?"

"I was twenty-three. A very sheltered twenty-three, thanks to strict, aging parents. I was also a very beautiful twenty-three, very naïve, and very excited about dating a worldly man like Damon Kincaid. I had no conception of the kind of monster I was falling in love with. When he invited me to spend the weekend on the coast, I was thrilled. I thought he was going to ask me to marry him. I was a fool and I paid for it. But the price was far too high and now I will have some of it paid back." Caitlin swung her cane fiercely, crashing it against the stainless steel window frame.

"Are you sure you know what you're doing, Caitlin? Kincaid sounds like a very dangerous man."

"Everything is planned down to the last detail," Caitlin said, regaining her control immediately.

"He'll recognize you. As soon as he walks into this house, he'll know who you are."

"No. After the accident the surgeons were forced to make several small changes to my face in order to repair the damage that had been done. A lot of little things got altered, the shape of my eyes and nose, for instance. Those changes, combined with the aging effect of the intervening years and a change in hair color, are enough. I don't resemble my old self very much. Even if I did, I doubt that Kincaid would recognize me. I was just another victim to him. The doctors wanted to get rid of the scar, too, but I refused. I made them leave it so that every time I looked in a mirror I thought about vengeance."

"Caitlin, this is crazy."

She turned around. "Now that you know the full truth, will you be leaving, Verity? Or will you stay here with me and lend me the shield of your friendship?"

Verity knew she had no option. "I'll stay. But I must tell Jonas what's going on. He has a right to know."

"Do what you think is best." Caitlin hesitated. "Thank you, Verity. I won't forget this, I promise you." Her eyes went to the painting and she stood looking at it as if mesmerized by her own creation.

Verity sighed. "I doubt if any of us will forget this." Leaving Caitlin staring at *Bloodlust*, she turned around and walked out the door into the gray hall.

And nearly collided with Jonas.

He clamped a palm over her mouth before she could say anything and motioned swiftly for her to be silent. Verity frowned at him over the edge of his hand but nodded her head in understanding. He released her, caught her wrist, and led her quickly toward the staircase.

Neither of them said a word until they were in his room. Then Jonas let go of her, shoved his hands into his back pockets, and stalked grimly across the room.

"What the hell was that all about?" he snapped.

"How much did you hear?" Verity countered.

"Enough. She's plotting some crazy revenge against Kincaid, isn't she?"

"She's the woman we saw on the bed, Jonas. She says Kincaid and Sandquist raped her. Sandquist is dead but she's determined to make Kincaid pay. She's going to do it by first denying him the painting he covets and then letting that same painting proclaim his guilt to the entire art world. Not bad, as vengeance goes. A little bizarre, but not bad."

Jonas swung around, his golden eyes harsh and dangerous. "That goddamned bitch is using you. I knew it. I damned well knew it. I just didn't know how until now."

"She wants some friends around when the big moment arrives. Surely you can understand that, Jonas."

"I'm not going to waste any time trying to understand that creepy female. I've got my hands full trying to understand you."

"Is that right?" Verity was becoming annoyed. Jonas's lack of charity toward Caitlin irked her. Couldn't he see the poor woman needed friendship?

"Damned right." He massaged the back of his neck. "What's more, I just talked to Emerson and we've all got something else to try to understand."

"You called Dad? I didn't realize you were going to talk to him."

"I wanted to see if he'd found out anything more about the man who attacked us. We do have a few other priorities in our lives besides crazy Caitlin."

"Don't call her that."

"Why not? She is crazy."

"There's nothing crazy about wanting revenge, especially for something as brutal as rape. Oh, never mind. What did Dad have to say?"

Jonas's eyes narrowed as he watched her. "The most important thing Emerson learned is that whoever that guy was who attacked us with the cannon, he wasn't sent by Reginald C. Yarington."

Verity's eyes widened. "You mean he wasn't a . . . a collection agent for Yarington?"

"No. Emerson checked and Yarington flatly denies it. Your father believes him."

"Then he really was just a thief or a vagrant looking for a place to spend the night?"

"It's possible. But things are getting a little too messy

around here, Verity. I don't like it. I got your father to persuade the Sequence Springs cops to run a quick check on
Caitlin."

"On Caitlin!"

"Yeah. They couldn't turn up a damn thing on her prior to
the moment when she hit the art scene in a big way. It's as if
she didn't exist before that."

"The accident changed everything for her," Verity murmured. "She changed her own identity and the surgeons
changed the way she looked. She was very afraid of Kincaid."

"The kind of disappearing trick she pulled with her past
takes planning and money and paperwork. It isn't just a
matter of changing your name and your face. It's as if she
didn't exist at all before she became Caitlin Evanger, eccentric artist. There's too much violence in the air, past and
present, Verity. In addition to the lack of Caitlin's past, I
don't like the fact that Kincaid showed up in our lives last
week, right after we got involved with Evanger, who, we
now discover, is planning to publicly humiliate him. At moments such as this, casual coincidences and flukish circumstances become highly suspect."

"What do you suggest we do?"

"Leave. Right now."

Verity closed her eyes and sank wearily onto the bed.
"You know I can't do that, Jonas. Too much has happened.
We have to see this through."

"We?" The single, mocking word hung in the air between
them.

Verity opened her eyes, shocked and stunned that he
would leave her alone at this juncture. "I guess I was assuming too much, wasn't I? Go ahead and take the car, Jonas.
I'm sure I can find my own way home when this is all over."

He groaned and reached down to yank her to her feet. His
face was harsh and each word was a knife slash. "Don't be

any more of a fool than you already are. You know damned good and well I'd never leave you alone here in this house."

She sagged against him in relief and her arms stole around his waist. "Thank you, Jonas," she said simply. "I'll make it up to you later, I promise."

"You can say that again," he vowed.

Chapter Seventeen

*C*aitlin had spared no expense recreating the scene she had chosen for the evening's festivities. The lilting strains of a dance that had originally been written for the lute swirled through the glittering salon. The music was being played on a classical guitar by an earnest young man adorned in shoulder-length hair, yellow tunic, and a pair of dark tights that looked suspiciously like exercise tights.

The musician was good. Jonas found it disturbingly easy to hear the four-hundred-year-old exuberance of the Renaissance tune that floated through the modern guitar strings.

In fact, if he narrowed his eyes a little and concentrated on the music and Verity, who was dancing in his arms, Jonas found the night's illusion almost too complete. The costumed people around him were as vividly attired as any Renaissance gathering would have been. It was true the modern fabrics used in the assortment of rented gowns, cloaks, tunics, doublets, and breeches were not as rich or as beautifully made as the originals would have been, but in the soft glow of artificial lamplight and the very real flare of the flames in the steel fireplace, it didn't matter. Polyester looked like silk, machined embroidery appeared handmade, and sparkling pieces of colored glass on hems and cuffs could be mistaken for gemstones.

But the greatest illusion of all, Jonas decided, was the one he was holding in his arms. Verity could easily have stepped from a sixteenth-century Italian painting. She was wearing the peacock-blue velvet gown he had chosen for her the day they went to San Francisco.

The deep, square neckline was embroidered with gold and silver thread and it framed the silken skin of her throat and shoulders. It was just low enough to hint at the soft rise of her breasts but not so low as to invite prolonged masculine stares. The snug, high-waisted bodice emphasized her slenderness and the full-skirted gown fell with formal grace all the way to her ankles.

Her hair was pulled back from her forehead, parted in the middle in the old, classic style and folded into a cascade of curls at the nape of her neck. A single blue jewel hung in the middle of her forehead in a style that had been very popular in the sixteenth century. The gem was attached to a fine chain that disappeared into her hair. Tonight Verity's hair looked as if it had been painted by Titian, Jonas thought.

Verity looked up at him, her eyes still reflecting the concern she had been feeling all afternoon for Caitlin. "Good thing we had advance warning that this was going to be a costume affair. I have a hunch every rental shop in the San Francisco Bay Area has been cleaned out for tonight's party."

Jonas took his eyes off her long enough to cast a quick glance around the room. "You may be right."

"It looks like everyone who is anyone in the art world accepted Caitlin's invitation."

"Like she said, a bunch of curiosity-seekers."

Five of the half-dozen people who would be bidding on *Bloodlust* tomorrow had arrived earlier and had been shown to their rooms but Jonas hadn't seen Damon Kincaid yet. He was beginning to wonder if the man was going to show up after all. Jonas hoped he wouldn't. The easiest way out of this mess was to have Caitlin's big plan for revenge go quietly down the tubes for lack of one of the participants. Once he got Verity away from this house, Jonas was certain he could talk some sense into her; get her to see that while Caitlin might have a legitimate desire for vengeance, she also had some serious mental and emotional problems. The woman needed professional help, not Verity's sympathy.

"You know," Verity went on in a soft, mischievous murmur, "you're the only male in the room who looks comfortable in a pair of tights."

Jonas heard the humor in her voice and turned his head to give her a wry glare. "Thanks. You certainly know how to hand out a compliment."

"It's the truth," she said more seriously. "You look right at home in that outfit. Everyone else in the room looks as if he's wearing a costume. You look real."

Verity's eyes moved leisurely over the costume Jonas had chosen. It consisted of a full cut white shirt gathered at the neck and cuffs, a black velvet tunic that ended above his knees, and, yes, a pair of black tights.

The tunic was belted with black leather studded with a lot of showy metal and a few false jewels. An equally flashy dagger sheath complete with a dull-edged fake blade hung suspended from the belt. Jonas had chosen a short black cloak to wear over the outfit. It fell to a point just below his waist. He had selected his costume and the one Verity was wearing because both had touched some responsive chord in his memory. He had seen people wearing clothes such as these when he had prowled the psychic time corridors.

"I am real, and don't you forget it," Jonas growled. "But I can't say the same for this costume. They didn't have zippers in the Renaissance. Or elastic. And back in those days the dagger would have been a legitimate weapon, not a piece of aluminum."

"At least you didn't wear that damn knife you carry around in your duffel bag."

"I'm wearing it."

Verity stared at him. "You are? Where?"

"On my hip. The cloak hides it."

"Good grief. Are you really expecting trouble tonight?"

Jonas shrugged. "I don't know what the hell is happening and that makes me nervous. The only consolation so far is that Kincaid hasn't arrived."

"Maybe he isn't coming after all," Verity mused. "I don't know what Caitlin will do if he doesn't show. She's been building herself up to this for so long that if things don't go the way she's planned them, I'm afraid she might go a little crazy."

"She's already crazy, if you want my opinion."

Verity's eyes flashed with sudden annoyance. "Just because you're a man doesn't mean you shouldn't be able to understand her need for vengeance. Can't you imagine the kind of emotional scars she's been carrying all these years? Can't you imagine what a woman must feel after being raped and brutalized?"

Jonas studied her intent expression. "I have a good imagination, Verity," he reminded her softly. "And I understand the need for vengeance. I know damn well what I would do to any man who tried to do to you what was done to Caitlin."

She searched his face and Jonas knew the exact moment when she saw the promise of hell in his eyes. Her own eyes widened for a moment and she trembled in his arms.

"Jonas?" His name was barely a whisper.

"That's right," he said softly. "I would slit his throat. So don't tell me I don't understand vengeance. Caitlin is entitled to hers if she's telling the truth about what happened to her. What I don't like about this whole thing is the elaborate plot and the way she's involving you. She has no right to do that."

"I'm her friend! And I know she's telling the truth. It's there in her painting."

"I also don't like the way this friendship between the two of you materialized out of nowhere a few weeks before she planned her grand scheme. And I don't like the way Kincaid found out about us. And I don't like the way that joker in the camouflage shirt showed up at the cabin with a gun. There are a lot of things I don't like about this scene, but most of all I don't like the fact that I can't talk you into leaving right now."

"Jonas, I would if I could. But I can't walk out on her. She needs me. She said so."

"She's got Tavi. Apparently that's the only person she's needed until now." Jonas saw the stubbornness in Verity's face and gave up the battle he knew he could not win. He tightened his hold on her and swung her around so that her blue velvet skirts shimmered in the soft light. "Oh, hell, forget it. We're here and it's going to be over soon. We'll stick it out and hope like the devil that Evanger knows what she's doing. In the meantime, I don't want you leaving this crowd unless I'm with you. Got that?"

"You don't think I'm in any danger?" she asked, clearly amazed by the notion.

"I don't know what to think," he admitted. "So I'm not taking any chances." A movement in the arched doorway caught his eye. "Damn. There's Kincaid now. So much for hoping he would short-circuit things by not showing up."

Kincaid had chosen to wear a plum-colored tunic over a white shirt and tights similar to the ones Jonas had on. Jonas wondered if Kincaid found them as uncomfortable as he did. Gave a man a whole new perspective on pantyhose. Still, the tights were remarkably flexible, he had to admit. There was a great deal of freedom of movement. A man could fight in a tunic and tights. That would have been an important consideration for Renaissance male fashion designers.

"Kincaid? Where?" Verity tried to turn here head so that she could see him.

"Christ, don't stare at the man," Jonas ordered, exasperated by her too-obvious fascination. "The last thing I want to do is attract his attention. Whatever is going to happen here is between him and Evanger and I don't want you any more involved than you already are."

"He's bound to see us sooner or later. The crowd is large, but not large enough to hide us."

"Well, we're not going to make things easier by going over and saying hi."

"Okay, okay. Sometimes you can be very short-tempered and difficult, Jonas. Has anyone ever pointed that out to you?"

"You have. All the time. Part of your duty as a shrew, I guess." He dropped his arm from her waist and propelled her toward the buffet table. "Let's get something to eat, my lady."

"I wonder what Caitlin's thinking now." Verity managed a swift glance at the artist, who was holding court on the other side of the room.

Jonas followed her gaze, his eyes narrowed in thought. Caitlin Evanger was certainly dressed for her role as a mistress of a Renaissance court salon tonight, he had to admit. Of all the people present, she was the only one who wasn't wearing a rented costume. Her dress appeared to have been handmade for her.

The gold-brocaded gown exposed a magnificent expanse of flesh above Caitlin's full breasts, far more skin than he would have allowed Verity to expose, Jonas decided. The huge, puffed sleeves were slashed to reveal red silk undersleeves. Evanger's short-cropped hair was hidden beneath a delicate, jewel-studded cap that had a long gold silk scarf attached. The scarf shimmered down the length of her back whenever she turned her head.

"Do you think he might recognize her?" Verity asked curiously.

"She said he wouldn't. She said she changed a lot after the accident, remember?"

"I know, but how could any man forget the face of a woman he had abused like that?"

Jonas didn't reply to that. He was in no mood to try to

explain a man like Kincaid to Verity. He didn't want to tell her that he had met a number of men who saw women only as objects of lust and that five or ten years after that lust had been satisfied, they would not remember either the woman's face or the satisfaction they had taken from her. Jonas didn't want to listen to another lecture on the evil tendencies of his own sex. He was familiar enough with them.

"Have some of this vegetable pâté," he ordered, smearing the green concoction on a triangle of toast. Verity glanced at him, eyes worried, her lips parting to say something. Jonas took the opportunity to slip the toast between her teeth, effectively silencing her. It was easier than trying to answer any of her questions.

"Caitlin just saw him," Verity whispered around the pâté. "Look at her. She's as tense as a bowstring."

"So are you. Calm down. This is her show."

"I'm scared, Jonas."

"This is a fine time to decide to get scared. Why didn't you get nervous this afternoon when I was ready to pack and leave?"

"I mean, I'm scared for Caitlin, not for myself. Why should I be frightened personally?"

"I don't know," Jonas admitted, aware of the discordant stirring of a few primitive instincts somewhere deep inside himself. "But if it makes you feel any better, I don't feel normal, either. Something's going on here." He watched intently as Kincaid made his way leisurely through the crowd to greet Caitlin. Caitlin greeted him with stiff formality but there was no sign of recognition from Kincaid. After the barest of introductions, Caitlin deliberately turned her back on Kincaid, who appeared unconcerned by the brush-off.

"Something more than what Caitlin told us?" Verity asked with unexpected shrewdness.

"It's possible. It's equally possible she's been honest with us but that she's made the mistake of underestimating her enemy. God knows she wouldn't be the first one in history to have done that."

Verity chewed on her lower lip. "Now you've really got me worried, Jonas. What if Kincaid has guessed he's being set up?"

"If Kincaid had any inkling of what was meant to happen tonight, I wouldn't give two cents for Caitlin's chances of getting her vengeance. In fact, I'm not sure I'd give two cents for her life."

"Jonas!"

Jonas ignored her small, choked cry. He tracked Kincaid's progress through the room, watching as the man moved graciously through the crowd, greeting acquaintances and introducing himself to others. He was a man completely in command of himself. A Borgia who had total confidence in his power. Jonas decided that if Kincaid had guessed what was meant to happen, Caitlin Evanger didn't stand a chance.

"Something tells me he knows something's up, Verity. He's too smart and too powerful to be taken unawares. Caitlin is a fool."

"Jonas, we've got to do something."

"Such as?"

Verity put her hand urgently on his sleeve. "I don't know. I do know I can't talk Caitlin out of her plan. She's convinced it will work."

"Then there's not much we can do except stand by in case Kincaid gets nasty."

The evening wore on toward midnight. In the dense crowd, it was relatively simple for Jonas and Verity to avoid Kincaid.

Simple, that was, until Kincaid sought them out.

"Ah, there you are, Miss Ames. Quarrel. I understood you two had been invited tonight," Kincaid said smoothly as he walked up to them with the easy attitude of an old acquaintance. He helped himself to a couple of canapes from the buffet table. "An interesting affair, isn't it? Falls a little short of the real thing in places, however. This food, for instance, is certainly very twentieth century."

"Not particularly," Verity countered crisply. "A lot of the

items on this buffet would have looked right at home on a Renaissance table. The egg-based dishes, the meats, and the pastas would have appeared familiar to someone from that era. A lot of modern cooking dates from the Renaissance. Of course, there aren't any pies with live birds inside, and I don't see any salted pork tongues or boiled calves' feet, but I expect the caterer had to make a few concessions to modern tastes. You're the expert, Jonas. What do you think?"

Jonas had heard the underlying hostility in her voice as she defended the buffet selections and he winced. Acting was apparently not one of his love's talents. Now that Verity had decided Kincaid was the bad guy, she was going to have a tough time hiding her dislike of him. He tried to gloss over the implicit rudeness, not wanting to alert Kincaid any more than he already was.

"I think you're right. The buffet table could have passed muster four hundred years ago. The caterer had an advantage tonight, however. He didn't have to worry about kitchen security."

"Security?" Kincaid cocked a handsome brow.

"In the Renaissance, food for an important gathering had to be prepared under tight security," Jonas explained patiently. "Everyone worried about getting poisoned."

"Oh, yes, that's right." Kincaid chuckled and helped himself to another canape. "Life back then must have been a constant adventure."

"That's an understatement. Did you ever get around to having the dagger authenticated?" Jonas asked conversationally.

Kincaid sipped his wine. "I did. And you were quite right. I hate to say it, but it appears I was taken. Not something I like to admit."

I'll just bet you don't, Jonas thought. "Did you speak to whoever handled the deal for you? Or contact the original owner?" He didn't know what made him ask that last question. He simply couldn't resist. He saw the attentive gleam in Verity's eyes and knew she, too, was remembering the man who had died in a bowl of linguini.

"There was no third party involved in the deal," Kincaid said casually. "Perhaps if I had been willing to pay a commission to someone qualified to authenticate the dagger, I wouldn't have found myself in the embarrassing position I was in when you spotted it for a fake in my office. As for the original owner, I'm afraid there's no going back to him for restitution. He's unavailable. The man had the bad manners to die a few years back. Shot, I believe, by a thief who got into his home one evening."

"How awful," Verity said with more depth of feeling than Jonas would have liked under the circumstances. "Was he a friend of yours?"

"Merely a business acquaintance."

"Did the police ever catch the murderer?" Verity persisted.

"I have no idea. I didn't follow the story." Kincaid dismissed the subject as he glanced around the throng. "So the mysterious, reclusive artist finally greets her public. I must admit she's doing it in grand style. Miss Evanger is a striking woman. Pity about the scar and that leg."

"She was in an accident," Verity muttered defensively. "She's lucky to be alive."

"Is that right?" Kincaid studied Caitlin from across the room.

Jonas gave serious consideration to throttling his lady. He contented himself with putting his arm around her waist and squeezing. Hard. She flinched and slanted him a reproachful glance. Silently he shook his head and she finally got the message. He saw the chagrin in her eyes as she realized she was getting too mouthy in front of Caitlin's enemy.

Verity's problem, Jonas decided objectively, was that she tended to be too mouthy most of the time and the tendency got worse when her temper was aroused.

"You'll be back here tomorrow along with the other bidders?" Jonas asked smoothly, hoping to distract Kincaid from his intense study of Caitlin.

"Yes. I can't say I appreciate the delay or all this nonsense Evanger is insisting upon, but I guess we must humor the eccentric artist. A relatively small price to pay for a chance at Evanger's final work," Kincaid replied absently. "What about you and Miss Ames?"

"We'll be at the auction, but we won't be bidding. We're here as Caitlin's guests," Verity volunteered.

Once again Jonas let his grip tighten unmercifully around her waist. Jonas didn't want Kincaid to have any more information than he already possessed. The whole damn situation was already too dangerous.

"I see. Miss Evanger must value your company," Kincaid said blandly. "Have you known her long? I understood she had few acquaintances."

"We've known her awhile," Jonas replied stonily, wishing Kincaid would leave before he pried any more information out of Verity. In the next moment, he got his wish.

"There's someone I should speak to across the room. A fellow collector. I'm surprised he's here tonight. He usually avoids this kind of gathering. If you'll both excuse me?"

"Of course," Verity said primly.

Kincaid's eyes went to her bare shoulders and the white skin above the blue bodice. "I hope you will honor me with a dance later, Miss Ames. Unless, of course, Quarrel objects?" He smiled blandly at Jonas.

"He does," Jonas said easily. "I keep close tabs on Verity. I'm sure you understand."

"For heaven's sake, Jonas," Verity exclaimed in exasperation.

Kincaid chuckled and moved off into the crowd. Verity rounded on Jonas. "Let's get something clear, Jonas. I don't particularly want to dance with that bastard, but I'm perfectly capable of making the decision and acting on it myself. I don't want you thinking you can pick and choose my dance partners for me."

"When it comes to partners like Kincaid, I'll make the decision and you'll abide by it," Jonas said calmly. He reached for another slice of pâté on toast.

"Dammit, Jonas, who the hell do you think you are to talk to me like that?"

"I'm the man you sleep with these days. That gives me all kinds of rights."

He could tell his imperturbable attitude was getting to her. Verity's eyes were glittering more brilliantly than the jewel on her forehead.

"Jonas, this is an asinine argument to be having right now."

"I couldn't agree more. Let's skip the argument and have something else to eat."

"How can you eat after talking to that man?"

"It's simple. I just put this cracker into my mouth and chomp down with both sets of teeth. Works every time."

"Jonas, that's the man in Caitlin's painting. Don't you understand? He's the one who . . . Oh, my God, the *painting*," Verity gasped.

"What about it?"

"I just realized. It's unprotected upstairs. Caitlin locked the door to her studio but that's the only precaution she took. But what if you're right and he is suspicious? What if Kincaid snuck up there and destroyed it before he walked into the party? That would explain why he was late arriving tonight."

"Verity, be reasonable. How would he know where the painting is or what Caitlin painted in the first place?"

"He knows there's a painting for sale and he must remember this house. In fact, it must look very familiar to him, because Caitlin admitted she never changed a thing in it. He'd know his way around the place. If he's at all suspicious about what's going on here tonight, it would be perfectly reasonable for him to sneak a look at *Bloodlust*. After all, this whole get-together is focused on that painting."

"Your logic is unassailable," Jonas admitted dryly. "But

what makes you think he could sneak up those stairs and find the room she uses as a studio with all the people coming and going around here?"

"I told you, he knows this house. He'd remember the back staircase. He'd know the big corner room on the third floor would make an excellent studio. The light would be perfect up there. Lord only knows how much else he'll remember." With sudden decision, Verity picked up her velvet skirts. "Let's go."

"Where?"

"To check on the painting," she hissed impatiently.

Jonas swore softly. "Not so fast. I'll go. You're staying here in the crowd."

"No, I'm not. I'll come with you. I want to see if anything's been done to *Bloodlust*."

"I'll check it out and report back to you. Word of honor."

"Jonas," she began in that tone of voice that told him she was about to put her foot down, "I said I'm coming with you and I mean it."

Jonas sighed and tipped up her stubborn little chin. He looked down into her defiant gaze and deliberately pitched his voice to a low and dangerous level. It was time she learned there were limits to the kind of orders he would take from her. He had been indulging her far too long.

"Listen closely, Verity. You're not leaving this room. I will check on *Bloodlust* for you but you will stay right here with all these people until I get back. I'm not taking any chances this evening. This subject is not open for further discussion. We are not voting on who gets to go upstairs and who doesn't. I'm making the decision and you will follow orders."

"Your orders?" she sputtered. "What makes you think I'll follow orders from you?"

"If you don't, I swear I will turn you over my knee and paddle you in front of all these nice people." He didn't make a threat out of it. He made it sound like a promise.

Verity was so shocked that for a few critical seconds she

couldn't find any words to fling at him. Jonas nodded once, satisfied that his message had been received and understood. He released her chin.

"I'll be back in a few minutes. Try to keep your mouth shut around Kincaid. You get too chatty when you get mad." He stepped into the crowd before she could recover.

Sometimes you had to get firm with a tyrant. History showed it didn't pay to appease one. Little tyrants turned into major nuisances if given a chance.

The hall outside the kitchen was empty. The light had been turned off. Jonas surveyed the narrow, shadowed staircase and decided Verity was right. It would be relatively easy for someone to make his way upstairs without being noticed, if he knew about the back stairs.

Reflexively he touched the hilt of the aluminum dagger and then dropped his hand in disgust. It would have been worth his life for a Renaissance lord to carry a fake. Jonas's hand moved under the black cloak to check the utilitarian knife that hung over his hip.

Theoretically there was no need for concern. Kincaid was safely occupied in the main salon. But Jonas was aware of a frisson of uneasiness as he loped swiftly up the stairs to the third level of the house.

The hall at the top was empty and dark. He made his way through the shadows, listening to the splatter of rain on the skylight overhead. One quick look at the painting would reassure him and he could then reassure Verity.

The door to the corner room where Caitlin practiced her art was still locked. Jonas tried it and knew a strong sense of relief when the knob failed to turn under his fingers. It didn't prove that Kincaid hadn't been inside, but it was an indication that all was still safe.

It wouldn't hurt to be certain. Besides, Verity would want to know if he had checked the painting itself, not just the lock on the door. Tyrants could be extremely demanding.

Reluctantly Jonas slipped the thin aluminum dagger out of

its sheath and inserted the tip between the door and its frame. He had heard that a credit card worked well on this kind of simple household lock but he hadn't carried plastic for nearly five years.

The dagger point did the job just fine. The lock gave way and the knob turned in Jonas's palm. He slid the fake weapon back into its sheath and stepped into the darkened room.

Something moved in the shadows and Jonas froze. A small pocket light switched on and he automatically looked away from it, trying not to let himself be temporarily blinded by it. The light revealed a gun locked in a beefy fist. It was pointed at him.

"Hold it right there. One move and I'll blow you away. There's a silencer on this. No one downstairs will hear a thing."

Jonas surveyed the dark, solid shape in front of him. He couldn't make out the features, only a general impression of size and strength behind the glare of the small flashlight. The hick accent was grating on the ears but there was no doubt the gun was rock steady. The man seemed quite comfortable with it.

"Are you up here to deliver an opinion on modern art or are you just lost?" Jonas asked.

"Shut up. Throw down that knife. Now."

For an instant Jonas thought the man had guessed about the real blade that hung beneath his cloak. Then he realized with a vast sense of relief that the man was referring to the aluminum dagger. Here in the darkness the thing looked amazingly real. Obediently Jonas removed the fake and tossed it aside.

"Don't move." The gunman put the flashlight down on a nearby table, making certain it continued to illuminate Jonas. He reached for an object that hung at his hip and flicked a small switch. Then he released it. "All right, let's go." He picked up the flashlight again and motioned toward the door with the gun.

"Go where?"

"Outside. I just alerted Kincaid. He'll be along in a few minutes. We'll wait for him at the back of the house."

"Kincaid's carrying a pager?"

"You got it. Now move."

Jonas weighed the odds and decided to take a realistic view. There was no way he could get the knife out of its sheath before the gunman pulled the trigger. He turned slowly toward the door.

"What about the painting?" he asked deliberately. If the man hadn't accomplished what he'd been sent up here to accomplish, finishing the job might provide a distraction.

"Forget the painting. I'll take care of it later."

Jonas glanced at the wall where *Bloodlust* stood. In the weak glare of the flashlight he could see that the painting was still draped in a white sheet. The intruder must have only recently arrived.

Jonas and the man behind him made their way slowly down the back stairs. Jonas indulged a few useless fantasies of accidentally encountering another guest or two who might have slipped away from the salon to search for a bathroom, but that proved futile. This part of the house was deadly quiet.

The gunman knew where he was going. He guided Jonas unerringly out the back door of the house. As they moved outside, Jonas got a clear view of the ski mask that shielded the man's features. They stood on the steps under the porch roof and waited.

It had been raining on and off for the past couple of hours but now the drizzle had turned into a steady downpour. The noise of it was a steady hum above the distant sound of the surf.

Kincaid appeared almost immediately. He stepped through the back door and eyed Jonas with cool satisfaction.

"So you got him, Tresslar.'" he said to the man with the gun. "Excellent. That proved simple enough and it takes care of the main problem."

Jonas shook his head. "Your problems are just beginning, Kincaid."

"No, my friend. They are nearly over. I would like to know a little more about you and where you fit in to this, but I'm afraid I can't risk taking the time to interrogate you. I don't want anyone realizing I've left the party. Don't worry, though. I will question the little redhead instead. I'm sure she'll be able to tell me a great deal about you."

Jonas fought down the cold rage that threatened to swamp him. "Verity knows nothing about any of this."

Kincaid's mouth curved faintly and his eyes glittered with an unnatural excitement. "We shall see. One thing is certain, I shall enjoy getting her to tell me what she does know. The experience should prove interesting. There's a certain sense of delicacy about her, a look of freshness that I find appealing. I have a feeling she will respond well to the stimulus of pain."

"I'll kill you if you so much as touch her," Jonas promised softly.

Kincaid's smile widened. "Brave words for a man who is about to become a ghost." He signaled to the gunman. "Get rid of him. Don't use the gun unless it's absolutely necessary. I would prefer the death to look like an accident. You know what to do."

Tresslar nodded. "Yeah," he said laconically. "I know what to do. But I didn't get a chance to check the painting, Kincaid."

"I'll take care of it myself later. Right now your priority is to get rid of him before he can cause any further trouble." Kincaid opened the back door and went inside the house without a backward glance.

"Well, that's that," Tresslar announced. "Out of sight, out of mind, I guess. Let's go."

Jonas gave him a thoughtful look. "Where, exactly, are we going?"

"To a place along the top of the cliffs where the fence is supposed to be broken. Kincaid described it to me. You, my friend, are going to have an accident. You'd had a few drinks, took a little walk outside to get some fresh air, and got too close to the edge of the cliffs. Real sad." He lifted the nose of the gun. "Move."

Jonas turned and went slowly down the porch steps. The cold rain drenched his face and hair within seconds but the cloak provided some protection for the rest of him. The only consolation was that the gunman was getting equally wet. The spongy ground made a good excuse for slow progress toward the cliffs.

"I said move, Quarrel. I haven't got all night."

Jonas deliberately stumbled in the mud but Tresslar made no attempt to get close enough to pull his victim back to his feet. He merely hefted the weapon with increasing impatience.

Jonas got back to his feet on his own. As he did so he slid the knife he had retrieved from its hip sheath into the gathered sleeve of his shirt. Then he undid the fastening of the cloak, as if he intended to discard its doubtful protection.

"Leave the fancy little coat alone. It goes over the cliff with you," Tresslar said.

It didn't take long to reach the cliff edge. Not nearly as long as Jonas would have liked. There was no time to create a distraction or come up with a brilliant plan of action for disarming Tresslar.

One thing was certain: whatever happened at the top of the cliffs was going to be messy and totally lacking in finesse.

"All right, this is the place." Tresslar swung the flashlight's beam along the broken railing at the edge of the cliffs. The unconnected posts jutted out of the wet ground at an odd angle.

Jonas swung around to face Tresslar, the edge of the cloak gripped in one fist in what he hoped looked like the white-knuckled grasp of a very nervous man. "You expecting me to jump? If so, you're in for a long wait."

"You want a helping hand? Glad to oblige." Tresslar

reached out and picked up one of the pieces of broken fence railing. Without any warning, he heaved it heavily toward Jonas.

Under ordinary circumstances, a man would have instinctively stepped back to avoid the length of splintered wood aimed at his head. But a step backward in this case would be a step into the sea.

Jonas realized what was happening as he saw Tresslar's arm move, but even so he was vaguely surprised at how difficult it was to stifle the instinct to get out of the way.

Jonas tightened his grasp on the edge of the cloak and swung around in a small, stumbling circle that could have been mistaken for an attempt at scrambling to evade the piece of wood.

It took Tresslar a couple of seconds to realize that Jonas hadn't flinched backward but had only turned around. By then it was too late. The cloak was swinging in a wide arc at the end of Jonas's arm. The heavy, wet length of it struck Tresslar's hand just as the broken length of wood thudded against Jonas's shoulder.

For an instant Jonas saw the psychic corridor in his mind and he wanted to scream in rage. The last thing he needed now was that kind of distraction. An image started to materialize, the picture of a man falling to his death over the cliffs. He was reaching desperately for the fence post and it was breaking free in his grasp. A frozen scream shaped the man's mouth.

Jonas saw no one else in the quick, strobelike image, but he knew instinctively that the victim had been pushed. He could feel the murderous intent that permeated the scene even before the ribbon of darkness started to snake toward him.

Then the old fence post bounced off Jonas's shoulder and fell to the muddy ground. During the brief, disorienting instant, Jonas's hand had never paused. He had continued the lashing motion of the cloak. He knew a kind of numb gratitude that he was able to continue functioning even through

the distraction caused by the image. He was definitely getting stronger. This time a part of his awareness stayed in the
present.

The swipe of the cloak wasn't strong enough to force
Tresslar to drop the weapon but it deflected his aim for a
crucial instant. Jonas was on him before Tresslar realized
what had happened. Jonas concentrated on the gun.

Tresslar yelped in fury, twisting powerfully in the mud.
Jonas hung on, using every trick he had picked up in five
years of surviving in port towns and backwater villages.

Tresslar heaved, slamming his free fist into the side of
Jonas's face. Jonas absorbed the blow and barely avoided
the knee to the groin that followed. He gritted his teeth and
set about breaking Tresslar's gun arm.

Tresslar screamed, the sound muffled by the sound of the
sea and the storm. He bucked upward again, partially dislodging Jonas. The two men rolled in the mud, coming up
against another fence post. This one mercifully did not give
off the vibrations the other one had.

The post gave beneath the impact. The softened earth
around it was not enough support to hold it in place.

Jonas felt the wood tilting in the mud and sensed what
was about to happen. He released his grip on Tresslar and
flung himself back out of the way.

The softened ground around the post gave way. The post
toppled over the edge of the cliff as Tresslar's weight proved
its undoing. More earth crumbled. Tresslar screamed again
as the world collapsed beneath him and then he was gone,
the gun still clutched in his fist. The flashlight vanished from
view simultaneously.

Jonas gulped air and crawled forward on his hands and
knees to peer over the edge of the cliff. He didn't dare get
too close.

There was nothing to be seen. The insatiable black sea
foamed far below, eager for another victim.

Jonas backed carefully away from the edge and jumped to
his feet.

It was as he pounded heavily toward the house through the mud that he remembered to check the knife he had shoved under his sleeve.

It was gone. He paused and glanced back over his shoulder. One look was enough to make him give up any idea of trying to find the knife in the dark without a flashlight.

He turned back toward the house and saw a familiar figure appear in the doorway.

"Quarrel! Thank God, I've been looking for you."

"Tavi! Where's Kincaid?"

"That's why I've been trying to find you. He disappeared a few minutes ago and so did Verity. Caitlin hasn't realized it yet. But I was watching him. I knew things were going wrong. I knew it. When I couldn't find you, I was terrified that something had already happened. . . ." She broke off and flipped on the porch light. She stared at Jonas, taking in the mud and the blood. Her somber face assumed a stricken expression. "What happened?"

"Later." He leaped up the steps and pushed past her into the house. "Did Kincaid leave in his car?"

"I don't know for certain. There are so many cars parked in the driveway. It will take ages to figure out if one of them is gone. But he must have taken her away in the car. It's the logical thing to do, isn't it?"

Jonas shook his head impatiently. "Not necessarily. Why would he want to call attention to himself? It's just as likely he's taken Verity away to stash her somewhere temporarily. He'll probably be returning to the party as soon as he's got her under control. Go tell Caitlin what's happened. Get everyone out of the salon and have them start searching the house and the grounds. We haven't got any time to lose. Hurry, goddammit!"

Tavi gasped and fled down the hall toward the main salon.

Jonas leaped up the back stairs, flinging open doors as he raced down the hall on the second floor. The odds were against Kincaid having tried to leave with Verity through the front door. Someone would have been sure to see him, and Verity would have been struggling. Jonas knew the man hadn't left through the back door, because he would have spotted him.

That meant Verity had to be somewhere in the big house.

Chapter
Eighteen

*T*he instant she spotted Kincaid slipping out of the crowded salon, Verity made her decision. She had no option but to follow him. There was every possibility that he had realized Jonas had left a short time earlier. She couldn't let Jonas be caught unawares.

A few people milled around in the downstairs hall but no one paid any attention to Verity as she walked swiftly toward the back of the house. In a matter of seconds she was out of sight of everyone, hurrying along the corridor that would bring her to the back stairs. She had to get to the third floor and warn Jonas that Kincaid might be searching for him.

Verity swung around the steel newel post, lifted her velvet skirts, and started up the stairs. She had raced up three steps when she heard Kincaid's voice in the hall behind her. A chill went through her as she realized he had just come in from outside.

"What a fortunate coincidence, Verity. I was just coming to look for you."

Verity stilled on the third step and turned to look at him. She forced herself to think clearly. Chances were that Jonas was still in Caitlin's third-floor room. The best thing Verity could do now was to keep Kincaid occupied.

"I was just going upstairs to my room to freshen up," she said with a bright smile. "Have you been outside? It sounds like it's pouring out there."

"It is. A very treacherous night." He walked toward her, a pale-haired demon moving through shadow. He halted at the foot of the stairs. He didn't bother to turn on the light. "A very dangerous night."

Verity didn't need the overhead light to detect the strange excitement in Damon Kincaid. There was something very wrong about him. Her fingers trembled and she found herself clasping the folds of her velvet gown with enough force to whiten her knuckles. But her smile never wavered. She had a special restaurateur's smile reserved for occasions when a difficult patron made a fuss. It was the one she used now.

"Were you getting some fresh air outside?" she asked pleasantly. "I don't blame you. It's awfully crowded in the salon." How much longer would Jonas be upstairs? she wondered. The next question was whether he would use this staircase or the front stairs when he returned to the party.

"I agree. The crowd is a bit much," Kincaid said easily. "Perhaps I'll join you upstairs." He put one foot on the bottom tread.

Verity sucked in her breath as she instinctively retreated to the step behind her. She wished she had turned on the light at the foot of the staircase. Light would be comforting right now.

She no longer tried to ignore her queasy stomach. In the shadows Kincaid was suddenly terrifying. He wore his Renaissance clothes with the nonchalance of a Borgia, looking as much at home in them as Jonas looked in his. The entire evening was taking on an air of unreality, aided and abetted by the elaborate masquerade arranged by Caitlin Evanger.

"I'm afraid I'm heading for a powder room," Verity managed to say brightly. "If you'll excuse me, I'll see you in a few minutes back in the salon." It took an incredible amount of courage to turn her back on him and start up the stairs with the air of a woman who was merely looking for a place to freshen her lipstick.

The tactic was a mistake. Kincaid leaped soundlessly up the stairs behind her and whipped an arm around her throat. Verity felt the cold steel nose of a small gun on her neck and the sickening strength in his arm.

"Not a sound, my lady, or I'll squeeze the breath out of your windpipe." Kincaid's voice implied he would like nothing better than to carry out the threat.

Verity didn't doubt him for an instant. Her father had a saying for such moments, she recalled. It flashed through her head: *Things have gone from sugar to shit*. Where was Jonas?

"What do you think you're doing?" Verity demanded in a husky whisper.

"Rearranging tonight's agenda. Let's go." He urged her up the stairs. "We'll give Tresslar a few minutes to finish the job he's working on now, and then I'll signal him and have him remove you to a less crowded location. I want to take my time having a little chat with you, Verity Ames. You're going to give me some answers to some questions I didn't have an opportunity to ask Quarrel."

Verity tried to turn her head and found the gun pressing into her throat. "What are you talking about? Who's Tresslar? And where is Jonas?"

"Tresslar is an employee of mine. And as for your friend Quarrel, I'm afraid he's no longer a factor in this interesting charade we're all playing. But I think it's safe enough to dispense with him because I have you. And you, Verity, will tell me all I need to know. But we'll conduct that conversation much later. I don't have time for it now. I've got to get back downstairs before too many people notice we're both missing."

"You're crazy! What have you done to Jonas?"

"Don't waste any time worrying about your ex-lover. He's out of the picture for good."

"Damn you, what did you do to him?" Verity's voice rose in spite of the gun and she started to struggle fiercely.

Kincaid responded by tightening his arm until Verity could no longer breathe. Panic raced through her as she grew dizzy. She twisted violently in his grasp, trying to hit him with her fists. The heavy velvet skirts she was wearing made it almost impossible to kick out at Kincaid's legs.

"Stop it, you little bitch!" Kincaid lost patience and slammed the barrel of the gun against the side of her head.

The blow wasn't hard enough to knock Verity unconscious but it dazed her. She collapsed weakly, nearly taking Kincaid down the stairs with her. He staggered beneath her unbalanced weight but recovered within a couple of steps.

"Be careful, Miss Ames, or I may decide it's more trouble than it's worth to keep you alive for a while."

Verity couldn't speak. The impact of the gun against her head had had a disorienting effect. The staircase wavered sickeningly as she tried to clear her fuzzy brain. By the time the world settled down again, Kincaid had yanked her to the top of the stairs. She took deep breaths, trying to gather enough strength to scream as he jerked her down the hall.

The back stairs had been built against the side of the house and did not bisect the corridor as the main staircase did. Kincaid and Verity emerged next to Jonas's room.

Kincaid didn't hesitate. "I think we'll stash you in your own room for now. Tresslar went through the house earlier and figured out which ones you and Quarrel were using. You'll be safe here until Tresslar can get up here to retrieve you." He came to a halt in front of the door, twisted the knob, and thrust Verity into the darkened room.

Verity reeled from the force of Kincaid's push. She stumbled, tried to regain her balance, and struck the bed. Desperately she reached out to grab a post. Once again she opened her mouth to scream. This time Kincaid backhanded her with such force that she sprawled across the bed. Her velvet skirts were flung high above her knees. When she rolled frantically to one side, they went higher, riding up above her thighs.

Kincaid dropped the gun on the nightstand and used both hands to subdue Verity. She still hadn't completely recovered from the blow against the side of her head and her resulting weakness made her an easy victim.

Furious with herself and enraged with Kincaid, Verity lashed out again and again as Kincaid anchored her heaving body with his own and slapped a pillow over her face.

Verity gasped as the stifling softness came down over her nose and mouth and then it became impossible to get a complete breath. She was going to die here in this terrible bed. Kincaid was going to suffocate her. Jonas might already be dead.

She could feel Kincaid's heavy body all along the length of her own. Dimly she realized he had an erection. The knowledge that he was getting sexually turned on by her death struggles inflamed her further. In desperation she dug her nails into his arms, determined to leave whatever scars she could.

"Dammit," he hissed as she scraped futilely at him. "Stop fighting me or I'll have to kill you now."

The bedroom door slammed open and the light came on as someone struck the wall switch.

"You're the one who's going to die now, Kincaid," Jonas said far too softly.

"Quarrel!" Kincaid sounded confused for an instant, as if he didn't understand what was happening. Then he reacted, rolling off of Verity.

Verity shoved the pillow aside, gasping for air. She found herself clinging to the edge of the bed. Another half-inch and she would fall onto the floor.

Jonas hurled himself into the room. But Kincaid already had the gun he had left on the nightstand. He wasn't aiming it at Jonas but at Verity. Jonas halted at the foot of the bed, his eyes full of the promise of death in a face that could have been carved from stone.

Kincaid sucked in air. "Don't come any closer or I'll blow her brains out all over that bed."

Verity looked up at him and realized that while Kincaid held the gun aimed at her, his whole attention was on the real danger in the room. He didn't let his gaze waver for a second from Jonas's tautly coiled body.

"What happened to Tresslar?" Kincaid demanded as he regained his self-control. He was still breathing hard, as if he had been interrupted in the middle of a sexual encounter.

"Tresslar's at the bottom of the cliff," Jonas said in the same soft voice he had used to tell Kincaid he intended to kill him.

"You're lying."

"Am I?"

"I don't know how you got away from him, but I'll worry about it later. It looks as though there will have to be some last-minute changes here. The three of us are going to make another trip down those back stairs. I will keep the gun under my cloak but it will be aimed at this redhaired bitch. Understand, Quarrel? If anyone tries to question us, remember that your lady here will be the first one to go. All right, let's move."

Verity obeyed with alacrity, but instead of getting to her feet as Kincaid stepped away from the bed, she simply dropped over the edge and fell to the floor. Her full skirts flared out as she rolled a half-turn and came up against Kincaid's leg. He staggered and fell heavily to his knees.

"Damn you, you bitch!"

Jonas was already moving, lunging toward his intended victim. Verity felt the floor shake as he landed on Kincaid. The gun flew from Kincaid's hand and skittered under the bed. Verity picked up her skirts and scrambled to her feet, backing away from the heaving, twisting bodies. Frantically she glanced around, trying to locate the gun.

Jonas and Kincaid fought with silent savagery but the battle itself was far from silent. They crashed against the furniture, sending small items flying through the air. The room was filled with the dull thud of body blows, grunts, and heavily drawn breaths. Both men were well matched and both were grimly determined. Verity was afraid to leave the room, terrified that while she was gone, Kincaid might gain the upper hand.

But she had to get help. She stepped out into the hall, preparing to scream down the house until someone came to see what was happening.

She nearly collided with Caitlin Evanger, who was hurrying along the corridor, a rapier in her hand. She looked like an avenging amazon. Tavi was close behind her, handsome face taut with fear.

"Caitlin, thank God you're here. Kincaid and Jonas are in there. We've got to get help." Verity turned to Tavi. "Go downstairs and get some of the guests. Have someone call the sheriff. Hurry, Tavi."

"It's too late," Caitlin whispered, her eyes feverish as she confronted the spectacle inside the bedroom. "The time has come."

Verity looked at Tavi. "What the hell is she talking about? Go get some help."

"She's right," Tavi said. "This isn't the way she had planned it, but it looks like fate has taken a hand."

"For God's sake, go call the law!"

Tavi didn't move. Caitlin was filling the doorway now, the rapier clutched in her fist. There was a jarring crash inside the room and Verity tried to see what was going on.

What happened next took place so swiftly that there was no time to alter the result. Jonas had landed a punch that had thrown Kincaid back against the wall that held the nineteenth-century rapier. Kincaid, blood coursing down his chin, glanced up and saw the weapon. He grabbed it by the hilt.

When he came away from the wall it was in a swift, skilled fencing lunge that drove the tip of the blade straight toward Jonas's chest.

Verity screamed as Jonas barely managed to dodge the

blade. Kincaid recovered from the lunge and prepared for another. He could take his time, his glinting eyes said, for he was the only armed man in the room now.

Verity shoved Caitlin to one side and snatched at the hilt of the rapier she held. All she could think of now was that Jonas needed a hand and this blade was the only weapon available.

Caitlin released the blade at once. "Yes," she said tightly. "Yes, yes, give it to him. Let him kill Kincaid with it. That's the way it was supposed to be."

Verity had the blade in her hand. She paid no attention to Caitlin's fierce words as she whirled to find an opening. All she needed was an opportunity to plunge the rapier into Kincaid while he concentrated on his intended victim.

She never got the chance to land her blow. Jonas had seen the blade in her hand. He spun aside from Kincaid's second lunge and the movement took him past Verity.

Jonas snatched the rapier from her hand as he moved by her.

"Jonas, no, don't touch it, it's the dangerous one!"

But the warning came too late. The moment his fingers closed around the hilt, the walls of the room began to curve around her and the psychic corridor opened in Verity's mind. She tried to shout a warning but the sound died on her lips.

She stood frozen in the doorway, her hands clenched at her sides as Jonas slipped into a fencer's crouch. She struggled to hold on to both realities simultaneously. It was the first time she had ever attempted it and she was startled to find it was even possible. But it wasn't easy. The two sometimes threatened to blend together, she discovered.

The present reality was suddenly overlaid with the sensation of a man's unrelenting fury. The fury was old and potent and timeless. It was also new and raw and reverberating through the bedroom.

Some things never change. A man's rage would always be a terrifying thing, whether it was very new or four hundred years old.

Verity couldn't tell if the rage was emanating from Jonas or from the terrible, writhing ribbons seeping down the corridor toward her. The coiling tendrils were the colors of midnight and blood and steel. The last time she had witnessed anything like them in the corridor was the night Jonas had come to this room with this rapier in his hand.

In the bedroom she watched the two men moving around each other in a deadly pas de deux. But in her mind she stood in the time corridor and watched another scene in which a man dressed very much as Jonas was dressed did battle with an enemy. The scene flickered and died and reappeared again in quick staccato bursts.

She closed her eyes in present time for a moment while she assessed what was happening in the corridor. She sensed the danger there and knew that someone had to deal with it. Jonas had his hands full. He must be waging a major battle just to keep his attention on the present. The past would be reaching for him through that rapier.

The only reason why the past wasn't swamping him was due to her.

She was acting as a magnet for the seething ribbons of emotion that flowed from the faltering image in the corridor. The tendrils of violence and emotion wanted Jonas but they were forced to hover impotently around her.

Instinctively she turned to search for Jonas but she couldn't find him in the corridor. She sensed his presence but he was not in sight. She stood alone watching the short, flickering battle scene.

The two men in the corridor circled each other with the same movements as the two in the bedroom. As the nearest one revolved slowly, rapier ready, Verity saw his face. It was the face of a man about Jonas's age and it was locked in the same taut fighting mask. It was the face of a man who meant to kill his opponent. For some reason the other man's face was more indistinct. The image winked in and out of sight, never progressing beyond the point where the man who was Jonas's age drove his rapier into the chest of the other man.

Over and over that one scene flickered in her mind. Over and over she was forced to watch the ghosts go through the motions of fighting and killing. It always ended the same way: blood welled and the image recycled.

And all the while the tendrils of emotions flowed from the image like blood from a wound. They sought Jonas, the one who had called them forth by touching the rapier, but they were forced to tangle around Verity's feet.

Verity was shaken as she had never been before. She was there alone with the image and the swirl of night and blood that was flooding the corridor. She sensed the dangerous, silent hunger in the ribbons of emotion that slithered around her.

"Verity!"

"Jonas? Where are you?" She whirled around in the corridor, searching for him.

"Stay where you are." Jonas's command came from a disembodied voice that seemed to fill the tunnel.

"Where are you?" she screamed in her mind.

"Trying to balance between the corridor and real time." And then came a disgusted oath.

"Shit."

There was an impression of momentary distraction and pain, then a cry from one of the women in the doorway in the bedroom.

Verity flicked open her eyes briefly, long enough to see the blood on Jonas's wet, muddy shirtsleeve. Kincaid had found a target.

But Jonas was moving quickly, ignoring his wound as he danced the deadly steps that brought him closer to his opponent.

For the first time Verity realized she hadn't known that Jonas knew how to fence. There was no doubt that Kincaid was an expert. She remembered the swaying dummy in his office that he used for practice.

"Verity. Pay attention, dammit."

Instinctively Verity closed her eyes again and found that she was inundated with violent tendrils of rage and pain. She was in the heart of a whirlwind now. She gasped as multicolored ribbons roiled around her, blinding her, buffeting her, seeking to break free and flow onward in search of Jonas. The storm rocked all her senses but she was able to hold herself steady.

She was the anchor.

Without any warning Jonas was there in the corridor, racing around a hidden curve, heading straight toward the maelstrom of emotions that was creating a storm around Verity.

"Don't move," he snapped.

Jonas stepped into the shifting currents of violence, fear, and rage that swarmed around her. It was as if he were searching for one particular tendril. At last he reached down and grasped a ribbon the color of old metal. He seized it and pulled it free of the others. When he lifted his hand it wriggled in his fist like a steel snake, eager to wrap itself around him.

"Jonas, no!" Verity screamed with sudden insight. "I'm the one who chains them. You must not touch that thing."

He turned to her, golden eyes gleaming. But he said nothing as he wrapped the steel-colored emotion around his arm. The other emotions seethed restlessly at Verity's feet, eager to assault Jonas. They were like a pack of hounds straining at their leashes. She was in danger of losing control over them now. Jonas should never have picked up that particular ribbon.

But Jonas was gone, racing away from her down the corridor with the metallic ribbon in his grasp. The ribbon reminded Verity more than ever of a snake that was preparing to feed.

Verity understood at last what was happening. Jonas had made a terrifying decision there in the corridor. He had deliberately taken hold of one of the most dangerous ribbons. She sensed that in doing so, he had subjected himself to a terrible risk. Neither of them knew how far he could stretch his control over his talent.

Verity opened her eyes and the psychic scene in her head wavered and became fuzzy. She tried to hold her attention simultaneously on the heaving ribbons at her feet and on the two men fighting to the death in front of her. She had no energy left for anything as productive as screaming.

Jonas was engaged in a series of lethal feints, thrusts, and parries that were being countered by Kincaid. But Kincaid seemed to be on the defensive now.

The blades flashed, tangled, and clanged. Jonas came up against the wall with a jolt that momentarily broke his defense. Kincaid, obviously tiring, seized the offensive and thrust forward with all his might.

Jonas threw himself to the side, going down on one knee. Then he lifted the tip of the rapier and thrust upward.

Kincaid looked startled at the maneuver and then he panicked as the sharp point flashed toward him. He interrupted his attack and scrambled awkwardly backward. Jonas rushed him grimly, coming up off his knee in a smooth, long lunge. He twined the rapier with Kincaid's weapon, catching it on his own blade. Using the leverage he had gained, he wrenched Kincaid's rapier out of his hands.

The blade clattered to the floor and Kincaid fell backward. He screamed incoherently and landed heavily on his side. Jonas had the point of the rapier at his throat before he could rise.

"I'm going to put this blade through your throat, you bastard. I warned you not to touch her. *I warned you.*"

Verity was aware of a great many things at the same time. She knew beyond a shadow of a doubt that Jonas was going to kill Kincaid. She sensed Caitlin's throbbing passion for vengeance.

And she felt her control slip away. The ribbons of emotion were getting ready to follow Jonas. All they needed was an opening.

The opening would be provided when Jonas slid the rapier into Kincaid's throat. The violence of death caused by the object to which they were attached would open the conduit the ribbons needed to come into the present.

Verity knew beyond a shadow of a doubt that Jonas would be destroyed or driven insane by the emotions of the past as they swept through the rapier into him.

"Jonas, no!" Verity darted forward and grabbed his arm just as his muscles were bunching for the kill.

He shook her off with such force that she went spinning against the bed. Florentine gold eyes glittered with relentless fury as he turned to look at her. A four-hundred-year-old ghost looked out of those eyes, but so did a twentieth-century man consumed by rage. "He was going to rape you. Kill you. I'll see him in hell for that."

Caitlin whispered hoarsely from the doorway. "Yes. Now. Kill him. *Kill him!*"

Kincaid looked from the face of the man who held him at blade point to the scarred woman in the doorway. "Who the hell are you?" he rasped. "What's going on here?"

"Kill him," Caitlin screamed.

Jonas started to plunge the rapier into Kincaid's soft flesh. Kincaid screamed and Verity leaped up from the bed. She caught hold of Jonas's arm one more time.

"No," she said tightly. "Not you, Jonas. Listen to me. You can't kill him. Everything in that corridor is waiting for you. I won't be able to hold those ribbons in the corridor if you kill him now. The past will devour you if you kill him."

"I'll take my chances."

"No, you won't. I won't allow it."

"Dammit, Verity," Jonas hissed.

Caitlin moved forward, her expression savage. "I agree. He has to die. Not for what he was about to do to Verity, but for what he did to me."

Kincaid stared at her. He licked at his lips, obviously seeking a way to buy some time. *"Who are you?"*

She looked down at him with the air of a woman pronouncing sentence on a condemned man. Then she smiled terribly. "Susan Connelly."

"No," Kincaid said in a thin scream. "No, you can't be."

"You're right," Caitlin said with an odd twist to her smile. "I'm not Susan. Not anymore." Her eyes flashed at Jonas. "Do it now while I can see the fear in his eyes."

"I won't let you use Jonas as your *condottiere,"* Verity warned fiercely. "This is your scene. You write the ending."

Caitlin stared at her. Then she lunged for the hilt of the rapier.

Jonas blinked, startled, and released the weapon into her clutching fingers.

Verity was instantly free of the corridor. It vanished along with the throbbing, hungry ribbons that had been swirling around her. She had time to see the metallic-colored one, cheated of its prey, rejoin the pack before the whole scene disappeared. It was a tremendous relief not to have to deal with two realities at once.

"You're all crazy! *Crazy!"* Kincaid leaped to his feet as the exchange was being made. He threw himself at Caitlin, clearly not expecting her to be able to use the rapier.

But Caitlin raised the tip of the blade as he launched himself toward her, bringing it instinctively into line with Kincaid's chest.

Kincaid had no chance to alter his course. His scream of rage and pain filled the room as he impaled himself on the rapier. He clutched the hilt in both hands as he slowly crumpled to his knees. His glazing eyes met Caitlin's as he sank to the floor in front of her. He looked stunned that such a fate could have overtaken him. Stunned that a woman could have done this to him. Then he looked very, very dead.

There was a shout from downstairs. Apparently someone had finally figured out something was going on upstairs.

Jonas glanced down at the dead man and then looked at each of the women in turn. "No question about it," he said meaningfully. "A clear-cut case of self-defense. We've got four eyewitnesses and we're all going to tell the same story. No sense confusing the authorities. Pay attention, ladies, while I give you the rough outline."

Chapter
Nineteen

*H*is arm hurt like hell. The anesthetic the doctor had provided when he stitched up the wound was wearing off, Jonas realized. But it was worth the discomfort just to have the opportunity to be the focus of Verity's anxious concern.

It occurred to him that he had never seen her fuss before, unless he counted the times she got upset because a sauce separated or a soufflé fell. It was strangely pleasant to have her hovering protectively. She hadn't left his side since the battle upstairs had ended, except to fetch and carry whatever he requested. The little tyrant had turned into a devoted handmaid.

Jonas told himself he'd better enjoy the service and attention while he could. Knowing Verity, it wouldn't last long.

"I think you should be in bed, Jonas," she said with a worried little frown as she checked his bandage for the thousandth time. "You know what the doctor said about shock."

"I'm not in shock," Jonas assured her mildly. "But just in case I'm on the verge, why don't you bring me something to drink? Whiskey might be nice."

"I've never heard of alcohol being good for shock."

"Trust me," he said. "Whiskey has been used for centuries

to cure everything from snakebite to shock. Works like a charm."

"If you say so." She hurried over to the bar that had been set up in the long salon at the front of the house. The remains of several half-empty bottles and a number of unopened ones still littered the area.

The bottles of liquor had been left standing where they were when the caterers and the guests had finally realized something dramatic had happened. Only the perishable food had been put away. Caitlin had asked everyone, including the elite group of bidders, to leave as soon as the sheriff's men had finished. The catering staff had promised to return early in the morning to clean up before the auction.

Verity's peacock-blue gown was gone, discarded for a pair of snug-fitting jeans and a teal-blue long-sleeved top that fastened with ten tiny buttons down the front. Jonas watched his boss bend over to find a glass behind the bar. The woman did look good in a pair of jeans.

Caitlin, Tavi, Verity, and Jonas were alone amid the aftermath of the aborted Renaissance ball. It was time for some explanations as far as Jonas was concerned; explanations that went beyond those that had been given to the authorities.

"I want some answers to a few questions," Jonas said as Verity put a cool glass into his hand. She sank down onto a footstool at his feet, close at hand in case he needed anything else. Jonas absently stroked her coppery hair with a sense of amused satisfaction. This was definitely a moment to be savored.

Across the room Tavi and Caitlin sat close together on the gray banquette that lined one wall. Neither woman had said much since the authorities had left. Caitlin seemed to have retreated into a world of her own and Tavi had not left her side.

The story given to the sheriff's men had been truthful up to a point. No outright lies had been told, but two of the six people who had been intimately involved in the evening's drama were dead. The other four had stuck to their story.

It was a simple, straightforward tale. Kincaid had apparently planned to steal *Bloodlust* and had hired the mysterious Tresslar to help him do it. For whatever reason, Kincaid had decided he didn't stand a chance in the coming auction. Jonas had interrupted the theft and nearly gotten himself killed. He had gone back to the house in time to find Kincaid trying to kidnap Verity, possibly because he knew she would be suspicious of his involvement when it was discovered that Jonas had gone over the cliff.

Startled in the act of trying to subdue Verity, Kincaid had lost his gun and had gone for the nearest weapon, an old rapier hanging on the wall. Caitlin had quickly supplied Jonas with a blade of his own. Kincaid had been defeated but had made one last bid to escape. He had flung himself at Caitlin, who was holding one of the rapiers. She had instinctively brought the blade up to ward him off, and the rest was history.

So to speak.

Simple and straightforward. The sheriff's men might not have liked certain parts of it, but it was a cinch they weren't going to get any other answers. Every eyewitness told basically the same tale.

"What do you want to know?" Caitlin asked quietly.

Jonas took a swallow of whiskey. "The little plan for revenge you outlined to Verity and me this morning was a complete lie, wasn't it? You never did intend to humiliate Kincaid in public. You intended to have him killed in private. By me. Let's start with how much you know about me." He felt Verity's tension as she put one arm on his leg. She was watching Caitlin closely.

Caitlin nodded slowly. "You have a right to know, I suppose."

"That's putting it mildly," Jonas remarked. "You said you heard me lecture at Vincent College a few years back?"

"I attended the lectures because I had already heard about the experiments," Caitlin said. She paused and then added gently, "I was a close friend of Elihu Wright. A very close friend."

Tavi shifted slightly and put her hand on Caitlin's. She said nothing.

Verity frowned thoughtfully. "Elihu Wright. Wasn't he the old man you said gave Vincent College the money to start the Department of Paranormal Research, Jonas?"

It was Caitlin who answered. "Elihu believed passionately in the existence of psychic phenomena of all kinds. He was determined to prove their existence and he gave millions to Vincent. In return he demanded to be kept thoroughly briefed on all research progress. When Jonas started testing, Elihu got very excited. He said that at last they had found a solid experimental subject. He was surprised at the type of psychic ability you had, Jonas. Elihu had been expecting to encounter telepathy or something more familiar. But there was no doubt about your talent."

"How much did he know?" Jonas asked.

"Everything." Caitlin looked at him. "Including what happened the day you went wild in the lab and nearly killed the technician. You never knew it, Jonas, but a great deal of data was recorded from that experiment. The research people went over it thoroughly and put together some theories. Those theories were all turned over to Elihu. The information was kept very secret but more tests were planned."

Jonas swore softly, feelingly. The bastards had intended to put him through that hell all over again. "Tests which never got carried out because I packed up and left the country."

Caitlin nodded again. "Elihu died shortly after you left. And the department itself was permanently closed. Psychic research was not deemed a respectable field of study for a classy college like Vincent. As Elihu's heir, I got possession of all the research reports that had been done."

"You were his heir?" Verity asked.

"I loved Elihu, not as a lover but as a friend. I met him in the hospital where I spent so much time after the accident. He was recovering from a heart attack. He became my friend and my mentor. He was the one who encouraged me to go back to painting. At that point in my life I didn't want to do anything, not even paint. But Elihu kept pushing me. We became very close. He had no family. His only passion was psychic research. When he died he left everything to me. He was extremely wealthy."

"It was his money you eventually used to buy this house?" Verity prodded.

"In part. But by the time Sandquist died, I was already becoming very successful on my own." She shrugged eloquently. "Money has not been a problem for me. Revenge was what I wanted. I spent hours, days, months, years thinking of ways to punish Sandquist and Kincaid. But they were always too powerful, too wealthy, and infinitely out of reach. Then Kincaid began collecting my paintings. I was stunned. At first I worried that he would recognize my style. I should have known better. My style changed drastically after what happened to me here in this house. And Kincaid had never been all that interested in my art before the rape."

"Besides, he thought you were dead," Verity said slowly. "Why was he so sure of that?"

"There was another woman in the car with me that night he ran me off the cliff. A hitchhiker I had picked up earlier. She was asleep in the backseat and never knew what happened. But I was conscious after the accident and I knew it was Kincaid who had tried to kill me. I knew I would never be safe. So I switched identities with the poor, dead woman before the authorities arrived. In the confusion, no one ever asked any questions."

"When you knew Kincaid had begun collecting your work, you saw the beginning of what might be a chance to get at him, right?" Jonas hazarded.

"Yes. Finally I had a hold, however tenuous, on him. I was wondering how to involve Sandquist, too, but then he went over that cliff one night."

Jonas's mouth twisted grimly as he remembered the muddy battle for survival he had waged at the broken fence.

"The same way I almost went over it tonight. Kincaid knew all about that particular spot at the edge of the cliff. My guess is he had used it previously. Probably to get rid of Sandquist." Broken flashes of impressions and images flickered through his mind again as they had when he grabbed the fence post to keep himself from falling. Another man besides Tresslar had gone, screaming, over those cliffs.

Tavi spoke up for the first time. "You think Kincaid killed Sandquist? But why?"

Verity glanced at her. "It's not unlikely that a couple of bastards such as those two might have had a falling-out. They might have been partners in crime but that doesn't mean they were best friends."

Jonas tangled his fingers in her hair. "True," he murmured. "Given the past they shared, the situation could have been ripe for blackmail, or it's possible Kincaid just decided Sandquist was a liability. After all, Sandquist knew a hell of a lot about Kincaid's doings here in this house. Drugs, sex, and violence. Plenty of motives." That fit, he decided. It made sense. He could easily envision Kincaid killing Sandquist. He sensed Verity's small shudder and his hand tightened reassuringly in her hair.

"At any rate," Caitlin continued softly, "when I realized Kincaid was avidly collecting Caitlin Evanger paintings, I began thinking of ways to use one of the paintings as bait. I had always dreamed of seeing Kincaid killed with the rapier he had used on me. I dreamed about it constantly, night after night." She touched the side of her face, then dropped her hand. "It was an obsession with me. But I didn't know how to use a rapier, and with this weak leg of mine, there was little chance I could become proficient."

Jonas took another mouthful of whiskey and thought that even with two good legs few people could have become skilled enough to take Kincaid in a fencing match. The man had been a brilliant fencer.

"But somewhere along the line you remembered that you had once seen me use a rapier," he said musingly. "In fact, I had nearly killed a man with it. Would have killed him if half a dozen lab workers hadn't found a way to knock me unconscious."

Caitlin looked at him. "I knew more about that experiment than you did, Jonas, because I read all the final reports. You didn't stick around to see what the analysis was."

"I knew what had happened," he told her harshly. "I didn't need any scientific analysis to tell me I'd nearly lost whatever passes for my soul that day in the lab."

Caitlin closed her eyes. "I'm sure you didn't. It must have been quite a terrifying experience."

"One I planned never to repeat," he assured her coldly. Verity shivered again under his hand.

"What you didn't learn that day in the lab was the conclusion the researchers came to afterward," Caitlin went on as if he hadn't spoken. "They decided their hypothesis was correct—that the more closely related your current environment or experience was to the past experience connected to the object you were holding, the more likely you were to be overwhelmed by those past emotions. That day in the lab, you nearly killed the lab tech because he was coming toward you with a hypodermic needle. It was only a sedative. You seemed very agitated that day when you picked up the rapier you were using for the tests. He wanted to calm you down."

"Those damn lab techs were always trying to use drugs to manipulate my responses," Jonas growled. "They knew I didn't want anything. I'd told them a thousand times I refused to mess up an already complicated situation with their medications. The lab tech made a mistake coming at me with that needle. I was already trying to handle a whole tunnel full of emotions left over from a time when men routinely worried about being poisoned."

Verity looked up from her position at his knee, her eyes full of understanding. "So when you saw the needle the lab tech was holding, you responded as if you were about to be poisoned by him. You reacted as the man who originally used that rapier would have reacted."

Jonas nodded grimly, his attention on Caitlin. "But you learned something else from those reports, didn't you? You discovered the real secret buried in them. You found out that in some cases, I don't just sense the emotions of the past, I can pick up other things as well."

Verity's fingers tightened on his leg. "What are you talking about?"

Caitlin looked at her. "I knew that he could not only tap in to the emotions of the man who had originally used that rapier, but that he could also tap that other man's skill with it."

Verity searched Jonas's face. "What does she mean, Jonas?"

Jonas finished the last of the whiskey. "I don't know much about fencing, Verity."

"Oh, my God," she whispered. The full impact of what he was saying widened her eyes.

"I know a few basic positions and moves, stuff I picked up because of my interest in old weaponry, but that's all. I've learned to use a knife over the years and I can handle a gun if I have to, but let's face it, a man doesn't have a lot of use for a sword or a rapier in this day and age. My interest in them was purely academic."

"You fought like an expert tonight," she whispered.

"As he did that day in the lab when he nearly killed the technician," Caitlin added. "That was the most significant conclusion the final lab report held. Somehow you have the capability of picking up the skills as well as the emotions connected with the man who used whatever object of violence you're handling."

Jonas lifted his head to look at Caitlin. "It's not that simple, Caitlin. It never was. That's what I tried to explain to the researchers. They wouldn't listen to me. They didn't understand what could happen in a situation where I deliberately tried to do that. I'm not sure I knew myself. I only know I didn't want to find out. Until tonight, that is, when I had no choice."

"You could have died." Verity clutched his leg so tightly that Jonas thought she would leave marks. "I sensed it. That's why I wouldn't let you kill Kincaid. I knew that if you took that final step, whatever lay in the past would somehow gain control of you. No one could survive that kind of takeover."

She knew, he realized. She understood all of what had happened back there in that corridor.

Caitlin frowned. "Why would he have died? All he was doing was tapping in to skills in addition to emotions. What's the difference?"

Verity shook her head. "You don't know what you asked of him when you set him up to kill Kincaid for you. If Jonas had killed a man while under the influence of those power-ful . . ."

Jonas tugged warningly at the fistful of red hair he had been toying with. "Never mind, Verity," he said softly. "She doesn't understand. No one understands except you and me. No one else knows what happens when we're together in that corridor."

Caitlin stared from one to the other. "What are you say-ing? That Verity is somehow involved in the process? Does she have a talent for psychometry, too?"

Jonas shook his head, annoyed with the woman. "No. She has another kind of talent altogether. One I'm not going to try to explain to you. It doesn't concern you."

Caitlin read the cold dismissal in his eyes and sighed. She looked at Verity. "I want you to know something, Verity. I never meant for you to be in any real danger tonight. Please believe me. I had a plan, but everything went wrong. Kin-caid must have second-guessed me somehow and come up with his own plan."

"What was your plan, Caitlin?" Verity demanded softly.

Caitlin looked at Tavi and then back at Verity. "It was simple enough. You've been bait all along. I intended to use you as bait again after the ball tonight."

"Bait!"

Jonas felt murderous all over again but he held on to his temper. It was the only way he could get the whole story. "Let's have it, Caitlin."

"Very well. You have a right to know. The pieces of my plan for revenge came together very slowly over a long period of time. I wanted Kincaid to die on that rapier. I needed him to die that way. But there was a problem. I knew no one who could or would kill a man in that way."

"Except me when I was under the influence of the past."

She nodded. "About a year ago I remembered you and your abilities and I got the first glimmer of a plan. But by then you had disappeared. You'd been gone from Vincent for four years and no one there knew what had happened to you. I finally found you down in Mexico. Money will buy anything, including very good private investigation services. But before I could think of a way to approach you and ask for your assistance, you came north on your own and went to work for Verity. Tavi and I went to the Sequence Springs Spa to meet you and to determine what the relationship was between you and Verity. I realized when I met you that you would never willingly help me, regardless of how much money I offered. You had the makings of a *condottiere* but you weren't a true mercenary. Money alone would not buy you. And I soon realized you didn't particularly like me."

"But there was Verity," Jonas supplied harshly.

Caitlin nodded sadly. "There was Verity. I realized almost immediately that the key to using you was Verity."

"That's why you were so eager to make me into your only friend in the world other than Tavi," Verity said bitterly.

Caitlin looked at her. "I want you to know that for me the friendship became real. I know you will never feel that way toward me now, but I will always remember your kindness and your generosity to me."

"Forget that bull and finish the story," Verity ordered.

"I think you can guess the conclusion. I came up with a plan after I saw you and Jonas together. I asked you here the first time so that Tavi and I could run a small experiment to make certain the rapier we had found would have the desired effect on Jonas. The rapier cost me a fortune. It was not one of the swords that came with this house. It was in the hands of a private collector and supposedly was associated with an old tale of rape and murder. There was a camera in Jonas's room that first night. We saw the strong effect the blade had on him. I knew then he still had the talent."

"Dammit to hell," Jonas muttered.

Caitlin ignored him, speaking earnestly to Verity. It was obvious she was weighted down with a dull guilt now that it was all over. Jonas could find no charity in his heart, however. He hoped the woman felt guilty for the rest of her life for having jeopardized Verity. He would have liked to take a little vengeance of his own right then, but he knew Verity would be furious if he tried.

"I made my plans for the Renaissance ball, knowing from what I had read in the research reports that the more closely the present resembled the past, the stronger the weapon's effect would be on Jonas. That rapier dates from the Renaissance, the era to which Jonas is most sensitive, and had been carried by a high-ranking nobleman who would have attended such affairs as the one I tried to reconstruct tonight."

"So the ball and the costumes and everything else were designed more or less to put Jonas in the mood for killing, is that it?" Verity asked tightly.

"I had intended Jonas to find Kincaid in your room after the ball tonight. I knew that if I put the blade in Quarrel's hand then, he would be swamped with the desire to kill Kincaid. That blade had once been used to avenge a rape. I was certain that when Jonas encountered a similar situation tonight, the past and the present would blend in his mind to the point where he could think of nothing else except killing Kincaid."

"How did you plan to get Kincaid to come to my room?" Verity asked coolly. "I'm hardly his type."

"Don't be a fool, Verity," Jonas growled.

She shot him a disturbed glance. "Well, it's true. I'm not

his type at all. You saw the kind of women who work for him."

"They were camouflage," Jonas said bluntly. "Socially acceptable. And not nearly as tempting to him as you would have been. I saw the way he looked at you that day when we went to his office."

"Jonas is right," Caitlin said heavily. "The moment I met you I knew you would be the perfect lure for Kincaid. He always had a lust for destroying innocence."

"I'm not exactly innocent," Verity exploded.

"Stop bragging," Jonas muttered.

"Well, I'm not innocent! Why does everyone keep acting as though I am?"

So much for the sweet-natured cosseting he had been receiving, Jonas thought with a flash of amusement. Verity was clearly annoyed now. The little tyrant did not like the accusation of naïveté. She failed to understand that the air of innocence about her was related to her genuineness, her integrity, her willingness to take people like Caitlin Evanger at face value. It had nothing to do with her sexual status.

For all her much-vaunted education and unusual upbringing, Verity Ames needed a keeper, Jonas decided.

"You and Kincaid would not have agreed on what constitutes innocence," Caitlin said gently. "I was certain he would find you quite interesting. I remembered his tastes all too well. I was once very much like you in some respects. I took people at face value. I believed in them. I dealt honestly with the world and expected the same in return. My sympathies were easily aroused. I could go on, but I'm sure you get the point. There is a freshness about you that Kincaid found deeply intriguing. Did you know that you were one of the first things he inquired about tonight when he was introduced to me?"

"No," Verity breathed. "No, I didn't know that." She looked dazed. Jonas stroked her hair soothingly while he stifled the remnants of his own murderous emotions. There was no point in getting all worked up about Kincaid again. The man was dead.

Caitlin looked at Verity. "I went to Sequence Springs without a clear-cut plan of action. I just wanted to check out Quarrel and his current situation. But once I met you, I knew I had all the elements for my little drama. You were the key that brought everything together."

"You mean," Jonas corrected roughly, "that you knew Verity was the key you could use to force Kincaid and me into a confrontation."

"With a little help from some stage props." Caitlin gestured wearily around at the shambles of the Renaissance ball. "You know, at first I thought it was merely a coincidence that you had fallen for exactly the type of woman I knew I could use to lure Kincaid. But now I'm not so sure. You and Kincaid were opposites in many ways. It's as if you, Jonas, represent the positive side of much that is considered masculine, while Kincaid represented the darkest elements in the male soul."

Tavi spoke up. "It makes a strange kind of sense that they would both be attracted to Verity. Jonas would instinctively want to protect her and Kincaid would instinctively want to defile her."

"What if I hadn't been the kind of woman you thought you could use to manipulate Kincaid?" Verity demanded.

"I would have had to find another way to throw Kincaid into battle with Jonas," Caitlin said quietly. "I was willing to wait until I had the perfect scenario."

"Since you did have me," Verity persisted grimly, "how did you plan to use me?"

Caitlin explained patiently. "It was only necessary that Jonas find you and Kincaid in a compromising position sometime during the evening. That was easy to plan. The bedroom you're in, the one in which I was tortured and raped, has a door that connects to the room Kincaid was assigned. He would remember that, of course. And I knew that he would not be able to resist trying the lock, knowing

you were on the other side. He would have found it unlocked. It was alarmed so that I would know the instant it
had been opened. Tavi would then have fetched Jonas and
told him she was worried about you."

"And I was just going to lie there in bed and blithely
invite Kincaid into my room?" Verity asked with asperity.

"I'm afraid," Caitlin said uneasily, "that you would have
been extremely sleepy and unaware of what was going on by
then. You probably would have thought it was Jonas coming
into the room. Kincaid would have assumed you were
groggy from too much alcohol. He would have been delighted with the opportunity your condition would have offered him. The idea of taking you while you were too dazed
to protest or even remember much about it would have appealed to his perverse nature. He would have known you
could hardly complain in the morning. What excuse could
you have offered for your condition? That you were too
drunk to fight him off? No, you would have kept silent.
Rape victims usually do."

"But I wouldn't have gotten that drunk," Verity exclaimed, shocked.

"Don't you understand, Verity?" Jonas asked harshly.
"Your good friend Caitlin was going to poison you. A real
Renaissance touch, that."

"No," Tavi protested earnestly. "She was only going to be
given a strong sedative, that's all. Just enough to make her
woozy. We never wanted to hurt her."

"I ought to kill you both," Jonas said quietly, too quietly.

"Me, perhaps," Caitlin agreed wearily. "But not Tavi.
Tavi tried to stop me all along. I can only assure you that I
never meant to put Verity into any real danger. It was all
arranged for you to show up in the nick of time, Quarrel.
The right rapier would be at hand and you would have been
predisposed to use it. The setting was perfect."

"Not quite," Jonas said dryly. "You made one major miscalculation. Verity was going to sleep with me tonight. She
wasn't going to be alone in that damned bedroom. If Kincaid

hadn't taken matters into his own hands, there would have been no confrontation between the two of us."

Caitlin lifted startled eyes to his. "But I had assigned that room to Verity and she knew that there were a half-dozen guests in the house. She wouldn't have risked the embarrassment of being seen sneaking down the hall to your room. Nor would she have allowed you to sneak into hers. You forget how much I've learned about her. She has a strong sense of the proprieties. For God's sake, she wasn't even comfortable bathing nude in a women-only spa!"

"Why is it so hard for everyone to understand that I'm not pure as the newdriven snow?" Verity demanded between set teeth. "Nor am I a prude. Not anymore, at any rate. Jonas is right, Caitlin. I had planned to spend the night in his room. Your whole plan would have gone awry if Kincaid hadn't taken the initiative tonight."

Caitlin stared at her for a very long time. "Then perhaps the whole thing was fate, after all," she finally whispered.

"The whole thing," Jonas announced grimly, "was a disaster. You put Verity's life in danger and you nearly got me killed. All to satisfy your need for vengeance. I've got no objection to vengeance, Caitlin, but you had no right to involve Verity or me. The only reason you and Tavi are still walking around in a healthy condition is because I know Verity would be furious with me if I took a little vengeance of my own. I give you fair warning, however. Don't come near her again, either of you, or I'll take matters into my own hands. Clear?"

"Yes," Caitlin said in a dreary, defeated voice. "Perfectly clear. Verity, I want you to know that the true casualty tonight is our friendship. I will regret losing it for the rest of my life. I had no idea when I first met you how important your friendship would become to me."

Jonas saw the spasm of sympathy that crossed Verity's face before she narrowed her eyes and asked coldly, "Tell me one thing, Caitlin. Did you know Kincaid was a fencing expert?"

"I knew. There is very little I didn't know about Damon Kincaid."

"Then you knew just how dangerous the whole thing was going to be for Jonas." Verity concluded tightly.

"There were risks involved. I realized that," Caitlin agreed. "But I didn't expect Kincaid to be armed."

"Your original plan wouldn't have worked," Jonas announced before Verity could lose her temper. His own anger was barely under control. "I wouldn't have let Verity out of my sight long enough for her to get into that kind of trouble."

Caitlin switched her gaze to his. "You let her out of your sight long enough for her to nearly get killed tonight. If my plan had prevailed she would never have been in any real danger."

Jonas's stomach tightened into a block of ice as he silently acknowledged the truth of that statement. He used his grip in Verity's hair to give her head a slight, exasperated shake. "Remind me to beat you later, Verity, for walking out of that party this evening. I gave you orders not to leave the crowd, remember?"

"I had to follow Kincaid when I saw him leave shortly after you did," she explained. "I thought he was after you."

"No, you did not have to follow him. You deliberately disobeyed instructions. But we'll get into that later." He glared at Caitlin. "So that's it? The whole story?"

"There's nothing more to tell," Tavi said aggressively. "It's over. Be done with it."

Jonas got to his feet, using his good arm to pull Verity up beside him. "Not a bad idea," he said to Tavi. "We're done with it, all right. Congratulations, Caitlin. Tonight's little drama had everything a Renaissance scheme needed—lies, deception, the betrayal of a friend, a desire for revenge, and the intent to kill. You would have done very well four hundred years ago. But Verity doesn't belong in that world. We're getting out of here. Go upstairs and pack, Verity."

"Jonas, it's nearly two in the morning."

"We'll find a motel somewhere along the way."

"But, Jonas . . ."

"If we don't find one we can drive on home. It's not that far."

"But, Jonas . . ."

He looked at her. "We're leaving, Verity," he said quietly.

She threw up her hands and surrendered. Without a word, she stalked out of the room.

No one said a word as they waited for Verity to return. When she came back downstairs with two suitcases and the peacock-blue costume, Jonas silently took her arm and led her outside to the car. He put her into the passenger seat. His arm hurt but he figured he could drive.

It was still raining as they drove away from the ugly house on the cliffs.

Half an hour later they found a motel that was still open. Verity fell asleep almost immediately, entangled in the reassuring warmth of Jonas's hard body. Jonas was not far behind her. The exhaustion that claimed them both went deep.

Verity awakened first, her eyes opening slowly to a room full of watery sunlight. The storm had passed. She yawned and stretched and decided she was almost back to normal. She felt Jonas stir beside her and she propped herself on one elbow to look down at him.

"How's the arm?" she asked first.

"Hurts. But I'll live." He smiled sleepily, one hand straying under the covers to find her bare thigh. "Providing I get enough cosseting and devoted attention, that is."

Verity ignored that. She had other things on her mind. "Jonas," she said very seriously, "Kincaid was a real expert with that rapier, wasn't he?"

"He was good."

"When you selected the metallic-colored ribbon from the bunch of tendrils around me in that corridor, you were deliberately picking up the one that would allow you to tap in to the skills of the guy who had originally owned the rapier, weren't you?"

"I was desperate. I knew I wasn't going to be able to dodge Kincaid much longer and I'm no fencer, Verity. Help didn't seem to be arriving very quickly."

"And I couldn't get at the gun," she concluded unhappily. "So you did the only thing you could think of in that moment. You took a terrible risk, Jonas."

"I had you there to help me," he pointed out gently. "I'm a lot stronger with you around. You know that, don't you? I didn't get swamped with that other man's emotions when I touched the ribbon. I was still aware of who I was and what I was doing. I knew damn well I was dealing with Kincaid, not some four-hundred-year-old ghost."

"Maybe the need to survive is stronger than any other force, past or present. You were fighting for your life, Jonas. That's a very powerful incentive to stay alert to present circumstances." Verity shook her head in rueful wonder. "Thank heavens the original owner of that rapier was a better fencer than Kincaid."

Jonas considered that. "'Better' isn't quite the word for it. In terms of actual skill, he and Kincaid were probably on about the same level. But there were two major differences that gave me the advantage."

"Which were?"

"The first difference is that the style of fencing has changed through the years. The guy who used that rapier four hundred years ago had been trained in a different technique than the one Kincaid used. Still, that might not have mattered too much in the long run. The handicap was mutual, so to speak. Kincaid couldn't predict what I was going to do and I couldn't predict his movements."

"So what was the second difference?" Verity persisted.

Jonas looked at her for a long moment before he said calmly, "The second difference was that Kincaid's fencing was of the modern variety in another crucial aspect. He had never been in a real duel. People don't fight real rapier duels in this day and age. I think he has very probably killed a couple of people, but he didn't do it while trying to dodge an untipped rapier. Facing a naked blade makes a big difference, believe me. You don't take the kind of chances you would take in a regular fencing match. At least a modern man wouldn't."

Verity swallowed as she realized what he was saying. "And the man who had used your blade had fought for real?"

Jonas sighed and leaned back on the pillows, his hands clasped behind his head. "Yeah. He knew what it was like to fight for his life with an untipped rapier. He knew how to take chances. I guess you could say I had the ultimate advantage."

Verity shuddered. "Whenever I think about it, I'm going to get chills."

"Then don't think about it," Jonas suggested pragmatically. "You know, I've been doing some thinking, myself."

"About what?" Her heart lifted. Had he been thinking about their relationship? she wondered.

"About the fact that I definitely am stronger around you. Your presence is changing things, Verity." Excitement laced his words now. "Do you realize I was able to use that ribbon of skill tonight without losing myself in the process? I've never been able to do that before. I stayed alert to my real time situation while I tapped in to something that was four hundred years old. I've never had that kind of freedom with my talent. The last time I tried it, I was swamped with another man's emotions and awareness. When I nearly killed that lab tech five years ago, I actually thought I was some character named Giovanni and I thought the tech was a Renaissance era assassin. But tonight I knew who I was and I knew who Kincaid was. It was an incredible feeling, using that ribbon without losing my sense of self-awareness. I wonder if . . ."

"Don't even think about conducting any more tests such as that one," Verity said with a shudder. "Jonas, we don't know what we're playing with. Your talent is extremely dangerous. I know something awful would have happened if you'd used that blade to kill Kincaid tonight. I was certain the violence of Kincaid's death would have allowed everything that I was trying to control in that psychic corridor to break free and flood you. We don't know what would have happened then."

Jonas contemplated that for a time and then nodded soberly. "You're right. As usual." He stretched out his unbandaged arm and pulled her down onto his chest. His lashes lifted and he looked deeply into her eyes. For a moment the gold in his gaze was so hot it could have melted steel. Then Jonas grinned slowly and wickedly. "You saved my ass, sweetheart. I wouldn't have made it without you. I owe you."

"You don't owe me. Your ass needed saving because you were busy saving mine at the time."

His grin broadened and he gave her derriere a proprietary pat. "Having saved two such valuable portions of our respective anatomies, we should probably celebrate in an appropriate fashion."

"Your arm . . ."

"It was not my arm I was proposing to employ in the endeavor."

She felt his manhood stirring against her thigh. "Not yet, Jonas. We have some more talking to do."

"About what?" He ran a finger along the upper curve of her breast.

"About what might have happened if the forces in that corridor had overwhelmed you, for one thing!"

"They didn't, so let's not talk about it."

"We can't ignore that kind of power, Jonas," she said fretfully.

"I've been living with the threat a long time. I've survived so far. And now I've got you. I'm in better shape than ever."

"Do you think you're the only person on the face of the earth who's faced with dealing with whatever comes through that corridor?"

"I don't know. There were other people being tested at Vincent College. Maybe one of them had some talent. Right now I don't know and I don't particularly care. All I want to do at this moment is make love to you."

"Does this mean you've decided not to beat me after all for leaving the party to follow Kincaid?"

Jonas squeezed her bare buttock. "Let's just say I'm feeling indulgent and will probably let you go unscathed this time. Also, with one arm in bandages, it would be hard to administer the kind of spanking you need. Too much like work. Maybe later."

"Don't hold your breath." Reluctantly Verity let herself be drawn into his sexy, teasing mood. There were still a lot of questions she wanted to ask, but she sensed that he would only stonewall her if she tried to get answers now. Jonas was making it clear that he did not want to discuss his frightening talent or the future. And this morning she was too glad to have him alive to want to push him.

"I'm not planning on holding my breath. I much prefer holding you. But in view of my somewhat incapacitated position, you're going to have to do all the work," Jonas told her.

Verity smiled with a feeling of sudden triumph. "I get to do the work? You've finally decided I'm not such an innocent after all?"

"Lady," he announced in grave tones, "this is your chance to prove to me that you have the makings of a siren, a scarlet woman, and a seducer of men. Show me what a heartless temptress you can be."

"You're on," she agreed and yanked the sheet down past his hips. For an instant she stared at the aroused, aggressive fullness she found there. "No, I take that back. You're up."

"You could say that."

She reached out to touch him intimately, loving the contrast between the rock-hardness of his shaft and the velvety skin that covered it. Some of the teasing light left Jonas's eyes and was replaced by a familiar male hunger.

"Oh, yes, sweetheart," he breathed, "that's it. Your hands always feel so good. So damn good."

Verity slipped her fingers down to cup the swelling mounds at the base of his shaft. She leaned forward and dropped a tiny kiss on one male nipple. Jonas's groan of pleasure came from deep in his chest. His legs shifted under the sheet and his fingers tangled in her hair.

Verity gave herself up to the joy of making love to him. She moved over him with growing delight, tasting him with the tip of her tongue, exploring him with fingers that were sensitive to every reaction they elicited.

She slid down the length of him, dropping warm, damp kisses in her wake until she reached the rough, curly hair that framed his manhood. Her own red hair spilled across his flat stomach as she boldly brushed her mouth against the pulsing hardness of him. Jonas's whole body seemed to clench in reaction. His hips lifted, silently pleading for more of the erotic attention.

Verity obliged willingly, thrilled by his response. It was unbelievably exciting to be able to excite this man. It gave her a heady feeling of feminine power that was unlike anything she had known.

"Jonas?" she whispered softly.

He grunted and used his palm against the back of her head to hold her where he wanted her. She took him into her mouth and Jonas sucked in his breath.

"That's it, babe," he gasped. "That's it."

He tasted hot and male and musky. Verity sampled him carefully and then bravely experimented with her teeth.

"Verity!"

She freed him and scrambled up to sit astride his thighs. Her fingers splayed across his chest as she gripped him firmly with her legs. "How am I doing?" she asked throatily as she eased herself down until he was at the entrance of her small passage.

Jonas opened his eyes, his expression taut with desire. "Don't worry," he muttered, "you have my vote for the Most

Wicked Woman of the Year award. Stop tormenting me and get on with the job."

Verity laughed down at him and then gasped as he tightened his fingers around her legs and pushed her bent knees farther apart. The action forced her to sink quickly, more quickly than she had planned, and he rose to meet her. He thrust himself swiftly and deeply into her.

"Talk about wicked seducers," she complained in a thick, husky tone as she tried to adjust to the sudden intrusion.

"Show me how much you want me, sweetheart."

She obeyed, glorying in the excitement they created between them, loving the feel of him deep inside her and the sense of possession she felt.

When their tightly wound spring of passion came apart in a shattering release, Verity collapsed across Jonas, clinging to him as if he were a lifeline in a storm. His body shuddered heavily again and again as he poured himself into her, then he held her fiercely against his damp chest.

When it was all over Verity opened her eyes and accepted the fact that she was in love with Jonas Quarrel. She was contemplating that when she happened to glance at the clock beside the bed.

"Jonas, the auction! I almost forgot." Verity lifted herself quickly, slithering to the side of the bed. "Hurry. It's due to start in an hour."

"What the hell are you talking about?"

She turned at the doorway of the bathroom. "Caitlin's auction," she explained impatiently. "Remember? As far as the bidders are concerned, nothing was canceled in spite of all the drama last night. It's true they all got kicked out of the house, but my guess is they'll be showing up at the appointed time this morning for the bidding. Those collectors aren't the kind of people to let a little thing like death and violence get in the way of getting hold of Caitlin Evanger's last painting. Heck, the story of what happened last night will only make *Bloodlust* more valuable. And when those bidders show up, I have a hunch Caitlin will go ahead with the auction."

"So what?" Jonas reluctantly swung his legs over the edge of the bed and winced. His hand went to the bandage on his arm. His expression was distinctly surly.

Verity ignored his change of mood and went into the bathroom. "So I think Tavi might be right. I think Caitlin will fall apart if she actually sells *Bloodlust*. She's obsessed with it."

"Personally, I do not give a damn." Jonas appeared in the bathroom doorway.

"Well, I do. Caitlin has been through too much to go under now."

Jonas lounged against the doorjamb. He folded his arms. "You're going to save her?"

"If I can." Verity stepped into the shower just as Jonas swore and muttered something under his breath. "What was that?" she called over the roar of the water.

"I said," he yelled back, "that you just lost your chance at the Most Wicked Woman of the Year award. Talk about innocence!"

Chapter
Twenty

*V*erity saw the cars parked in the driveway of the gray house as soon as she and Jonas rounded the last bend of the cliff-edge highway. She sat forward nervously, hoping she wasn't too late.

"Hurry, Jonas."

"Calm down. This is a crazy idea to begin with, but there's no point in working yourself up into a frenzy over it."

"You don't understand. Tavi was right to be so worried about the sale of *Bloodlust*. Nobody knows what will happen to Caitlin if she auctions it off."

"If you want my opinion, Caitlin Evanger is a survivor," Jonas grumbled. "She won't commit suicide just because *Bloodlust* is out of her life."

"She might not kill herself," Verity agreed slowly, "but I have a feeling she'll commit professional suicide. Tavi thinks she'll never paint again."

"No loss."

"That's not true! The woman is a brilliant artist."

Verity was charged with anxious energy. She threw open the car door before Jonas had switched off the ignition. Without waiting for him she broke into a run, heading toward the front door of the house. She rang the bell, and when there was no immediate answer she pounded on the door.

"They're probably all on the third floor in the room where the painting was stored," Jonas said, coming up behind her. He reached around Verity and turned the doorknob. The gray door swung inward, revealing a silent hall. "Go to it, heroine."

Verity needed no urging. She dashed down the hall toward the stainless steel staircase. The house was far too quiet, she realized as she pounded up the stairs. Jonas loped behind her, keeping up with her without appearing to exert himself. He had a knack for doing everything in a nonchalant fashion, Verity decided resentfully. Even running. The perfect Renaissance courtier. She was already wet under her arms.

Then she remembered that Jonas did not make love to her nonchalantly. The realization made her feel better.

Breathing heavily, she reached the top floor and raced down the hall to the studio. The door stood open and as Verity came to a skittering halt she saw that she had guessed right.

Five very serious people—three men and two women, ranging in age from thirty to seventy—were standing in front of *Bloodlust*. Their gazes were riveted to the painting. Caitlin stood beside it, leaning most of her weight on her ebony cane. Her striking face looked drawn and grim.

It was Tavi who turned first to see who stood in the doorway, and her eyes flickered with faint hope. The five bidders paid little attention to the newcomer, and Caitlin merely glanced at Verity and shook her head.

"You shouldn't have come back," Caitlin said. "We're almost finished here."

"I had to come back." Verity drew in a deep breath and walked into the room. "I'm your friend, remember? One of the only two friends you've got."

Tavi closed her eyes and a tear trickled down her cheek. "It's too late," she whispered. "It was always too late."

A portly man in a gray suit spoke up. "I believe the last bid was mine. Are there any more bids?"

"Not so fast," Jonas advised laconically from the doorway. He surveyed the room full of collectors. "I know that what happened here last night makes *Bloodlust* more interesting than ever, but I'm afraid you're going to have to contain your enthusiasm for a while. Verity is in charge right now."

The portly man scowled. "What do you mean, she's in charge?"

Jonas smiled lopsidedly. "You're about to suffer at the whim of a tyrant. It's an interesting experience."

"What the devil is going on here?" one of the women bidders demanded. "I'm here to conduct business. I am prepared to top Rossander's bid."

Verity glanced at her. "Save your money. The painting is not for sale." There were shocked gasps on all sides. She ignored them and kept walking toward Caitlin. En route she passed the worktable that held Caitlin's tools. She snatched up a small blade used for cutting canvas. Then she went straight toward *Bloodlust*.

"Hey, wait one goddamned minute," someone shouted, apparently realizing belatedly what was about to happen.

"Jonas," Verity said quietly, not looking back at him.

"Sorry, folks," Jonas said mildly. "But I work for her. Anyone moves, he's going to have to move through me."

Five stunned faces turned toward him. No one moved.

Verity came to a halt in front of *Bloodlust* and looked at Caitlin who hadn't taken her eyes off of her. "You don't need this painting any longer, Caitlin."

"What are you going to do?" Caitlin asked in a dull voice.

"I'm going to get it out of your life. Permanently." Verity lifted the small blade and began slashing the canvas into ribbons.

There were a few screams of protest from the crowd of horrified bidders, but no one dared to try stopping her. There were advantages to having someone like Jonas in one's employ, Verity thought wryly.

Methodically she completed her task, taking her time and doing a thorough job. When *Bloodlust* had been reduced to a pile of tatters, she turned to Tavi.

"Burn it."

Tavi nodded and quickly knelt to pick up the picees of the destroyed painting. She scooped up everything and hurried out of the room.

"Goddammit," the man called Rossander said fiercely. "Goddammit to hell. You just destroyed a fortune, lady. *A fortune*. I ought to—"

"That's enough," Jonas said from the doorway. Rossander, who had started to take a step toward Verity, came to a sputtering halt.

Verity ignored both of them. She was watching Caitlin. "*Bloodlust* is not going to be the last Caitlin Evanger painting after all, is it, Caitlin? The past is behind you. Now you can start living your present and your future."

Caitlin's masklike face slowly began to crumble. A silvery moisture appeared in her eyes. Verity stepped forward and took Caitlin into her arms, holding the tall woman while the tears streamed down her face. And then Verity, too, was crying. No one moved. A few minutes later, Tavi reappeared in the doorway.

She went to where Verity and Caitlin stood, put her arms around both of them, and cried, too. She touched Verity gently. Verity looked at her and saw that Tavi was smiling a little through the dampness.

"Thank you," Tavi said softly. "I think it's going to be all right now."

Verity nodded her understanding.

"Auction's over," Jonas quietly told the five confounded and irate bidders. "It's time to leave."

Nobody argued with him.

Three days later Verity left her kitchen in search of Jonas. She had really had it this time. The man had disappeared with a six-pack out of the No Bull's refrigerator right after he'd finished washing the noon dishes. He knew perfectly well she expected him to give her a hand cleaning out the cupboards this afternoon. She had distinctly told him so this morning. He was supposed to be a handyperson in addition to being a dishwasher.

Verity made her way up the path toward her father's cabin with steely determination. She knew exactly where to find both men.

She was not disappointed. They were lounging on the porch, drinking beer and reading. Her father was immersed in a fishing magazine and Jonas, bare to the waist, was scanning Sequence Springs's one daily newspaper. Neither man looked up as Verity came to a halt at the bottom of the steps, her hands on her jeaned hips and fire in her eyes.

"Well, well, well, what have we here?" she demanded. "Practicing for early retirement, are we? I've got jobs for both of you and you know it. Dad, you said you'd clean out the freezer this week. So far you haven't gotten close enough to risk frostbite. And as for you, Jonas, you were supposed to help me clean out cupboards this afternoon."

Jonas didn't look up from his newspaper. "I forgot."

Verity was outraged. "The hell you did. Just like you forgot to send out those letters to the museums, the ones I distinctly remember telling you to write yesterday?"

"I'll get to them one of these days," he assured her, turning the page. "I'm in no hurry. I've already got a good job. Why should I want to leave it to go do consulting work for some museum?"

"How about for the very good reason that consulting work would be in your field of expertise?" she snapped. "Not to mention the additional fact that it pays a heck of a lot better."

"Dishwashing is my field of expertise and I can live on what I'm making now."

"Don't be ridiculous."

This was not the first time they'd had this argument. In

fact, they'd had a lot of arguments since returning from Caitlin Evanger's house three days ago. Verity knew in her heart that she had been responsible for starting every one of those arguments.

She couldn't help it. She was pushing Jonas and she knew it. But she had to do it. She had to find out how soon he was going to leave. It was easier to force the issue than to wait in cold dread for him suddenly to announce one day that he was departing. Verity had never been the type to wait for fate to overtake her.

"Leave the man alone, Verity," Emerson advised blandly. "He's still healing. That was a nasty gouge he took from that rapier."

Verity bit her lip, instantly contrite. "Does your arm hurt very much today, Jonas?"

"Let's just say I'm in excruciating pain but bearing up admirably." He casually turned another page of the newspaper with his injured arm.

"See? What did I tell you?" Emerson said.

"If you're in so much pain," Verity said, "then you'd better make an appointment with the doctor."

"I've already got an appointment to have the stitches removed tomorrow. Don't fret about it, Verity." Jonas swallowed beer, frowning over a story on the back page of the paper.

"If you're in pain, you can make another appointment right now. Use the phone in my office. I pay workmen's comp for this sort of thing, you know."

"Somehow, I don't think workmen's comp is going to cover a rapier wound in the arm," Emerson remarked. "Jonas didn't even get the injury while working at the No Bull."

"Well, if it's not bad enough to see a doctor about, then Jonas can darn well help me with those cupboards," Verity said loftily. "And after he's finished, he can get started on those letters I told him to write. There's plenty of work to be done around here and I intend to see that it gets done, or else."

"Or else what?" Jonas asked from behind the paper.

His total lack of concern was the straw that broke the camel's back. Already seething with anxiety, frustration, and anger, Verity went up in flames.

"Or else I'll fire you and get someone else who knows how to do the job," she vowed, taking fierce satisfaction from having had the last word. She spun around on her heel and strode briskly toward her own cabin.

"That does it."

Something in the inflection of Jonas's too-quiet words brought Verity to a halt. She glanced over her shoulder in time to see him crumple the beer can in his hand and toss it aside. The newspaper followed, landing in a heap on the porch as Jonas got deliberately to his feet.

Verity felt the first trickle of doubt. "That does what?" she demanded aggressively.

Jonas stood on the top step, his thumbs hooked into the waistband of his jeans. His bare chest and smoothly muscled shoulders looked very broad and strong and male in the warm afternoon sunlight.

"Threatening to fire me is going too far, Verity, even for you. With a woman like you a man has to draw the line somewhere." He started slowly down the steps. "I've put up with a lot from you, boss lady. I've tolerated your scolding and your lectures and a lot of bullshit about proper eating habits. I let you talk me into a situation that nearly got both of us killed. All in all, I think I've been very indulgent with you. Don't you think I've been indulgent with her, Emerson?"

"Too right," Emerson muttered sympathetically. "Very indulgent."

"But enough is enough," Jonas continued, his eyes gleaming with righteous indignation. "I've had enough of your nagging and your shrewish behavior. Most of the time, being the gentle, easygoing soul that I am, I try to rise above it. But for the past three days you've been impossible to be around. The only time you shut up is when we're in bed. Unfortunately I can't keep you in bed twenty-four hours a day. I'm beginning to see why it used to be a man's goal to keep his woman barefoot and pregnant."

"Jonas!" Verity swung her astounded gaze to her father. "Are you going to let him talk to me like that?"

"Don't look at me." Emerson spread hs hands wide. "I'm just an innocent bystander."

Jonas went intently toward her. "You've gone too far when you start threatening me with my job. I've always given you a day's work for a day's pay and you've got no legitimate complaints, lady."

Verity took a couple of quick steps backward as she realized belatedly that Jonas was dangerous in this mood. "Jonas, don't you dare touch me. You work for me. You'd do well to remember that. You take orders from me. I'm giving you an order right now and you'd better follow it or I'll . . . I'll . . ."

He never paused, just kept striding toward her with a relentless expression on his face.

For possibly the first time in her entire life, Verity's nerve broke. She whirled and ran for the safety of her own cabin. She had never seen Jonas in this mood, and age-old feminine instinct warned her that the only safety lay in flight. She would give him a piece of her mind later when he'd had a chance to calm down. She'd chew him up one side and down the other later. She would read him the riot act for his behavior.

Later.

When it was safe to go near him again.

He caught her before she reached the front steps of her cabin. He came up behind her, moving silently, and clamped a hand on one of her shoulders. He spun her around so quickly she lost her balance. Before she could regain it, the world turned upside down and she found herself hanging over a broad male shoulder. She pounded on his back.

"Jonas, you bastard, I'll strangle you for this."

"One of the first things a would-be tyrant ought to learn is not to make threats she can't back up," he advised, striding through the front door of her cabin. "Machiavelli was very clear on that point."

He set her on her feet, sat down on the nearest chair, and yanked her over his knee.

"Jonas, don't you dare!"

Verity couldn't believe it when the flat of his palm landed heavily on her bottom. The tight jeans she wore provided no protection whatsoever.

She yelled in outrage and pain, and when the second blow came she tried digging her fingers into his thigh and kicking her legs wildly. He was impervious to her struggles and her angry cries.

"Damn you. Damn you, damn you, damn you."

"Tell me why you've been on my case for the past three days," Jonas ordered between blows. "Tell me what the hell I did to deserve the kind of abuse I've been getting around here lately."

"You're going to leave," she accused furiously. "I know you're going to leave. It's just a matter of time."

"So what are you trying to do? Speed up my departure?" He smacked her again.

"*Yes.*" Verity lost her temper completely and dug her fingernails fiercely into his leg. Enough was enough.

Jonas yelped. "Ouch! Dammit, you little . . ." The blows stopped abruptly. "You're trying to get rid of me?"

"I just want to know where I stand. I want you to make some kind of decision. I can't handle not knowing what's going to happen."

"Why all the concern about my leaving? You worried about having to advertise for more kitchen help?"

"No," she shrieked furiously. "It's not that. I just want to know how much time I have left with you. I love you, you big, dumb, *condottiere* bastard."

"Repeat that," he ordered thickly.

"I said I love you." Verity wriggled off his thighs and wound up kneeling in front of him on the floor. She shoved her disordered hair out of her eyes and glared at him as she got to her feet. "I realize that fact doesn't speak well for my intelligence, but that's the way it is. I can't seem to help myself. But I have to know when you'll leave me. I refuse to live in fear from day to day. Can't you understand that? Maybe I have been pushing you for the past three days. I suppose I was spoiling for a fight. Anything to clear the air."

"Did it ever occur to you to just ask me flat out what my plans were?" he roared as he massaged his leg where she had left the imprint of her sharp nails.

She blinked uncertainly. "No," she admitted softly. "I guess I didn't know how to phrase the question. I haven't had a lot of experience with handling the beginnings and endings of affairs. It's a hard question to ask, Jonas. Maybe I didn't want to hear the answer."

"For a supposedly intelligent woman, you show an amazing amount of stupidity at times. I'm not going anywhere. I happen to like it here in Sequence Springs, Verity Ames. God knows why, given my present conditions of employment, which include everything from low wages to a difficult boss. But we'll go into that later. Right now we have something else to clear up. You said you loved me?"

Verity cleared her throat. "Well, yes." That had sort of tumbled out accidentally in the heat of the moment, she decided. She hadn't meant to spell it out so plainly. It made her terribly vulnerable and Verity discovered she did not like being vulnerable. Especially not to this man. But she didn't have much choice.

Jonas was eyeing her assessingly. "What is this? You no longer consider me irresponsible, unreliable, and unacceptable?"

Verity flushed, her palm going surreptitiously to her stinging rear. "I know you a lot better now than I did when I first said that. I'd trust you with my life," she said simply. "In fact I already have trusted you with it. It's true you do irritate me from time to time. You're far too casual about certain matters, including your career. But I know now that if you make a commitment, you'll fulfill it. If you said you were going to do something, you'd do it."

"And if I said I intended to stay here in Sequence Springs with you, you'd believe me?" he asked, his voice gentling.

She nodded warily, afraid to acknowledge the hope that was building in her heart. "But I was afraid to ask you for fear you'd tell me you had to leave. If not right away, then soon. I didn't want to hear it. But a part of me had to hear the truth. I can't stand not knowing."

Jonas stopped rubbing his leg and propped his elbows on his knees. He laced his fingers and leaned his chin on his hands. His golden eyes were deep and brooding as he contemplated her. "So you started pushing me, waiting to see what would happen when the blow-up finally came. Well, you found out, didn't you?"

"No. All I got for my efforts was a beating. That's not an answer." She got to her feet and walked toward the window.

Jonas followed, coming up behind her. "That was no beating. That was a display of extreme masculine displeasure. Besides, we're even. I may never walk properly again. I think you ruined my leg."

"You deserved it."

"I'd never really hurt you and you know it." He settled both hands on her shoulders and pulled her back against him. He put his face into her tangled hair. "You do know that, don't you?"

"Yes, I know that," she admitted reluctantly. It was the truth. She would never have any need to fear this man. He had already given her ample proof that he would fight to the death for her.

"I'm not going anywhere, little tyrant. It would take a nuclear bomb to remove me from your vicinity. I need you, I want you, and it dawned on me a few days ago that I'm in love with you. You should have realized it before I did. You have such great insight into my character."

"Oh, Jonas." She turned in his arms, her eyes shining. "Do you mean it? You love me?"

He smiled down at her. "I said it, didn't I?"

Her smile was shaky with relief. "Then you mean it," she whispered. She buried her face against his chest. "You wouldn't lie to me."

"I couldn't lie to you," he said quietly. "We're bound together, you and I, in a very special way. Maybe whatever holds us together in that psychic corridor links us outside as well. Maybe that's why I wanted you so badly the first time I saw you. Maybe that's the real reason I traveled a couple of thousand miles to find you."

She knew then, with sure instinct, that he was right. "But do you think our psychic link is a strong enough basis on which to build a relationship?" she asked hesitantly.

Jonas locked his fingers in her hair. "I have a hunch it provides a much stronger foundation than most relationships have. Besides, we haven't got a *relationship*. We're in love."

"But is it really love?" Verity persisted thoughtfully. "I believe you when you say you think you're in love with me, but maybe you're just misinterpreting that sense of being psychically linked to me. Maybe there isn't any word for the kind of connection we share, so you're willing to label it love but in reality it could be . . . Mmmmmph."

The last of her lecture on the subject of the reality of love died beneath Jonas's forceful kiss. He didn't release her mouth for a long time, not until she had gone soft and compliant in his arms. Then he slowly eased the kiss until his lips were just barely brushing hers. He murmured softly:

> *"My lady has for too long sworn that no man's will*
> *would bind or bend her.*
> *But I have braved the thorns that guard her secrets.*
> *I claim the victory and the treasure.*
> *Now I think it's time my lady learned the art of sweet*
> *surrender."*

"Where do you get that awful Renaissance poetry you're always quoting?" Verity asked admiringly as she wrapped her arms around his waist.

Jonas laughed with wicked triumph as he picked her up and carried her down the hall toward the bedroom.

"I make it up as I go along," he told her.

"I was afraid of that."

She pulled his head down to hers so that she could kiss him with the thoroughness he deserved.